# STRANGE
# ANGELS
# &
# BETRAYALS

THE **STRANGE ANGELS** SERIES
BY LILI ST. CROW

**STRANGE ANGELS**
**BETRAYALS**
**JEALOUSY**
**DEFIANCE**
**RECKONING**

# STRANGE ANGELS & BETRAYALS

## LILI ST. CROW

razor
bill

Strange Angels and Betrayals

RAZORBILL

Published by the Penguin Group
Penguin Young Readers Group
345 Hudson Street, New York, New York 10014, U.S.A.
Penguin Group (USA) Inc., 375 Hudson Street, New York, New York 10014, U.S.A.
Penguin Group (Canada), 90 Eglinton Avenue East, Suite 700, Toronto, Ontario, Canada M4P 2Y3
(a division of Pearson Penguin Canada Inc.)
Penguin Books Ltd, 80 Strand, London WC2R 0RL, England
Penguin Ireland, 25 St Stephen's Green, Dublin 2, Ireland (a division of Penguin Books Ltd)
Penguin Group (Australia), 250 Camberwell Road, Camberwell, Victoria 3124, Australia (a division
of Pearson Australia Group Pty Ltd)
Penguin Books India Pvt Ltd, 11 Community Centre, Panchsheel Park, New Delhi – 110 017, India
Penguin Group (NZ), 67 Apollo Drive, Mairangi Bay, Auckland 1311, New Zealand
(a division of Pearson New Zealand Ltd)

Penguin Books (South Africa) (Pty) Ltd, 24 Sturdee Avenue, Rosebank, Johannesburg 2196, South Africa

Penguin Books Ltd, Registered Offices: 80 Strand, London WC2R 0RL, England

10 9 8 7 6 5 4 3 2 1

ISBN 978-1-59514-492-8

Library of Congress Cataloging-in-Publication Data is available

Printed in the United States of America

# STRANGE ANGELS

LILI ST. CROW

*For Gates, who caught the line when I threw it.*

## Acknowledgments

If not for Richelle Mead (who talked to Jessica) and Jessica Rothenberg (who talked to Miriam) and Miriam Kriss (who talked to me), this book would have never grown past a small snippet that someday I'd maybe, probably, sort of get around to. Thanks to them, Dru's story got to come out.

Thanks are also due to Gates, who was my first and best reader. If this story rings true at all, it's because of his suggestions and not-so-gentle shoves.

There are also the usual suspects to thank: Mel Sanders, the other half of my writing brain, who listens to me obsess over every story; Christa Hickey and Sixten Zeiss for all the love and coffee; Maddy and Nicky for being my strength.

I could go on and on with the thanks, but I will content myself with thanking you, gentle Reader. Without you I am just muttering at the wind. Let me thank you the way we both like best, by telling you a story. . .

*A fronte praecipitium, a tergo lupi.*

# PROLOGUE

**didn't tell Dad** about Granmama's white owl. I know I should have.

There's that space between sleep and dreaming where things—not quite dreams, not fully fledged precognition, but weird little blends of both—sometimes get in. Your eyes open, slow and dreamy, when the sense of *someone looking* rises through the cotton-wool fog of being warm and tired.

That's when I saw it.

The owl ruffled itself up on my windowsill drenched in moonglow, each pale feather sharp and clear under icy light. I hadn't bothered to pull the cheap blinds down or hang up the curtains. Why bother, when we—Dad and me—only spend a few months in any town?

I blinked at the yellow-eyed bird. Instead of the comfort that means Gran is thinking about me—and don't ask how I know the dead think of the living; I've seen too much *not* to know—I felt a sharp annoyance, like a glass splinter under the surface of my brain.

The owl's beak was black, and its feathers had ghostly spots like cobwebs, shadows against snowy down. It stared into my sleepy eyes for what seemed like eternity, ruffling just a bit, puffing up the way Gran always used to when she thought anyone was messing with me.

*Not again. Go away.*

It usually only showed up when something interesting or really foul was about to happen. Dad had never seen it, or at least I didn't think so. But he could tell when I had, and it would make him reach for a weapon until I managed to open my mouth and say whether we were going to meet an old friend—or find ourselves in deep shit.

The night Gran died the owl had sat inside the window while she took her last few shallow, sipping breaths, but I don't think the nurses or the doctor saw it. They would have said something. By that point I knew enough to keep my mouth shut, at least. I just sat there and held Gran's hand until she drained away; then I sat in the hall while they did things to her empty body and wheeled it off. I curled up inside myself when the doctor or the social worker tried to talk to me, and just kept repeating that my dad would know, that he was on his way—even though I had no clue *where* he was, really. He'd been gone a good three months, off ridding the world of nasty things while I watched Gran slide downhill.

Of course, that morning Dad showed up, haggard and unshaven, his shoulder bandaged and his face bruised. He had all the ID, signed all the papers, and answered all the questions. Everything turned out okay, but sometimes I dream about that night, wondering if I'm going to get left behind again in some fluorescent-lit corridor smelling of Lysol and cold pain.

I don't like thinking about that. I settled further into the pillow, watching the owl's fluffing, each feather edged with cold moonlight.

My eyes drifted closed. Warm darkness swallowed me, and when the alarm clock went off it was morning, weak winter sunshine spilling through the window and making a square on the brown carpet. I'd thrashed out of the covers and was about to freeze my ass off. Dad hadn't turned the heater up.

It took a good twenty minutes in the shower before I felt anything *close* to awake. *Or* human. By the time I stamped down the stairs, I was already pissed off and getting worse. My favorite jeans weren't clean and I had a zit the size of Mount Pinatubo on my temple under a hank of dishwater brown hair. I opted for a gray T-shirt and a red hoodie, a pair of combat boots and no makeup.

Why bother, right? I wasn't going to be here long enough for anyone to care.

My bag smacked the floor. Last night's dishes still crouched in the sink. Dad was at the kitchen table, his shoulders hunched over the tray as he loaded clips, each bullet making a little clicking sound. "Hi, sweetheart."

I snorted, snagging the orange juice and opening the carton, taking a long cold draft. I wiped my mouth and belched musically.

"Ladylike." His bloodshot blue eyes didn't rise from the clip, and I knew what that meant.

"Going out tonight?" That's what I said. What I meant was, *without me?*

*Click. Click.* He set the full clip aside and started on the next. The bullets glinted, silver-coated. He must have been up all night with that, making them and loading them. "I won't be in for dinner. Order a pizza or something."

Which meant he was going somewhere more-dangerous, not just kinda-dangerous. And that he didn't need me to zero the target. So he must've gotten some kind of intel. He'd been gone every night this week, always reappearing in time for dinner smelling of cigarette smoke and danger. In other towns he'd mostly take me with him; people either didn't care about a teenage girl drinking a Coke in a bar, or we went places where Dad was reasonably sure he could stop any trouble with an ice-cold military stare or a drawled word.

But in this town he hadn't taken me anywhere. So if he'd gotten intel, it was on his own.

*How? Probably the old-fashioned way. He likes that better, I guess.* "I could come along."

"Dru." Just the one word, a warning in his tone. Mom's silver locket glittered at his throat, winking in the morning light.

"You might need me. I can carry the ammo." *And tell you when something invisible's in the corner, looking at you.* I heard the stubborn whine in my voice and belched again to cover it, a nice sonorous one that all but rattled the window looking out onto the scrubby backyard with its dilapidated swing set. There was a box of dishes sitting in front of the cabinets next to the stove; I suppressed the urge to kick at it. Mom's cookie jar—the one shaped like a fat grinning black-and-white cow—was next to the sink, the first thing unpacked in every new house. I always put it in the bathroom box with the toilet paper and shampoo; that's always the last in and first one out.

I've gotten kind of used to packing and unpacking, you could say. And trying to find toilet paper after a thirty-six-hour drive is no fun.

"Not this time, Dru." He looked up at me, though, the bristles of his cropped hair glittering blond under fluorescent light. "I'll be home late. Don't wait up."

I was about to protest, but his mouth had turned into a thin, hard line and the bottle sitting on the table warned me. Jim Beam. It had been almost full last night when I went to bed, and the dregs of amber liquid in it glowed warmer than his hair. Dad was pale blond, almost a towhead, even if his stubble was brown and gold.

I've got a washed-out version of Mom's curls and a better copy of Dad's blue eyes. The rest of me, I guess, is up for grabs. Except maybe Gran's nose, but she could have just been trying to make me feel better. I'm no prize. Most girls go through a gawky stage, but I'm beginning to think mine will be a lifelong thing.

It doesn't bother me too much. Better to be strong than pretty and useless. I'll take a plain girl with her head screwed on right over a cheerleader any day.

So I just leaned down and scooped up my messenger bag, the strap scraping against my fingerless wool gloves. They're scratchy but they're warm, and if you slip small stuff under the cuff, it's damn near invisible. "Okay."

"You should have some breakfast." *Click*. Another bullet slid into the clip. His eyes dropped back down to it, like it was the most important thing in the world.

Eat something? When he was about to go out and deal with bad news alone? Was he *kidding*?

My stomach turned over hard. "I'll miss the bus. Do you want some eggs?"

I don't know why I offered. He liked them sunny-side up, but neither Mom or me could ever get them done right. I've been breaking yolks all my life, even when he tried to teach me the right way to gently jiggle with a spatula to get them out of the pan. Mom would just laugh on Sunday mornings and tell him scrambled or over-hard was what he was going to get, and he'd come up behind her and put his arms around her waist and nuzzle her long, curling chestnut hair. I would always yell, *Ewwww! No kissing!*

And they would both laugh.

That was Before. A thousand years ago. When I was little.

Dad shook his head a little. "No thanks, kiddo. You have money?"

I spotted his billfold on the counter and scooped it up. "I'm taking twenty."

"Take another twenty, just in case." *Click. Click.* "How's school going?"

*Just fine, Dad. Just freaking dandy. Two weeks in a new town is enough to make me all sorts of friends.* "Okay."

I took two twenties out of his billfold, rubbing the plastic sleeve over Mom's picture with my thumb like I always did. There was a shiny space on the sleeve right over her wide, bright smile. Her chestnut hair was as wildly curly as mine, but pulled back into a loose ponytail, blonde-streaked ringlets falling into her heart-shaped face. She was beautiful. You could see why Dad fell for her in that picture. You could almost smell her perfume.

"Just okay?" *Click.*

"It's fine. It's stupid. Same old stuff." I toed the linoleum and set his billfold down. "I'm going."

*Click.* He didn't look up. "Okay. I love you." He was wearing his Marines sweatshirt and the pair of blue sweats he always worked out in, with the hole in the knee. I stared at the top of his head while he finished the clip, set it aside, and picked up a fresh one. I could almost feel the noise of each bullet being slid home in my own fingers.

My throat had turned to stone. "'Kay. Whatever. Bye." *Don't get killed.* I stamped out of the kitchen and down the hall, one of the stacked boxes barking me in the shin. I still hadn't unpacked the living room yet. Why bother? I'd just have to box it all up in another couple months.

I slammed the front door, too, and pulled my hood up, shoving my hair back. I hadn't bothered with much beyond dragging a comb through it. Mom's curls had been loose pretty ringlets, but mine were pure frizz. The Midwest podunk humidity made it worse; it was a wet blanket of cold that immediately turned my breath into a white cloud and nipped at my elbows and knees.

The rental was on a long, ruler-straight block of similar houses, all dozing under watery sunlight managing to fight its way through overcast. The air tasted like iron and I shivered. We'd been in Florida before this, always sticky, sweaty, sultry heat against the skin like oil. We'd cleared out four poltergeists in Pensacola and a haunting apparition of a woman even Dad could see in some dead-end town north of Miami, and there was a creepy woman with cottonmouths and copperheads in glass cages who sold Dad the silver he needed to take care of something else. I hadn't had to go to school there—we were so busy staying mobile, moving from one hotel to the next, so whatever Dad needed the silver for couldn't get a lock on us.

Now it was the Dakotas, and snow up to our knees. Great.

Our yard was the only one with weeds and tall grass. We had a picket fence, too, but the paint was flaking and peeling off and parts of it were missing, like a gap-toothed smile. Still, the porch was sturdy and the house was even sturdier. Dad didn't believe in renting crappy bungalows. He said it was a bad way to raise a kid.

I walked away with my head down and my hands stuffed in my pockets.

I never saw Dad alive again.

# CHAPTER 1

"**Miss Anderson?**" **Mrs.** Bletchley's voice droned through my name.

I'd propped my cheek on my fist and was staring out the window at the cold wasteland of a baseball field, waiting for the chimes to sound. Foley High School didn't believe in bells. Instead, a sound like a cell phone ringing would echo through the room when it was time to go run on the treadmill in another classroom.

The pencil in my hand rested against blank paper, and I brought my gaze around slowly, sudden silence in the room meaning all eyes were on me.

I hate that.

Bletchley was round-faced, white-haired, and plump. The other teachers probably thought she was a kind, harmless soul. She had small dark hazel eyes behind steel-rimmed glasses and carnelian lipstick feathering off the edge of her lips. Her hands, when they weren't clasping a yardstick like a cane, were constantly picking at the bottom edge of her lumpy cardigan. She alternated between three sweaters: primrose, blue with knitted roses, and a bilious yellow one with a Peter Pan collar. Today it was the yellow.

She looked like a weasel getting ready to steal its next chicken. The kids called her Mad Dog behind her back, and she could smell weakness.

There are two species of teacher—the soft and the hard. Soft teachers might genuinely want to help, or they might have been broken in. They're usually nervous and afraid of kids, especially high school boys. The hard teachers are another thing entirely. They're like sharks—machines made for eating, with a finely tuned sense for blood in the water.

"Were we *paying attention*, Miss Anderson?" You could have stropped a knife on Bletchley's tone. A tide of whispers ran through the room. Bletch had picked her target for the next thirty minutes, and it was me.

I just *love* being the new girl.

I really shouldn't have even opened my mouth. Hard teachers are like bullies. If you don't react, pretty soon they think you're stupid and they leave you alone.

The half-Asian goth kid in front of me shifted in his seat. He was tall and skinny, with a mop of wavy dark hair. The back of his neck was visible as he bent down in his seat, the collar of the black coat he never took off sticking up at the corners but folded down in back. I stared at his nape under the dark curls.

*What the hell, might as well.* "Fort Sumter," I said.

Silence. Bletchley's eyes narrowed behind her steel-rimmed glasses, and I'd opened my mouth. So I jumped in with both feet.

"You asked where the first shots of the Civil War were fired. It was Fort Sumter. April 12 to April 13 of 1861." I delivered the words in a flat, bored monotone, and the whispers turned into the particular type of silent laughter a hard teacher hates most.

Who knew sophomore American History could be so fun?

Bletch eyed me for a moment. I wasn't quite a known quantity yet, so I might actually get away with it. The goth kid in front of me squirmed again in his seat, making it creak.

The teacher visibly decided to pick on someone else, with a look that promised me trouble later. "Thank you, Miss Anderson." Her pause lengthened as she tapped meditatively on the desk with her yardstick. Her ankles were swelling out of her oxfords, despite the heavy dark nylon socks she wore under a long waddling denim skirt. They looked like circulation socks—the kind they give diabetics.

*Gran used to wear those when her ankles pained her.* My skin chilled as I slumped in the hard plastic seat, not daring to look out the window again. Bletch might just as easily circle back to me. I hadn't told Dad about the owl on my windowsill. Was he still home?

The unsteady, sinking feeling in my stomach got worse. I stared at the boy's neck in front of me, but he shifted again, tugging at the corners of his collar with nervous fingers.

*Don't move,* I wanted to whisper. *She's looking for her next victim.* If I'd been all there in the classroom instead of worrying about Dad, I might have done something like smacking him on the back of the head to save him, since I didn't give a good goddamn if I was sent to the office or signed up for detention or whatever.

The axe fell. "Mr. Graves." Bletch's eyes lit up.

The kid in front of me stiffened, his shoulders going tense.

Blood in the water. I tried not to feel guilty.

"I certainly hope you're taking notes. Since Miss Anderson has answered the question about the *start*, perhaps you can tell us about the *causes* of the Civil War?" Her eyebrows went up, and the predatory gleam in her eyes reminded me of cottonmouths in glass aquariums, staring lidless before they opened their mouths and made that awful ratcheting sound. The thumps of snakes hitting the glass echoed in my head, along with the smell of red beans and rice, body odor, and incense.

We were a long way away from Florida. The proprietor of that little occult store had given me the genuine willies, what with her filmy eyes and the shifting mass of stuff trailing behind her—a cloud of disturbance regular people wouldn't see, but would feel like a cold draft. She'd given me a long, measuring look before Dad snapped his fingers and informed her that she was talking to *him*, thank you very much, ma'am.

*I should have told him about the owl.* The sudden certainty was chilling, and my fingers turned numb, prickling with cold.

"Um. Causes of the Civil War. Uhhh . . ." The kid in front of me stumbled, and Bletch had him. She spent the rest of the class period picking on him, even though he eventually came up with the right answers—when she let him get a word in edgewise. By the time the chimes rang for the end of the round, even the back of his neck was red. I felt bad about it, but I didn't let it slow me down.

The halls were the usual crush, jocks snapping like sharks, cheerleaders simpering, and the rest of us just trying to get by. A contingent of stoners clustered around a locker, and I'm sure I saw a brown paper bag change hands. I glanced back—nope, no teachers in sight. A girl from art class looked right past my tentative wave and swished away, her backpack sagging dispiritedly from one shoulder.

I hate being the new girl.

The cafeteria was a surf-roar of noise and the smell of floor wax and industrial food. I had some change for the bank of pay phones between the caf and Death Alley leading down to the office, so I

plugged it in and dialed the number written in my Yoda notebook—
the last in a string of similar numbers scrawled in pencil or blue
pen. The phone had been on when we moved in, listed under the
last tenant's name, and it was easier just paying the bill for a while.
I couldn't be expected to memorize every goddamn phone number.
Or at least, that's what I'd told Dad when he ragged me for having
them written down.

He told me to watch my mouth and stopped bugging me about
it. Domestic harmony, thy name is Anderson.

The handset rang in my ear. Once. Three times. Five.

He wasn't home, or he was working out, not picking up. I thought
about skipping the rest of the day, but he'd be pissed off and I'd just
get another lecture about the value of education. If I dared to point
out that education wasn't everything and high school wouldn't teach
me how to exorcise a room or put down a zombie, I'd just get *another*
lecture about how I was supposed to be normal.

Just because he hunted things out of fairy tales didn't mean I had
any right to skip school. Oh no. Even if he was pretty blind without
me, since only the maternal side of his family was the one gifted with
what Gran always called "the touch."

Some touch. I haven't figured out if it meant "crazy" or just
"spooky." The jury, you could say, is still out on that one.

Dad never seemed sad or unhappy about missing out on the
woo-woo train. Then again, Gran never did stand for much of what
she called "moping," and I couldn't imagine her being any different
when Dad was a kid. Weird as it is to think about him being gawky
and adolescent—but I've seen the pictures.

Gran was big on pictures.

I hung up after fifteen rings and stood staring at the phone,
chewing on a hangnail. It hurt like hell, and there was a healing

scrape on my left-hand knuckles from the heavy bag. Other girls don't have fathers who yell at them to work through the pain, to hit harder, to *get in there and kill it kill it kill it!* Other girls never filled thermoses with holy water or handed ammo through a window while their fathers held off skittering things like giant mutant cockroaches. That had been Baton Rouge, and that had been *bad*. I'd had to drive Dad to the hospital and lie about how he got the chunk taken out of his calf.

Sometimes it was hard to tell where the lying to the normal world ended and the bullshit posturing necessary in the Real World began. There's so much paramilitary hanging out under the edge of the Real World that the macho bull snorting reaches epic proportions.

The phone just kept ringing.

"Screw it," I said under my breath, under the surf roar of noise echoing from the cafeteria. I didn't even get my fifty cents back; the machine ate it.

For a second I stood there, just looking at the phone like it might suddenly give me a good idea. It smelled like damp wool and wet concrete in here, as well as formaldehyde carpet and the exhalation of two thousand kids. Not to mention sweaty stocking feet and food pried from underneath Ronald McDonald's bumpers. School smell. It's the same pretty much everywhere in the U.S., with only slight regional differences in the foot-sweat and served-roadkill departments.

The crowd noise from the caf hurt my ears and made my head ache like one of Mom's migraines. I was hungry, but the thought of going in there and elbowing through the line, then finding a place to sit where I wouldn't be required to look at anyone or share a table with some jackass kids just seemed like too much hassle.

If I went home and Dad was there, I'd get The Lecture. If I

went home and he *wasn't* there, I'd just wait and worry. If I went through geometry and art class this afternoon I'd go bazonko nuts, even though art class was generally the most enjoyable part of the day. And forget about the waste of time they called "civics class." I'd seen more real-life civics on afternoon CNN. That is, if you define *civics* as "blowhards with expensive hair."

None of these classes taught you anything *real*. I'd rather be with Dad on stakeout or doing what he called "intel runs"—going to occult shops or bars, places where people who knew about the Real World, the dark world, got together and spoke in whispers between shots.

Like the tea shop where Dad's old buddy August hangs out in New York, where you step up to get into the bar's dark gloom—and you step up *again* to get out. Or the bar in Seattle where the proprietor has tusks growing out of his lower jaw and a warty broad face that looks like something that lives under a bridge and eats goats. Or the nightclub in Pensacola where all the flashing strobes of light look like screaming faces when they hit the floor. And that country store out on a back road near Port Arthur, where the woman sitting in her rocker on the front porch will have what you need in a paper bag sitting right next to her, while the dust streaks and twinkles on the window, even at night. There are places like that all over—where you can buy things that shouldn't or don't strictly exist.

If you're willing to pay. Sometimes in money. Most times in *information*. And other times in something less tangible. Favors. Memories. Even souls.

Maybe I could do some recon of my own, find Dad a good place to plug in. The watering holes for the Real World are hidden from the normal world, but they always stick out like a sore thumb to me. I think it's because Gran always had me play "what's on the table" —

that game where you shut your eyes and try to remember everything she'd set out for lunch or dinner, canning or quilting.

That sounded better than putting up with the same bullshit everyone my age has to put up with. So I turned and went the other way, toward the doors that would lead out to the soccer fields and baseball diamond. I could cut across the fields and maybe slip out through the greenbelt—Foley was one of those schools with an open campus, a rarity anymore. I had that extra twenty, enough to sit in a café or coffee shop where nobody would bother me before I put on my serious face and started following the tickle of intuition.

The cold outside was like a slap to already-stinging cheeks. It still smelled like iron, the way a penny tastes when you suck on it. I walked with my head down, my boots crunching frozen weeds, my nose immediately running.

*What a choice. Skip school and freeze your ass off, or go back inside the building where it's warm and get bored literally to death.*

"Hey! Hey, you!"

I ignored the voice, swiping at my nose with the sleeve of my sweatshirt jacket. Footsteps crunched behind me. I didn't hunch my shoulders—that's a dead giveaway that you've heard someone. If it was a teacher, I was going to have to come up with a reason why I was out here, and I began to think about exercising my creative lying muscle.

*They should have a class for that. Who would teach it? I wonder if it would grade on a curve.*

"Hey! Anderson!" The voice was too young to belong to a teacher. And it was male.

*Shit.* Just my luck. The bullies don't usually mess with me, but you never know. I set my heel down in the gravel and whirled, my

15

head coming up and my hair falling in my eyes despite being mostly stuffed under my hood.

It was the half-Asian goth kid from American History class.

He was too tall, and the long black coat flapped as he skidded to a stop. He'd pushed his collar up again, and the cold made his cheeks and nose cherry red under his mop of dyed-black hair. He wheezed for a second, his narrow chest heaving under a Black Sabbath T-shirt, and peered at me through strings of hair. His eyes were an odd pale green, but his hair managed to keep them from doing more than peeping out every once in a while. In a few years he'd probably be a real looker, with those contrasting eyes and the thick wavy dark hair.

Right now, though, he was in that funny in-between stage where every part of a guy's body looks like it was pulled out of a different parts catalog. Poor kid.

I waited. Finally, he got his breath back. "You want a cigarette?"

"No." *Jesus, no.* He had the type of baby face most guys would curse at in the mirror, at war with its own nose and cheekbones. The kind of face some half-breeds get stuck with if they don't draw the pretty card. It made him look about twelve, except he was so *tall*. The hair was maybe an attempt to look like he really was "sixteen, honest." He had nice boots, steel-toed combat numbers laced up to his knees. To top it all off, an inverted crucifix dangled from a silver chain, against his bony sternum.

I backed up another step and took another look at him. Nope. Nothing of the Real World on this kid. I didn't *think* so, but it's better to check. Better to check twice and be relieved than only check once and get your ass blown off, Dad says.

*Dad. Is he gone already? It's still daylight, he's probably okay.* I didn't like the way my chest was getting tight.

The kid dug in a pocket and fished out a crumpled pack of Winstons, the corners of his eyes crinkling. At least he hadn't drawn the really slit-eyed card a lot of half-breeds have to play, where they look like they're squinting to beat Clint Eastwood the whole time. "You want one?" he asked again.

*What the hell?* I stared at the crucifix. Did he have any idea what that *meant?* Or how quickly it could get him in a lot of trouble, in some places?

Probably not. That's why the Real World is the Real World: because the normal world thinks it's the only game going.

"No thanks." *I want a cup of coffee and a club sandwich. I want to sit down someplace and draw. I want to find some place where the sunlight doesn't get in and I don't feel like a total alien. Leave me the hell alone. I should have told Dad about the owl.* My conscience pricked me. "Sorry about Bletchley."

He shrugged, a quick birdlike movement. All of him was birdlike, from his beak of a nose at war with his caramel-skinned baby face to the restless way his fingers moved. He tapped a cigarette out of the pack and produced a silver Zippo, lit the cancer stick, exhaled a cloud of smoke, and promptly went into a coughing fit.

Jesus. Here I was freezing my ass off with Cool Goth Boy. Some days were so much worse than others it wasn't funny. "It's okay," he said when he could talk again. "She's a bitch. She does that all the time."

*Glad to know I didn't interrupt anything.* I stood there with no real idea of what to say. I settled for a shrug of my own. "See you."

"Are you skipping?" He fell into step beside me, ignoring the fact that I was *walking away*. "Off to a good start."

*Leave me alone.* "I don't want to deal with it today."

"Okay. I know a place to go. You shoot pool?" He managed not to choke himself on another drag of cigarette smoke. "I'm Graves."

*When did I invite you along?* "I know." I looked back down at my boots, marking off time. "Dru." *And don't you dare ask what it's short for.*

"Dru." He repeated it. "You're new. Couple of weeks, right? Welcome to Foley."

*State the goddamn obvious and bring out your suburban Welcome Wagon.* I couldn't see any way to ditch him just yet, so I just made a noise of assent. We crossed the soccer field in weird tandem, him shortening his stride out of respect for my lack of grasshopper legs. I sized him up as we walked. I'd give myself better odds in a fight, I decided. He didn't look very tough.

Still, I was walking into the woods with a kid I didn't know. I stole quick little glances at his hands and decided he might be okay. At least I could kick his ass if he tried anything, and the greenbelt wasn't very big.

He tried again. "Where you from?"

*A planet far, far away. Where nightmares are real.* "Florida." The question always came up, sooner or later. Sometimes, mostly when I was younger, I lied. Most of the time I just pretended like I'd always lived in the last place we'd come from.

People don't really want to know anything about you. They just want you to fit into their little predetermined slots. They decide what you are in the first two seconds, and they only get nervous or upset if you don't live up to their snap judgments. That's one way the normal world's like the Real—it all depends on what people *think* you are. Figure that out, play to what they expect, and it's clear sailing.

"Yeah, you sounded a bit down-South. Big change for you, huh? It's going to snow." He announced it like I should be grateful to him for telling me. The strap of my bag dug into my shoulder.

I tried not to bristle. *I do not sound Southern. I sound like Gran a little bit, but that's all.* "Thanks for the warning." I didn't bother disguising the sarcasm.

"Hey, no problem. First one's free."

When I glanced up at him, he was smiling under his hair. It almost threatened to eat his nose, that hair. The proud, bony nose was putting up a good fight, though, and he looked miserably cold. He didn't even have any gloves.

For a second I toyed with the idea of telling him something. *Hi. I'm Dru Anderson. My father went way-out wack after my mom died and now he travels around hunting things that go bump in the night, killing things you only find in fairy tales and ghost stories. I help him out when I can, but most of the time I'm deadweight, even though I can tell you where anything inhuman in this town is likely to hang out. I'm skipping school because I won't be here in another three months. None of it goddamn well matters.*

Instead, I found myself almost smiling back. "You should wear some gloves."

He peered at me, shaking his hair away. His eyes turned out to be green with threads of brown and gold, thickly fringed with dark lashes, change-color eyes. Boys always get the best eyelashes; it's like some kind of cosmic law. And half-breed kids get some kind of extra help there from genetics, too. Once he grew into that nose and his face thinned out a bit, the girls would like him a lot. Maybe it would even go to his head.

"Ruins the image," he said. Silver glittered in his left ear, an earring I couldn't quite make out.

"You'll goddamn well freeze to death." We reached the end of the soccer field and he took the lead, going to the right along a dusty footpath. Bare branches interlaced above us, and the dry smell of fallen leaves tickled my nose with dust. The brick pile of the school behind us would soon be out of sight, and that made me happier than I'd been all day.

Graves snorted, tossed his hair back as he took another drag. The smoke hung in a feathered shape for a moment as he exhaled, but I blinked to clear my eyes. "Hey, we've got to suffer for beauty. Chicks don't go for guys with gloves."

*I'll bet chicks don't go for you at all, out here in Stepford Podunk.* "How would you know?" I stepped over a tree root, my bag bumping my hip.

"I know." He shot me a look over his shoulder, his hair almost swallowing his grin, too. "You never said if you liked shooting pool."

"I don't." I felt a little guilty again. He was trying to be nice. There was one in every school—some guy who thought his chances were better with new girls. "But I'll beat your ass at it, okay?"

I decided I could wait to find the local paranormal hangout. Dad would probably give me another version of The Lecture if I went looking for it alone. There was that one time in Dallas when he found me trading shots of Coke with a pointy-eared goggle-eyed gremlin and about had a cow—

"Fine." He didn't even sound insulted. "If you can, *Dru*."

I thought about telling him Dad had taught me to shoot pool when we were low on cash, and decided not to. Maybe if I embarrassed the kid he'd leave me alone.

CHAPTER **2**

**I got home a** little after five, riding the jolting, bumping bus all the way from downtown. Graves had wanted me to hang around and shoot a few more games, but the place—an all-ages pool club with a jukebox and indoor basketball and tennis courts—was loud and full of funky smells, as well as being jammed with kids who should have been in school themselves. So I bailed and had to figure out the bus. I'm used to figuring out the public transportation in just about any part of America, and this place actually had a good system.

Dad's truck was gone, but he'd left the light on in the kitchen and a fifty-dollar bill next to a note. *Don't wait up. Order pizza. Homework before TV, kiddo, and do your katas. Love you. Dad.*

Other dads actually sat at the dinner table. Mine left me a fifty and a reminder to do my goddamn katas.

I was cold anyway, so I dropped my bag in the kitchen and bashed my way out into the garage, the big broken-spring door rattling as the wind teased at it. The heavy bag creaked, swaying a little, but I shucked my coat and shivered in the middle of the concrete floor instead.

Dad liked karate, and he was big enough that it was a good choice for him. But I'm built rangy, like my mom, except she had nice chestworks and a pretty curve to her hips. I'm just angles except for the breasticles, which are more trouble than they're worth, especially when it comes to boys. I don't have the kind of muscle mass you need to meet a punch with direct force.

So for me, it's tai chi and what Dad called "The Basic Dirty-Fightin'" when he was sober and "Six Great Ways to Bounce an Asshole" when he'd had a few Beams. I like tai chi—I like the slow way each movement flows into the next and the breathing smooths everything out. It's still hard work, because your knees always have to be a little unlocked, and after a while it really murders your quads and hamstrings, but it's nice.

*Push-pull. Part the horse's mane. Catch the swallow's tail.* Warmed up and loosened, and feeling a little better, I finally inhaled and exhaled, as close to at peace as I guess you can ever get. The outside world rushed in as soon as I opened my eyes, and I began worrying about Dad again before I even opened the door to the kitchen and stamped through, making a lot of noise I really didn't have to.

It's the only way to fill up an empty house.

I dug through the fridge and eventually settled on a bowl of Cheerios. I'd scarfed a greasy slice of pizza at the pool hall, and the thought of more half-cardboard cheese didn't appeal to me, even with pepperoni. So I wolfed the cereal, spiked a glass of Coke with some of Dad's Jim Beam, and wandered up to my room to lie on the bed and look at the light on the ceiling. Every room is different, and the way outside light reflects up onto the spackle stuff smeared on most ceilings is unique. I could probably describe pretty much every place we've ever lived in terms of ceiling light.

The worst part about Dad being out on hunting runs was the way whatever house we were in got really creepy around dusk. Night is when most of the stuff in the Real World comes out to play—and by *play* you can mean "have a little fun," "go grocery shopping because sunlight burns like acid," or "make unwary people disappear, yum yum." Take your pick.

I pulled Mom's red-and-white quilt around me, snug as a bug in a rug, and sipped at the Coke until my taste buds burned off a little — I'd made it about half and half, and began to get a warm glow after a while. My clock blinked its little red eyes, and darkness gathered deeper and deeper in the corners. The wind made the glassed-in screen door on the enclosed back porch rattle.

When we lived in apartments, I would play the game of listening to the sounds in the building as everyone came home, and imagining stories for all of them. Most apartment buildings aren't quiet if you're really listening. After a while the noises begin to seem like family, and you catch the rhythm of each separate life in your building working together to make the melody called home. One place we lived, the guy next door played the cello after dinner every night. That was nice to listen to, even if the *other* guy down the hall beat his wife once a month when rent came due.

Houses are different. They creak to themselves, muttering, when night comes around. An empty house around dusk starts to talk, no matter how newly built it is. I used to play music to cover it up, but after a while the thought that I wouldn't be able to hear if anything was sneaking around the hallways got to me.

When you can see apparitions and poltergeists in living, solid color, that sort of thinking usually does start getting to you.

So I mostly listened and waited on nights when Dad was "out." Night gets kind of strange when you're waiting for someone to come home. I've seen shit on TV you wouldn't believe, stuff that only happens when you're alone and nobody can verify the sighting. Once Dad found me curled up on the floor of the mobile home we were renting in Byronville, clutching a baseball bat and sound asleep while a *Twilight Zone* rerun blared out of the television. I'd eaten a TV dinner and my hair had gotten into the empty tray. After that he made me promise to go to bed and not wait up, but that just meant that I fell asleep sitting up in bed and thinking about all the ways things could go wrong.

Things can go very, very wrong. They go wrong all the time in the normal world, and the Real World just means they go wrong with teeth and claws, quicker than your average bear. August called it "the Situation." Dad called it "gone south." Juan-Raoul de la Hoya-Smith called it *"mala* goddamn *suerte, chingada."*

I didn't know what Dad was after this time. He hadn't said anything on the way from Florida. That was a little unusual — normally he had me looking through the boxes of old leather-bound books he picked up here and there, searching for odd bits of information. Or helping him make bullets and sharpen the knives, bouncing ideas off me or quizzing me on tactics. I'm probably the only sixteen-year-old girl in a three-hundred-mile radius who knows how to distinguish a poltergeist from an actual ghost (hint: If you can disrupt it with nitric acid, or if it throws new crap at you every time, it's a poltergeist), or how to tell if a medium's real or faking it (poke 'em with a true-iron needle). I know the six signs of a good occult store (Number One is the proprietor bolts the door before talking about Real Business) and the four things you never do when you're in a bar with other people who know about the darker side of the world (don't look weak). I know how to access public information and talk my way around clerks in courthouses (a smile and the right clothing work wonders). I also know how to hack into newspaper files, police reports, and some kinds of government databases (primary rule: Don't get caught. Duh).

Hey, even if you've got great intuition you can't just walk up to people and ask them about the resident exorcist or the last unsolved murder that was committed during the new moon. You *also* can't ask them about the haunted houses that serve as nodes or the local werwulfen hangout—where the burgers aren't just rare, they're raw. And served in big bloody piles.

Sometimes you have to go digging to find the pattern behind events that to other people just look like random bad luck.

*Get information and you'll find a pattern*, Gran said. *Find the pattern and you have your prey*, Dad said.

He also said, *Don't let the backwoods woo-woo take the place of logic.* He said that a lot.

I wondered where he was and took another gulp of Coke and Beam. My CD player was across the room, the concrete-block-and-plywood bookcase empty except for my clothes. There was another pile of clothes and my CD case in front of the closet, and other than my mattresses and the nightstand, that was about it. The lap of luxury at Casa Anderson. I'd stopped putting up posters or hauling my books upstairs. It wasn't worth it and Dad didn't care as long as the laundry got done. To my everlasting relief, he'd also stopped with the starch a few years back. The military made him big on spray starch, but I point-blank refused to touch the stuff after a while. He finally gave up doing it himself, and I manfully restrained myself from pointing out that the world didn't explode when he did.

And they say maturity is just for adults.

The house was empty. It started talking, groans and squeaks as the wind outside rose. Everywhere you go, the air changes around dusk. Sometimes it's soft and sweet, or whistling just enough to make you feel happy to be inside and snuggled up.

When something bad is coming, it's different. Like a moan, only with big glass teeth.

Tonight the wind had that sound. I hoped Dad would be home soon. Once I finished my drink I fished in my bag for a pencil and paper and started to draw. The long curved lines turned into a frilly iris, one of Gran's favorite flowers. I got into it, shading the different textures of the petals, imagining the colors—vibrant purple, snowy white, the green of the stem. I'd drawn a lot of irises, especially after Mom died and Gran got me paper and a pencil to keep me busy while she worked in her cabin.

When I think of right after Mom died and Dad disappeared for the first time, the smell of paper and the sound of Gran scrubbing something—she was always cleaning—mixes together with the feeling of a pencil in my hand. She was always washing the floors with hawthorn water or wiping down the windows, in between the other tons of work that had to happen to keep the cabin running right. Like collecting eggs or feeding the pigs or splitting wood. I still can't pass a house without looking for the best place to put a woodpile, and I always spin the eggs once clockwise on the counter before breaking them.

Somehow she found time to keep the place clean as a whistle and rinsed down with all sorts of floor and window washes—hawthorn, mountain ash, true rowan, sometimes yarrow or lavender. Bundles of wild garlic and onions strung up everywhere, and Gran working on her spinning wheel late at night, the thump and whirr getting into my chest as I cried myself to sleep, missing Dad, wanting my mommy, terrified and lonely and not understanding.

What does a five-year-old understand about "dead"? Or "forever"? Or even about "be back in a while"?

Full night fell. The clock blinked on and on. I got up to go to the bathroom a couple times, taking the quilt with me. Once I went downstairs for another Coke and Beam. Dad would give me another Lecture—probably the one about Responsible Choices and Adulthood, and how I wasn't close to either yet—if he ever guessed I drank while he was out. But since he put the stuff away at a pretty steady rate himself, I don't think he ever twigged.

I went on to drawing simple shapes—the lamp on my nightstand, the bookshelves, the closet doors. Then I sketched the pile of laundry in front of the closet, taking care to shade everything just so. The clock kept blinking. I finished the second glass of Jimmy Beam lightly misted with Coke and fell asleep with the pencil still in my fingers, a jagged line sliding down the pad of paper in my lap, opened to a fresh page.

When I woke up in the morning, Dad still wasn't there.

# Intermezzo

**H**e **walked down** a long corridor, picking his way carefully in booted feet. The concrete was crazed with broken lines and slick with fat rivulets and lakes of something best not to name; he stepped over them like a kid stepping over sidewalk cracks, break your mother's back.

A buzzing had started in my head. I wanted to open my mouth, tell him not to go down that hall, that Something Invisible was looking at him. But the hall was so long, and it was so hard to think through the hornets in my head. They were having a fine old time building condos inside my skull, and the buzzing spread through my bones as if I'd stepped on a live wire.

I didn't use to have these buzzing dreams often. Lately they've been once a month or so, usually just before I start my period, cramps and weird sleeping going hand in hand. But this one wasn't the usual buzzing dream, where I am flying over rooftops, or even the worst dream of all that ends with me in close darkness, surrounded by stuffed animals.

No. This dream was hyper-colored. I could see every hair on his head, the fine lines of lavender in his blue irises, the nap of his favorite green Army jacket, every line and crease on his polished combat boots. The gun gleamed dully in his hand, held loosely, professionally.

There were fluorescent lights overhead, their buzz echoing the idiot noise in my head. That's why I couldn't speak, you know—that sound just destroys anything you might say, like static on the television screen will eat whatever you're thinking for hours at a time. You can just sit and stare. Like some brain-sucking thing has, well, sucked your brain.

Time slowed down, getting all stretchy and elastic. Each step took a century, and by the time the door came into view—just a plain steel door, with those fluorescents noising overhead—the hornets weren't just crawling through my bones and brain but touching my skin with fleshy little prickling feet.

There was something behind that door, something that smelled of iron and cold darkness, a freezing shiver up the spine. It was like the feeling I got in that broken-down house on the outskirts of Chattanooga, my first job with Dad, right before a poltergeist started throwing little shards of glass hard enough to bury them in rotten drywall with little sounds like puckering lips.

Or like that small podunk in South Carolina where the local voodoo king sent the zombies around because Dad was cutting into his business by breaking the hexes the king had been throwing at people who got in his way—or who wouldn't give him what he wanted. I'd had to use every scrap of anti-hexing Gran taught me and a few things from our books to break through some of those old, nasty curses, and Dad had lost some serious blood fighting off the zombies. That had been bad.

This feeling was worse. Much, much worse.

Don't go in there, *I wanted to say.* There's something in there. Don't do it.

*He walked down the hall, and the buzzing got so bad it shook everything out of me, the dream running like colored ink on wet paper, and as it receded I struggled to say something, anything, to warn him.*

*He didn't even look up. He just kept walking toward that door, and the dream closed down like a camera lens, darkness eating through its edges.*

*I was still trying to scream when Dad reached out his free hand slowly, like a sleepwalker, and turned the knob. And the darkness behind it laughed and laughed and laughed. . . .*

## CHAPTER 3

**I came awake all** at once, with a jolt like five shots of espresso hitting my bloodstream at full speed. The pencil had snapped in my fist, and I was clutching the two broken pieces. My head felt like a bowling ball being cracked by a giant's fingers, and I moaned and blinked. Gray light coming in through the window was empty, sterile, and infinite.

The house was a still, cold cave.

I pushed myself up, head throbbing and ribs aching. I'd fallen asleep and slid over to the side, my back against the wall and my artist's pad digging into my stomach. I rubbed what felt like a half-ton of sand out of my eyes and listened for the heater, for the sound of breathing, for the creaks of Dad moving around.

Nothing. And my alarm clock was turned off. I vaguely remembered something noisy happening earlier and me fumbling for it, almost spearing my palm with the broken pencil.

I rolled up out of my mattresses and shuffled barefoot into the hall. The quilt wrapped around my shoulders wouldn't keep me warm enough. I made my way down to the other bedroom at the end of the hall, the one next to the stairs.

The door was open but the blinds were down. I peered in. Dad's cot was there, and his metal footlocker. A wooden box sat by the door, Dad's private box; I didn't lift the lid. The cot was neatly made, and I thought it hadn't been slept in. You could always bounce a quarter off Dad's cot, though, even five minutes after he got up.

*No problem. He's downstairs; he fell asleep over the table again. Or he's in the living room with the TV on mute, bandaging himself up. Go down and look. You'll see. He's there.*

My heart knew otherwise. It pounded inside my ribcage, each pulse accompanied by a sick squeeze of pain inside my skull and a flip-flop of my stomach. I made it down the stairs like an old woman, holding on to the icy banister.

Silence like the heavy quilt wrapped around my shoulders.

There were boxes in the living room, and my orange beanbag chair. Dad's camping chair sat at its usual precise angle to the television. The red eye of the cable box blinked, and I could almost hear it flicking on and off, it was so quiet.

Dad wasn't in the kitchen. Dirty dishes still piled in the sink, and the house was *cold*. I shuffled out into the hall and punched the buttons to turn the heater on.

The heat pump soughed into life with a *wump*. It was so loud in the stillness I jumped, pulling Mom's sunrise quilt closer around my shoulders. Then I walked slow dream-like down the hall and to the front door, unlocking both deadbolts and yanking it open.

The cold hit me like a hammer, stinging my eyes and robbing the breath from my lungs. The front yard lay under a sheet of white, bits of the broken picket fence buried under mounds of heavy wet snow. The driveway was a pristine carpet.

Dad's truck was nowhere in sight. The entire neighborhood dozed under its cold, thick blanket.

I think that's when I knew. I shut the door, locked both deadbolts, and went up the stairs at a stumbling run, my head pounding and my entire body jolted by each footstep. I banged down the hall and into the bathroom, where I slammed the door and started heaving over the toilet. I didn't produce anything but bile, even though I retched so hard tears squirted hot out of my burning eyes. I stopped long enough to cry, my forehead against the cool white porcelain of the toilet, and then I had to pee so bad I nearly wet myself. While I was sitting on the toilet I had to retch again, so I bent over and tried my best to swallow whatever came up.

I don't know how long it lasted. By the time it was over I could only think about one thing at a time.

*He might come back,* I told myself. *What if he got stuck in the snow? It happens. He got stuck somewhere. Or something.*

Except there wasn't enough snow for him to get stuck in. The truck was heavy, and it had chains in a box under the passenger's seat. Dad was too cautious to let something like weather get in the way of an operation. Or in the way of coming back to get me.

*Then he called and you missed it because you were passed out.*

That couldn't be it either. He wouldn't call; he would just come home. If he got fatigued or the mission went sideways, he would come and collect me and we'd blow town. It had happened before. Since he'd picked me up from the hospital when Gran died, he'd always come back for me. It was like sunrise, or the tide.

*So something's happened to him.*

I rested my forehead on my knees, staring at my jeans rucked around my ankles. My underwear was white cotton, startling against the dark blue denim.

The practical part of me that got the laundry done and kept track of the boxes spoke up, in its calm, cool whisper. *Did you hear me, Dru? Something's happened to him.*

"I know," I whispered. It was the only sound other than the heater's sighing. My heartbeat and my whisper were loud as thunder. My mouth tasted foul.

*So something's happened to him. Maybe he'll come home.*

Maybe he would. The best thing to do was wait. I was *supposed* to wait for him. If it had gone sideways, he would come get me and we'd pack and leave town ASAP. It was standard operating procedure. The old SOP, to be done ASAP, all CYA and BYOB. All the little paramilitary letters lined up in a row, a private language none of the kids at school had to know.

*What if he doesn't? Answer me that, Dru. What if he doesn't?*

That was what I was trying not to think. He'd always come home before, sometimes at dawn. He'd *never* been completely gone overnight, or left in the morning without leaving me a note. He called to check in. It was just what he did.

My forehead was fever-hot. So were my cheeks. My hair hung down in curling strings, dark brown with threads of gold, darker and stringier than Mom's. I felt greasy all over, and the zit on my temple hurt along with the rest of me. My stomach rumbled. I was hungry.

I decided to get up. I couldn't crouch on the toilet forever. Dad would come home; he *would*. I'd wait for him.

In the meantime, I'd take a shower. I'd clean up the house so I had something to do, and so when he came home he wouldn't have to look at a mess. That would make everything all right. He might be wounded or tired when he came home, so I'd get out the first aid kit and make sure everything was ready for whatever had happened to him.

*Yeah. Do that, Dru. That'll make everything just about okay. Just ducky.*

I wiped and stood up, stepped out of my jeans and panties, and dragged Mom's quilt back into my bedroom. I grabbed fresh clothes and went back to the bathroom to clean myself up.

First a shower, then I'd clean up the kitchen. After that, the living room. I'd get out the first aid kit and restock it.

Yeah. That was what I'd do.

So I did it.

# CHAPTER 4

**I**t started snowing again late in the afternoon, big wet spinning flakes from a sky like smooth-beaten iron. I went outside to look at the driveway, shivering in Dad's green Army sweater. I didn't have much in the way of winter clothes; pretty much all my wardrobe was summer stuff since we'd spent so much time below the Mason-Dixon. We'd been down south for at least two years, between the Carolinas, Baton Rouge, Chattanooga, Atlanta, and Florida. If I tanned at all instead of burning, I might have looked even weirder up here with the goddamn polar bears.

I tilted my head back and looked up into infinity. Snow whirled out of the half-darkness, each flake bigger than a quarter and very wet. They stuck to my hair, still damp from the shower. Dad's sweater was way too big for me, and I had the cuffs turned down so they covered my fists, clenching and releasing. I had to take a deep breath to uncurl my hands before I trudged back inside.

I'd already done three loads of laundry and cleaned up the kitchen. The heater was going; it was nice and warm. I was organizing the boxes in the living room, unpacking some and arranging things. I'd already gone through some of the ammo cache and organized the clips according to the guns they were for. Dad would be oiling the rifles soon—it was about that time of the month. Taking care of your gear is essential, especially when you're after things that may or may not be able to mess with complex machinery and electronics. That's why Dad didn't carry a cell phone, they were like magnets for poltergeists and other things.

I tried not to think about it.

My stomach growled and I felt weird, like my head was full of rushing noise. I drank four glasses of tap water through the afternoon, sucking them down in between whatever I was doing, and that helped with everything except the roaring tornado between my ears.

Snowy light came through the windows; the blinds were pulled up. I could see a stretch of the front yard and the clogged street. Some cars had struggled by during the afternoon, none of them fishtailing, all of them wearing snow chains and rattling into their own driveways down the street.

None of them was Dad. I checked every time I heard the clattercrunch of chains or the sound of an engine. They all trundled past to their warm garages, ignoring our lonely house out at the end of the lane. Dad had picked this house because it was solid, but also because it stood apart from the others—which is more of a rarity than you'd think in the Midwest, since they have all that prairie space to shut out.

I was on my knees putting the last clips in the box when I heard something tapping in the kitchen.

*Tip-tap. Tip-tap. Taptaptap.*

My skin chilled, gooseflesh rising hard and fast on my arms. My head jerked up, hair falling in my eyes. It wasn't frizzing today, for once. Go figure—the day I stay home from school I have good hair.

*What the hell is that?* It wasn't the screen door on the enclosed porch back there rattling; I already knew that sound.

The gooseflesh didn't go away, little nuggets of ice under my skin.

*Tap. Tap.* Like little rubber-covered sticks drumming hard against a windowpane. My mouth had gone dry and my fingers were numb. Then I got the taste of oranges and salt in my mouth, and I knew something bad was about to happen. Gran called it an "arrah"; it was only later I found out she meant "aura." Like before a migraine, or the envelope of light Gran always said you could see around people if you had enough of the touch.

With me it was always oranges, and salt. Not real oranges, either. I can't explain it better—it's like wax oranges, maybe.

*Oh shit. Shit.*

The strangest thing of all was how calm I was. The light was failing—even if snow bounced back streetlight shine, it was getting darker. I always expect creepiness around dusk, and I had the howlin' heebie-jeebies anyway.

I got up, my legs turning to wood and shaking like an earthquake had hit. Then I scooped Dad's spare bowie knife off the top of a half-unpacked box. The living room looked like a bomb had hit it; I realized I'd just been unpacking half a box and wandering on to the next. The taste of oranges got stronger, and the tapping came again, a creaking, scratching sound, like small nails against a window.

I held the knife the way Dad taught me, flat along the forearm with the hilt clasped in my hand. That way you can hit someone in the face with the pommel and you can get your triceps and lats—some of the stronger muscles in your body, especially if you do triceps dips or lat pulldowns—into the action. And if you slash up you have your biceps getting busy too, plus you can keep better control of the knife.

*Go quiet, Dru.* It was Dad's voice in my head, now. A soft whisper, like he was teaching me how to concentrate on a target. *Go quiet and take cover on that side of the hall. It's coming from the kitchen. Do it like I taught you.*

I edged down the hall, cursing the boxes set along the side I should have been taking cover against. The kitchen light was on, sending a rectangle of golden glow into the hall and covering the foot of the stairs. The heater clicked off, and the tapping sped up.

*Taptaptaptap.* Pause. *Taptaptap. Taptap.*

My heart lodged in my throat, a chunk of beating meat. The big muscles in my thighs trembled like I'd just finished running a hard mile and a half. I slid slow and easy down the hall, little bits of the kitchen coming into view.

The thing they don't tell you about in situations like these—and by "they" I mean horror movies, which are generally better training for this sort of thing than you'd think—is how your field of vision constricts, everything getting narrower and narrower. You can't see enough, and peripheral vision plays tricks on you. The eyes flick around frantically, trying to take everything in and failing miserably. I stepped in front of the stairs and saw the sink, the stove, a slice of the kitchen table.

The window over the sink was empty, full of snowlight. I let out a soft breath through my mouth, as quiet as possible. My heart pounded in my ears like a drum solo in a pair of headphones. The taste of wax oranges got stronger, turned thick and cloying. Rotting in my mouth.

*Tap. Taptaptaptaptap.* The tattoo of skritching sounds grew stronger, almost frantic.

I stepped into the kitchen.

The back door was set to one side of the counters, Dad's chair at the table with its back to the wall holding the pantry. When he sat down he could see the back door and the entry to the hall, keeping his back to the safest quadrant. The door itself was a prosaic little number, a latticed glass window on top and a flimsy wooden panel with a deadbolt and a chain probably stronger than the door itself on bottom.

My gorge rose hot and thick, fighting with my heart for control of my throat. I choked and almost dropped the knife. I could see it clearly through the squares of double-paned glass, darkening because the enclosed porch was getting dim and dark, light bleeding out of the sky as the snow whirled down.

There was a zombie at my back door. Its eyes swung up, and they were blue, the whites already clouding with the egg rot of death. Its jaw was a mess of meat and frozen blood; something had eaten half its face. Its fingertips, already worn down to bony nubs, scraped against the window. Flesh hung in strips from its hand, and my stomach turned over *hard*. Black mist rose at the corners of my vision, and the funny rushing sound in my head sounded like a jet plane taking off.

I'd know that zombie anywhere. Even if he was dead and mangled, his eyes were the same. Blue as winter ice, fringed with pale lashes.

The zombie's gaze locked with mine. It cocked its head like it had just heard a faraway noise.

I let out a dry barking sound and my back hit the wall next to the hallway, smacking my hip against a stack of boxes.

Dad bunched up his rotting fist, the meat chewed away from fingerbones by something I didn't want to imagine or even *think* about, and punched his way through the window.

# CHAPTER 5

**I would have stood** there forever, staring in dreamy terror at the thing that used to be my father as it battered itself against the back door—if it hadn't been for the phone. It rang shrilly under the sound of snapping wood, and something about that garbled screech jolted me into action. I screamed, a high, girly cry of fear, and dropped the knife. The chime of it hitting linoleum was lost in the groaning noise of breakage as the zombie forced its way through the back door, staring at me. Zombies do that—if something catches their attention they turn blindly toward it and don't stop until they've torn it to bits.

Unless, of course, whoever *made* the zombie had given it a target. Then they don't pay much attention to anything except shambling around in the darkest corners they can find, instinctively avoiding notice as they work their way toward their objective. Not too smart, zombies—but they're determined. *Way* determined.

I should know, I'd watched Dad kill more than a few. Zombies are like cockroaches—you never see them until there's too many of them, and they hang on hard to whatever semblance of life bad contamination or dark magic's given them.

I scrambled back into the hall and bolted for the living room. Each step took a lifetime. My boots slipped on the carpet; I banged into a box and screamed again, diving around the corner and into the living room as the zombie let out a weird bellow. They don't talk, the reanimated. Instead, they let out a whistling groaning noise like a cow in terrible pain, air forced through dead frozen vocal cords. Usually when someone hears that sound, it's the *last* thing they hear, because zombies are eerily quick when they have their next snack in sight.

That's another thing about them. You can bring something resembling life back to a dead body once the soul's gone, sure. But whatever you stick in there always ends up *hungry*.

The nine-millimeter was under the arm of Dad's camp chair in a Velcro holster. I hit the ground hard and scrabbled for it, moving too fast to bother scrambling upright, my feet tangling over each other as I heard light shuffling footsteps and the crunch of broken glass. The zombie blundered into the hall and I heard a god-awful racket—it must have tripped over a box.

My fingers were the size of sausages and clumsy, too. I ripped the cold metal of the gun out of the holster, Velcro tearing free and the chair spinning as I shoved it away. I rolled over onto my back, hearing Dad's voice in my head again.

*Easy there, sweetheart. Don't point that thing at anything you don't intend to kill. Always treat a gun like it's loaded.*

I *hoped* it was loaded. I knew it *probably* was—Dad wouldn't have a piece on his camp chair if it wasn't. I've been shooting since I was nine and even Gran had a gun in her house and I knew gun safety, didn't I? It was why I was Dad's helper. I knew the right way to handle a firearm and the wrong way, too, and the thing blundered around the corner, fixing me with its terrible rotting eyes that were now unholy, glowing blue. A spark of red revolved far back in the pupils, and I *smelled it*.

Zombies smell worse than anything you can imagine if you haven't been hunting things on the dark side of the world. It's a ripe, gassy odor, like rotting eggs and meat gone bad, crawling blind with maggots. It's roadkill and decayed food and body odor all rolled into one package and tied up with puke.

I screamed again, but all that came out was a whistling sound, because my throat had locked up. I pointed the gun and pulled the trigger.

*Click*.

Oh shit.

The safety was on. The thing lunged for me, its atonal bellow rolling free of its throat again—

—and it *fell*.

*Take the goddamn safety off*. I scrabbled with the gun as the zombie splatted onto the carpet. It was covered in snow, wet and running with rot, and it wore Dad's favorite green Army-surplus coat. It had tripped over a box partly blocking the entrance to the living room.

My breath sounded harsh as a crow's caw as the safety clicked off. I lay on my back and pointed the gun.

Dad's eyes met mine. The zombie scrambled to its bare, rotting feet—his *shoes* were gone, where were his boots?—and stretched out its hands, bits of flesh falling and plopping on the carpet. The stink roiled through my nose, filled my head, and I retched as I pulled the trigger.

The first bullet went wide, blowing out part of the living-room wall. I was still screaming and dry-sobbing as the zombie ratcheted forward, falling toward me, its teeth snicking together as its ruined jaw ground shut again and again, practicing the chewing motion that would eat its prey alive. I kept pulling the trigger.

I didn't even hear the shots, though they must have been deafening. All I heard was my own sobs.

It fell on me. Slime splashed and black blood splatted on my face. It burned like acid. It was cold like the snow outside, and it *stank*. Its jaws clicked twice, it shuddered, and a gout of something black and disgusting smashed out of its mouth.

I was still screaming. Couldn't get enough breath, so I was making a high, whining sound. The gun clicked. I was pulling the trigger, but I'd emptied the clip.

The zombie was truly dead. There was a hole in its chest, nicely grouped shots. You have to damage the heart or the thing keeps coming. It's something about the process of making a zombie, the meaning of the heart keeping the whole body going—or so the books say. But I hadn't been thinking about the books. I'd been blindly following training, aiming for the bodyshot like he had taught me.

*Don't aim for the head if you've got a choice. Don't pull. Squeeze the trigger, sweetheart.* Dad's voice, in my head. With the never-ending refrain repeated so many times, I could have said it in my sleep: *Don't point that thing at something you don't intend to kill.*

I thrashed wildly, smashing the thing on the head with the gun, hammering on it and struggling free of deadweight. Still making that high, whining sound, I crawled fast as I could across the living room until I reached the corner farthest away from the zombie. My left hand got rug burn. My right was full of the empty gun.

I put my back in the corner and heard myself babbling. Weak, incoherent sounds bounced off the empty white walls. I was cold and covered in stinking, burning goo.

The zombie lay facedown. Runnels of filth caved through its rotting skin. The smell was *unbelievable*. It wore Dad's jacket and Dad's jeans. Once you've taken the heart out, a zombie rots real quick. Even the skeleton decomposes into dust.

I started to cry.

The babbling turned into one word, over and over again.

"Daddy? Daddy? *Daddy?*"

He just lay there.

The zombie just lay there.

# CHAPTER 6

**The mall was** open because the snowplows had come out. The main drags were clean and clear. They took winter seriously around here and had everything salted, sanded, scraped, and plowed to within an inch of its life. The buses were still running, too.

Life doesn't stop out on the prairies for a little snow. Canned Muzak still has to play, after all, and if they closed the malls, who would play it?

I stared at the small McDonald's cup. It was full of coffee that had been steaming hot and now just kind of sat there. My eyes burned, full of sand. I'd scrubbed the zombie rot off my skin and thrown some clothes on, shoved all the cash I could find—Dad's billfold was gone, probably tucked into the truck somewhere or, more likely, taken—into my messenger bag and hightailed it out of the house, stopping only to turn the heat off, for some weird reason. The back door was shattered and the smell was incredible, thick as Crisco in the nose.

*Did anyone hear the shots?* I didn't think so—there had been no sirens, and our house was a pariah, set apart like it had a disease. We heard nothing from our neighbors, and that was the way Dad liked it. The snow would muffle everything, too.

*If it had killed me, nobody would even know I was dead. I'd be lying there, and . . .*

My brain stopped working, stalled like a choked engine. I shuddered, the plastic chair squeaking. The mall was as brightly lit as Heaven and people were wandering around, shopping like there wasn't a decomposing zombie in my living room. Down on the lower level of the food court a fountain splashed, water rilling musically down squares of Art Deco concrete and sculpted, welded steel.

The Styrofoam cup was a white circle with a brown ellipse inside it, a conical, textured shape. I could draw it. My pad was in my bag, shoved in there with hysterical haste like everything else.

Drawing sounded good, except I couldn't do it with my hands shaking so bad. I shivered again. I couldn't have told you what I was wearing, only that I'd changed clothes after scrubbing the zombie goo off me.

*I shot him. I shot Daddy.*

I kept bumping up against the memory—Dad's blue eyes with their rotting whites fixed on me, a crimson spark dancing in the depths of the clouded pupil, no longer perfectly circular but fringing at the edges as the tissue died. The gun jolting against my hands. The *smell*.

I realized I was making the sound again, a low whining at the back of my throat under the fountain's wet splishing, and killed it. I couldn't afford to have someone look too closely at me.

I'd just killed my dad.

*Hello, Officer? Can you help me? My dad got turned into a*

*zombie. You know, we've been traveling around getting rid of things that aren't real, and this time they hit back. I really need someplace to stay—but can you make sure I have some holy water or something wherever it is? And some silver-jacketed bullets? That'd be sweet. Yeah, that'd be totally cool. Thanks. And while you're at it, can you tell the guys with the straitjackets that I'm really sane? That would help.*

The coffee trembled inside the cup as I touched its rim with two fingers. Soon the mall would start closing down. It was a weeknight. Where would I go? I couldn't get a hotel room with the ID I had on me, unless I tried the bad part of town, and that would cost more cash than I wanted to spend right at the moment. Speaking of cash, I needed to find a way to get more if I ran out, and—

I couldn't even think about planning that far ahead.

*I shot my daddy. Jesus Christ, I shot my dad.* Tears rose hot and thick in my throat. The awful scratching sound at the back window turned into someone pulling the cheap plastic chair opposite me away from the table and dropping down into it, grinning at me through a mop of curly dark hair.

"*There* you are. Skipping two days in a row. Someone call the cops." Graves set an Orange Julius cup on the table—I'd chosen a place with my back to a wall, jumping nervously anytime someone walked behind me on their way to the restrooms. It was the spot with the best sight lines, and someone had put a fake potted plant behind my chair. Awful kind of them.

I stared at Goth Boy instead of the coffee cup now. The silver earring in his left ear was a dangling skull and crossbones. The faint satisfaction I felt at finally getting a clear look at it was drowned in the panic rising in my throat, thumping behind my heart.

He shook dyed, dead-black hair out of his eyes. They were more green than hazel now, cradled in the slightest of epicanthic folds, and the even caramel of his skin was something to hate him for. "Hey." The grin faded, spilled out of his face. Today he wore a Kiss T-shirt and the usual black coat, and when he put his long hands on the table I saw he was wearing fingerless black gloves. The inverted crucifix winked at me from its silver chain, and my gorge rose again, pointlessly. "Are you okay?"

I almost laughed. I was *not* okay. I was not anywhere near okay. I was about as far away from okay as it was possible to get. My eyes swiveled back down to the coffee cup.

"Jesus. What happened?" He leaned forward, putting his elbows on the table. I almost flinched.

*Don't get too close to me. I just shot my dad.*

"Hey. Dru. *Hey.*" He snapped his long brown fingers. "Hello. Sitting right here. What happened?"

*Oh Christ.* The lump in my throat went down, after a short wrestling match. I swallowed convulsively twice and found my voice, weak and watery but still mine. "Fuck off."

His eyebrows shot up. He had actually scraped his hair back behind his ears with both hands, and now he looked very young as he stared back at me. His mouth thinned out, and I thought he was actually going to get up and walk away.

Then he settled back in his chair, arranging his long, gawky limbs as best he could, and picked up his cup. He took a long slurp of whatever was in it, and his eyes turned even more greeny-gold. They caught the fluorescent light and glowed at me.

Graves just sat there like he had all the time in the world.

I finally picked up my coffee cup. It seemed like the thing to do. The crap inside it was ice-cold, but it tasted better than the remainder of the zombie's smell in my mouth. I took a gulp, set the cup down, and grimaced. My face wrinkled up, and I almost spewed cold ash-tasting coffee sludge across the table.

He didn't move.

I listened to the soft strains of canned Muzak, trying to place the song. It was hopeless. Some pop anthem strangled by the gods of commerce. The words curdled in my chest. I couldn't tell anyone what had happened.

Who would believe me? That's why it's the Real World, the night world, and not the normal world. People don't want to know—and the things that eat people or grow fur or tell the future don't *want* people to know. It's a perfect marriage, complete with lies.

Pressure mounted in my throat. I had to say *something*. I leaned forward, resting my elbows on the table too. "I can't go home tonight." The hitch in my voice almost turned into a sob.

His eyebrows drew together. He was perilously close to unibrow; I guess nobody had held him down and administered a good plucking to the caterpillar climbing across his forehead. His earring winked at me.

Graves took another slurp. The unibrow wriggled. Then he pushed the cup away. His knuckles were chapped, I saw. I guess chicks didn't dig hand lotion either, in his book.

"Okay," he said quietly. "Do you have a place to stay?"

I blinked at him. *Oh, no. Christ. Don't try to solve my problems, kid. You have no idea.* "I'll find somewhere." It was the truth. Even if I had to go back to the house. The thought sent a cold chill up my back. Could someone have called the cops? No, they would have caught me in the bathroom—but it was snowing. Maybe the cops couldn't get out to our house in all the snow. But the snow did funny things with sound, and our house was so far away from everyone else's.

The hamster wheel inside my head started up, trying to fig-

ure things out from this new angle—and running smack into a
wall again.

*You're taking this really well, Dru. You just shot your dad. How
are you going to explain this to the cops?*

Well, technically, with as fast as zombies rotted, there wouldn't
be anything other than a broken door and a bullet hole to explain. I
could say it was there when we moved in, that my dad worked nights,
and that's why he couldn't come to the door—

A dry sob caught me unawares. I folded my arms across my
stomach and hunched over. I rested my forehead on the cool, slick
material of the table, and it felt good. Almost as good as the cold
porcelain of a toilet when you're really, really sick.

My stomach roiled again.

*Don't throw up, Dru. Don't you dare throw up on that floor.*

Dad's voice echoed in my skull now, the usual mantra while I
worked the heavy bag. *Work through it, sweetheart. Come on. One
more for Daddy. Do it. Come on, girl, that's not going to cut it! One
more for me! Come on!*

"Jesus," Graves whispered. He sounded a lot older than a
sophomore now. "How bad is it?"

My teeth chattered. I almost choked on a laugh. *How bad is
it? It's so bad you have no idea. That's how bad.* "Just go away," I
said to my knees. How had I managed to tie my boots? I didn't even
remember getting dressed. I was out in public here at the mall. What
was I wearing?

Jeans. I could feel socks. I had my boots on. I plucked at the
edge of my T-shirt and saw it was red. I was wearing Dad's spare Army
jacket, and there was a heavy weight in the right pocket that had to
be something deadly.

*Jesus Christ, I'm armed in public. Dad would kill me.*

"Dru?" His voice had gotten deeper. "How bad is it? You really can't go home?"

I blinked. I had my gloves on, and someone was talking to me. I uncurled, sitting up. The world fell into place, colors and sounds not running like tinted water over glass. The Orange Julius was across the food court, and its sign suddenly seemed like the most wonderful, brightest beacon of hope in the world.

I smelled french fries, hot grease. I wanted to eat. My stomach growled so loudly I hunched my shoulders, hoping he couldn't hear it.

Graves shifted in his chair again. Then he pushed his paper cup across the table. "Take a drink. Your coffee's cold." Still in that quiet, oddly adult voice. No teenage bluster at all in the words.

I grabbed it, sucked at the straw. The taste of strawberries and fake ice cream exploded against my tongue, cutting through and erasing the stink of reanimated death.

He hauled himself up to his full gawky height, scraping the chair back unmusically against the flooring. "Stay here, okay? Just for a second."

I nodded and took another long swallow. He strode off, using those long grasshopper legs to his advantage. By the time I finished the smoothie he was back, sliding a tray across the table. It was a bacon cheeseburger and fries, with a vanilla milkshake I grabbed at. I wolfed the burger in what seemed like two bites while Graves settled back in his chair, tapping his fingers at the edge of the table. He didn't shuck his coat, but he did take a few fries. He'd even brought packets of ketchup, and the only reason I didn't tear into one was because the thought of the thick red inside made the food back up in my throat.

I slurped the last of the vanilla shake and thought of throwing up. Graves hummed along with the Muzak, tapping at the table's edge. He was offbeat, but it didn't seem to bother him much.

"Thanks," I said finally, shoving my hair back behind my ears. The curls had turned to frizz again.

"No problem." He shrugged, bony shoulders moving. "First one's free. Look, you really can't go home? What happened?"

*I shot my dad. But it's okay, he was one of the walking reanimated.* The bacon cheeseburger fought for freedom. I put down the revolt with a slight burp that tasted like fake dairy product and slightly-less-fake beef. "You wouldn't believe me if I told you."

"Try me." He leaned forward, resting his elbows on the table. His mouth had pulled in on itself, compressed into a thin line, and his gaze was dead level.

I stared at his right hand, the way the fingers lay against the slickness of the tabletop, the nails bitten down to the quick. His knuckles were still red and chapped, like he'd been outside a lot in the cold. He still had really good skin. A little bit of lotion would probably fix him right up.

*I could draw his hand. I bet I could. I'd have to shade it more than I normally do to get all the textures down.* "I just can't go home," I heard myself whisper. "Not until tomorrow." *Maybe not even then, either. I don't know.*

Graves was silent for a few moments. His hand was tense against the tabletop, all relaxation spilling out of his fingers. Muzak swelled through horns and synthesizers, echoing through the food court like the noise inside my head. I finally placed the song.

It was, of all things, an inoffensive rendition of AC/DC's "Highway to Hell." Dad liked that sort of music. Every new town we landed in, it was my job to find the oldies station and the classic rock station. I didn't know what Dad would think about one of his favorites having its nuts cut off and played over a mall speaker system.

*He's not going to be thinking about anything ever again, Dru.* The tears rose again. I snuffled, swallowed hard, and glared at Graves, daring him to say something about me blubbering like a kid.

Finally, he sat back, taking his hand off the table. "Do you have a place to sleep?"

*I wish I did.* "I'll find somewhere." *A flophouse hotel, or I'll ride the buses all night. Or something.*

More silence between us. I heard a high, cawing laugh, and glanced over at the Orange Julius to see two blonde girls giggling behind their hands. They had a pair of jocks with them, one strapping dark-haired guy I'd seen at school and another who looked like his cousin or brother.

I felt a million miles away from them. Normal goddamn teenagers, acting like idiots in front of a fast-food place. The dark jock put his arms around one of the girls and picked her up. She shrieked with laughter, the sound as bright as new spilled pennies. Her shirt rode up, showing the supple curve of her back. It was snowing outside and there was a zombie dead in my living room, and here this girl was, dressed like a hooker and laughing.

My hand curled into a fist. I took a deep breath.

"I know a place." Graves said it quietly, leaning forward across the table. He braced his thin elbows and rested his chin on his fist. "If you want, you know."

*Oh, Jesus. Not now.* "Why is it there's always a guy who thinks he can get something out of the new girl?" My fingernails dug into my palm. "Every goddamn town, it's the same thing. Some guy thinks he's God's gift to the displaced."

"I just asked if you wanted a place to sleep." Graves hunched his shoulders defensively. "Jesus."

Then I felt bad. It wasn't his fault I had a dead zombie in my house. The back door was open; the place would be freezing in the morning. I couldn't think about going back until daylight.

*Then what will you do, Dru?* Dad's voice in my head, as if he was giving me a test. *What's going to happen then? You need a plan. Right now you're running on rabbit.*

Graves was still peering at me, his eyes darker greenish under his curly mass of hair. His earring winked again, a hard clear dart of light.

"Sorry." My throat ached. How loudly had I screamed? Had anyone heard the gunshots? I couldn't stop wondering about it. "It's been a bad day." *You have no idea how bad it's been.*

"No problem." He spread his hands, brushing away the apology. His coat whispered as he shifted in the creaking plastic seat. "So, I'll take you someplace you can sleep tonight. Someplace safe. Okay?"

"How much?" I had some money—usually there was no shortage of cash where Dad was concerned; liquid resources were critical to our type of lifestyle. But if Dad was really, truly gone, I had to take careful stock of what I had and make sure I could get more before I started spending like a maniac.

And his billfold was gone. He might've tucked it in the car. But . . .

"I keep telling you, first one's free." He glanced around the food court. "You want to play some air hockey? Good way to get your mind off stuff."

*I don't know how I'm going to get my mind off zombies, kid.* But it was something to do. I couldn't just sit here until the mall closed. I'd explode. Or start crying. Or something else guaranteed to draw attention to myself.

"Sure," I heard myself say.

His face lit up. "Cool. You finished?"

I pushed back my chair and felt my back spasm as I hauled

myself upright, wincing and sucking in a sharp breath. I'd probably pulled something, trying to get away from the zombie. "Yeah, I guess. Graves?"

"Huh?" He shook his hair down over his face, but the grin still remained. It made him look a little bit older, cutting lines into his baby face.

"Thanks." The word wasn't adequate, and I searched for something else to say. "Nice gloves."

"Hey, you know." He scooped up the tray and my still-full cup of ice-cold coffee. The unibrow waggled at me, and then he actually, of all things, *winked*. "Chicks dig guys in gloves."

I actually laughed. Call it a miracle.

# CHAPTER 7

"**You're kidding,**" I said for the fifth time. "In the *mall?*"

"It's warm and it's safe. It opens up in plenty of time to get to school in the morning." Graves ran his hand back through his hair and checked the hallway. "Come on."

I'd never been behind the scenes in a mall before. They're huge places, and the stores are only half of it. Behind each store and threading through the entire complex were maintenance hallways and office space, just a thin doorway away. Graves loitered in the hall leading to the restrooms until it was clear, produced a thin rectangle of plastic—it looked like a credit card—to slip the lock on one of the doors with the ease of long practice, and motioned me through. He looked over my shoulder when he did, and his face was a lot older than usual, but it smoothed out by the time he pulled the door closed and made sure it was locked.

Muzak filtered into the maintenance hallway only faintly, for which I was unendingly grateful. My right hand ached, both from the kickback of the nine-millimeter and from air hockey. He played a mean game, this beaky little boy, and it was take-no-prisoners time once I beat him in the first two rounds.

I hadn't thought about zombies for five-whole-minute stretches, while lunging over the top of the table. It was easier not to think when you were moving.

Our footsteps echoed on bare concrete. The walls were unpainted, and dust grimed the corners. "How often does anyone come through here?"

"Not very. The maintenance staff is gonna want to go home just like everyone else; if anyone's left after they lock up it'll be a miracle. Even the janitors leave early on days like this." He took a right and led me into a confusing tangle of corridors that all looked the same. It was warm, at least, and I suddenly realized I was exhausted.

I shifted my bag higher on my shoulder, the strap cutting through Dad's jacket and my T-shirt. The wool of my gloves rasped against my hands. "You do this often?"

"When I have to." His shoulders hunched, but he slowed down so I could keep up with him. "We have to stay back here for a little while, until everyone's cleared out. Then it's safe, and we can play."

"Play what? More air hockey?" I just wanted to take my boots off and sit down somewhere. A crying fit sounded good, too. *Really* good. Not to mention a hot shower and some television, while I was at it.

"If you want. Anything *we* want. They've got cameras, but most of 'em don't work. The parent company that owns the mall is too cheap to put in real cameras, so most of 'em are dummies anyway, and the ones that do work don't have any tapes or anything. Come nighttime, this place is a playground. There's shit here you wouldn't *believe*."

I wanted to ask him if *he* had to go home sometime soon.

Decided not to. His home life was his own problem; I had plenty of my own.

Graves turned sharp left, and I found myself in a cavernous space with a huge garage door pulled down, dumpsters lining the walls on the other side. A cardboard-crushing machine telling everyone to *Reduce Reuse Recycle!* with a cheerful cartoon mouse waving under a yellow-painted sun glowered at us. I shivered, hearing the wind pick up outside the big garagelike door. Thin fingers of cold air caressed my face.

It wasn't the low moan of the wind at dusk, but something about it was hungry and ugly just the same. The shivers plucked at the aching muscles of my back, made the rug burn on my left hand prickle.

I kept expecting to hear the tapping again, or the screaming sound of dry tendons working, or a shuffling step.

"You okay?" Graves had turned to face me and stood with his hand on a stack of pallets leaning against the wall. He'd pushed his hair back, tucking some of it behind his ears, and I had to admit he wasn't bad-looking, just babyfaced and beaky. I could see the adult face underneath, in the way his bones held his face up. Even if his eyes stayed muddy instead of greenish.

*I'm not going to be okay for a while. I just have to figure out what to do.* I swallowed a lump in my throat, my stomach unhappy with the sheer amount of grease in a mall bacon cheeseburger. "Copacetic."

"Okay. You can't tell anyone about this." He hesitated.

I could have told him now wasn't the time for him to be having second thoughts. "I don't have anyone to tell. You're about the only person I know here." *Cut the crap. I'm tired.*

He nodded, chewing at his lower lip, then turned and shimmied sideways behind the cardboard crusher.

*You have* got *to be kidding me.* I took a deep breath, hitched my bag around so I could squeeze through the narrow slice, and followed.

There was barely enough room for me and none at all for my bag. Still, I struggled through, almost hit my head on something metallic, and whispered a curse. Graves fiddled with the wall and—miraculously—a door opened inward. "They forgot about this once they put the dumpster and stuff down here." His voice echoed and fell flat. There was a click, and warm electric light played over the dirty concrete wall in front of my face. I squirmed around the side of the door frame and almost fell into another hallway. "This used to be an office when it was a loading dock for Macy's. When they did the big remodel two years ago they closed this all up, bricked up the back of the office and stuck all those dumpsters and stuff against the wall. I wondered if you could still get in here, and whaddaya know. Neat, huh?"

I looked around. There was a bathroom off to one side, through a half-open door. The rest of the office looked just like a studio apartment. "How the hell did you get the sleeping bag in here?" I didn't have to work very hard to sound impressed.

He pointed up, a faint blush starting on his cheekbones. Two ceiling tiles were removed, the rest discolored and dirty. The only light came from a naked bulb dangling from an extension cord. "I lofted some stuff up through there. Welcome to Casa Graves, babe."

The sleeping bag lay on a camp cot, and a flimsy plywood bookcase with a Discman and a stack of CDs stood next to a pair of tangled headphones. Jimi Hendrix leered at me from a poster tacked up on the wall. Another poster of a woman's gigantic fake breasts cradling a cold Bud Light bottle stood above a coffeemaker and a hot plate, with a shelf of dishes and packages of Top Ramen stacked neatly underneath. Black T-shirts hung on a folding rack, and a few pairs of jeans were folded up underneath.

It reminded me of Dad's room, always kept military-neat no matter where we landed. No matter what city we were in, I could always find anything in Dad's room in seconds flat.

*Dad.* The lump in my throat refused to go away. I realized Graves was standing, his hands in his pockets and his shoulders hunched up even further, in the middle of the room next to the cot. His face was a study in disinterest, but I caught the darkening of his eyes and the shadow of hurt around his mouth. He was waiting for me to say something cruel.

I was starting to wonder about this kid.

"It's nice," I managed, around the lump. "It's cozy." It was so warm sweat prickled along my lower back. I slid my bag off my shoulder and felt like an idiot for wondering about his home life. I stripped my gloves off and stuffed them in my left coat pocket, trying not to stare at the breasts-and-Bud poster.

"There isn't a shower." Graves's shoulders dropped down from their hunch, relieved. He stripped off his gloves with two quick movements and tossed them on the bed. They looked like crumpled imposters on its neatness. "But the bathroom works fine, and if I have to I can get a space heater through the roof. It's safe. Nobody remembers it's still here. Close the door, willya?"

I did. The hinges were held on with clumsily attached screws, and I was suddenly sure he'd rehung the door to make it swing inward—after monkeying through above the ceiling tiles. This kid was smart.

I set my bag down near the bookcase and wondered if I should slide out of the green Army coat before I felt the heavy accusing weight in its pocket again. I couldn't remember if I'd shoved a fresh clip in the gun.

*Sloppy, sweetheart. Always check your ammo.* Dad's voice again. I could almost forget the zombie's howling bellow and the tip-taps of its bony fingers against the glass. The low moaning sound it made, an unmodulated groan. The sound of my own screams drowning out the gun's blunt roar.

I shivered again.

Graves had shrugged out of his coat and tossed it on the cot as well. The entire room smelled like healthy teenage boy, a mix of hair, testosterone, and Speed Stick or Right Guard or one of those deodorants with heavy masculine names. "You can take your coat off. You want some coffee? I've got some Coke, too, but it's not cold. And I've got Doritos, if you're still hungry. Noodles, too."

"No, I'm good." I picked my way over to the bookcase and peered at the paperbacks. He liked horror novels, lots of Stephen King, Richard Matheson, Dean Koontz. But there was also a copy of Sun Tzu's *The Art of War* and a stack of books about the Spanish Civil War, as well as a thick, well-read history of World War II. And—good Lord. There was a whole shelf of romance novels, with pink bodice-ripping covers. Right over the bottom shelf of heavy, thick math textbooks.

This guy was getting more interesting all the time.

"I read a lot," he said behind me, a little unsteadily. "I can't get a TV in here." There were shuffling sounds, and when I looked back over my shoulder, I saw he was making coffee despite his shaking hands. "Sure you don't want a Coke or something?"

He was nervous, blushing, and almost stammering. It was kind of endearing.

"Maybe some coffee," I volunteered, diplomatically. "This is really cool, Graves. It's like your own little world."

"No teachers and no jocks." He made a short snorting noise that tried to be a laugh. "Come on in and sit down. You look tired."

I *felt* tired. But it was weird—I felt safer than I had last night at home. There was no wind moaning at the windows, and I didn't have to wait for the worst—it had already happened. Just having someone else near, talking while he made coffee, was enough to make me feel better.

I folded myself down next to the bookcase and hugged my knees. "You live here?"

A shrug, seen from the back. "Here and other places. Wherever I want." He vanished into the bathroom with the coffeepot. "We can go out the other way once the mall's closed down."

*Another way out? Smart, kid. Never have just one escape route.* I put my forehead on my jean-clad knees and let out a long breath I hadn't been aware of holding. Trembling spilled through my bones as Graves splashed in the bathroom. He finally came out, and a few minutes later the smell of coffee filled the small studio. It reminded me of Dad—he always needed caffeine in the mornings. I made his coffee the way he taught me, the way they made it in the Marines— strong and bitter enough to eat a silver spoon. Gran had boiled hers in a percolator, and Dad wasn't far behind. I was probably the only kid in three states who knew how to run an old-timey coffee bubbler.

"Hey." Graves had appeared right next to me, crouching down. Strings of wavy hair fell in his face, and he pushed them back with a quick flick of his long fingers. "You okay? You hurt anywhere?"

The question struck me as absurd. I hurt all over, every muscle in my back was tight, my legs ached, my shoulders felt like lead bars, my arms were heavy—and my heart, speared with something dark and terrible, hurt worst of all. My hands shook. Even my *hair* ached, now that I was sitting down, not moving from one thing to the next. I opened my mouth to tell him so, and a dry, barking sob interrupted me halfway.

"Oh shit." He sounded really alarmed, and he dropped down next to me. "Dru? Jesus. Dru?"

I couldn't answer him. Sobs racked me, horrible sounds like I was being strangled because I couldn't keep them back but I tried so hard my teeth locked together, grinding. My jaw creaked, and I couldn't smell the coffee after a while because my nose was full.

Graves put one bony arm around me and didn't say anything while I cried. It was decent of him, and I liked him for it. I was almost sorry I was going to have to blow town and leave him behind.

* * *

He gave me the cot and the sleeping bag, and I passed out clutching my messenger bag to my chest, Dad's coat on the floor next to the bed. When I woke up hours later, Graves was gone. There was a scrawled note attached to the inside of the door with a wad of spearmint gum.

*Went to school. I'll bring your homework back. ~~You should really stop skipping~~*. There was another line, more heavily crossed out, that I couldn't decipher, then: *Stay as long as you want. I'll be back.*

I dug in my bag until I came up with my watch, a waterproof Swiss number Dad had bought in New York when I was twelve. He'd left me with August for about a month while he was up near the Canadian border doing something or another. Even though August was pretty cool and knew more about the Real World than a lot of books, he still wasn't real company, like Dad. And besides, he always made me stay inside while he was out "working." A whole month in

New York and all I knew was one street in Brooklyn.

It was a little after 3 p.m. I'd slept for a long time; my head felt heavy, my mouth sandy and nasty, every muscle stiff and my back hurting like a sonofabitch. I'd definitely pulled something getting away from the zombie.

The thought hurt, but not as much as I thought it would. It was like pinching your toes after they've gone to sleep. Dad was a zombie. Had been a zombie. Whatever.

*What am I going to do now?* I stood staring blankly at the note on the door for a little while, just breathing and feeling the inside of my head full of cotton wool.

A thought swam through the fuzziness, linking up with the memory of August's close, stuffy apartment. *Contacts. Dad has contacts. I should go find the list and let one of them know.*

We weren't the only ones hunting down ghosts, poltergeists, flickers, bad hexes, chupacabras, gator spirits, bad voodoo, or anything else you care to name. There's a whole underground movement, checking in at occult and Army-Navy surplus stores, passing along information and trading tips on how to best clean out a haunted house or take down a sucker, how to disperse a poltergeist or where the next wave of weird crap moving through a region is coming from.

I shivered at the thought of suckers, gooseflesh rising hard and hot on my arms, spilling down my back. They were bad news, like werwulfen—though wulfen were generally not dangerous to people like Dad, having their own running feud with the suckers to keep them busy.

I shut my eyes. Why hadn't I told Dad about Gran's owl? He might have listened and not gone out that night.

Which made it my fault, in a fuzzy sort of way. And the house was standing open, getting colder and colder, with a hole the size of Texas in the back door and a stain on the living-room carpet, plus a bullet hole in the living-room wall.

*What am I going to do?*

First things first. I was *starving*. I needed food, and I needed to think. I had to make a list of Things To Do. I'd have to go back to the house during daylight. Daylight was safest. I needed to get the ammo together, and all the weapons. I needed to pack up, and I needed to find Dad's truck.

Our battered blue Ford truck rose up inside my head like a beacon. If I could find the truck, I could make it out of town and figure out what to do next. Gran's house up in the Blue Ridge was still standing solid—we'd been there a few months back, swinging through to check in on it—and mine under the terms of the trust fund she and Dad had set up. I could hide out there. Once I was up in the mountains, I would have a little space to breathe. Nobody would come looking for me there—it took two dirt roads and a piece to even get close, as Gran always said.

Dad deserved a funeral service. There wouldn't be anything left of him but greasy dust and bits of bleached bone, though. Zombies fall apart amazingly quick.

One scorching tear trickled down my cheek, then another. He wasn't going to come stamping in the door yelling, *Dru, honey, get your ass up!* He wasn't going to walk in tired and heavy, lock the door, and ask me what was for dinner. He wasn't ever going to quiz me about sage smudging, hex-breaking, or poltergeist-clearing ever again. Or even leave me a note reminding me to do my katas.

I came back to myself with a jolt and looked down at my watch. It was buckled on my wrist now, my clever little fingers doing the work for me. Thirty minutes had passed while I stood staring at the note on the door. My back ached, every single muscle glued to its neighbors and protesting. I needed some aspirin in the *worst* way.

I had money. I could make it up to the food court—but what if someone saw me behind the mall's scenes? Would I get in trouble I couldn't lie my way out of, or would someone start watching the halls and catch Graves on his way back?

*Oh, for God's sake. You've got plenty of problems without worrying about him.*

But you don't blow someone else's bolt-hole. It's like a law among hunters. And if Dad was gone, I was the only one left to do the hunting.

*That* was a scary thought, and one I pushed away as soon as I could.

I stamped back to the bed and dug in my bag. It was deathly quiet down here, but even if I made any noise someone outside wouldn't be able to tell where it was coming from, would they? How often did people scurry down to the dumpsters during the day, anyway? Who used the cardboard crusher?

My artist's pad was a bit worn around the edges from being smashed into my bag all the time. I flipped through it, looking for a clean sheet so I could leave a note for Graves.

The strength went out of my legs, and I sat down hard on the concrete floor, my teeth clicking together as my ass hit.

There was the drawing of the iris I'd been working on, shaded lovingly. Then the doodles of shapes, the closet door, and my nightstand. The pile of laundry. On the next page the pencil had dug into the paper, rasping harshly and shading giant blocks of shadow. I didn't remember drawing this, but I knew I had. Who else could've?

It was the back of a warehouse or another large building butted up against an even larger one, broken windows suggested with slices of pencil shading. There was a busted-down chain-link fence, and in front of the fence was something familiar—a truck crouched like a big cat.

*Our* truck. I'd know that camper anywhere. My mouth went dry and copper-tasting. My heartbeat thudded in my throat and ears.

*I don't remember drawing this. I fell asleep after drawing the laundry—I know I did!*

But I'd *dreamed*, hadn't I? A bad dream, about . . . what? Dad, and a door. And something behind the door. The more I looked at the building crouching behind our truck, the more certain I was that something horrible had happened in there, something that ended up with Dad getting turned into a flesh-eating, shambling horror.

The pencil had been broken in my hand, digging in with sharp edges when I woke up. The drawing had obviously been done quickly, using shortcuts I knew about from years of scribbling sketches. It was ridiculous, impossible. Gran would have been proud of me for displaying a new talent, but I wasn't so happy about it at all.

I was still staring at the drawing's heavy, thick strokes when a scratching sound from the wall brought my head up. I dove off the bed and rolled, grabbing the jacket and ending up full-length on the floor, my hand squirming for the gun just like Dad taught me. *Get down first*, then *return fire. Making yourself a target while you fire back is bad business, sweetheart.*

Sanity caught up with me just as the door swung inward. Who else knew I was down here?

Graves hopped through the door and shook his head sharply. He was soaking wet and shivering, water dripping from his curly hair and the hem of his long black coat. His lips were almost blue, his nose bright red and dripping, and his cheeks looked yellow-raw. "It's c-cold as sh-*shit* out there," he stuttered, and blinked owlishly at me

69

as he swept the door closed, a black backpack hanging wetly from one sodden bony shoulder. "And snowing again. I had a hell of a time getting back in here. I brought you something."

I felt ridiculous, lying on the floor, but he didn't seem to notice. He shut the door and stamped, shaking himself like a golden retriever just come up out of a freezing lake. Water flew.

I clicked the safety back on and eased my finger off the trigger. Clambered to my feet, leaving the gun in my coat. "It's snowing again?"

"God, is it ever. You wouldn't believe what I went through to get inside the mall. Here." He dug in his backpack, shaking more water out of his hair. I could see the melting ice sticking to the dark strands. He was *soaked*.

"Jesus." I crossed the small room and tried to take the backpack away from him. "Get out of that coat, your lips are blue. You'd better get into something dry."

"She's already trying to get my clothes off," he announced to the ceiling, refusing to relinquish his bag. "You sound all Southern when you—hang *on* for a second. Jeez, patience is a *virtue*. Slow down, it's for you."

The backpack yielded a smaller paper bag that smelled like meat and fries. I got him out of the coat and was looking around for someplace to hang the heavy dark material when he dropped the pack, pulled his wet shirt off over his head, and shook all over again, splattering me with cold water and bits of ice.

"What did you do, roll in it? Jesus." I rescued the bag of food. "Where did you get this?"

"Place on Marshall that never closes. I worked there one summer. They do good food. Start eating, don't wait for me. You want some coffee?"

He headed off for the bathroom, his shoulder blades like fragile wings under copper-tinted skin. There was a bloom of red across his shoulders from the cold, and he was already unbuttoning his pants. He had nice musculature, a bit scrawny but developed, at odds with his baby-cheeked face.

A flush worked its way up my neck, found my cheeks. I looked quickly away, found a hanger and got his coat hung up where it could drip onto the floor.

He came out of the bathroom with a towel around his waist and another one scrubbing at his hair. I dug in the bag and found three cheesesteak sandwiches and a triple order of curly fries. They smelled *divine*. "Wow. What do I owe you?"

A flash of a grin eased his face. "First one's free, kid. Start eating; you probably haven't had anything all day, have you? They even canceled school, for once. Bletch was madder than a jock with his balls kicked in. It took me a couple hours to get to the place out on Marshall and another—" He broke off, looking down at me with one half of his unibrow cocked. "You'd better eat. I didn't haul it out here for nothing."

At least he was looking a little less like a half-melted Popsicle. "Christ, will you put your clothes on?" Dad walked around shirtless whenever he wanted to and I was sure I wasn't a prude, but still.

"I thought you were trying to get me *out* of my clothes." He snorted his particular sarcastic laugh, half bark and half yip of pain. "Start eating."

"Really, what do I owe you?" *And where do you get your money, kid? Do I care?* There were all sorts of questions about why a kid would live in a mall, but I wasn't so sure I wanted to know. His problems were just that—*his*. I had enough on my hands.

"Told you, first one's free." He actually *winked*, his eyes more brown than green today. He grabbed a shirt and pulled it over his head, took a handful of other clothes while I looked down at the floor, that strange heat swamping my cheeks like water filling up a footprint.

"You bought me dinner the other day, remember?"

"But I *didn't* buy you a Marshall Street Special. I wasn't sure you'd be here, but then I thought you'd probably still be sleeping. You were passed out pretty hard when I left this morning." He dropped down next to me wearing an Iron Maiden T-shirt and dry jeans. The towel landed with a thump near the duffel bag that held his dirty laundry, and he picked up one of the sandwiches. "Hope it's still warm."

My coat was lying on the floor right next to him. It looked innocent, but I knew what was in the pocket. What would he say if he guessed what I'd been about to do?

Just who *was* this kid, anyway? "Why are you doing this?"

His shoulders hunched again. He took a massive bite of cheesy steak sandwich and closed his eyes. The floor was hard and cold, and I wondered where he'd slept last night. I hadn't even thought about it before.

He chewed, his hair hanging in damp black strings over his eyes, and shrugged. "Mrfle."

*What the hell does that mean?* I decided to let it go. He'd brought me down here, after all, and I wasn't one to throw stones when it came to abnormal living arrangements. "Thank you. I mean, it's been bad. Thanks." The urge to tell him something, anything, rose in my throat.

He swallowed, his Adam's apple bobbing. "Want to talk about it? It's cool if you don't."

*What could I tell you that you'd believe?* At least when I had Dad I wasn't so lonely.

*Dad.* I heard that weird bellow again, air forced through a frozen throat. What had the zombie been trying to say? Anything?

Tears prickled my eyes for the thousandth time, hot and hard. The lump congealed in my windpipe. I had to breathe deep. I was starving, and I don't think straight when I'm hungry. "My dad." I unwrapped my sandwich and took a bite.

It was really good, salty and cheesy and full of fat and carbohydrates. The bun was fresh, and it was still warm.

"What about him?" Graves said it carefully, and I could have laughed.

"It's not what you think. He's dead." The word sounded strange in my mouth. A single syllable that didn't belong to my Dad. It belonged somewhere *out there*, and putting it in a sentence with him was wrong, even though I knew it was true.

If he was surprised, he hid it really well. His eyes got really wide and very green. He took another bite, chewed thoughtfully. Snagged a handful of curly fries and stuffed them in his mouth, still watching me. Waiting for the other shoe to drop.

I reached over to the bed and fished my artist's pad out of the tangled mess of the sleeping bag. I opened it to the drawing of Dad's truck. "Do you know where this is?"

He took the paper. His eyes widened briefly, again. He swallowed again, throat working. His earring glittered at me, like a signal. "This is really good."

*Duh, I've been drawing since I was five.* "Thanks. Do you know where that is?"

"No." He waited, his eyebrows up. His mouth made a little inquisitive movement, and he licked the grease off his fingers.

*Shit.* "I have to find it. I have to find our truck so I can . . . Well, I have to find it." I took a bite, swallowed it without tasting, and

73

laid down the sixty-four-million-dollar question. "Will you help me? Please?"

"Help you find that building?" He shrugged. "Sure, I guess. It'll take a while with all the snow. The radio said it won't stop for a week. We're in for a regular old whiteout."

I waited for him to ask more questions, but he didn't. Instead, he just ate, watching me between bites. When he finished the first sandwich, he started on the second. I listened to the silence outside the walls, chewing reflexively. It might have been cardboard for all I could taste.

He was halfway done when he stopped chewing and looked at me. "What kind of trouble are you in?"

*I don't know yet. I wish I did. If I told you, you'd think I was crazy.* "It's pretty bad." That was about all I could say.

"Okay." He shrugged again. "Sounds interesting. We'll start looking tomorrow. But we'll have to do it after school."

My jaw threatened to drop.

His shoulders hunched again. "You think I want to live in the corners like this for the rest of my life? I've got a plan. I'm going to get my GED and go to community college; then I'm going to go to real college. I'm going to be a mathematician. They get paid crap until they get tenure, but after that it's pretty cool. I'm going to be a physics professor."

*A physics professor?* I tried to imagine him as an adult, or as a teacher, and failed. The effort made my brain hurt. He was just so gawky and young. "Everybody's got to have a goal." Odd relief bloomed under my breastbone, filled my entire chest. "You don't skip school?"

"No way. It's a one-way ticket back to foster care if I fly above the radar, you know." The thoughts crossing his face went too quickly for me to even guess at before the wall went back up behind his eyes. "That was my first time, with you." He grinned, a fetching, lopsided smile that he ended up stuffing more curly fries into. "You're a bad influence, Dru."

*You have no idea, kid.* I was startled into another laugh. The sandwich tasted pretty good after that.

## CHAPTER 8

**N**ight came quickly, and when Graves decided it was safe
he led me back out through the maze of passages. The mall
was deserted, lights turned down low. The fountain on the
first floor was shut down too, its surface placid and quiet. Silence
wrapped around all the chairs upended on the tables in the food
court, tiptoed down the halls, sheathed the stores in darkness. In
here, you couldn't hear the wind. We might as well have been on
another planet.

Graves leaned over the waist-high barrier and yelled wordlessly
into the mezzanine, the sound ricocheting off floor and ceiling, a
weirdly distorted echo bouncing back. He surveyed the result with a
satisfied air. "See? Pure liberation. You do it."

I let out a shattering war-whoop, the kind I used while sparring
with Dad or doing my katas. Graves flinched, but his own yell rose
with mine. My cry broke on a laugh, his did the same, and he pushed
at me with his bony shoulder, almost toppling me over. I pushed

back, and I suppose that's when I started thinking he was a friend instead of just some kid.

The noise died away. "Sometimes I play the games in the arcade by myself," he said meditatively. His eyes glittered in the half-dark. "It's nice having someone else around. You want to play some air hockey?"

I almost shuddered at the thought. "No thanks." My wrist still hurt, along with the rug burn on my left hand. And my back was still unhappy, despite the ancient bottle of Tylenol Graves had stashed in his bathroom. "Can I just walk around?"

"Sure. I'm going to check a few things out. Stay away from Sears, they have a working camera last I looked." He grinned, then whirled on his toes and strode away with a bounce in his step, his long black coat fluttering

I stood there for a few minutes, my eyes closed. Dad's jacket was heavy and warm. The mall was dark, only the barest of night-lights on in store windows. Grates were pulled down to close the stores off, everything from rolling iron contraptions to glass sheets stopping ghosts from shoplifting. The chill of possibly getting caught walked along my shoulders. If any cops showed up, I'd get busted for possession of a weapon and God alone knew what else.

*Stop worrying, Dru.* I sighed, the tension leaving my neck for a few seconds. I felt a little naked without my bag, but I couldn't carry it everywhere. *If you could get caught, Graves wouldn't be here. He's smart enough.*

Matter of fact, he was distressingly smart. He didn't *look* like a math geek; I wondered if the goth bit was camouflage. It's not every teenage boy who wants to be a physics professor when he grows up. He probably had a nice rational mindset that would think I was batshit if I started telling him about some of the things I'd seen.

What did I care, anyway? It wasn't like he was going to be a permanent fixture in my life.

*You have other problems. Start by figuring out how Dad got turned into a zombie.*

I needed to go back to Dad's books and do some research. The second and last group of zombies we'd run across had been near Baton Rouge. And that had been straight-up voodoo like that guy in South Carolina, not native to the Midwest. There might be other stuff in the books about zombies, stuff we hadn't looked at last time because we hadn't needed it. I'd been too busy with unhexing to really pay attention to Dad putting the corpses down again.

The books were in the living room. Had the neighbors even heard the gunshots? The thought was like poking at a sore tooth with your tongue. All I could answer was probably not, since there hadn't been any sign of cops when I'd left. But still . . .

I didn't know nearly enough, and sneaking around a mall at night wasn't going to answer the questions.

*Just what are you thinking of, anyway, Dru?* I turned to my left and stuck my hands in my pockets, the cold weight of the gun against my right-hand knuckles. If I inhaled really deeply, I could smell fabric softener and the ghost of Dad's aftershave. It wasn't nearly as comforting as it should have been.

I put my head down and ambled along the gallery, past the Hillshire Farms—breathing out smoky meat and processed cheese even through the glass door—and a chain store selling cheap jewelry by the ton. My boots made almost no noise against the short, tough-as-nails industrial carpet, and it was dark.

It was nice to be in here after everything was closed up. The silence was vast and downy, like soft feathers. The half-light was restful; it hid everything. There was nobody around to see me if I chose to smile or frown, nobody looking to see what I was wearing, nobody I had to lie to or watch out for. I could stare in the windows or stop outside Victoria's Secret, examining spindly lingerie-clad mannequins spotlit for the night, and nobody would think I was strange.

It wasn't as cool as I thought it might be. After about ten minutes of wandering around I began to get a little nervous. I couldn't even hear the wind. With that much silence, the inside of my head started to get a little crowded with other sounds. Remembered sounds.

Like the tapping of fleshless fingers on glass. Or the hideous, scratching, frozen-throated bellow of a zombie.

*Someone* turned *him into a zombie.* It was the thought I'd been avoiding ever since I'd pulled the trigger again and again. *You don't just happen to trip and fall and turn into one of the reanimated. Someone did it* to *him. Who? Probably the same someone he was after.*

Someone, or some*thing*? The thing behind the door? I was awful certain my dream was real, and that I'd seen Dad's next-to-last moments on earth.

Which led me to the not-so-comforting thought that I might start dreaming of really gruesome things. It wasn't going to be fun if I did. Gran had never taught me much about dreams; we'd been too busy during our waking hours. All she'd ever said was, *Dreams are false friends, honey Dru. They don't show you what you need or what's sure; they most just show you nothin' you can hang onna peg. Just maybes, that's all.*

I stopped just outside the movie store and rubbed at my forehead with the heel of my left hand. If I rubbed hard enough, I wondered if I would come up with something that would fix the huge hole in the world.

Things like this weren't supposed to happen. It was like a regular bad dream, except it *kept* happening. Dad was gone. Really gone, not just coming back near dawn bloody and exhausted. He was irrevocably, absolutely, finally gone.

Just like Gran. Just like Mom.

I was alone. The fact that I'd been trained to be self-sufficient wasn't comforting at all. I wanted my dad.

I was just about to go down *that* particular mental road when I heard something I shouldn't have, something that froze me in place, staring at the blank TV screens that during mall hours showed whatever movie the employees had been told to push that week. My own reflection—curly wild dark hair, big white-ringed eyes, glaring white cheeks, and camo jacket—stared at me, replicated in each glass shield.

The crash and tinkle of broken glass was followed by a crunch and a low, sonorous growl that scraped not only at my ears but *inside* my head, dragging through the center of my brain. Pain flared behind my eyes, and I pitched forward, catching myself on the window with my left hand and forehead. The jolt clicked my teeth together *hard*. Copper bloodtaste spilled down my throat as my heartbeat slammed into overdrive, pounding so hard in my belly and chest black spots whirled and danced through my vision.

I found myself on my knees, shaking the growl out of my head. The pain vanished as soon as it had arrived, and I was only disoriented.

*Get up, Dru!* Dad's voice barked at me. *Get under cover! Do it now!*

I set my teeth and breathed in the way Gran taught me, pulling myself back into a compact ball inside my own skull. The growl slid into a lower, purely physical register, and I lifted my head, peering with watering eyes down the long empty hallway broken only by potted plants, benches, and carts full of useless crap covered for the night. There was a ruddy glow creeping up the walls, and I heard a rushing crackle under the growl.

Now that the thing wasn't echoing inside my head, I could think. I scrambled on hands and knees to the shelter of a huge potted palm, probably fake, and smelled smoke. I wasn't sure if it was real smoke or just my own panic. My right hand dug in my jacket pocket, the weight of the gun cold and reassuring. I slid it free of the fabric, bringing it up nice and easy and clicking the safety off as the growling swelled, plucking at the outside of the small ball I'd made of myself inside my head.

Another thing they don't tell you about this sort of thing is how much it makes you want to pee. I *really* wanted to find a bathroom, my bladder suddenly incredibly, painfully full. No time for that—I slid over to the side and peeked down the hallway.

*Whatever it is just broke the glass on a second-floor window.* Then I realized entrances to the top level of the parking lot were on the second floor, and a quarter of the way up this arm of the mall was one of those entrances. It was just past the shop with the funny-smelling lotions.

*What the hell?* I breathed in, tasted smoke and something else, something icy and fresh, with an iron undertaste.

Outside air.

Then it padded into view, long and lean against shifting shadows. It was the size of a pony, covered in weird glassy hair, shaped like a mother of a big shaggy dog. My head hurt, the way it did when an apparition was getting ready to materialize, draining the warmth out of the air and sucking up all the ambient energy most people barely recognize they're swimming in.

I sucked in another soft breath, catching myself before I made a noise. It was a close call. *Be quiet, Dru. Be really quiet. This is so not good.*

I suppose I get a prize for stating the obvious, even inside my own skull.

The dog-thing inhaled, snorting through a nose the size of the Grand Canyon. As it exhaled, its jaws parting and the huge obsidian teeth sliding against each other, it made a sound like a match applied to a gas leak. Smoke fumed off its shoulders, lifted from its spine.

It *ignited*. Orange and yellow flame raced along its back, dripping down the glassy fur, spattering the flooring. The scorch of it rolled down and hit the back of my throat—burning plastic.

The thing was on fire.

I was stupid. I gasped. I couldn't help it.

It heard me.

Its blind fiery head swung around, questing. Then it snorted, and the heat of it rolled down the hall and brushed the leaves of the fake palm tree above me. The quiet rustling was almost lost in the sound of its claws snicking as it loped unerringly forward.

A burning *dog*. The size of a Shetland pony. Running straight at me.

I scrambled to my feet, my mouth dry and tasting like thick liquid copper. I bolted. My boots slapped the linoleum as the thing let out a howling growl with the rush and crackle of flame underneath it, belching with foul, sulfur-impregnated, roasted air.

I put my head down, barely aware I was screaming like a goddamn cheerleader in a horror movie, and ran for my life.

# CHAPTER 9

**pounded down the** hallway and jagged to the left as the mezzanine opened up in a well of darkness, my legs thick with terror and refusing to work right, the gun clutched uselessly in my right hand as my arms pumped. The escalators were turned off for the night, but I skidded around the corner and took the frozen stairs three at a time anyway, my hips and shoulders jolting each time I landed. The thing behind me—*it's burning*, the rational part of my brain howled, and the other part, the part Dad had trained into me, replied with an iron imperative to *fucking move I know it's burning!*— gave out another roar as it thumped into something with a crash, and the whole thing began to seem like a nightmare. I'd wake up any second now, safe in my bed, with Dad downstairs watching cable.

It smelled horrible, rotten eggs and burning foulness. I ran like a rabbit, fleet with terror, my boots slapping down with little squeaking sounds. Something that sounded like Dad was screaming in my ear, but I didn't listen. I *couldn't* listen.

Instinct saved me. I threw myself aside as a bullet train of compressed air screamed past, holding the smearing crimson and orange of the burning thing, stretched out in a full leap. I fell heavily, not bothering to try and stop myself, barking my head on something. Warmth dripped down the side of my face. I scrambled to my feet and tripped again, knocking over chairs—overflow from the food court, a nice little nook where people could sit and eat their fast food while looking at the fountain—

*The fountain!* The click inside my head was so loud I almost didn't hear the burning thing howl again, a long, cheated rasp of ignited rage. I made it to my feet with hysterical speed and bolted, my back burning with pain and something torn loose in my side.

Behind me. It was behind me again, and it was fast. I couldn't hope to outrun it. Twenty feet between me and the fountain, and I wasn't going to make it.

*MOVE!* Dad's voice bellowed in my head, as if we were in Louisiana again with the cockroach things scuttling in the basement and the ammo clips jittering in my shaking hands.

I *moved.* I don't know how. One moment I knew I wasn't going to be able to get there in time, the next I was *there.*

Water gushed up in a sheet as I threw myself over the lip of the fountain in a wide receiver's dive, getting a sudden mouthful of chlorine and stale chill, my head barked something else—the concrete holding up some ridiculous Swiss-cheese sheet metal the water cascaded down while the fountain was turned on. More pain jolted down my neck. I was really racking up the score here. If this was a video game I'd be yelling at the stupid screen right now. Or throwing my controller at it.

The burning thing howled. Spattered with filthy mall-fountain water, it landed heavily as I scrabbled, a gout of foul-smelling steam belching up. Heat rolled through the water clawing at my arms and legs. I grabbed the sheet metal and *pulled* with both hands, my right clumsy because of the gun clicking against the rattling flimsy edifice. I pushed myself aside and fell again as the creature smashed spastically into the metal with a hollow *bong* that would have struck me as goddamn hilarious if the water hadn't been boiling. I landed hard again, breath driven out of me in a howling scream, and heard a yammering electronic sound. Had that been going on the whole time?

It slid down the metal and landed with a splashing jolt.

Steam drifted in great eddies from the once-placid water. The fountain bubbled and buzzed. I scrabbled for the stone ledge and just made it, hopping up and perching like a frog with trembling legs.

"Holy shit," someone was saying, someone with a high trembling voice very much like mine. I felt my lips shape the words, numbly. My hair dripped in my face and something warm and sticky was in my eyes. "Holy *shit*. Jesus Christ."

I coughed, water blowing out of my nose. Red drops pattered in the bubbling froth of the fountain. I was bleeding, but it didn't seem important. I was soaked to the skin and my fingers ached around the butt of the gun. My clothes were too heavy, full of blood and sulfur-stinking water now. I was shaking like an epileptic.

"Jesus Christ," I whispered. "Jesus *Christ*."

A slight movement caught my eye and the gun leveled itself, my finger cramping on the trigger. My gasping shallow breaths were suddenly audible even over the racket. Smoke and steam drifted in the air. Dots of coolness spattered me from overhead. The sprinklers were going. It was raining inside the mall. The burning thing lay in the water, twitching hard enough to send up little splashes and waves of froth.

Graves stared at me. He was on the other side of the fountain, wreathed in steam, his mouth ajar and his eyes wide.

*Where the hell did he come from?* The gun didn't care. My arm was straight, my aim was good, and I could hardly miss from this range. I gasped, my ribs heaving as I struggled to *breathe*, to get enough air into my starved lungs. I made harsh racking sounds, coughing at the reek in the steamy air. It was a sauna in here, and the sprinklers weren't helping.

Graves rose, his hands palm-out, the classic *don't shoot* stance. His mouth was ajar and his eyes were dilated. His gaze kept flicking between me and the thing thrashing in the fountain as it drowned in something inimical to it, still superheating the liquid. It was dying; I knew it was dying. I choked on the smell, shaking, but the gun didn't waver.

"Dru—" He shouted it, over the wailing of the fire alarm. My entire arm cramped with the need to do something.

I pulled the trigger.

# CHAPTER 10

The second shape—the thing that was leaping for Graves—was longer, leaner, and its fur was shorter, gray instead of glassy and smoking. A white streak bolted up the side of its long, oddly-shaped head. It stretched out in full leap, its snarling muzzle starred with ivory teeth sharper than knives, strings of saliva pouring out of its mouth. My first shot went wide, and the thing bowled past Graves, knocking him aside as easily as I might shoulder a grade-schooler out of the way. Goth Boy went flying, his coat flapping once with a sound like a sheet snapped out to lay flat while making the bed, and the gun spoke again.

I tracked the thing just like Dad had taught me, training taking over. Blood bloomed on its pelt. It looked like a steroid-pumped fur rug, muscle rippling under its fur, and its eyes were alight with unholy yellow.

The werwulf screamed a high yip of pain and tumbled off to the side, landing on the fountain's lip with a sickening crack. I would like to say I hopped gracefully down off my perch, but the truth is that I fell and scrambled around the other side of the fountain, looking for Graves. Cordite pulled sharp against all the other smells filling the mall. I retched once, a heave that came all the way up from my toes and kept crawling.

Graves shook his head, dazed. He'd levered himself up on his elbows, blinking in befuddlement. He saw me, and his eyes widened. They were a thin ring of green around a dilated pupil, the whites rolling like a terrified horse's. Still, the green rim was a line of emerald fire.

"Get *up!*" I screamed, and scrambled to my feet, grabbing his arm in my left hand and hauling with every ounce of strength I had left over. He came up a little more gracefully than I might have under the circumstances, and his cheeks were flour-pale, spots standing out high along the arches of his cheekbones. The silver earring swung, smacking my face as he ran into me, blind with fear. *"Move, goddammit!"*

It wasn't my voice. It was Dad's harsh bark transplanted to my throat.

I had no idea whether I'd wounded the werwulf enough to keep it down or not, and the walloping electronic noise plus the steam was making it hard to think. I *had* to think if both of us were going to get out of this alive.

*This one's all about you, Dru.* No Dad around to bail me out.

Our feet slipped in spilled water. I dripped blood and fell heavily to my knees in the tide. That was why it was my fault—if I hadn't tripped, almost biting a chunk out of my tongue when I landed, the werwulf would have hit me instead of Graves. They collided with rib-snapping force, and he screamed the high girlish scream of a squirrel in a trap.

I yelled something unrepeatable and shapeless anyway, brought the gun around, and *kicked*. My boot connected solidly with the werwulf's sleek canine head, and, like a gift, the thing crouching over Graves's body turned around and snarled at me, the eyes glowing like diseased sunlight, its gray streak shocking against the wiry darkness.

My voice cracked as I screamed, and I squeezed the trigger again. The sound was deafening. Gore splattered, the nine-millimeter's barrel smoking with cooked splashback. The werwulf spilled away, its muzzle gaping.

I'd shot it in the jaw.

It fell over the lip of the fountain and began to throw up stinking gouts of reddish, steaming water, the smell of cooked fur adding to the thunderous stench.

Graves moaned soundlessly under the noise of the alarm. I realized it was a *fire alarm*, and cursed in a long gasp. The boy's shoulder was shredded. The wulf had bitten him.

*Shit. Oh shit.*

I struggled with myself. The best thing to do was leave him. He was *bitten*, and that was bad news. I needed to get the hell out of here quick. The cops and the fire brigade would be here any second despite the snow, and how was I going to explain all this? Even my well-honed talent for creative lying wasn't up to the task.

Graves opened his eyes. He stared at me, his mouth working under the braying alarm. Water plashed. I snapped a glance at the wulf, which was rolling around holding its jaw with two lean, furry hands, producing an amazing bubbling howl with each heaving of its ribs. I looked back at the boy and for a second, I couldn't remember who the hell he was or what I was doing here. All I could think of was the hideous, horrible smell as Dad's body rotted away right in front of me.

I was on my own. *This one's all about you, Dru. You're making the call now.*

"Get up." I didn't recognize my voice this time, either. "Get the fuck up, kid. We've got to go."

Amazingly, he set his jaw and struggled to his feet, holding his shoulder. Blood spilled between his fingers, black in the dimness.

*First thing to do is get us away from that wulf. It'll heal quick and it'll be pissed. We can't go back to the room; it'll come after us there and we'll be trapped like rats in a hole. Where can I take him? Think!*

There was only one place. I had to hope the cops weren't there — and that nothing *else* was there, either.

Which meant I had to get Graves moving, treat him for shock, and navigate both of us through a blizzard.

*Oh, jeez.* Blood dripped down the side of my face, warm and wet. My back spasmed, and I'd pulled something in my arm, too. I was a song of aches and pains, and I wanted to lie right down and let them do whatever they wanted to me as long as I didn't have to move or think anymore.

Great.

# CHAPTER 11

Once I'd scrubbed the blood off both of us and gotten a pressure bandage onto Graves—the strips of his shredded shirt, actually, ripped up in the food-court restroom—the long dark coat buttoned up didn't look half bad. Neither did he, except for being so pale and shock-eyed.

I got us out of the restroom and up onto the second level of the mall into another one just in time. We weren't leaving a trail of water and blood now, though we still both stank to high heaven. I used plenty of paper towels to scrub the worst of the gunk off, shivering as adrenaline wore off and the fact that I'd just been dumped in a fountain by a big burning thing and shot a werwulf in the *face* occurred to me over and over again.

Like this. I'd look in the mirror at the long nasty gash along my hairline and think, *I'm going to have a scar when that heals.* Then my mind would shiver sideways, and I would hear the zombie again, tapping its bony fingers on the back door. Or the streak-headed werwulf's snarl. Or the burning thing's thrashing as it drowned.

And I would let out a hurt little quivering sound, clapping my hand over my mouth in case any of the cops were looking around the mall. I didn't think they would—there was a clear trail of scorching from the broken windows to the fountain, and it was so messy around there it wouldn't be immediately obvious *what* had happened.

The thing that worried me more was the wulf. Had he been rabid, newly changed, or just pissed off? Wulfen don't normally go after humans; there is too much fresh raw meat you can get easily in a supermarket. The exception is right after they shift the first time, but it would make no sense for a first-time wulf to want to get *inside* a building. From what I've heard, they usually want to run out and get some fresh air.

The thing that worried me most of all was a big burning dog the size of a Shetland pony. Had it been after me? After Graves? Or just pissed off because it had to buy some new clothes?

I didn't hear any footsteps, but after a while the alarm shut off. I waited. Graves was propped against the inside of a stall, shivering so hard his teeth clicked together rapidly. He was in shock, and I didn't know what to do for him. The bite—would he begin to change? I should have left him behind. You don't fool around with werwulf bites. You just *don't*. It was a law. When he started to get hairy and hungry, I'd have to—

*Christ no. Don't think about that.* I checked my watch again. Still ticking, even though it took a licking. Just like me.

My legs shook, tired all the way down to the bones. My head was full of cotton wool. I hurt *all over*, adrenaline fading in fits and starts.

I went to the entrance to the restroom, where the hallway

did a sharp bend so nobody could peek into the girls' pee-palace. I listened with every fiber of my being, focusing out, my entire body becoming an aching pair of ears. The compact ball of my *self* inside my head relaxed too, sending little fingers out, searching for any disturbance.

I heard nothing. No voices, no sounds of movement.

*Okay. How do I get us out of here?*

I could bet that the werwulf, if it was still alive, had fled. They're strong and unholy quick, but they avoid the authorities just like suckers. A cadre of cops with firepower and vests can cause plenty of damage, and neither wulfen or suckers want to be caught in the open like that. It attracts too much attention. They live by staying at the edges of things, under the cover of night.

Of course, the cops and other authorities didn't want news of the weird getting out; it might cause a panic. Cops, EMTs, firemen— they cover up this sort of thing as a matter of course, consigning it to the dead-file section. Dad always argued with August about whether it was a Conspiracy or just the human need to have things fit into neat little boxes.

So neither side, Real World or officialdom, wanted to meet each other face-to-face. Even if cops had vests and greater firepower, a wulf could wreak a lot of havoc. They're expensive to replace, fine officers of the law. Freelance hunters like Dad have to make do with even more firepower and sneaky cunning, understanding their prey in order to think three steps ahead of it.

Too bad I was just a kid. Dad was the brains of the operation. I just tagged along and told him where to find the biggest weirdness, or broke a hex or two. I mean, I was a great *accessory*, the best weirdness detector around, but he was the boss and the brains and the one with the guns. I was worse than useless on my own, and I had someone else to worry about now, too.

But *the situation is what the situation is*, Dad always said. There was nothing else to do but keep going. If I stopped now I'd drown without even a bubble.

"What's going on?" Graves whispered. He sounded about three years old and scared of the dark. "Jesus Christ, what's going on?"

"It has nothing to do with Jesus," I whispered back, checking the gun for the fiftieth time. If I'd had a spare clip for the gun I'd have racked it in, on the theory that it was better to have a full one than a half-empty one if something else happened.

*Dad, you should be proud of me. I'm thinking like you. Trying to, anyway.*

I just hoped I could think enough like him to keep us both breathing.

Graves blinked at me. "You shot it." His voice shook like a bad engine. "I thought you were going to shoot me."

*I should. Dad probably would.* I shut my eyes, leaned the back of my head against the tiled wall, my wet hair finally stopping its dripping. "I wasn't aiming at you."

"What was that thing?" His hand clamped over his shoulder, the pressure bandage mercilessly tight. "It had teeth. It had big teeth. It smelled."

"It was a werwulf." *I shouldn't tell him anything. I should put a bullet in his brain. Dad would put him down as a casualty before he changes. Once bitten, you have twelve hours, sometimes less. That's a fact.*

And a wulf who knew about a hunter was a liability. Dad always said "liability" like it was a filthy word. To him, it probably was.

"You *know* about these things?" The question ended on a squeak.

I shushed him. If he made noise and the cops heard it—were they still around? I checked my watch again. Eight thirty-eight p.m., or 1638 hours if you were all military. Fifty-three minutes since I'd moved us to this bathroom. Was it enough time for the cops to clear a scene this weird?

Outside it would be getting colder. I was bruised and exhausted. I walked cautiously past the stalls to the sinks, where I took another deep breath in, all the way down to the bottom of my lungs, and looked in the mirror.

There was that long but freshly scabbed-up gash along my hairline, but if I left my hair down I'd just look wet and scruffy. Anyone out tonight would probably be wet as well. If I could get us downtown I could probably hail us a cab—if the cabbie was suicidal—and take it to three streets over from my house, and hope nothing was waiting for me inside.

Yeah. And I could fly to the moon, too. If it was bad enough to shut the mall down early, there was little chance of a cab, right? But these people were serious about snow. Maybe they had everything scraped now.

There was a sound behind me. Graves floundered around the end of the stalls. "Don't leave me here." At least he didn't shout it, but he might have thought he was shouting, his voice was so hoarse and constricted.

My throat closed up on me. Dad had told me over and over again what to do if something happened to him. I usually tuned it out—who wanted to think about *that*? Not me, that's for sure. But still . . . *Don't take on any weight; you'll drown. You remember that if anything happens to me. You take care of yourself, Dru. You be strong and do what you have to do.*

But this kid wasn't a sucker or a werwulf yet. He was just a kid.

He'd brought me food and let me see his private hideaway. I got the idea he didn't do that a lot.

He'd *trusted* me. I couldn't just leave him.

Could I?

"I'm not going to leave you." I sounded funny even to myself— breathless, as if I was running up a hill. "You're going to have to do what I say."

Amazingly, he smiled at me. "You're bossy." His pupils were still huge, but a little color had begun to come back into his face, especially along his cheekbones. "I like bossy chicks."

*Jesus.* At least someone around here was feeling better. "Shut up. You're going to have to do *exactly* what I tell you to do. Got it?" *Or we'll get arrested. Or maybe just killed.*

"Sure. You do this to all your dates?" It was a type of courage over a screaming well of panic. He was really a brave kid, or maybe it was just the shock.

"I don't date." *I never stay anyplace long enough to date.* "Is that silver?" I pointed to his earring, forgetting I still had the gun in my hand until he flinched. He covered it well.

"I guess so. The guy I bought it from said it was."

"What about that? The chain?" This time I used my left hand to point at his necklace. *My bag's down in his room. I need my bag.*

It was too risky. All of this was too risky. If I went back down to Graves's little bolt-hole, we could be caught by the cops (bad) or caught by the possibly rabid werwulf (even worse), healed and ready for round two. They recovered *quick.* I had to get both of us out of here.

*I need my bag.* The urge was like the urge to pee. I wanted my bag the way little kids want a hug after they've scraped their knees, the way you want sunshine after a long rainy month, or a drink of water in the desert.

"The chain's silver." Some sense came back into his eyes. Giving him questions to answer was a good idea.

"Good. I'm going to go get my bag. You stay here."

That made his eyes wide and wild, the pupils shrinking so the green irises showed. "Don't *leave* me here!" He scraped himself away from the stall, his voice bouncing off tiles.

I shushed him again. "Look," I whispered fiercely, "you don't know how to move under cover. I'm going to go down and get my bag. I'll come back for you and I'll take you somewhere safe."

"It's not safe here?" Sarcasm tinted his tone, but at least he said it quietly. "Jesus. What was that thing?"

"Werwulf. I told you." I looked nervously at the entrance, hoping nobody heard us, hoping nobody was in this part of the mall. Were they gone? It wasn't like the cops to clear a scene in under an hour. Then again, if it just looked like a really weird vandalism thing, they might not stay too long. There had to be plenty of other stuff happening out in the world tonight. Bad weather always strains the emergency infrastructure.

I chewed my already-sore lower lip, tried to think. I *needed* my bag, and I needed to get us both out of the mall and back to the only safe place I knew. How would Dad do it?

If I thought about it that way it seemed almost doable. Almost. Except for the not-having-any-idea-what-to-do-next part.

"Stay here." I was already thinking about cover, plotting out routes and backtracks.

Graves grabbed my arm with surprising strength. "Dru. Don't leave me. *Please.*"

I opened my mouth to tell him to shut up and do what I told him, but then I got a good look at him. Deathly pale, the high spots of feverish color still standing out on his cheeks, about ready to fall over by the way he swayed on his feet, his fingers biting into my upper arm. His other arm hung limp and useless.

If I left him here in the girls' bathroom, I might come back and find him unresponsive or already changing. I struggled to *think* clearly, but my clear-thinker seemed busted. I should have left him there. Dad might have shot him just to cut down on the variables; he would *definitely* be telling me to get a move on. The longer I stayed here, the more dangerous it was.

I didn't have anyone else, and I was the reason Graves had been bit. It must hurt like hell.

"Dru." He couldn't speak louder than a sandpapery whisper, and his fingers dug in with feverish strength. I was going to bruise there, too—if I hadn't already. There didn't seem to be an unbruised place on my body. We were both in pretty bad shape.

Another thought rose: Graves's arm awkwardly around me while I cried. He hadn't asked questions or tried any funny business.

I couldn't leave him here.

"All right," I told us both. "Stay right behind me. Move the way I do. We're going to try to stay under cover. How many different ways can you get me down to your room?"

The relief crossing his transparent face bit me hard in the chest. If he hadn't been so pale, he would have looked like Christmas. "Four or five. Take your pick." He swayed, caught himself, and tried to straighten. "I'll keep up. Just don't leave me."

Four or five different routes was good news, if I kept him conscious enough to navigate me. "Okay." I tried again to think clearly, failed just as miserably as before. "I need my bag, and our best option's a bus route that's still going out east. Are any going to be running?"

"The 53." He nodded, his hair flopping in his face. Even his nose looked pale, for God's sake. "Runs all night, even when it snows. I can get you there."

I took an experimental step toward the entrance. He swayed after me, and I thought I had maybe twenty minutes before I had to hold him up.

*Move it, Dru.* "Okay," I said again. "You and me, Graves. Let's go."

# CHAPTER 12

**The buses were** still running. Chained up and slow as hell on their nighttime schedule, but they were still running in the right direction, and we had our first bit of luck catching the 53 almost as soon as we got to the stop across the main thoroughfare from the mall.

We looked normal enough, shivering and cold; bus drivers don't look too closely if you don't seem actively inebriated. A cab was a lost cause—it also occurred to me during the wait at the bus stop that cabbies are probably inordinately curious about their passengers. *That* was no good.

I watched my house from the corner, shivering in my boots. Graves slumped against me. He'd been almost okay on the bus, but now his head hung and strings of wet curly hair fell in his eyes, curtaining his milk-pale face. His eyes were dilated again, and his lips were close to blue.

Snow in my front yard was pristine. The truck was still missing from the driveway. The light in the living room was on, a rich golden glow in the gloomy orange snow-city light. Thick flakes of white whirled down; both of us were covered in the stuff because I'd dragged Graves off the bus two streets away. He'd almost pitched headfirst into a drift, and we had to walk in the road because of the snowplows racking up mountains of frozen, slushy chunks of ick in the gutters. The sidewalks were damn near iced over and impassable, and sand crunched under my boots. Our tracks would be obliterated in less than half an hour.

*Can werwulfen track through snow? Especially if they have a blood trail—I'll bet they can smell it.* I shivered at the thought. I didn't even want to think about what the burning dog and the werwulf had been looking for.

Because there was only one answer for that, wasn't there? It was an answer I'd run up against on the bus, the gun a cold weight in my pocket and Graves slumped against me, his head bobbing a little bit as we were bounced around.

It looked like nobody had messed with the house. It looked like the shooting had gone unnoticed. Snow made sound carry itself around weird, and the house had been pretty closed up. I wondered if anyone would have found me yet if the zombie had done what it set out to do.

Now *there* was a nice, happy thought.

There was no cover, but I didn't want to struggle around through the drifts to the back. For one thing, I didn't want to see the shattered debris of the door the zombie had come through any sooner than I had to. For another, Graves was slumping more and more heavily each passing second. I was doing okay keeping him moving, but I didn't feel up to carrying him if his legs gave out.

"Come on." I didn't say it nicely. I all but dragged him up over the mountain range of road-snow piled at the bottom of our driveway. Then it was slogging through snow midway up my shins, each step dragged down with powdery, icy weight. My nose dripped and my cheeks were raw. My fingers felt like frozen sausages. Graves started making a thin noise in the back of his throat, like he was going to pass out.

I didn't blame him. I bet his shoulder hurt like hell. Wulf bites are messy; they grind a lot when they clamp down. He was lucky to still have some use of his arm, his hand tucked limply in his pocket to keep him from looking like Frankenstein's monster. The wound had been still raw and messy when I peeled up the bandage to check it, just after we got off the bus; a good sign for him not changing just yet but a bad sign for him possibly staying out of unconsciousness.

I dug in my coat pocket for my keys. "Don't you dare pass out on me now, soldier," I hissed. The strap of my bag cut into the space between my shoulder and neck, and with Graves's unwounded arm over my shoulders I felt like Atlas holding up the world. I was so tired even my eyelashes hurt. My back was a solid chunk of pain, my side flaring with a red sensation, just under a really bad stitch, with each breath.

The key went into the doorknob; it took me two tries and a round of cursing before I could get the deadbolt open, too. I pushed open the door and was faced with the remnants of zombie stink, not too bad considering how we both smelled now. The house'd had time to air out through the back, I guess.

Graves stumbled. I propped him against the hallway wall and closed the door. Then I got out my gun and I swept the house just like Dad had taught me. Every place we lived we went through the drill, covering fire angles and searching as a two-man team. He also made me do it alone while he timed me. I'd only done it four or five times with the stopwatch in this place, but that's enough when you've been doing something like that for years.

The living room was a shambles, but the only sign remaining of the zombie was thick, fine powder-ash ground into the carpet, a meaningless smudge inside tattered clothes. There was a bullet hole in the wall, and another one lower down I hadn't noticed before.

*A little paint and spackle will fix that right up.* I shivered, let out a shapeless sighing sound like a sob. My nose ran, clear snot dripping down my lip. I wiped at it with my sodden coat sleeve and continued.

The kitchen was icy and unfamiliar in the dark. The back door hung on its hinges, sound except for a huge hole in the middle of it. There was plywood in the garage—I could nail something up there and hang a blanket over it for insulation. The enclosed porch was cold and dank, smelling like a root cellar, and the glassed-in screen door was miraculously undamaged. I wrestled it closed through a wad of wet snow and looked for something to brace it with, found exactly nothing, and gave up. The snow would drift up against it and keep it closed if I was lucky. Besides, if we had to get out in a hurry, I couldn't lock or block it. I still hadn't swept the upstairs.

Upstairs everything was as I'd left it. The whole house was still. Quiet as a tomb.

Downstairs, Graves's eyes were half-closed. "Nice place," he mumbled, but the words had a slurred quality I didn't like. His lips were bluer than I liked, too. Pale drops of sweat and water stood out on the ashen gray his skin had turned into, and his pupils were so dilated I could barely see the irises, just dark holes.

I locked the front door and got him upstairs, bullying him up each step. I was sweating and clammy by the time we finished. Then the hard part started. I got him out of his wet clothes, ignoring the snickers as I stripped him down to his tighty-whiteys. He went into my bed under the blankets, and his eyes closed the rest of the way. He sighed just like an exhausted little kid and was out.

I dropped my bag, shucked my coat, and started struggling down to sports bra and panties. I didn't think he'd die of hypothermia—he'd been bitten, and the fever from the bite might help.

*What, so he can tear open your throat when he changes?*

I wasn't thinking clearly. I was so cold I didn't feel cold anymore, which was a bad sign. I just felt tired. So goddamn tired.

I climbed into bed, stacking the blankets on top of us. Then I took him in my arms, shivering. He was icy, I wasn't much better, and he was making that thin, hurt sound again. I realized I was lying on his shoulder and tried to rearrange myself, managing to move so I wasn't grinding down on his injury. His shirt, torn up and used as a bandage, was chilly and tacky-wet.

"What're y'doin'?" His tongue was too thick for his mouth. I hoped he wasn't changing. His skin was smooth enough against mine.

All the wulfen I'd ever seen were bad shadows in the rearview mirror, or looking just like everyone else who hung out in a bar catering to the Real World. In other words, weird as all get-out. If he changed . . .

I couldn't even finish the thought. My bones had turned to lead bars, along with my eyelids and even my wet hair. If we both died of hypothermia, all of this would be academic anyway.

Graves shifted uneasily, stilled. The prickle of hairiness would give away the change, and the sound of bones crackling. Dad had talked about it—the sound of their bones reshaping, the snarling, the fur rippling out.

*God, I hope that's not happening.* I let out a long, shaking breath. "Warming you up."

"Jesus." His eyes dropped closed, struggled open. "Y'cold."

"So are you." The gun was on the nightstand. If he changed, he'd probably start to scream when his bones began to remodel themselves. I'd have enough time to take care of the problem.

*Dru, you're not thinking straight.*

I knew I wasn't. But I was so completely exhausted.

The wind started to moan outside, but inside my room everything was hushed. My fingers and toes hurt, needles rammed all the way through flesh and bone. I hoped we weren't going to lose toes to frostbite. But it wasn't as cold as it could have been if it was still snowing, was it?

I couldn't think. My head was full of mud. I should have warmed him up and gotten something over the hole in the back door. Snow would trickle into the porch if the screen door didn't stay closed, and I'd have a hell of a time cleaning it up.

A little warmth began to steal back into me, then a little more. Graves's cheeks flushed, and he started to sweat. He stopped making that noise, and would jerk himself awake every time his eyelids fell. The time between those little twitches got longer and longer, his breathing evening out.

"Dru?" he finally whispered.

"What?" I roused myself with an effort. *Tired. Got to get up and fix the back door. Then have to think of something. Something I have to do.*

I couldn't remember.

"Are you naked?" His eyes fell shut again, and he made a little hitching sound like a snore.

*Oh, for Christ's sake.* But I fell asleep before I could work up the energy to be pissed off.

# CHAPTER 13

**I woke up with** a pounding headache, stiff and sore all over, with a back made of torn-up iron bars and something wrong with my left arm because Graves's heavy goddamn head was lying on it. I sat bolt-upright and flinched as still, cold air met bare skin. I was sweating—he was *warm*. Sweat cooled rapidly on my back and shoulders. My mouth tasted like day-old coffee mixed with ash.

Graves was on his back. He didn't protest when I scrambled painfully out of the bed, because he was utterly, deeply asleep, his hair lank over his face, his nose lifting proudly. The very, very slight suggestion of epicanthic folds made his closed eyes exotic, the fan of his charcoal lashes even and regular against his cheekbones. The bandage was crusted with blood and something yellow, traceries of blue-black spreading along the vein map up his neck and down his arm, onto his chest.

*Doesn't look good, does it?*

I looked around for clothes. I still smelled traces of the burning thing from yesterday all over me, but I needed to get something on my shivering skin. I was also hungry as hell.

First things first, though. I pulled on a pair of jeans and a sweatshirt, scooped the gun off the table, and went into Dad's room. I came back with nylon rope—good for rappelling, tying down a load in a pickup, and, not so incidentally, for tying up a kid who might turn into a werwulf.

Werwulfen, especially new ones, have a real problem with silver. That part of pop culture is real enough. The chain around his neck wasn't rubbing red blisters into his skin, which was a good sign. Neither was the skull earring, pressed against his cheekbone by the way his head was turned slightly to the side. A pulse beat strong and steady in his throat. He was skinny but had a lot of good muscle—and if he started to change on me, he would have the kind of hysterical strength that could throw me across the room without thinking twice about it. Or even noticing.

He'd be too busy looking for his first chunk of raw meat.

*What am I going to tie him to? The mattress? Jesus, a fine time to wish I had a four-poster.*

Fortunately, Dad taught me a lot about knots. A trucker's hitch will cinch someone down—it just gets tighter the more you struggle— and if he couldn't get enough leverage, he couldn't come after me. First I trussed his wrists and elbows, then his knees and ankles; then I ran four more lines between the mattress and the box spring. *That* was a trick. Each one I secured with a trucker's hitch.

If he had to go to the bathroom, he was out of luck. I could always get a new mattress. I couldn't buy a new trachea.

With that done, I washed up. No hot shower for me—I couldn't afford the time. But clean clothes and a scrubbed-clean face does wonders for any girl's mood—even if that face is dead white, hectic flares of color on the cheeks, and with pupils wide enough to look half-wild. The zit on my temple had vanished, and no more seemed to be rising.

Go figure. My hair was a total loss, though. Humidity and cold made me look like the Bride of Frankenstein, except without the cool white zigzags.

*That* made me think of the streak-headed werwulf, and I shivered. I found a dry pair of sneakers because my boots were still sopping wet, and was ready to start solving problems.

Downstairs, snow had spilled in through the screen door on the little porch, and it was bastard cold. I looked longingly at the box of Cheerios on the counter—my stomach growled just thinking about it—but went to hunt in the garage for plywood instead. My scrounger's luck was good, and in less than ten minutes I had the snow cleared away and plywood bracing the screen door; I nailed more plywood up outside over the hole in the actual back door. I swept up broken glass, listening to the wind moan outside. My fingers were numb and my breath made little clouds in front of my face. I began to regret ever waking up.

I rigged some blankets on a line over the back door to insulate it, taping it down with duct tape, every girl's best friend. Then, finally, I turned up the heat and shivered through my first bowl of cereal. The milk burned, it was so cold. The entire house smelled like fresh air plus a faint, rapidly fading taint of zombie. I was so hungry I didn't even mind.

As soon as I finished the cereal, I put a fresh clip in the gun and checked on Graves. He was still out cold, breathing through his nose and mouth the way little kids do. The house began to warm up, and I sat on the stairs for a long time, hugging myself and staring down the hall at the boxes and the bullet holes blown in the wall.

*What are you going to do, Dru?*

The hollow place inside me didn't answer. I knew I should get up and eat something else, but I just kept staring at bullet holes. Nothing sounded good now that I had a lump of cold cereal in me.

I held the gun loosely in my right hand. If Graves started to change . . .

*Well,* technically you've already killed one person, sweetheart. Dad's voice, cool and calm, like every time I was being an idiot. *One more shouldn't be that hard. Just wait until he changes and put him down. You should have done it at the mall.*

Still, it was oddly comforting knowing there was someone in the house who wasn't going anywhere. Kind of pathetic, but I've spent so many nights alone waiting for Dad to come back it was nice to hear the silent sound that means someone else is breathing in the same space. So what if he'd turn into a big hairy beast and try to kill me? The first time a werwulf changed it was unstoppable until it got blood.

That's what the books said. I didn't have any reason to doubt them. Or Dad, who said the same thing.

*This is rapidly getting out of hand.* Dad's phrase, delivered with a straight face and usually a gun in either hand. *What are you going to do next, Dru?*

I needed a plan. The trouble was, I didn't have one.

"I suppose I should get the living room cleaned up," I said to the quiet. "Wait for him to wake up. Then we'll see."

The hollow place inside me wasn't satisfied by that. Dad was dead. He wasn't coming back. I was alone in the world, and I'd gotten some kid who had tried to help me bitten by a werwulf. There were other things I had to think about, but I was damned if I could remember them. I felt very small and very alone, sitting there on the stairs.

*Racking up the score here, kiddo.* I shivered, hugging my

knees. The snow was really coming down, wind moaning against the corners of the house. It was 8 a.m. and dark out there, except for the directionless glow between the whirling quarter-size flakes from reflected city light. *Gonna need a new back door. Unless you're blowing town.*

I *couldn't* blow town. Graves would need someone to explain to him what was going on. And someone had killed Dad.

That was what I'd been trying not to think. I mean, I'd killed Dad. But it hadn't *really* been Dad. You can't make a zombie when someone's still alive.

You just can't.

*Someone turned him into a zombie. You don't wake up one morning as one of the reanimated. Someone killed him and turned him into a zombie. He wasn't in good shape, either. There was a lot of trauma to those tissues—they rot quicker when they're injured before they die.*

I felt like I was in one of those snow globes—you know, where you shake them and the entire inside fills with whirling white. Everything inside still and motionless, surrounded by floating bits of ice. I was trying not to think what I had to think next, and succeeding only in filling my head with static.

I don't know how long I would have sat there if I hadn't heard a sharp, surprised half-yell from overhead.

Graves was awake. I hauled myself up and trudged up the stairs, the gun cold and heavy in my hand.

I didn't want to do what I thought I was going to do.

*Tough luck, chickie babe. You have to.*

\* \* \*

He stopped struggling against the ropes as soon as he saw me. The blankets had rucked up away from his toes. The room was warmer, and sweat plastered his long, dead-black hair to his face.

We stared at each other for a few moments. Then he lifted his chapped fingers—lying on his side, it was about all he could do. His voice was husky, and he said the absolute last thing I'd expect a kid who'd gotten bit by a werwulf and tied to a bed to say.

"Kinky." He arched one half of his unibrow, his eyes burning green around the holes of his pupils. He didn't look ready to sprout hair or fangs.

We were coming up on twelve hours since he'd been bit.

"I never figured you for the bondage type," he continued. "How the hell am I going to piss?"

Smart kid.

The gun was loaded with one in the chamber. I clicked the safety off, praying that the next five minutes would go well. I advanced nervously into the room, giving myself plenty of time. The knots looked like they were holding just fine.

"I'm going to ask you a few questions." I managed to keep my tone even. "If you give the right answers, I'll cut the ropes off and we'll go from there."

He licked his lips. His eyes flicked between the gun and my face, and he went very still.

Something told me he knew I wasn't bluffing.

That was great. Because I wasn't so sure. I couldn't kill him on my bed. I couldn't shoot someone like that. Sure, I'd shot the werwulf. It had been just like a video game, just like Dad trained me.

But . . . I *knew* this guy. I couldn't shoot him. He was *human*.

He was the closest thing to a friend I had now.

I stood beside my own bed, near our scattered sodden clothes from yesterday. I leveled the gun. "First question. Where did you get your necklace?"

He swallowed. He'd gone ghost-pale. His pulse throbbed frantically in his throat. "Hot Topic, in the mall. You're not going to shoot me, Dru."

*I wish I was half as sure as you sound.* I was nerving myself up for something, that was for goddamn sure. "Do you know what it means?"

"Hell, I just got it because it was on sale. People leave me alone if they think I'm crazy and into that cult shit." His Adam's apple bobbed as he swallowed convulsively. "Christ, you're not going to shoot me, are you?"

*It's either that or have you tear out my throat. Twelve hours is the limit for werwulf changes. If you haven't changed by now, there's only a couple of reasons why.* I leaned down a little, bracing the gun in both hands, and put the barrel to his temple. Kept my fingers carefully locked outside the trigger guard, because accidents can happen. "Do you believe in ghosts, Graves?"

He swallowed again. His throat worked. "Shit, I don't know. Don't shoot me. Please." His voice cracked.

If he knew about the Real World, he would have answered differently. Was he lying?

I didn't want to think so. He hadn't acted like he knew jackshit about it. So that narrowed down the reasons why he wasn't getting all hairy.

I swallowed. My throat was as dry as the stuff you drop into water to get fog for parties. Frozen carbon dioxide. It burns like hell and you can use it in swamps to make gator spirits angry. "Answer this question very carefully, kid. Are you a virgin?"

The silence was so long I thought I was going to have to ask him again.

"What the hell?" He sounded honestly perplexed.

"Yes or no? *Are you a virgin?*" I lost control halfway through. My voice spiraled up into a scream.

He flinched, and I ached to hit him. I wanted to hit *something*, that's for sure. I wanted to *do* something instead of just stand there and threaten him.

"Sonofa*bitch answer me!*" My voice bounced off the walls, made the whole room whirl around me. My blood pounded in my ears. Adrenaline poured through my blood, copper winding me tighter and tighter.

"*Yes!*" he screamed back. "Yes, I'm a fucking virgin, *don't shoot me goddammit fucking please!*"

I froze. My fingers were cramping outside the trigger guard.

His chest heaved. Tears slicked his cheeks and his eyes were squeezed shut. He strained against the ropes without moving, and my entire body had gone cold.

Almost twelve hours, and he was a virgin.

It might be okay after all.

I didn't recognize the hoarse rasp coming from my throat as mine. "All right." I eased the safety back on with a click, *after* I pointed the gun away. Far, far away from both him *and* me. "All right. Fine. All right."

Graves made hoarse little sobbing sounds. I backed off, retreating from the bed.

Jesus. What had I done? I should have asked him that first off instead of putting a gun to his head. I felt sick.

I stumbled for the bathroom and threw up every inch of cereal I'd eaten. Then I cried too, shaking over the cold porcelain. I had to blow my nose three times. When that was done, raw-eyed and sore, I went slowly back down the dark hall into Dad's room. I found a spare holster and put the gun in it, and I got out a bowie knife. The knots would be cinched down too tight to loosen now.

Graves was lying on the bed with his eyes closed, his lips moving soundlessly. I'd just scared the shit out of him.

*So what? Better to scare him than get your throat ripped out. The first time a wulf changes, it's unstoppable.*

I told Dad's voice to take a hike for once, and began sawing through the ropes. "You were bitten by a werwulf. I had to be sure," I said as I avoided cutting his forearm. My hands were shaking just a little. "Just stay still. We'll have you out of these in a jiffy."

He didn't say anything.

I managed to get the ropes around his ankles and knees cut through, then the ones at his elbows and wrists. He just lay there, limp, breathing heavily.

"I'm sorry." I sounded five years old. The words were empty. It was the kind of thing you say to someone when you've broken a toy or something, not when you've just held a gun to their head and shouted at them. "I had to be sure. If you're a virgin, it's okay; you won't change like a regular wulf. The imprint won't take, because you're a closed door. At least, that's what Dad told me. He was almost always right. I—"

"Shut up," he whispered. His eyes squeezed shut. Tears made his lashes into a damp mat. "Leave me alone."

I backed away on my knees, holding the knife. "I'm sorry. Really. I just—"

"I said, leave me *alone*. Shut *up*." His voice broke.

I wiped at my cheek with my fingers. There wasn't anything else to say. So I just made it to my feet with each piece of my body creaking and left him alone.

# CHAPTER 14

**sat on the** stairs again, listening to the heater run and the silent un-noise of snow outside. I heard Graves moving around—the toilet flushing, water running, shuffling feet and creaks I hadn't had a chance to learn in this new place yet. Each house has its own set of sounds, and each person sounds different.

He didn't sound like Dad. But still, just hearing someone breathing and walking around was better than nothing. *Way* better than nothing.

My eyes were hot and grainy. I stared at the gun in my hands. Nine-millimeter, dead black, and heavy, its nose sleek and sharp. It was a good gun.

*What are you going to do, Dru? Go back to high school and be prom queen? What the hell. Why not?*

The answer was right around the corner—I just couldn't think of it. There was something I was missing, something I was trying not to think. It had to do with that door, and the concrete corridor, and the dream hanging heavy in my head, like a lead bowling ball.

*Someone turned Dad into a zombie. While he was out hunting. So someone knew about what he was doing, right?*

But who could know? What had he been after? He hadn't said anything to me.

The questions revolved inside my head. Then the thing I'd been forgetting since waking up slid into place with a click like racking a bullet into the chamber.

*Contacts. Dad had contacts. I should call someone.*

Relief so intense it was ridiculous poured through my entire body at the thought. Someone adult, older than me, better-armed and more experienced, who could come out and . . .

. . . do what? Set up housekeeping? Adopt me? Take me on as an apprentice? Make everything okay?

Yeah. Sure. None of the other hunters Dad had let me hang around with were in the *least* parental. But they were older, right? And they'd be interested in something that killed him. They were his friends. Combat buddies. Comrades in arms.

Right?

I closed my eyes. Leaned against the wall, dangling the gun in my right hand.

The stairs squeaked. Graves shuffled down each one like it hurt. There was a dragging sound.

I didn't open my eyes.

When he sat down beside me I was only mildly surprised. We sat like that for a few minutes, until my eyelids flew up and the world came rushing back into my head again.

He had Mom's sunrise quilt from my bed wrapped around his shoulders, and his face was set. He'd pushed his hair behind his ears. He was barefoot. The house was warm enough now.

The messy lacerations of wulfbite were closing, angry pink instead of bleeding crimson or the crusted yellow. The blue-black mapping of his veins had vanished. Their bites heal really, eerily fast. Nobody knows why.

The ticking silence of the heater filled up the space between us. We both fit on the step, he was so birdlike thin.

I'd told him I was sorry. Did he have any idea how sorry I was?

He sat there for a while, fidgeting in that way of his. Then he spoke, quietly. Almost gently, as if I was crying. "Why'd you do that?"

*I had to.* "You might have changed."

"Changed." He said it so flatly I almost might not have known it was a question.

"Into a werwulf. Like that thing back at the mall that bit you."

"A vherr-what?"

"A werwulf." I considered spelling it for him, decided not to. "As in howl at the moon, silver bullet, Lon Chaney type of thing. Only it's not really like that. They're responsible for some disappearances, but mostly they eat a lot of raw meat and play head games with each other. Humans aren't enough fun. Plus they've got a running feud with the suckers."

"Suckers?"

*You don't even want to know.* Dad *never even wanted to know.* "I had to know if you'd change."

"So you tied me up and asked if I was a virgin? Help me out here." He shifted, wrapping the quilt more tightly around his bare shoulders. He was shirtless. Of course—his shirt was ruined and his coat was probably still wet.

I glanced down. He wore a pair of my workout pants. They hit him at mid-calf and sagged around his narrow waist. Boy had no hips at all. "It's near twelve hours. Generally, if you don't change by then there's a reason, and you're probably safe. If you're bitten while you're a virgin, some of the transfer of werwulf stuff doesn't get done. It's all theory, but virgins have a higher incidence of not changing." I watched him out of the corner of my eye, waiting for the leaning backward that would tell me he'd stopped listening. People don't want to hear about the Real World, and if you ever try to explain, they just quit listening real early.

He didn't move. Just stared at me. I took a deep breath and forged ahead. "It has to do with magic, I guess. Stuff like that. See, when a werwulf bites and doesn't finish his kill, there's an . . . an imprint, I guess you could call it. If you're a virgin, the imprint doesn't get made right. It's like you're a closed door, and once you have sex that door is opened and some things can take hold. Infect you, almost." I looked down at my knees, just talking to hear myself talk now. Or maybe I was afraid of what he would say once I shut up. "Congratulations. You're mostly safe from wulfbite for the rest of your life. Like . . . like an inoculation." It was a pretty good explanation, and about the sum total of my knowledge of werwulfen. The silent house ate the words. I couldn't think of anything else to tell him.

"Well. That's comforting." He swallowed so heavily I heard it. "Look, Dru, I—"

"I'm glad you didn't change," I said all in a rush. "Because I don't know what I'd have done."

"Shot me." The raw edge of anger smoked under the words. I closed my eyes against it, leaned against the wall. "I guess. Right?"

*Yes. No. I don't know. I shot someone else.* Hopelessness turned into a rock inside my chest.

"Dru?" As if I wasn't listening.

"Fuck off." *Don't lecture me.*

He persisted. "That was real, wasn't it." It wasn't a question, but he was still trying to convince himself. "I saw a huge-ass dog burning and running after you. I saw the thing that bit me, and the bite's closing up like I'm Wolverine or something. It was *real*."

"Bingo. You get a prize." The gun was so heavy. If I let it slip through my fingers and tumble down the stairs, what would it do? Probably go off and kill someone else. Just my luck.

He asked the question that got everyone in trouble. "What else is real?"

*You don't want to know.* "You wouldn't believe me if I told you." *Some things you just have to see for yourself. But you're not going to see it, are you? You're going to head for the door and leave me to get through this myself. It'd be better for you if you did, I guess.* Sour heat boiled in my throat. I pushed it down before it could make my eyes prickle.

"You could tell me and see. I mean, I was okay with everything else, wasn't I?"

Wind mouthed the corners of the house. It wasn't as lonely a sound as it usually was, because someone was sitting right next to me. "You got bit for it. I'm sorry." There they were again, those two pale little useless words.

"Well, you're an interesting chick, Miss Anderson." When I didn't reply, he moved, bumping his shoulder against mine. "Did you feel me up when you were tying me down?"

*What?* My jaw threatened to drop. "Um, no. Did you want me to?"

"Well, it would have been nice." His shoulder bumped mine again. "Can I ask you something?"

I didn't answer. He was going to ask me anyway. People don't say that if they don't want to pry something out of you.

But he surprised me. "What happened to your dad? I mean, really happened?"

"He got t-turned into a z-zombie." I thought I was going to choke on the words, but they came out. Hoarse and broken, but they came out. "Someone did it to him." There it was. Someone had beat Dad up *bad*, and then turned him into one of the reanimated.

I'd said it out loud now. Any chance of waking up and finding it all just a Really Bad, Really Lifelike Dream was now straight in the scupper, as Gran always said.

"A zombie. Okay. Whew. All right." Graves let out a huge sigh, like he'd just finished carrying a heavy container up a steep hill. "So what are you gong to do?"

*How the hell should I know?* "Make some lunch, I guess." I used the wall to push myself up to my feet. The heater clicked off. "You want something to eat?"

"I wanted to ask you something else." His chin tilted up a bit, and he met my eyes. The skull and crossbones earring fell back, touching his hair. He'd taken off the necklace, and his muscle moved in his bare chest under the quilt. "You got anyone you can call? Like your mom or something, since your dad's . . ." Graves had to swallow before he said the word. "Dead? He's dead, right? That's what zombie means."

I shrugged. "It means dead and reanimated. My mom's dead, too. So is my grandmother." *Everyone's gone. They all keep disappearing on me.* The words were full of old bitterness. "I'm going to make lunch. You must be hungry."

"So you just live here by yourself? In this house?" He was a persistent one. He scrambled up off the steps, wrapped himself up in the red-and-white quilt like a mummy, and shuffled after me.

"For a while. Until I can't anymore." I led him into the kitchen and flicked the light on, setting the gun on the counter within easy reach. "Pretty much all I feel like making is grilled cheese. You want some?"

His eyes roved the surface of the counters like he was looking for contraband. "Why was that dog thing after you?"

That was another question that bothered me. I shrugged. "I don't know. Do you want some goddamn lunch or not?"

"Sure, I'll take some. If you promise not to hold a gun to my head." By the time I rounded on him he was smiling, and had both his hands up in *hey, man, I'm harmless* mode. "Just kidding, Dru. Lighten up, okay?"

*Lighten up?* I stared at him like he was crazy before getting the cheese and butter out of the fridge. *I tied him down and nearly shot him, and he's telling me to "lighten up"?*

The grin widened, his eyes very bright green now, no hazel tint left. He shook his hair down over his face and puckered his lips, making kissing noises. That strange heat crawled up my cheeks again. It got to me and I laughed, with the butter in one hand and the cheese in the other. We had bread in the freezer—it probably would have frozen on the counter too. That's a good way to keep it fresh down South, especially if you eat a lot of toast. Or grilled cheese.

"That's better." He leaned against the counter, wrapping himself more securely in the quilt. "We're in the same boat, you know. I don't have anyone either. Not anyone I can call or anything. I've been on my own since I was twelve."

*Great. What am I supposed to say to that?* I got the frying pan out. He didn't mention the plywood and taped-down blankets over the back door. I didn't mention the closing and healing flesh on his shoulder. We were mostly silent, and the wind moaned against the corners of the house.

But I opened up a couple cans of tomato soup and dumped them in a pot, and I didn't feel quite so lonely. Having someone in the house—someone who wasn't going to leave just yet—helped. I even poured him a glass of milk.

Call me domestic.

# CHAPTER 15

"**H**oly *shit*." **Graves** peered into the ammo crate. "Jesus. Was your dad a survivalist?"

He was helping me clean up the living room. He didn't ask about the bullet holes in the wall, or about the faint, horrible smell of rotting zombie. He also didn't ask about the clothes he'd seen me scoop carefully up off the floor and set to soaking in the washing machine. Dad's clothes were torn up and stinky, all his weapons and his billfold missing, along with Mom's locket on its supple silver chain.

I didn't want to think about that.

Snow whirled down thick and steady outside, each flake a muffled erasure of the world. The radio said some people had lost power, but not us. Not yet. I was glad about that—even with the duct-taped blankets the kitchen was chilly, the heater working overtime until I scrounged up more blankets and another two pieces of plywood to create a baffle. It worked pretty well, actually.

Especially since I'd braced the door to the porch.

I opened up the fire-safe box, sure I'd find what I was after. After a bit of digging through papers—birth certificates for both of us, my immunization records, a fat file of records from each school I'd attended—I found the ragged red address book, duct tape clinging to its vinyl cover. Dad's kill book would be in the truck, but contacts were always kept separate.

*Okay, Dad. Let's see who can get me out of this, since you've ended up a stain on the living-room rug. A stain I should vacuum up, by the way. In a fresh bag so I can keep it.*

A hot bolt of nausea scored through me. That was no way to think about my dead father, was it? But it was either find something snarky to say or start crying, and if I started sniveling now, I might never stop.

Dad hated sniveling. "Bingo," I muttered.

"I mean, what do you use all this stuff for?" Graves continued. I'd given him a pair of Dad's sweats, but he'd turned down my offer of a Peter Frampton T-shirt. So his narrow back was pale and goose-pimpled despite the heater. I could have found him something else to wear, but he made such a big deal over the Frampton I decided he could go shirtless if he was going to be picky. I mean, it's not like it was David Cassidy or something.

I kept trying not to look at his bare skin, though. It made me feel weird. "Hunting." I closed the top of the safe box, made sure it was shut and locked down. "Get out of there, that's live ammo."

He was still poking around. "This isn't really a grenade, is it?"

"Of course it's real. You won't clean out a roach-spirit nest with a fake grenade. Get *out* of there, you're not trained."

"Did your dad teach you how to use this stuff?"

"Most of it. He told me to leave the AK-47 alone, though." I paged through the address book, deciphering Dad's scrawl. Most of the numbers were down South, with a smattering in California and up around Maine. Nothing *near* the freaking Dakotas. I even recognized some of them—the hunter in Carmel who surfed almost every day unless he was too injured from clearing out sucker holes with a team of hard-faced mercenaries; the women who lived out on the back bayou miles away from anywhere and kept the gator spirits pacified and cleared out; August in New York who swore in gutter Polish when he drank with Dad and could make a thin shining yellow flame spring from the tip of his index finger if he was in the right mood.

Graves almost choked. "You have an AK-47?"

*And a flamethrower, but that's in the truck.* "Only for emergencies." I found a scrap of paper tucked three-quarters of the way back with a number in our new area code. Nothing else. No name, no inked cross that meant it was a safe number for me to dial, no ident info.

Great. Who would take a plane ride out here just to make me feel better? I'd have to explain what happened to Dad, too. Or as much as I knew about what happened to him. Which wasn't much. But still.

The way my stomach turned over at the thought threatened to push out every bit of grilled cheese I'd eaten. It was my fault; I hadn't told him about the owl. "Jesus," I whispered, staring down at the number. It was on the back of a receipt from an occult shop in Miami, the one where Dad had found a glassy shard of obsidian good for taking down chupacabras. He'd FedExed it out to Tijuana for Juan-Raoul de la Hoya-Smith.

The goatsuckers were really bad around Tijuana. Juan-Raoul said it was the heat and the *tamales*.

Dad had stayed closeted with the dreadlocked, scary-looking owner of that shop for a good two hours after it closed, while I wandered around looking at things and getting hungrier and hungrier. When he'd reappeared, his face had been stony-set and white, and he'd stayed up drinking in our hotel room all that night. I'd ordered room service and watched old cartoons until I fell asleep.

Now I wondered if Dad had gotten this phone number there. I wondered if it was safe—the inked cross meant "safe"; the slashed circle meant "unsafe except in an emergency"; and no sign could mean anything.

It was Dad's handwriting, no doubt about it. Nobody else had access to the book, and there was his way of making a 9 from the bottom with a single line. I wondered whose number it was.

I was going to have to go to a pay phone and find out. It was the only number in this area, but it didn't have a mark next to it. It wasn't like Dad to forget a thing like marking a safe contact.

It wasn't like him at all. But he hadn't been himself since that shop with the cottonmouths hitting the glass with hard, padded sounds, making that horrible ratcheting noise. I looked up at the living-room window. The blizzard wind made a low chuckling sound, mocking me.

"Dru? You okay?" Graves was suddenly there. I hadn't seen him moving as I stared at the window, lost in thought.

Woolgathering, Gran would have called it. As in, *Don't woolgather when they's work to be done, Dru. Go milk the goats and look'n fer eggs, and when you come back I'll teach'n you how to use a pendulum. Won't that be fun?*

Only with her thick Appalachian accent, it sounded slow as molasses inside my head. I could get out the pendulum now, but it wouldn't be any good when I was wishing and hoping too hard.

Sometimes things like pendulums or tarot cards will just tell you what you want to hear, not the truth. Gran always said you should see it for yourself instead of using "crutches," but the crutches were good when you didn't have time to put yourself in a trance or wait for a dream or omen.

"I'm fine." I shook the idea away and copied the number on a plain piece of anonymous scrap paper, then shoved it in my pocket. The receipt was Evidence, and we Minimized Evidence, so it went back in the book. The contacts went back into the fireproof box, and I looked around the living room. There was nothing to do for the time being while we were snowed in, so I searched for something to say to get the conversation off me. "You can't go anywhere in this kind of weather, you know."

"I thought I'd just stay with you anyway. Seeing as how you're so interesting." He waggled his eyebrows, but the effect was lost under his mop of hair. He rubbed at his shoulder gently, the pink traces of werwulf bite already fading. The scars would be white and star-shaped before long, little puckers where the teeth had punctured the skin. "Besides, I can't get back into the mall just yet. Or any-where else."

The quick healing was eerie, and the wounds just *looked* wrong, the way all wounds from the Real World do.

*I'm sorry.* I didn't say it. Instead I pushed myself to my sock feet and shivered, staring out the front window. The snowflakes were amazing, thick and cottony. "How often does it snow like this?"

"About four or five times every winter. School will be back open tomorrow; they'll have the snowplows going all night. You should think about going."

*Yeah. I'll get right on that.* I rubbed at my temple, where the zit was gone. It still hurt a little, though, deep under the skin. I hate those zits that burrow underground. You think they've vanished, but no, they just barricade themselves right next to the bone and hurt.

And my back twinged as I stretched carefully. "I don't have any big dreams to keep me in school. What are you, a guidance counselor?"

"You have to think about the rest of your life." He sounded serious, just like an ABC After School Special, pushing his dead-black hair away from his forehead. "Seriously. High school isn't forever. If it was, I'd kill myself."

*That makes two of us.* "High school doesn't even *matter.* When I turn eighteen I'll be able to smoke and vote, not to mention get a decent job."

"Not if you keep skipping. The way to get a decent job is to play the game well enough in high school, so you can get into college on a good GPA. That way you don't end up poor and sucking on forties out in the Circle K parking lot, like my stupid stepdad." Graves stretched. His eyes had turned a sleepy moss green. "Can I have another sandwich?"

"You know where the kitchen is." *I need to find the truck. Then I need to find out who did that to Dad. And who this number belongs to.* My left hand curled into a fist, shoved inside my pocket to touch the paper. It was the only lead I had for now.

I thought Graves would keep bugging me, but apparently he was *really* smart. He left me alone in the silent living room with its faint horrible smell that lasted even after I got the ancient vacuum cleaner out and sucked every last trace of ash into a fresh bag.

It was the only way I had to keep some piece of Dad. He deserved a funeral. He deserved to be buried with Mom.

*That* was the wrong thought, and it made everything even worse. Something inside my chest was tearing open, and it was hard work

to try to keep it closed over. That's the funny thing about old hurts—
they just wait for a new heartache to come along and then show up,
just as sharp and horrible as the first day you woke up with the world
changed all around you.

I taped the bag shut and tucked it in the fireproof box; then I
had to lean over the top of the box for a while, shaking and keeping
the sobs muffled in my throat while Graves clinked around in the
kitchen, listening to the weather report on the radio and occasionally
bursting into snatches of song.

I was glad he was in a good mood.

# CHAPTER 16

The bad part of the storm lasted not a week but three days, and Graves turned out to be a halfway decent cook. I'm no slouch in the kitchen—Gran took care of that—but Goth Boy was better. He made me omelets and was a fair hand with coffee, even though he did it too weak like most civilians. He slept in Dad's cot, dragged into my room and neatly made each morning.

I got the idea he was on his best behavior. It was kind of nice to half-wake in the middle of the night and hear someone breathing, though. Like I was in a hotel room with Dad. I would half-smile and roll over, and I slept pretty okay.

By the third day I was sick of the house and in a state of nervous tension that had me working the heavy bag in the garage, shivering as sweat steamed on my skin and I popped punches like a boxer, shuffling, and did my katas. It hurt, but I was used to that, working through the flinches as my muscles reminded me I'd mistreated them.

The tai chi helped a little bit. The breathing and the quiet move-ments—full moon rising over the water, single whip, play the gui-tar—cleared out the inside of my head. It was the only time I wasn't chewing myself into little mental bits. The problem was, as soon as I stopped, listening to the broken garage door bend and flex as the wind plucked at it, all the problems started crowding back inside my skull again.

At least while I worked out I could sometimes hear Dad's voice in my head. Better than nothing. But I didn't touch the weight bench in the corner. Dad was always picking up cheap barbells at garage sales, since it didn't make sense to tote them around the entire continent with us. The bench itself was a remnant from two cities ago, and one of the first things I'd pitch if I was packing to leave.

Except I kept thinking Dad would stamp out into the garage, growl a greeting, and expect me to spot him for a set or two.

I worried about the truck outside in this kind of weather, I worried about *finding* the damn truck so I could get out of town, and I most especially worried about whatever had turned Dad into a zombie.

The snow had blown itself out, and the weather report said it would be clear and chilly the next few days. School was set to open up, and Graves had a bad case of cabin fever as well. He was getting tired of wearing Dad's clothes, since they were all pretty much too baggy for him. I washed his jeans and he even condescended to compliment my long-sleeve Disco Duck T-shirt. We watched cable until I could hum along with all the advertising jingles again. We could agree on old sci-fi B movies, but he didn't want to watch the horror flicks.

I didn't blame him. So we stuck mostly to cartoons.

The fourth day turned over into the quiet cold before dawn,

and I woke up in my bed with Graves leaning over me in only his tighty-whities, shaking me with a clammy-cold hand. "Someone's at the door," he whispered, and I bolted out of bed so fast we almost cracked skulls.

"Who is it?" I grabbed a sweater and struggled into it, hearing the knocking—dull thuds muffled by the acoustics of snow—that hadn't managed to dent my dreamless sleep.

Or had I dreamed? I couldn't be sure.

I made it halfway downstairs just as the thudding stopped. Graves bumbled along behind me until I turned around and gave him a glare, putting a finger to my lips. He froze in the act of opening his mouth, scratching at the lower curve of his ribs on the right.

Three more thuds, each very distinct. I froze, my skin going cold and prickling, every hair on my body standing straight up and doing its best to escape my skin.

I knew that feeling. Gran had called it the singing willies. Dad called it the tingles.

I called it *something nasty on the other side of that door.*

And me without a gun or anything.

It tasted like old sludge and rust, the tang of iron against the back of my palate in that special place ordinary people don't have. Dad said he always knew when I was getting the tingles by the look on my face, and it must have been true, because Graves went white as milk under his coloring, his nostrils flaring and his messy hair quivering as he shook like a dog caught between cowardice and outright peeing itself with fear.

I caught something shifting over the surface of the door, a ripple like blue lines, just caught out of peripheral vision. The bolt of pain searing through my head caught me unaware, and I let out a hard, whistling breath.

I snapped a quick glance at the entrance to the living room. Stopped myself—the blinds were up, I hadn't pulled them before bed. No cover. There were weapons up in my room. I'd have grabbed one on the way out, but if a cop was at the door—or another adult authority figure—I would have gotten myself in trouble.

*This is getting ridiculous.*

One last knock on the door, a playful tap. *Little pig, little pig, let me in.*

I let out a soft, shallow breath, just a sip of air. Pointed at Graves, pointed upstairs, and made a gun with my forefinger and thumb. Raised my eyebrows meaningfully.

He nodded, the pink scars on his shoulder standing out vividly against pale skin. His undies had ridden up into the crack of his narrow ass, of which I was treated to a full view as he turned and tried to go as quietly as possible up the stairs.

I settled down into a crouch, watching the door, my entire skin alive and alert to every sound I could possibly pick up. Whoever it was, they were on the front porch, waiting. I knew it as surely as I knew my own name. It's like being able to see the heat shimmer off pavement on a summer day, the disturbance created by something weird standing in the normal world. The blue lines trembled on the edge of being visible, the house's space rejecting something inimical.

Every place we lived, I usually snuck out of my room the first night and traced the windows and outer doors with the wand Gran left, feeling my will bleed through the rowan wood and into the fabric of the walls themselves. She called it "wardin'" or "closin' up the house." Dad called it "that old Appalachia foolishness," but never very loudly, and he never stopped me.

Too much of what Gran taught me was useful. He just made a

token protest, that was all. I never pointed out that the protest was ridiculous, considering *his* line of work. It was just one of those things.

Sometimes I almost saw those thin blue lines running like lightning over the physical texture of the walls and windows. This time, it seemed like they were getting stronger, the lightning crackling together and concentrating, repelling something.

*Holy shit.*

The stairs creaked. The house responded, singing its almost-morning song under a blanket of snow. Yesterday the front yard had been a carpet of white, only barely broken by nubs where the picket fence stood guard, buried under a drift.

The front door did not creak. It just stood there, radiating the secret of something behind it, running with blue light I could almost, *almost* see. My palms had gone slick with sweat, my mouth cotton-dry and tasting funny, like morning and rust all swilled together.

*That's not rust, Dru. That's blood.* The voice of instinct announced it quite calmly. *It's something weird and it smells like blood. It's on your front porch, maybe looking at the dead plants in plastic pots you never bothered to move. If you look out the window in the living room, what do you want to bet you'll see it grinning back at you?*

A faint rattling, scratching noise touched the door. I began to feel woozy, thinking of Dad's bone-scraped fingers screaking against glass.

*Little pig, little pig, let me in.*

There's a lot of things in the Real World that can't cross a threshold without an invitation. Zombies aren't one of them—but maybe this thing was, and maybe the old ritual of closing up the house Gran had taught me was doing some good.

Maybe? No, *definitely*. "Not by the hair on my chinny-chin-chin," I mouthed, as Graves tried to move quietly down the stairs behind me. A board groaned sharply under his weight, and he let out a breath and froze.

The sense of presence leached away, like oily water sliding down a drain. I heard a thin sound that might have been a chuckle or a scream, depending on how far away it was.

I sat down hard on the stairs because my legs wouldn't hold me up. They were shaking too bad, and weak as wet noodles.

Graves handed me the gun over my shoulder. I took it, not having the heart to tell him the thing at the door was gone. My legs jittered like I'd had a jolt of pure caffeine laced with terror.

Well, I certainly had the terror. It spilled through me, dark as wine and tasting of ash and metal.

"It smells bad," Graves whispered. "What is it?"

*I don't know enough to even guess. Except just one thing — it's bad. Really, really bad.* I swallowed four or five times, my throat dry as silicon chips. "You can smell that?"

"Yeah. It smells nasty. Something rusting." His nostrils spread slightly as he inhaled, taking in a gulp of air that flared his rib cage. Muscle stood out in his neck and shoulders. He was shaking, too.

"That's not rust. It's blood." We both let out the breath at the same time, me at the end of my sentence, him as if he'd been waiting for me to exhale. "Are you psychic?"

"Me? No. I can't even get a date." He gave me a glance, and his eyes burned sickly phosphorescent green. Against his deadly paleness, the ethnic coloring of his skin drained away to stark white, the glow of his eyes was an insult. "It's gone, isn't it."

"It is." I wished my legs would stop shaking. "I don't know what it was." *But I can guess, can't I? It pretty much means one thing — something so bad even Dad would turn tail and run hard from it.*

*I just hope I'm wrong.*

* * *

Dawn came up clear and cold, snow throwing back thin sunlight under an aching-blue sky brushed with high white horsetail clouds. I put on Dad's Army sweater and his surplus coat, threw on a pair of jeans, stepped into my boots and stamped downstairs. I squinted at the ammo box, which was better than staring at the grease-dusty stain on the carpet.

Did I want to go around armed in broad daylight? It was looking more and more like a good idea. But still, the thought of getting caught with a firearm, no good ID, and no good explanation why I was packing heat was daunting.

To say the least.

"I still think I should go with you," Graves said. He leaned against the door to the living room, hands stuffed in his jeans pockets.

I shook my head, my braid bumping my shoulder. I'd drenched my hair in conditioner and braided it back, wanting it out of the way. "Dad would kill me if I dragged a civilian into this." I winced inwardly as soon as I said it, soldiered on. "Best thing for you to do is forget you ever saw any of this and go back to getting through high school." *Since something hinky is knocking at my front door and I can't blow town unless I have the truck. You're already too involved.*

"Yeah, well." He shrugged, thin shoulders rising and dropping. "Fat chance. What are you going to do, anyway?"

I cast another longing look at the ammo crate and picked up my backpack. The glare of snow outside made the bare walls even whiter, the bullet holes next to Graves standing out in sharp relief. "I'm going to make a phone call."

"Who you calling? Ghostbusters?"

*I suppose you had to make that joke sooner or later.* I mentally reviewed everything in my backpack, ran over how much money I had again. "I don't know yet."

"You don't know who you're calling?" His unibrow peaked on either side, forehead wrinkling as he mulled this over. "Jesus."

"Look, I've been doing this most of my life. I can do without the editorial." I thought about it for a few more moments, then strode over to the smaller weapons crate and dug for a few seconds, coming up with a switchblade. I pressed the button and was rewarded with a *snick!* as the suicide spring unleashed the stiletto. I studied the silver coating along the flat.

Silver doesn't belong on the edge where it can be sharpened off. If you load a blade along the flat, it might disturb the balance, but it stops a lot of things cold. And I could explain a military-surplus stiletto-style switchblade a lot easier than a firearm. I was pretty sure I could even talk myself out of getting detained if all I had on me was a blade.

I pressed the button and used the top of the weapons crate to close the knife, stuffed it in my jacket pocket.

Graves shrugged and peeled himself away from the wall. "I'm going with you."

"Look—" But he was already gone. I heard him take the stairs two at a time and guessed he was heading for his coat.

What could I say? He'd already been bitten. Once the Real World gets its teeth in you, it's hard to go back to nine-to-five and Happy Meals.

And . . . well, I listened to him moving around upstairs and could almost pretend he was Dad.

My conscience pinched me, *hard*, right in the middle of my chest. *Dru, you can't let him in on this. He's already been banged around and bitten. He might get worse if he gets mixed up further.*

But I was a kid too, and on my own. I wanted some help and he was looking like the best help I was going to get.

It wasn't fair.

But I'd gotten him bit—I wasn't naïve enough to think the burning dog and the werwulf had just been in the neighborhood and wanted an Orange Julius after closing hours. Not with something tapping at my door before dawn, too. Something the blue lines of Gran's warding—which seemed much stronger now than ever before—had sat up and taken notice of.

It wouldn't be decent of me to drag him along any further. He'd just end up getting hurt—he didn't have any experience at all.

I swallowed, hard. Slid my bag's strap over my head, pulled on a stocking cap, and yanked my gloves on. It looked bastard cold out there. When I stepped out the front door the air was like a dry suckerpunch to the lungs; I gasped and started shivering immediately, hunching my shoulders and wrapping a scratchy wool Army-surplus scarf around my neck. *Jesus. This isn't people weather. It's Popsicle weather.*

I was fairly sure Graves would lock up on his way out, so I crunched carefully down the porch steps. I was miserably unsurprised to see the snow in the front yard was still pristine. Whatever had knocked at the front door hadn't left any footprints.

Great.

I was already caked with snow up to my knees by the time I made it onto the street. The plows had come by again that morning, so the going was treacherous but not impossible. Dru Anderson, Fearless Teen Hunter of the Weird, slipping and sliding on crusted ice. But Jesus, if I had to stay home I'd start chewing on the walls.

And who was to say that something wouldn't come back once the sun went down, and bring someone with it that the warding wouldn't stop? My best chance was to try to make contact with someone now.

"*Dru!*" Graves yelled.

I didn't hunch my shoulders, just kept going. My boots had some good traction, but I couldn't go faster than a sort of skating crawl.

"*Dru! Wait up!*"

Kept going. Once I hit the cross-street I could hook down and get to the bus shelter, and hopefully the buses were still running on time. Maybe he'd get tired of yelling once I made it clear I wasn't listening.

Crunching sounded behind me, a fast light patter that sounded wrong. Then Graves all but plowed into me from behind, grabbed my shoulder, and we almost went down in a heap on the frozen roadway. I grabbed at his wrist, locked it, and found some solid footing, almost spinning him in a half-circle before he jerked his arm away much harder than he should have been able to.

I stared at him; he stared at me. His mouth was half-open, short light breaths puffing vapor into the chill. His cheeks were already raw and reddened, and his hair was even wilder than usual, almost standing straight up and spitting sparks. The effect was startling. He looked like a cat rubbed the wrong way with a balloon.

"Jesus," I gasped. "What the hell?"

"I'm going *with* you," he announced. Like I was stupid. "For Christ's sake, Dru."

"You're going to get yourself killed. And maybe get me killed too. Let *go!*" *And Jesus, how did you run like that?* A nasty supposition halfway rose in the back of my head, but I killed it. I had enough problems. I yanked my arm free.

He set his jaw stubbornly, and the breeze turned knife-sharp. My hair felt like it was freezing to my head, and the layers I was wearing weren't helping as much as I'd thought they would inside the house.

"You got me into this." His hand dropped to his side, and he squared his shoulders. "I got bit by something that shouldn't be *real*. None of this should be fucking *real*. And you're telling me to be a good little boy and run along home. No dice. I told you the first one's free, Dru, but this ain't the first one. This one you're paying for, and you're taking me with you. You *owe* me."

"I don't owe you anything." I knew it wasn't true even as I said it. If I hadn't been hiding in the goddamn mall, would the burning dog-thing have come to the house? Good luck getting the thing off my back then. He'd saved my life—and even if he didn't know it because he was a babe in the woods, *I* did.

*Andersons pay their debts*, Dad always said. *And quick, before they mount up.*

But what about the thing knocking on the front door? Someone knew where I lived now.

Someone—or some*thing*.

My stomach turned hard and sour. Graves stared at me like he was trying to will a hole in my forehead. Little ice crystals touched his hair, and his cheeks weren't just red now, but flaming. We were both shivering.

He didn't even have a scarf. For a native of this place, he seemed woefully unprepared.

I didn't even know what to do; I was just making it up halfass as I went along. "My dad is dead." The tone I used—flat, normal, as if I was talking about dinner—surprised me. Snow muffled the words; they plopped down exhausted as soon as they left my lips. "I'm sorry I got you into this. Do me a favor and go home so you don't get any further in."

"Hey, I don't know if you noticed, but I don't have a picket fence and fireplace to go back to. I'm on my own like you are, and for longer, too." He hunched his shoulders, already looking miserably cold. "I could've just left you sitting there in the mall. I got involved because I wanted to, and now I'm *in* it. So can we get moving before I freeze to death, or is that too much to ask?"

I took a step back, found my footing, and turned. Headed off down the street. Some of the neighbors had cleared their sidewalks, but most of them hadn't bothered. The gutters were mounded with snowplow ick.

Graves crunched along behind me. I tried to ignore him. *Good one, Dru. What the hell do you need him along for? He's only going to drag you down. Or you're going to drag him down.*

But he caught up with me as we reached the end of the block, and I didn't step away or try to keep ahead of him. He didn't say another word for a long time, and while that was okay, I kind of wished he'd talk to me.

It might have stopped me from thinking scary, scary thoughts.

# CHAPTER 17

The coffee shop was one I'd never been in before, and it was jammed with people in heavy winter coats, the windows fogging with collective breath. I watched the street for a bit, Graves sitting across from me and fiddling with a paper cup, his legs stretched out and his knee bumping mine every once in a while until I shifted.

"All right," I said, finally, when I'd watched the traffic moving on the street for long enough. I took a gulp of my hot chocolate, found it was cold. "We go over it again. I'm going up to that pay phone. I'm popping in the change and dialing. I'll see who answers and play it by ear. As soon as I hang up, you get up and meet me up at the corner. If I walk up on the building side, you peel away, take the 34 bus, and meet me at my house in a few hours. If I walk up on the street side, it's safe to act like you know me. Got it?"

I got an eye roll and a shrug in response. "I got it, I got it. Very James Bond. You really *have* been doing this a while." He didn't look at me, staring at the line going up to the counter. His face squinched up as if he tasted something bitter. "This place really reeks."

I shrugged. It was just a regular chain coffee outlet, with hordes of overpriced crap crowding the shelves and rickety tables, the kids behind the counter scrambling to keep up with the nonfat, soy chai, double shot, sugar-free, dry foam, drip please, do you have a sugar substitute? People shuffled up to the counter, got their froofy java, and shuffled out the door, usually jabbering away on cell phones about something useless or meaningless.

None of them knew about the Real World. None of them were so scared their bones felt like water.

"They don't have a clue." I scooped up my not-so-hot-anymore chocolate and scraped my chair away from the table. My back still hurt, twinges running down either side of my spine like a river.

A lady the size of a pickup truck in a massive blue parka—so large she looked practically square from the back—manhandled her kid up to the counter. The poor kid looked about five, bundled up against the cold, a wide slick of snot running down his upper lip, which he kept wiping at with a crusted sleeve. He stared raptly at the wall below the counter as his mom jabbered at the tired-looking blonde girl behind the counter. The curve of the wall seemed to fascinate him, since it bulged out to hold the coffee machines off to their left, and he ran his mittened hand along it until his mother jerked him back like she wished she had a choke collar on him. He let out an indignant sound and she shook him the way a dog will shake a puppy, but without a mama dog's gentleness.

My stomach turned into a cold lump. "Not a single goddamn clue," I repeated, and tossed my still-full cup into the trash on my way out the door.

The cold was full of exhaust and a bitter metal tang that probably meant more snow. I crunched down the sidewalk—a sheet of deicer pellets that looked like blue rock salt lay unreeled in front of every downtown business—toward the pay phone. I was pretty sure it worked; it'd given me a dial tone earlier when we walked past toward the coffee shop.

I dug in my pocket for quarters and the number, copied onto a blank anonymous scrap of notepaper. I ran over the plan again, trying to look for weak spots or angles, anything I'd missed, and I suddenly wondered if Dad had ever felt this way. This *responsible*. Throat dry, stomach churning, worry like a diamond-eyed rat chewing inside my head with bright, sharp teeth.

When I was little, I used to think he could do anything. He'd show up at Gran's every few months, sometimes with bruises or walking a little slow, and Gran would bake a cake, lay out a supper with everything he liked. It got to where I could tell when he was coming in by how early Gran got up and started cooking in the morning. She always knew before he would come bouncing up the washboard driveway, even though the house had no phone.

I remembered him picking me up and whirling around until I was dizzy while I shrieked with laughter in the front yard, a field of daisies and grass Gran hacked at with a machete every once in a while. Or him taking me out into the woods a little later and teaching me to shoot—first plinking with a BB gun, then with a .22 rifle, and last of all with a pistol and a shotgun. That was my twelfth summer, the one before Gran died.

I shook the memory away and stepped up to the half-booth. The mouthpiece slipped against my gloves, and I consoled myself that not a lot of germs would be able to live on it when it was this goddamn cold. I plugged the quarters in and dialed, then stuffed the paper back into my pocket. *Leave no trace, Dru girl. Think about what you're doing.*

I waited, heart pounding, a nasty sour taste filling my throat up to my back teeth.

Ringing. The phone worked, at least. Two rings. Three. Four. Someone picked up.

They didn't say anything, though. Instead, there was the peculiar not-quite-dead sound of a line with someone breathing on the other end. I listened, counting off the seconds. There was faint, indecipherable noise in the background, like traffic.

*One one thousand. Two one thousand. Three one thousand.*

There was a hissing sound, breath escaping between tongue and teeth, not quite whistling.

*Six one thousand. Seven one thousand. Eight one thousand.*

"Don't hang up, little girl." Male. Sounded pretty young, too, but something in the spacing of the words was off. Like an accent, and unlike.

My entire body flushed hot, then chilled. I tasted wax oranges and salt, but faintly. *Nine one thousand. Ten one thousand.*

"Quiet as a mouse." There was a short, bitter little laugh, as if the guy at the other end had a mouthful of something foul. "Fine. When you're ready for more answers, come find me. Corner of Burke and 72$^{nd}$. You can just walk right in."

*Fourteen one thousand. Fifteen one thousand.* I jammed the receiver back down in its cradle and stepped back, breathing heavily, all my muscles threatening to turn into noodles. *Jesus. Jesus Christ.*

I glanced around. The dangerous taste of oranges intensified, coating my tongue. *Shit. What now?* My legs took care of moving me away from the phone, hugging the building side of the walk. There were even dry patches where the building overhangs kept the snow off.

I didn't wait to see if Graves peeled off and headed for the bus. I hoped he'd be smart.

*Burke and 72nd.* I had to find a map. The transit center would have one, and it was a good place to lose a tail. I wasn't sure if someone was following, but the thick, clotted citrus filling my mouth warned me. Sometimes Real World baddies can get a lock on you even over the phone line, Dad said—hey, they were psychic, too. It was why we bothered being cautious about phone numbers—and my best bet was getting enough distance to confuse whoever it was.

There hadn't been an inked cross, so it wasn't a safe number. But he, whoever he was, might not know for sure it was me. Hopefully he wouldn't know if Dad had given the number to another hunter, if there had been a backup, or just *who* I was.

*Too much you don't know, Dru. This might have been a mistake.*

Still, now I knew something. I knew where a trap was. Where there was a trap, there was a way to spring it and find out who was behind it. If I was careful, and lucky.

*You might be careful, but you're just a kid. Dad should be doing this. He was smart and strong, and if someone turned him into a walking corpse, you don't have a chance.*

But I was all there was. What else was I going to do?

*Skip town. Get the hell out.*

Yeah, right. In the snow. With no car. *That* sounded like a way to get caught by something or someone. And not a nice way, either.

I put my head down and lengthened my stride, still sticking to the building side. The sky was a freezing, aching blue, clouds blinking over the lens of the heavens. Some of them were heavy gray, a thick billowing edge trailing infinity in its wake.

I didn't look back to see if Graves was doing what I'd told him.

He was on his own for the next few hours, until I was sure it was safe for me to go home.

Until I was sure I wouldn't bring anything home *with* me.

The transit center was two streets over. I stood looking at a map of downtown and finally found Burke and 72nd on the edge, where the streets started to bleed away into the suburbs. Only one bus went out that way. I checked the sky, traced the route with my fingertips, looked for escapes. There weren't any.

*This would be a lot easier if I had the truck. Come on, Dru. Plan. Use that brain.*

I stood staring at the transit map, willing it to show me something different. I needed to make sure my trail was clear, go home, and plan.

A bolt of glassy pain lanced through the center of my brain. I sucked in a breath, flinching, but it passed as soon as it had come, leaving only a ringing sound in its wake, like a wet wineglass stroked just right. Everything else was drowned in silence like deep water.

I looked up.

The world stood frozen in sharp detail. The buses were caught mid-idle, clouds of breath hanging out of everyone's mouth, each puff of exhaust or breath solid like wax castings. A guy in a long dark coat was flicking away a cigarette butt, its smoke trailing thinly from his fingers like a leash. People stood, balanced on one foot or another, like the movie of life had just hit pause and someone had forgotten to tell me.

A snow-pale fluttering moved atop one of the buses. I stared.

There, on top of the long, blunt-nosed shape, Granmama's white owl fluffed its wings, pinned me with a yellow stare. Its head cocked to the side, as if to say, *What's up, boss?*

It was hard to move. Clear air had hardened to syrup around me.

The best I could manage was a swimming amble, fighting against drag. Three steps, four, toward the bus, which stood with its door open, the driver inside motionless, a CB handset to his mouth and his eyes shut, in the middle of a blink.

The world snapped around me like a rubber band. Sound flooded back, engines and coughs and people talking, the low moan of the wind. I stood for a moment, staring up at the driver as he finished jabbering into the radio and glanced down at me.

"Getting on the bus, kid?" He had Santa Claus apple cheeks and a full white beard, and a kerchief of the American flag knotted around his neck. His knuckles were swollen and reddened, and he looked as cheerful and nonthreatening as you'd want someone to be behind the wheel of several tons.

I climbed aboard, heart thumping, showed my bus pass, and took a seat a quarter of the way back—close enough to the driver that delinquents or crazies in the rear wouldn't bother me, but far enough back the driver wouldn't notice much of anything I did unless I had some sort of vomiting seizure or something.

The way I felt, a seizure might've been an option. I had to struggle to breathe deeply.

I was sweating under my coat, scarf, and hat. But my teeth kept wanting to chatter, and goose bumps prickled hot and hard on my arms and legs. I folded my arms, trying not to feel as if I was hugging myself for comfort, and when the bus started up and began lurching, I wondered if the owl was still on top. Or if anyone would see it.

*Way to go with the woo-woo, Dru.* But there was a curious comfort—Gran had taught me about running on intuition. If her owl was here, I didn't have to worry much about being led astray. I just had to go with it, and I didn't have to convince Dad that it was serious and for real instead of just kid fears or an overactive imagination. Sure,

I was supposed to watch out for stuff he couldn't eyeball, and he always said my instincts were good. . . . But still, I guess adults have problems with this sort of thing, even when they know the monsters are out there.

I'd never had the world stop around me before. And the owl had never shown up during broad daylight. It was a nighttime thing, a dream thing.

I shivered again.

*Watch your ass, Dru. Just because you're getting a message doesn't mean it's a good one.*

It was just what Dad would have said. Gran might have just nodded, her peaky gray eyebrows going up in that particular way, the one that meant I'd just stated something so obvious it didn't bear repeating or remarking on.

I swallowed a sudden wave of homesick loneliness. The taste of oranges faded as the bus wallowed through a turn, tires rasping and gritting on sand-covered roadtop, and crept out of the transit center. I looked steadily out the window, my eyes pricking with hot tears, and waited for the next thing.

* * *

Two hours later the sky had turned into a pale gray bruise, small stones of snow were pattering down, and my mouth tasted like I'd been walking in a citrus grove again. I heard that same ringing, like a gong after its tone has faded but before it stops vibrating, and pulled the stop cord. My hand just flashed out and caught it, really without any direction on my part.

Running on intuition is like that. You never know what crazy shit's going to happen next.

"Keep warm out there," the driver said as I passed. He'd said the same thing to every ever-loving person who got off. I just pulled my cap further down, almost to my eyebrows, and hoped I wouldn't slip and fall on my ass when I hit the ground outside.

I exhaled sharply, looked around. The bus shelter here was a shell of plastic, scarred with graffiti, and warehouses slumped all around under the iron-dark sky. The light had deepened but was failing fast, sunshine struggling to make it through whirling snow. It was late in the afternoon, and it gets dark quickly in winter this far north.

Real dark, and real quickly.

I cast around. Considered spitting to get the taste of wax oranges off my tongue. The snow hissed, driving in small particles against the bus shelter, and Granmama's owl glided in on soft muffled wings, a cleaner white than the dirty sky.

*You know, I'd be diagnosed crazy if I told a shrink about this. What the hell is an owl doing out here?* But I followed carefully, my soles crunching against snow that started to creak when I stepped in it. What sidewalk there was wasn't cleared out here—I had to fight through a shin-deep freeze, scramble over a heap of dirty crap thrown up by snowplows, and cross the street. Then there was another waist-high mountain of exhaust-blackened, sand-laden snow to scale, and the mouth of a dark alley to navigate. The owl glided in noiselessly as if on a string, a tongue sliding through a gap in broken teeth. The warehouses on either side were abandoned, *Sunshine Meatpacking* on one faded sign spackled with chunks of frozen stuff plastered there by the wind.

The alley had been sheltered from the worst of the snow. It was stacked with wooden pallets and other assorted junk. Good for an ambush, especially with the shadows growing by the second. The owl floated above me in a tight circle, then sailed down and around a bend.

Great. A blind turn in an alley. Dad would be motioning me back to the open end of it to keep watch. He'd go from cover to cover, but I was just strolling down the middle as if I was on rails.

Tiny little dots of snow drifted down one at a time, the alley only getting a desultory sprinkling. The wind rose with a moan, tiny ice pellets whispering wherever they touched a flat surface. I slipped my right hand in my pocket, touched the switchblade's cold handle. My fingertips were frozen solid, not stinging anymore.

The alley made an L shape, and the bend was choked with junk on either side. I halted, peered around the corner, saw more daylight.

*Looks okay.* I looked up—no owl. The oranges vanished, leaving only the cold and the sudden miserable feeling that I was being watched.

I slid through the gap between pallets and headed down the other half of the alley. There was less trash here, but it looked older and more rotten—a drift of decaying newspaper over a shape that might have been human.

I flinched nervously. Looked again and it was just a busted-down old couch. Overflowing trash cans, one with condensation frozen on its sides, frost flowers blooming across the galvanized surface. I shuddered at the thought of what they might have in them and hurried past, because the end of the alley suddenly seemed brighter.

I came out, blinking, in a weedy, trash-strewn vacant space. At the far end, a chain-link fence sloped drunkenly back and forth. It looked weirdly familiar. And there on the other side . . .

I turned in a full circle. Yep, there were the two buildings squinched together, broken glass staring out into the cold night. I'd seen them from a different angle. I finished the turn, squinted at the chain-link fence. Let out a disbelieving sigh, my breath louder than the snow.

Our truck hunched on the other side of the fence. It was buried under a hood of deep snow, but I'd know the camper shape anywhere. And under the snow it was faded blue, the blue of a summer sky, the best color in the world.

"Holy shit," I whispered. The buildings behind me crouched, groaning like they intended to get up and hobble for a hot bath.

I took another two steps forward, through a knee-deep drift. The wind smacked me, rising and moaning eerily, loaded with stinging snow-buckshot. My jeans were sodden, clinging below the knee, and I couldn't feel my feet. I lurched forward again, tripped over something buried under the snow, and fell headlong. My palms hit snow, and I hoped there was nothing sharp under its soft white blanket.

*Good one, Dru.* I floundered up to my feet, shaking like a dog to get the powdery stuff off me. Considered cursing, but another bolt of pain slung through my head, this one jolting down my neck and spreading across my sore, aching back. I let out a half-garbled sound and hunched, crossing my arms over my belly, cold burning against my cheeks.

I pulled back into my own head with an effort, clenching myself like a fist. My eyes ran with hot water, and I lurched to my feet, aware of how the light was draining from the sky.

*Get to the truck.* It was Dad's voice again, urgent but calm. *Get to the truck NOW. Run, Dru. Run.*

I made it up and staggered. My feet were so cold I didn't think I could run, but I gave it a go just as a low, hissing growl sounded behind me and something snapped like a flag in a high breeze. Snow flung itself up and the wind screeched. I leaped like a fish with a hook through its mouth.

"*Down!*" someone yelled, and habit grabbed me by the scruff. You don't hesitate when someone yells like that.

I hit the snow again, full-length, and heard something roar.

*Goddamn, that sounds like a shotgun.* I floundered, rolled over on my back, and the world turned to clear syrup again, snowflakes hanging suspended, the sky flushed with one last long red smear of dying sunlight, and the werwulf hanging in the air over me caught in mid-snarl, a long string of saliva flying back to splat on the lobe of one high-peaked, hairy ear. Its eyes were like coals, and the white streak up the side of its head was familiar—I had time to see almost every hair etched on its pelt, as well as the ruins of a shredded pair of canvas pants clasping its narrow hips. Its legs bent back the wrong way, fully extended for the leap. Its long, lean face was screwed up in a snarl of pure hatred.

It hung there for what seemed like forever as I struggled against deadweight, a scream locked in my throat—and the world snapped again, with a sound like ice breaking over deep cold water. Something hit the thing from the side, and it tumbled, turning in midair, landing impossibly gracefully, kicking up a sheet of snow as it slid.

"*Get up!*" that voice yelled again. It wasn't Dad's, but I know the sound of a command under fire. I scrambled, made it to my feet, found out I'd lost my stocking cap, and bolted for the truck again.

I made an amazing running leap as my back tore with pain again, the chain-link fence sagging under my weight. Fingers and toes madly scrabbling, I muscled up and made it just as that huge booming sound repeated. Definitely a shotgun, but I wasn't waiting around to find out. Adrenaline and terror boosted me up over the fence—I dropped a good five feet and jarred myself a good one when I landed, almost biting a chunk out of my tongue. It was ten feet to the truck, the longest ten feet of my life. I skidded on something icy under the snow and fetched up against the driver's side, grabbed onto the mirror, and snapped a glance over my shoulder.

Someone crouched in the snow, shotgun socked to his broad shoulder and trained on the streak-headed werwulf. I saw a flash of black hair, lying down sleek and wet, before the gun spoke again. The wulf howled and tumbled away, a high arc of blood spattering free.

My brain kicked into overdrive. *Gun. Get a gun. Keys.* I dug in my left coat pocket, dragged my keys out—spilling out a few spare pieces of paper and a gum wrapper—and found the truck key. My fingers tingled madly. *Lock might be frozen, oh God, help.*

The key went in easy. I twisted it—and was rewarded with the little silver bar of the lock inside clicking up. I tore my key free, dropped it on the driver's seat, and dug underneath the seat for the flat, heavy steel box.

The field box. It held a gun, ammo, and a couple other things you might need in a hurry if the situation went south. I was never supposed to touch it, but this was an *emergency*, dammit.

Another snarl. The sound almost made words. A werwulf's mouth probably wasn't built for human speech, but it sounded terribly, horribly almost human. As if an intelligent, murderous dog was trying to cry out.

"Come on, pretty boy. Let's see what you've got." He sounded like he was having a grand old time, whoever he was—I couldn't see out through the windshield. I got the box open, and let out a relieved half-sob. The modified Glock lay there, three clips next to it, I racked one, chambered a round—it seemed to take forever—then ducked back around the driver's door, gun pointed down.

Now that I wasn't half-blind with fear, I saw a jagged hole in the fence, just big enough to duck through. The field was now trampled, snow flung all over the place and dead grass sticking up in spikes. How had that happened?

They circled each other, the boy—because he didn't look any older than me—moving with fluid grace, his boots light atop the snow and landing like it was solid ground. The wulf limped and slipped, favoring its left side, and snarled again at him, the sound rasping at my brain like sandpaper. The streak up the side of its head glimmered just like the snow.

"I'm behind you," I warned him, wishing my voice didn't squeak halfway through. My throat was dry. The wulf's coal-like eyes flicked toward me, back at the boy as he took another step, getting its attention again.

"You should get out of here," the boy said conversationally, and I couldn't believe what I was hearing. Or seeing.

He had no footsteps. No footsteps at all. The powdery snow didn't give under his feet.

"I'm armed." I edged forward, raised the gun as he slid out of my field of fire. The circle they were drawing around each other was getting smaller with each step. "Besides, I've got some questions to ask you." I raised the gun, sighted just like Dad taught me, and put some pressure on the trigger. Snow whirled down, the flakes getting bigger, the clouds overhead losing their bloody light as the sun slid under the horizon.

The werwulf snarled again, its lean muzzle wrinkling. Blood spattered loose, the snow steaming where it landed. My palms were sweating, wool gloves sodden with melted snow and my own fear. *Hold it steady, Dru. Don't point that thing at anything you don't intend to kill.*

It eyed the boy, and me, and a shadow of madness crossed its glowing gaze before it backed up two steps, shook its slim head, snarled again—then whirled and bolted.

He fired, and so did I. The wulf howled as bullets struck home. I aimed for its back and knew I'd hit it as soon as I fired; the shotgun blast probably wasn't as effective. The wulf nipped smartly through a boarded-up window, leaving behind only a chilling howl echoed by the wind. Snow blew—and I half-turned, training the gun on the boy and breathing so hard my ribs heaved hysterically.

He lowered the shotgun and gave me a sidelong glance. His eyes were blue, like mine—but a very light cold blue, like the sky that morning before it clouded over. Winter blue. I saw this before the last bit of pink dusk faded out and the eerie orange half-darkness of snow reflecting city light replaced it, softening the sharpness of his profile.

"Who the hell are *you?*" I coughed once, rackingly, but the gun didn't waver. A thin thread of melting snow slid down the back of my neck, and a few wayward curls that had worked free of the braid bounced in my face. "And why did you tell me to go halfway across town?" *And why the hell did Dad have your number?*

He was silent for fifteen seconds, his head tilted as if listening. "We'd better move," he said finally. The odd spacing between his words didn't go away. "This is an old haunt of *his,* but still useful. *His* other pets will come back in force, sooner rather than later."

*What's this* we, *white man? And whose other pets? I've never heard of werwulfen being* pets *before.* "Who the hell are you?" I was only faintly relieved to see that he had a shadow, but his boots rested lightly on the snow, not disturbing it a bit. *Jesus.*

That earned me another sidelong glance. "It's Reynard, Christophe Reynard, nice to meet you. Can you drive, little girl?"

I backed up carefully, testing my footing with each step. My boots crunched right through the top crust of the snow and kept sinking until they hit dirt. "Of course I can drive. I've got my permit and everything." *And two sets of fake IDs for if I need to look a little older than I am.*

"Then you'd better see if that thing starts. Go on." He didn't move, staring at the hole in the wall the streak-headed wulf had squeezed through. He wasn't even breathing hard. His mouth drew down at the corners, that was all. "The cold around here can play havoc with batteries."

It was just the sort of thing Dad might have said. "Who the hell *are* you?" I repeated.

"I told you." Apparently deciding it was safe, he turned away from the warehouse, holding the shotgun easily. "Maybe the silver load in those pellets will poison Ash before he gets home to tell tales, but don't count on it. You need to get that truck started, Dru."

I gave a nervous little jump. *What the hell?* "How do you know my name?"

He gave a slight nod, like I'd confirmed a guess, and I swore at myself again. *Way to go, Dru, falling for the oldest trick in the book.*

"I know a lot about you." He looked like he meant it, too. Snow whirled down, flakes now the size of dimes, and following every eddy and swirl of wind. "I know you should be in school, I know you're alone, and I know you're scared. You shoot me, and you'll have more questions *and* a dead body on your hands. Go home."

I wasn't about to give up so easily. Either he was a safe contact and Dad had forgotten to mark it—which wasn't like Dad at all—or he was someone I might have to threaten to get some information out of. And if he vanished now I might never find him again, phone number or not. "What did you do to my father?" I felt like my hands were shaking, but the gun was steady as ever.

"Your father?" He measured me with those burning blue eyes. I realized he wasn't dressed for the weather—just a black long-sleeve T-shirt and jeans, snow beginning to cling to his sleek dark hair and eyelashes. Heavy engineer's boots were clumped with snow despite the way he stood balanced weightlessly on the crust, and there was a spray of it up his left side, like he'd rolled or landed in it. "I told him to leave well enough alone, that's all. I told him he was lucky to have made it this far. And I told him what I'm going to tell *you*. Go home and lock your doors, and leave the night to us."

My jaw threatened to drop. His eyes actually *glowed*, holes punched through darkness to a sterile place full of fox fire. And when he smiled, baring teeth whiter than the fresh snow already beginning to cover up evidence of the fight, I saw fangs that should have looked like a cheap set of Halloween falsies. But they didn't, because they were growing out of his jaws, upper and lower canines too long, front teeth subtly modified to hold flesh down or tear it free so the animal could get at hot blood.

"Ohshit," I whispered, and my voice seemed very small. My entire body shivered, drawing up against itself. Have you ever been so scared your flesh starts literally crawling on your bones? Yeah. Like that. "You're a . . . You're one of *them*."

"I am Kouros. A *djamphir*." His chin lifted a little when he said it, like it was a title or something. His hair ran with wet gleams, like it was oiled. "And you're nothing more than helpless right now. Go away."

*Helpless my ass.* I swallowed bitter iron. *He's a sucker, Dru. Get out of here. OhGod get out of here.* "Tell me what happened to my father." It was hard, but I kept my eyes on him. I wanted to look at the buildings behind him. Somewhere in there was a long concrete corridor I'd seen before, and a door that still might have something behind it.

Only, would that something be anything I wanted to see?

His smile widened, the teeth prominently displayed like an animal's warning grimace. "Some other time. Soon, since you'll be seeing me again. Now go home, little girl. And lock your doors."

There was a sound like ripping paper, and he simply *winked out*, snow spraying up in an impressive fantail. I let out a scream and squeezed off a shot, tracking the smear of *something wrong* bulleting through the air. It passed close enough to touch my cheek, flipping a few stray curls, and a flat, eerie little laugh echoed before falling dead against the snow. A breath of scent slid by my face, like warm apple pies.

I lost sight of it slipping away down what was certainly the way in or out of here, a long channel, probably a dirt driveway under a blanket of snow. I swallowed sourness, tasted a bitter citrus rind against my tongue, and knew I had to get out of there too.

I didn't want to. I wanted to find that corridor and see if anything of Dad was left down there. There just wasn't *time*.

Instead, I clumped past the truck, the way the smear had fled. The scent of apples and cinnamon trailed slightly before the wind whisked it briskly away. And about fifteen feet past the back bumper, my boots sinking through and hitting gravel—a good sign—there was something else. A spray of crimson drops sinking into the white.

I'd hit him. Whatever he was.

I got the hell out of there.

# CHAPTER 18

**Five or ten** miles an hour through blowing snow, chains rasping against ice and packed, sanded muck as well as a fresh, fast-falling layer of slippery whiteness that spun like feathers in the cone of my headlights. The drive home was no fun. I was shaking all over despite the heater blasting away, and when I finally made it into the driveway past 9 p.m., I parked at an angle that could only be described as drunken.

The lights were all on, solid gold shining warmly through thin windows. The blinds in the living room were finally down, though. My teeth were chattering by the time I got to the front porch, and I saw the shadow of something moving in the living room.

I hoped it was Graves, but my right hand went reflexively into my pocket and curled around the switchblade. I stood staring at the front door for a second—*probably right where something else stood a day ago*, I thought, and shivered harder. The memory seemed to belong to someone else, a long time ago and far away.

The locks chucked, and the door yanked open. "Jesus Christ," Graves said. "Where the hell have you *been*? Whose car is that? Are you okay?"

I let go of the switchblade, finger by finger. All of a sudden I was so glad to see him it wasn't even funny. He'd come back and waited for me so I didn't have to come home to an empty house. He was right—nobody had twisted his arm into approaching me at the mall *or* taking care of me. And he really sounded worried.

I didn't blame him. I probably looked like hell.

The porch creaked as I looked at him, blinking back something weird and hot. It overflowed, and one tear tracked its way down my cheek.

"Oh, shit." He was in his sock feet, and stepped out onto the porch, grabbed my arm, and dragged me into welcome warmth. I leaned against the wall inside the door as he closed and locked it, and just closed my eyes.

"We need to talk," I managed around the lump in my throat.

"No. Really?" If the words had been loaded with any more sarcasm they would have staggered. As it was, they only fell flat. "What the hell happened?"

"That's my dad's truck." The shivers were coming in waves now. "I found it. I found the guy attached to the phone number. He kn-kn-knows something."

He took it calmly. "Huh. You should get out of those clothes. You're dripping on the carpet."

Then again, Graves didn't know—and I couldn't explain—about the streak-headed werwulf and the boy who stood on snow as if it was a dance floor. It's not the sort of thing you can explain to someone who's only touched the Real World once.

I wasn't able to tell him that the boy was probably something more inhuman than the wulf who had ended up shredding his shoulder. That the boy wasn't a *boy*, was probably older than any adult I ever knew. And that he'd probably turned my dad into a zombie, and I was next unless I could come up with a plan, and a good one.

*Why* would he turn Dad into a zombie, though? I mean, suckers aren't the only thing that can turn people into hungry walking corpses. It happens all the time. Voodoo, burial in contaminated ground, black sorcery, working at big chain retail stores—there were endless ways someone could end up reanimated.

Still, they like to play with their prey, the suckers. Zombification is only one of their tricks.

They call themselves all sorts of tribal names, but hunters call them only a few things—suckers, *nosferatu*, "those undead bastards." And they're one of the few things everyone, no matter their personal feuds or dislike, will band together and try to kill. There were even whispers of werwulfen sometimes working with groups of human hunters to take a nest out. Wulfen and suckers don't get along; nobody knows why.

But why would a wulf and a burning dog *and* a sucker be after Dad *or* me?

It was the same mental ground I'd been retreading for hours, not getting anywhere. Now that I wasn't concentrating on driving, it was worse. *But why did Dad have his number? What was Dad doing out here? He didn't mention anything to me. He always had me help him find out what we were hunting.*

If Dad was hunting a sucker and he wanted me out of the way, why wouldn't he warn me or leave me somewhere safe? Why would he take me along and not talk about it?

I stared at the boxes stacked in the hall. It smelled red in here, like tomatoes and spice, and Graves put an awkward arm over my shoulder. "Look, I made some spaghetti. I also stopped by the mall and got some of my clothes and stuff. So, um, why don't you just get cleaned up and dried off, and you can tell me what's going on? You look cold."

I *was* cold, a chill that had nothing to do with the weather running through the center of my bones. Ice in the marrow, a buzzing in my head. The circular mental motion started again, my brain struggling over the same rut it had been in since I turned the key and the truck ground into life.

*Go over it again, Dru. Think it through.*

Suckers *could* make zombies. I knew that much. As a matter of fact, it was one of the questions you asked first when you ran across the reanimated—was it voodoo, burial somewhere weird and bad, suckers, or something else responsible for controlling the shambling corpse? If it was just someone buried in contaminated ground, you could fix it easily enough. If it was voodoo, you could find out who had access to corpses *and* a nasty habit of raising them.

If it was a sucker bringing the rotting bodies up from the ground or making their own corpses, though, you were pretty dead unless you had luck or backup. I was running low on both.

"Dru." Graves shook me a little, peeled me away from the wall. Peered down into my face, his unibrow puckering. "Come on. You look like you've seen a ghost." He caught himself and gave his peculiar, barking laugh. "That's pretty possible, isn't it?"

*You have no idea, kid.* I found my voice. "Pretty possible. Yeah." It took an effort to step away from him. I barked my shin on a box and winced a little. "I'll go get cleaned up. Spaghetti sounds good."

"Ragu." He shrugged. "It was all that was around. You want me to reheat some?"

*I know it was all that was around; Dad loved Ragu sauce. With tons of garlic.* My heart gave a squeezing twist. "Sure. Thanks." My stomach grumbled a little, despite being closed up tighter than a bank after hours.

His face eased. He let go of me and tried a tentative smile. "No problem. I was worried about you."

*You know what? So was I. I'm already as good as dead. There's no way I can fight a sucker. He's just playing with me.* There it was, the stark truth. "Yeah. Me too." I made it down the hall and up the stairs, stripped out of my wet clothes—my back twingeing every so often, reminding me that I'd wrenched it again—and crawled into some sweats and a T-shirt. The side of my head, where I'd clipped it on the fountain, stung softly. My ribs ached, and I had to wriggle around in the bed gingerly until I found a position that didn't hurt. I lay still, trying to make the no-pain last as long as possible, hearing Graves humming a little, off-key, downstairs. I stayed awake only long enough to pull the blankets a little higher up and feel a moment's worth of regret at not eating when he was going to all the trouble.

Then I blinked out.

* * *

*I don't often dream of my mother.*

*When I do, it's always the same. She is leaning over my crib, her face bigger than the moon and more beautiful than sunlight, or maybe it's just that way because I'm so young. Her hair tumbles down in glossy ringlets, smelling of her special shampoo, and the silver locket at her throat glimmers.*

*But there is a shadow in her pretty dark eyes; it matches the darkness over the left half of her face. It's like the shadow of rain seen through a window, light broken in rivulets.*

"Dru," she says, softly but urgently. "Get up."

I rub my eyes and yawn. "Mommy?" My voice is muffled. Sometimes it's the voice of a two-year-old, sometimes it's older. But always, it's wondering and quiet, sleepy.

"Come on, Dru." She puts her hands down and picks me up with a slight oof! as if she can't believe how much I've grown. I'm a big girl now, and I don't need her to carry me, but I'm so tired I don't protest. I cuddle into her warmth and feel the hummingbird beat of her heart. "I love you, baby," she whispers into my hair. She smells of fresh cookies and warm perfume, and it is here the dream starts to fray. Because I hear something like footsteps, or a pulse. It is quiet at first, but it gets louder and more rapid with each beat. "I love you so much."

"Mommy . . ." I put my head on her shoulder. I know I am heavy, but she is carrying me, and when she sets me down to open a door, I protest only a little.

It is the closet downstairs. Just how I know it's downstairs I'm not sure. There is something in the floor she pulls up, and some of my stuffed animals have been jammed into the square hole, along with blankets and a pillow from her and Daddy's bed. She scoops me up again and settles me in the hole, and I begin to feel a faint alarm. "Mommy?"

"We're going to play the game, Dru. You hide here and wait for Daddy to come home from work."

This is all wrong. Sometimes I hide in the closet to scare Daddy, but never in the middle of the night. And never in a hole in the floor—a hole I didn't even know was there. "I don't wanna," I say, and try to get up.

"Dru." She grabs my arm, and it hurts for a second before her grip gentles. "It's important, baby. This is a special game. Hide in the closet, and when Daddy comes home he'll find you. Lie down now. Be a good girl."

I protest, I whine a little. "I don't wanna." But I am a good girl. I snuggle down into the hole, because it's dark and warm and I'm tired, and the shadow on Mommy's face gets deeper. Only her eyes glitter, glowing summer blue instead of their usual soft laughing brown. She covers me up with a blanket and smiles at me until I close my eyes. Sleep isn't far behind, but as I go down I hear something and I understand she's fitted the cover over the hole, and I am in the dark. But it smells like her, and I am so tired.

I hear, very faint and far away, the closet door close, and a scratching. And just before the dream ends, I hear a long, low, chilling laugh, like someone trying to speak with a mouthful of razor blades, and I know my mother is somewhere close, and she is desperate, and something very bad is about to happen.

# CHAPTER 19

**S**chool started right up again the day after, and the day after *that* Graves talked me into going. I think he didn't know what else to do, and I gave in after only a token shouting match.

What the hell, right? I was already dead. All I had to do was wait for the blue-eyed boy to find me again. I mean, Jesus, I was just sixteen, right? Dad's truck was back in the driveway, but if I blew town I'd just die on some highway, probably at night, seeing something loom in the rearview mirror, or I'd get run off the road and ripped up in a ditch somewhere.

It was only a matter of time.

So, why not? Why not just do what he said?

At least it got me out of the house, where I was only prowling the rooms, getting more and more jumpy, looking at the stain on the living-room carpet, snarling at Graves when he tried to get me to eat. I'd managed to get the engine-block heater on the truck plugged in so it wouldn't freeze, even though the garage door was still broken and useless. That was about all I could do other than roam through the house like a madwoman, staring at everyday objects as if I'd never see them again.

I spent the nights crouched in the living room with the blinds up, my back against the wall, looking out at the wasteland of snow that was the front yard and jerking myself into wakefulness every time I dozed off. After the first night I figured I'd better put the gun down, and when Graves nagged me about going to school—probably because he thought I was getting a little weird—I told him I would to shut him up.

I didn't have the heart to tell him he was sharing a house with someone marked by a sucker. I mean, why rain on his parade? I tried to get him to go back to the mall, somewhere, *anywhere* away from me. It wasn't safe around me, but he stubbornly refused, and what could I do? Beat him up? I *could*, but why expend the effort?

I was so tired. So, so deathly tired. At least during the safe hours of sunlight at school I was surrounded by other people, and I was fairly sure I could sleep.

Bletchley, however, had other ideas. "Are you *with* us, Miss Anderson?"

I stared at the whiteboard at the front of the classroom. It was a valid question. *Was* I with them? I didn't think I'd ever been with them. Not the normal people, at least. Maybe there were one or two of them who had what Gran called "the touch." Maybe there were even a few of them who'd seen something weird or inexplicable, but they'd probably forgotten it as soon as they—

"Miss Anderson?" Bletchley was delighted. Her egglike eyes swam behind her spectacles, and she picked at the bottom of her sweater—the blue one with knitted roses, this time.

I just kept seeing Dad's face, half-chewed, the bony twitching of his fingertips. Blood on snow, and feet in heavy boots resting lightly on the unmarred top crust. The streak-headed werwulf snarling, its top lip lifting. And the hiss of the burning dog as it landed in the fountain, sulfur and stink and—

"No," I said finally. "I don't think I'm with you, Bletch."

In front of me, Graves slid down in his seat as if making himself smaller. I almost thought I heard him whisper, *shit*.

I heartily agreed. But I was too tired to deal with Bletch's crap. My eyes were full of sand and my entire body hurt.

A ripple went through the classroom. Bletchley stiffened and opened her mouth, but I was awake now. A nice nap ruined, not like first and second period, where I'd just put my head down on the desk and tuned the entire world out.

"As a matter of fact," I continued flatly, "I was just wondering why I was sitting here listening to you, when you obviously don't like anyone under twenty-one very much. It's like you only think real life starts when you can legally buy a beer or something. But then I realized another thing. You're scared of us."

"*Miss* Anderson—" Bletch began, but the words just kept spilling out. *Despite* the thin little voice in my head telling me that I shouldn't be saying the things I was thinking. Even if they were true.

Adults probably listen to that voice a lot. Did Dad ever stop telling me what he was thinking? What *hadn't* he told me?

I opened my mouth and had no idea what would come out next. "You probably thought teaching would be easy. A whole classful of helpless little snots for you to bully." I grabbed for my bag, made it to my feet, and almost knocked the whole desk over. Barked my hip a good one, and it added to the garden of bruises and scrapes all over my body. Pretty soon the sucker-boy would find me and I wouldn't feel anything ever again. "More every year, and they're always so easy to push around. Because you've got the power, right?"

"Sit *down!*" she hissed. Bright spots stood out on her withered cheeks, just as if someone had stamped her with one of those ink things they pop on your hand at clubs to prove you've paid the door fee.

I wasn't going to sit down. She probably didn't think I would, either, but maybe she figured it was worth a try.

"You've got all the power, and nobody would listen to us anyway. Because we're just kids. Who cares about *us?*" I ducked through my bag strap. It was too heavy, but that was because of what was in it. Graves made a restless movement, his hair and coat rustling.

Bletch inhaled and opened her mouth again to tell me to sit down or shut up. If I gave a damn, it might have even stopped me— that's what they count on, the hard teachers. They count on the weight of authority to get to you before a protest can even get halfway out of your mouth.

Fury ignited behind my breastbone, a hot glow like coals blooming into something sharp and dangerous. It was the same old crap— someone thinking they can push you around because you're young, because you're helpless. You had to just sit there and take it because you were under a certain number, because you weren't a real person yet; you could be picked up and dropped like a toy, left behind or thrown away—

"I don't think so," I continued, right over the top of her. "I think every goddamn kid you ever bullied is going to haunt you one day. And *I hope you choke on it!*" I didn't realize I was yelling until I had to fill my lungs with a gasping sound that would have been funny if not for what happened next.

Bletch's eyes bugged out of her head. She buckled, grabbing at her desk with one claw, the other clutching vainly at her throat, and made a hoarse, inhuman cawing noise.

The first one to start screaming was a pretty little brunette in the front row. I thought her name was Heather; she was wearing, of all things, a cheerleader's uniform. Why she bothered with umpteen feet of snow on the ground was beyond me. But right now her face was distorted with shock, and she let out a shriek that might have done a train justice. The sound made a few kids jump, and another one—a brunet boy with a thick neck and a jock's varsity jacket—let out a high-pitched squeal that harmonized oddly.

I finished gasping for air and stared at the teacher, who folded down like a piece of wet laundry let loose from the line. She thudded to her knees, and her face turned a weird plummy color. The bugging of her eyes began to seem natural and inevitable, but a faint alarm sounded in the back of my head. Other kids were screaming now too.

My gaze snapped away to the whiteboard. It was chattering madly against the wall, held on only by brackets. The instant I looked at it, there was a hollow cracking sound, and it fell, slamming onto the floor and actually *breaking*, a gigantic rip zigzagging horizontally across it.

A sensation like steam escaping through a valve slid through me, a sense of exquisite release.

Bletchley gasped and fell on her side, but regular color started to return to her face. She was breathing now. Someone retched in the back row, and my head snapped aside as if I'd been slapped, my cheek stinging. The air was thick with crawling electricity, suddenly hot as summer and humid like a thunderstorm was approaching.

Graves sat utterly still in the middle of kids who were getting up out of their chairs or screaming. His eyes were green flame, and his earring winked, a single silver star. His mouth was slightly open, as if he'd just had a hell of a good idea and was giving it such deep consideration the rest of his face had declared a vacation.

I turned around, my legs shaking like I'd just finished a hard five-mile run, and made it to the door. A new noise cut through the bedlam—the chimes for class ending, ringing in the middle of the hour. Now *that* was weird.

I let out a jagged sound that might have been a laugh, and fled.

\* \* \*

I was four blocks away and still moving at a pretty good clip when his hand tangled in my coat, getting a good handful of my hair too, and he yanked me backward. I'd've gone down in a heap if he hadn't shoved me upright, but as it was I overcorrected and we both fell over into a small mountain of dirty scudge-snow shoved aside from the street. I wasn't wearing my gloves or a scarf. Snow burned my hands as I tried to struggle to my feet. My bag got tangled up, and Graves cussed me a blue streak, finishing up with, "—the hell did you do *that* for?"

"Boy," he continued, bouncing up off the frozen-solid drift like he was one of those weighted-at-the-bottom dolls, "you sure know how to throw a party. I've been bitten, beat up, tied to a bed, James Bonded out, and now you finish off by choking a goddamn *teacher!*"

I didn't try to say I hadn't been touching her. There was no point. I'd been ill-wishing her—*hexing*, Gran called it, and to those with the touch it wasn't small potatoes. I was pretty good at untangling hexes and curses, but not so good at throwing them at people, mostly because Gran wouldn't hear of it. *Cain't hex, cain't heal,* she would always mutter, especially when the men from the county were out assessing property tax. *But hexin's a strong medicine, Dru. You mind me now.*

To Gran, "strong medicine" could be good or bad, just like the laxatives she was forever talking about. *Good for makin' the mail move smooth, but too much and you shit yer brains out. Mind me now, Dru.*

I'd once set out to ask her how exactly such an operation as the moving of the brain out through the digestive system was accomplished, but I'd lost my nerve.

Graves reached down, grabbed the front of my coat, and yanked hard enough to rip fabric, succeeding in hauling me to my feet again. "You'd better tell me what's going on. Or I swear to God, I'll —" He peered down at me. "Jesus Christ. You're leaking."

If by "leaking" he meant "sobbing like a girl," I guess so. I wiped at my nose with my sleeve, snorted out a bray of a laugh, and went back to sobbing. Tears slicked my face, and I shoved him away. "Fuck *off*! I don't *need* you complicating things! I'm *dead*, goddammit! Don't you get it? I'm *fucking dead*!"

He shook dirty snow out of his hair. "You're not dead. You're too goddamn annoying to be dead. Now come on. They called 911 for Bletch — I don't think you want to be here when that starts happening."

*Jesus, why won't you just leave me* alone? I was about to yell again, but sirens started in the distance. It was like a slap of cold water across the face, and I realized I was indeed crying completely and messily, and I was covered in dirty snow, I was pretty sure my socks didn't match, I was a song of different aches and pains, and I hadn't washed my hair in two days. I felt greasy and cruddy, my back felt like it was on fire, and the heavy weight in my bag was definitely not my smartest move.

I was being utterly idiotic. The realization woke me up out of whatever stupor I'd been wandering in for days now.

I hitched in a shuddering breath, trying to get some kind of calm back, failed miserably, and didn't protest when Graves grabbed my arm and started off down the sidewalk.

"Why can't I have a normal girlfriend?" he asked the air over his head. "I finally meet someone I like and she turns out to be crazy. Oh, well."

"*Girlfriend*?" I half-choked, almost spraying snot out of my nose. *Good one, Dru. You didn't brush your teeth today, either. Sloppy, very sloppy.* I was going to break out in a huge way after all this. It was going to be Zit City on the Anderson face. But right now my cheeks were so flaming hot it didn't matter.

He gave me a sideways glance, and I really saw the guy he was going to be in a few years lurking under his baby face and the wild hair. His cheekbones were going to come out and he was going to be one of those pretty half-Asians. He already had good skin, even if it was reddened by the cold. "Well, jeez, you know."

Was he *blushing*? So was I, if the lava flow covering my face and spilling down my throat was any indication. He kept glancing at me, and I couldn't look away.

For Christ's sake. The lunacy just would not end.

I wiped at my nose again, wished for a Kleenex. "I don't—" I began. *I don't date. I don't have time, even if you are one of the better kids I've met. And—*

He shrugged, his cheeks going a deeper tomato red that had nothing to do with the snow. The flush spread down his neck, even. We were about even in that department. "It was a joke, Dru. God. Just relax, will you? Come on." He kept dragging me. Admittedly, I didn't put up much of a fight. But still . . . "A whole day at school ruined. You're gonna wreck my GPA."

"I thought you were going to take your GED anyway." My lips were numb. My hands were too; I stuffed them in my coat pockets. The sirens whooped and brayed, getting closer.

"I want to get into a *college* so I don't have to be *poor*. GPA still *matters*," he informed me in the tone reserved for gormless idiots. "But hey, I've been good all year. Might as well take a couple days off. Now, you wanna tell me what's going on? I've been thinking you probably don't want some stupid kid messing up whatever you've got going, but I told you, I'm *in* it now. I might as well know what I'm facing, right?"

I looked down at the sidewalk. My face was still sweat-hot, prickling in the cold. Feet had worn some of the snow down; deicer, rock salt, and sand had done the rest. Ice rimed the concrete, but it was pretty passable, all things considered. It was a nice clear day, clouds lowering around the rim of the horizon but not closing the lens of the sky just yet. The only problem was the cold, knifing straight through every article of clothing.

"That stain in your living room is about the size of a body." Graves let go of my arm, but I kept walking next to him, powerless to stop. "And your dad . . . I'm not stupid, Dru."

*I know you're not.* "You wouldn't believe me." I was mumbling like a kid caught out after curfew.

He didn't look at me, but his shoulders hunched. He turned the corner just as the ambulance roared by, and I followed. Once we were a block away, the siren shut off abruptly and it was possible to talk again.

Graves gave me a sidelong glance. He wasn't red anymore, but the new weight in his gaze was uncomfortable. "Yeah? Try me." Two steps further, and he hunched even more, an oddly fluid movement.

"I keep seeing it. In my dreams. That thing that bit me."

I hadn't told him I'd seen the streak-headed wulf again. It just didn't seem like good news to give him. "That's normal. It's like, post-traumatic stress or something." I swallowed drily. The last of the sobs hitched to a halt. After crying that messily your head gets clear, whatever chemical it dumps into your blood giving you a lightheaded buzz.

"Is it normal that I can smell people now? *Really* smell them, and *really* smell what they had for lunch? And is it normal to be able to see in the dark? Like, as if it was day? And what about being able to move quicker than I should be? It's like I'm dialed to superhero now. Is *that* goddamn normal?"

I stopped, staring at him. He kept walking, paused a few steps away, and looked over his shoulder. "Come on, keep up. It's cold out here."

"You really . . ." *This is what comes of not shooting someone when you have the chance. Dad would have shot him. But he didn't turn into a fur rug!* "You didn't change. You shouldn't be having effects like that."

"I thought you said I was safe."

"I thought you *were*." My cheeks were now cold, stinging wet. I shivered. Once I started I couldn't seem to stop. The high-octane trembling ran through me like ice water. "Where are we going?"

"Nuh-uh." He shook his head, dark hair swinging. Most of the snow had been stripped free, the rest melting, water clinging to the strands. He was a blot of black on the gray and dirty-snow day, hardly the most inconspicuous kid. "Your turn. What the hell happened to you? You've been set on 'weird' ever since you left me in that coffee shop. Not that you have to stretch very far for it."

"I . . ." I held my breath, let it out in a sharp sigh, and decided to take the plunge. What was he going to do, laugh at me? "I saw someone. I have this . . . thing. . . . Anyway, I found my dad's truck by following this thing I have. It tells me stuff sometimes. There was a—the wulf that bit you, it was there." *I don't know anything about this, and that's wrong. I should be hitting the books to find out all I can, and hitting them hard.* "And a sucker showed up."

"The thing that bit me?" His face squinched up, hard, as if he'd tasted something bitter. "And a sucker?"

*How the hell am I supposed to explain?* "As in, *blood* sucker. We call them all sorts of names—*nosferatu*, undead, sucker, you know—"

"You're a *vampire hunter*? Jeez. Really? Or do they call it something different?" He sounded amused and thoughtful, rather than uncomfortable, at the thought.

"They just call it hunting. And not just vampires." *You're taking this really well.* "Other stuff, too. Whatever's dangerous and messing with people. My dad did it; I helped. Something killed him and turned him into a zombie. Probably this sucker—they can do it. Anyway, the sucker ran the wulf off and told me to go home. He's going to come kill me."

"Why? I mean, doesn't it make more sense for him to kill you there? Not that I'm in a hurry for you to bite it, you know." He actually hopped from foot to foot like a bird, impatient. "Come on. Keep moving. Your lips are turning blue."

"Leave my lips out of this." But it was awfully cold, and as soon as I started moving I was reminded that I hadn't put on a sweater, either. How *had* I gotten out of the house this morning? I suddenly wanted a hot shower more than anything else in the world. "They like to play with their victims. They get bored, I guess."

"Doesn't make much sense," he repeated.

*Haven't you ever had a cat?* "Like so much about this does?"

"It does, actually." He slid out a pack of Winstons, offered it to me, and frowned when I shook my head. "I mean, look at all the shit on TV. It's all over—witches and werewolves and all that sort of stuff. No smoke without fire, right? My stepdad used to say that."

It was by far the most information he'd ever given about his family. We were just sharing all over the place, Graves and I. The houses around us watched with their prissy little doors shut tight, blinds drawn down, driveways empty. "It's not like it is on television. You need to get that through your head right now. It's dangerous and dirty and smells bad and—"

He tapped out a coffin nail and lit up, stuffing the pack back in his pocket. His breath was already a cloud of smoke. "Yeah, well, so is sex and drugs and everything else worth doing. So what's our next move? You're the expert here."

*I'm no expert. I'm just a kid.* "I don't . . . I mean . . . my dad did all the planning." I couldn't believe I'd just said something so mealy-mouthed.

"So? What would he do?" Graves's coat flapped. He exhaled a stream of tobacco smoke. His nose wrinkled. "Gah. This doesn't even taste good now."

"Then why do you do it?" *He would get everything together and go back to those warehouses, looking for the "scene" so I could tell him what happened. He would take me to canvass the occult stores and the bars where they know about the Real World and find out who this Christophe is and where he sleeps—if he could cajole the information out of someone. He'd barricade the house or move somewhere else.*

But there was no way I could find a lease on my own without some serious work, and a hotel would be expensive and full of nosy adults unless it was a flophouse, which would be expensive and full of nasty people looking to take a bite out of a teenage girl.

I could make sure all the windows and doors at home were barred to evil—Gran had taught me that. It wouldn't stop a zombie—but I had someone with me now, right?

And I had guns. And grenades.

*Great, Dru. So you could blow both yourself and your new friend up? Dad told you never to mess with the grenades!*

But Dad wasn't here. I was on my own. Except, well, for Graves.

Who shrugged, taking another drag and screwing his face up hard. "Habit. I'm an addict, okay? Can we get back on topic? What would your dad do?" He didn't look like he was going anywhere. He looked, in fact, determined to stay put.

It was probably a bad thing. It might get him killed. But I couldn't help feeling relieved.

I couldn't help being glad he was around.

"He'd make a daylight run." I was shivering so hard the words almost got chopped into bits. "Where I found the truck. He'd go back and start digging where that streak-headed wulf scuttled away to. Track it if he could."

"Streak-headed?" He waved it away as soon as I opened my mouth, his cigarette trailing a line of smoke. "No, don't tell me. I've got a better question. Was that you? Did you do that to ol' Bletch?"

I swallowed the lie I meant to tell. "I guess so. It's called a hex. I've never thrown one before." *And that's something to worry about too. Where the hell did that come from? I've never been able to do that.*

But I'd never been so angry before, had I? Or so hopeless. And I was doing new things all the time now. The *touch* was getting stronger.

"Then how do you know it was you?" He looked down at his feet, obediently carrying him over the sidewalk. Stopped and motioned me around an icy patch; there was only room for one person to walk. "Looked to me like she had a heart attack once someone called her a bully to her face."

"Did I call her a bully? I don't remember that bit." I shuffled, picking my way around the ice. The glare of sunlight off snow pierced straight through my head, and I was suddenly very aware of my empty stomach.

There was a sound of moving cloth. "It was great, Dru. You said what everyone's been thinking for *years*."

"I'm glad you approve." *Still, I hexed her. Dammit. Gran would have a cow. Dad would take one look at my face when I got home and give me the Lecture About Using Gifts Responsibly.* My bag was too heavy. I fussed with the strap, trying to get it to not cut into my shoulder.

Graves's half-yipping laugh came again. "I was about to stand up and applaud, but people started screaming."

When his coat came down on my shoulders I gave a half-startled, nervous sidling step or two, almost dumping myself on the bank of road-snow. Again. "Are you crazy? It's fifty below out here!"

He shrugged, his thin shoulders moving under a ragged red wool sweater that had seen better days. He *had* brought a lot of his clothes over, and it was a relief to see him in something new. "You're making me cold, you're shivering so hard. I'm used to this, Florida girl. Just say thank you, okay?"

I winced half-guiltily, remembered I *had* told him about Florida. "You're nuts." But the coat was warm, and I pushed my arms through the sleeves. My bag bumped my hip, and as soon as we got home I'd have to clean it out. "Let's go home. I want some lunch and we can plan."

"Sounds good."

We walked in silence for a little while, crunching under each footstep like little bones clicking and breaking. I smelled him on his coat—healthy boy, deodorant, testosterone, cigarette smoke, and the faint tang of fried food. My cheeks tingled, but I didn't blush. Instead, I stared down at my feet, moving independently of me like good little soldiers, and hunched my shoulders so I could take a deep breath. Funny, but you don't really realize how personal it is to smell someone. He wasn't Dad, but he was right here with me.

I bit my lip, then I opened my mouth. "Graves?"

"What?" He sounded wary. I would too, if I was dealing with a crazy girl who had just hexed a stupid history teacher and told me all about suckers and wulfen.

"Thank you." The coat was really warm; I could see why he wore it. The shivers began to ease. The clearheaded sense of being cried out and ready to get to work dawned over me like a blessing.

I could tell he was grinning by the sudden feeling of warm sunshine on my back. "No problem, Dru. First one's free."

# CHAPTER 20

**T**he truck was still parked cockeyed in the driveway, and the phone was ringing when we let ourselves in. Graves went straight to turn the heat up, and I reached the phone just as the tinny repeated shriek ceased. "Probably the school calling to tell on you," he said, with his bitter little bark of a laugh.

There were a lot of missed calls lately, but the thought of *that* one sent a chill up my spine. "Jesus. I suppose you could pretend to be my dad." I struggled out of his coat, now wet with slushy ice near the hem since he was so tall it dragged when I wore it. My shirt held a faint ghost of cigarette smoke now, too, as well as an even fainter ghost of deodorant.

"You've got some kinky ideas, Miss Anderson." The heater wumped into life. I passed him in the hall and headed straight for the first weapons crate.

The gun came out of my bag, and I discovered I was sweating. What had I been *thinking*? It was loaded, one in the chamber, and

the safety (thank God) on. Going to nice suburban schools meant I
didn't have to worry about metal detectors, but it was still stupid to
pack heat to Foley High.

Dad called it "the rabbits"—when a hunter got stupid, blunted
by fear or the walloping unreality of the Real World. I suppose a
better term would be shell shock, or even monster shock.

I was about to strip the gun and set it back in the box when
my head jerked up. A half-second later, the doorbell rang. I jerked
around, my nostrils filling with the smell of coppery rust. It mixed
uneasily with the sudden wax-citrus tang in my saliva.

*Ohshit.* And something occurred to me—it was broad daylight,
sun splashing off the snow.

Suckers don't go out during the day. So it was *something else*.

But *what*?

There was a fast, light flurry of taps on the door. And the
shimmer of something weird behind it, clearly visible. The blue
lines of warding weren't visible, but I could *feel* them, thread-thin,
running together and humming. Gathering themselves like blue
lightning.

If whatever-it-was took two steps to the side, it could peer in the
huge, uncovered window and see me crouching near a weapons
crate, my frozen hands locked around a nine-millimeter and my legs
suddenly cramping.

*OhGod. Not right now.*

But you don't get to choose what comes after you, and when. If
you did, life would be a lot simpler, wouldn't it?

Graves appeared in the doorway to the living room. His eyes
were wide, white-ringed, and he looked almost as scared as I felt. His
cheeks were cottage-cheese pale under their even goldenness. For an
ethnic boy, he certainly got pretty white.

"What do we do?" he mouthed, and I didn't even try to pretend there wasn't serious bad news standing on the porch.

I snapped a glance at the front window and the wasteland of snow that was the front yard. *Jesus. I've got him to protect, too. He's not trained for this.*

I motioned him back with one hand, eased myself down to the floor, and began to crawl-slink along the carpet, gun in one hand. I checked and rechecked to make sure the safety was on, and was careful to point it away from my fool head.

More light taps. The sense of breathing, amused impatience welling up behind the door sent chills down my spine. Crawling over the discoloration on the carpet gave the chills more weight. There was a faint, rotting tang of zombie, not enough to make me gag but enough to make me wish I didn't have to slither over it.

I made it to some halfass cover—a row of boxes to one side of the television. The angle was bad, but I could at least see a slice of the porch and, hopefully, whatever was at the door.

Dust got in my nose as I shimmied behind the boxes. The urge to sneeze filled my nose, trickled down my throat, and damn near made my eyes water. *Do this right, Dru. You'll only get one shot.* I got my legs up under me as another flurry of taps hit the door.

I rose, carefully, slowly. Peered over the top of a box holding spare clothes and blankets.

The angle was indeed bad. But through the glass, I could see a moving shadow as whatever was out there shifted weight, probably from one foot to the other.

Assuming it had only two feet.

But weird stuff usually only came out at *night*. This was wrong, all wrong. I pointed the gun carefully, braced myself. The top of my head felt very, very exposed, poking above the boxes.

"Dru—" Graves half-whispered. There was a queer sliding noise, ending with a click.

*What the hell was that?* The shadow moved slightly.

"Dru—" Graves, again. Like we were in class and he was trying to pass a note or get someone to copy from.

*Yeah, sure, like this kid's ever copied. Puh-leeze.* "Shut up," I whispered, as quietly as I could. *Should I take a shot through the wall? I thought the angle was better over here. Dammit.*

"The door," Graves whispered. "The locks are moving."

*Oh shit.* I scrambled to my feet and launched myself over the boxes. It was an amazing leap—I don't even remember my wet boots touching the floor on the other side. I piled into the hall past Graves, shoving him down and aside. The door, its locks rotating and clicking into the open position, the knob turning slowly and paradoxically too fast for me to stop it; I barely got the safety off, raised the gun as the door blew open, a wave of intense cold streaking down the hall.

The lightning-crackle of the warding didn't even slow him down.

The blue-eyed boy's fingers closed around my wrist, and he casually twisted the gun free. It clattered on the floor, thankfully not going off.

There's one thing to be said for your dad leaving you a fifty and a reminder to do your katas. When a bad guy busts into your house and grabs you, you can punch him in the face hard enough to make him stagger back, blood pouring from his patrician nose.

Red blood. Not black, and not sheened with the opalescent slug-trail of sucker blood. Memory clicked inside my head—the drips on the snow that night had been red blood too.

Suckers bleed black; there is no hemoglobin left in them. It was why they needed fresh transfusions all the time. I hadn't thought of it before, too tired and scared to think anything *like* straight.

Too late now.

*What the hell?*

He stumbled back, his hair no longer dark-wet and sleek but light brown and shaggy, and I took a step, foot coming down solid and other leg bending, knee jackhammering up, and I got him a good one in the nuts—or would have if his arm hadn't swept down and smashed right above my knee, harder than anything human had a right to hit, deflecting my knee just a little bit. A burst of apple-pie scent came out of somewhere and hit me in the face.

Graves finally let out a yell. The blue eyes flickered past me, but I was already moving. Dad always said that the nut shot was great if it went through, but a girl always had to have a backup—because a guy won't expect you to go for the nuts *and* for something else.

I guess since the groin is the center of a guy's world, he rarely guesses it isn't the center of *yours*.

My fist, already folded up, headed for his throat like an express train. Next came the open palm, the heel of the hand striking just under the nose and driving up so the nasal promontory broke and slid into the brain. If I could just move fast enough.

*Work it, Dru! Harder! Harder!* Dad's voice, yelling—but there was no time for that, because there was a shattering roar behind me and something bulleted past, something long and lean, moving faster than it had any right to, hard to look at because it was blurring like clay under fast-running water. It hit the blue-eyed boy and threw him back at least six feet, and they were still going when the boy's head clipped the lintel and they tumbled out the door, onto the porch, and out of sight.

*What the—?* But I was already moving, forgetting the gun and tearing for the front door. The noise was immense, a growling roar mixed in with high-pitched but unmistakably male laughter, along with thumping that shook the whole house.

That was Graves. Hairy and moving like a bullet on speed.

*He wasn't supposed to change!* It seemed to take forever to reach the door, and by that time they had shattered the porch railing and dumped off into the front yard. There was a sickening *crack!* and an amazing fountain of snow jetted up.

"*Stop it!*" I screamed, but they weren't paying any attention. There was so much snow it was hard to see what was happening, but it looked like the blue-eyed boy had Graves—or what had been Graves—by the scruff and was flinging him around.

I took three steps, launched myself off the porch, and flew just like Supergirl, fists outstretched. I tackled the blue-eyed boy *hard*, all the breath driven out of me and my shoulder giving a huge burst of pain, and knocked him ass-over-teakettle. We went down in a tangle of arms and legs, and I gave the kid a good sock in the stomach before I realized what he was yelling.

"*I'm here to help you, fucking morons!*"

I rolled free, snow stinging my hands and face, and leaped to my feet just as Graves launched himself again. Time slowed down; my hand shot out and grabbed a fistful of his wild, curly hair—wilder and curlier now. He wasn't furry all over, but he was *changed*, something inhuman shining out through his burning-green eyes and the air hardening and shimmering around him like heat off a black sidewalk.

I gave a huge yank, only mildly concerned at the fact that I shouldn't have been able to move fast enough to catch him. The world had gotten very, well, basic, and the fact that this new kid was bleeding red had just truly made its way through a haze of adrenaline.

*Better not rabbit anymore, Dru. Come on. Control the situation.*

My abused shoulder gave a howl, but I held on grimly; Graves's legs flipped out from under him, and he let out a sound like that dog in the cartoons reaching the end of his chain and getting roinked but good. I let out a hurt little cry, my fingers cramping, and Graves hit the ground, his hair—vital, curly, springing with harsh life—slipping free of my hand.

"Where the hell did you get *that*?" the blue-eyed boy snarled. His face was a mask of blood, the right half already puffing up and discolored from my first punch. He was, again, not dressed for the weather—a black V-neck sweater about as thick as a piece of paper, jeans, and black sneakers caked with snow. I caught another breath of a good, spicy apple smell, and wondered if one of the neighbors was baking.

Sunlight gilded his hair, bringing out blond highlights in the brown. It looked like a new, expensive shaggy cut, and when Graves snarled at him he snarled back, lips peeling back and exposing teeth that were only bluntly human. They both made rumbling sounds— Graves like a huge-ass, very pissed-off dog, and Blue Eyes like metal rubbing against itself.

"Just hold on a minute." I reached down. Graves had struggled up to sit on his haunches in the snow. He was still actually growling, a low deep thrumming sound that rattled my teeth. Just to be safe, I put a hand on his head—not that I'd be able to stop him if he launched himself now, but it was worth a try. "Graves? Hold on a second, please."

"He can't hear you," Blue Eyes said. "The beast has him."

"Screw *you*," Graves snarled, and I was really happy to hear that.

Werwulfen don't talk. Not in their animal form, anyway—the streak-headed one hadn't been able to do much more than make weird noises. Their mouths aren't made right for talking once they shift into their other form.

Talking was a good sign, and it meant *not-werwulf*. But that was *definitely* what he'd been bitten by, he hadn't changed in twelve hours, and he'd been a virgin, right?

It should have meant he was safe. But Graves was doing all sorts of things he wasn't *supposed* to. I wished again I knew more about all this, instead of just what Dad and I could piece together with the help of some moldering leather-bound books passed from hunter to hunter and kept behind the counters of *real* occult stores, not brought out until a hunter presents his bona fides.

Books I should have been spending some serious time with instead of moping, by the way.

"Just everyone hold on. Hang on for one red-hot second." I dug around in my memory, pointed at Blue Eyes with my free hand. "You. Christophe, right?"

He actually gave me a correct little half-bow, spreading his arms, and I began to feel a little faint. Because even though he didn't have fangs now and his hair was sticking up, powdered with snow, he *still* rested on the top crust of a drift like a feather. My eyes struggled with what my brain was seeing, gave up, attacked the problem again, and decided since he was standing in a flood of bright sunlight, he was Something Else.

*But you saw the fangs, Dru!*

"What the hell *are* you?" I wished I hadn't ditched the gun, but told myself again that it had been a good idea—one of the few good ideas I'd had in the last couple days. What was I going to do, start shooting in broad daylight? That would have been a fine how-do-you-do. The wind shifted, and I smelled apples again. My mouth watered.

His smile stretched, became a model of lunatic good cheer. "I could ask you the same thing, little girl. Why didn't you tell me who you really were?"

"You knew my name." I struggled with the lunatic urge to pat Graves's head. *Just stay still for a second; let me question him.*

"The name is *not* the thing," Christophe said, tipping his head back a little and addressing the cold blue sky. The sky that was, in fact, the exact shade of his eyes.

Go figure.

His gaze swung back down to me, and he shrugged. "Should we move this conversation inside? That is, if you can keep a leash on your little lapdog there."

Graves stiffened, but he didn't move. The thrumming growl coming from him petered out, and he rose, slowly, his heels coming down and the rest of him unfolding fluidly. "What is he, Dru?" Thank God, he sounded at least reasonably calm. "He doesn't smell right."

"Look who's talking." Christophe folded his arms. He should have looked ridiculous with snow plastered all over him, but somehow he didn't. "I told you, I am *djamphir*. I am of the *Kouroi*. I hunt the beasts that fill the night. And you, Miss Anderson, are like and unlike. Why didn't you tell me what you were?"

"You killed my father." But I didn't sound so sure. I wasn't so sure, now. "What, I was supposed to trade baseball cards with you?"

"I didn't kill your dear Papá. I warned him away, but he was determined. He had a bone to pick with Sergej." His face twitched, a shadow rolling over it as I watched, fascinated. "Don't we all."

"Sergej?" The name sent a thin glass spike of pain through my skull. My skin chilled, and I realized we were all standing out in the goddamn snow. "Who's that?"

Christophe stared at me like I'd just asked what oxygen was. Then he bent over, wheezing, and I realized he was laughing.

*You know, I thought I'd gotten used to weird, but this is something else.* I'd dropped my arm. Now I grabbed Graves's sweater and pulled him back. He came without resisting, his head dropping forward like a little boy's. "I don't feel so hot," he said, very softly, and coughed.

"I'm not surprised." My teeth were gritted so hard the words had to struggle free. "I think we have some reading to do." I didn't want to turn my back on Laughing Boy, so I had to walk backward, high-stepping to get my feet out of the snow. The front yard looked like a tornado had hit it. Thank God nobody was home in the middle of the day to see this.

I almost went down hard on the porch steps; Graves grabbed the railing and we swayed drunkenly. Step by step, we retreated up, Graves leaning on me heavier and heavier. The vitality was running out of him like water out of a broken cup. Laughing Boy stopped wheezing and watched this with interest.

"I don't suppose you'll invite me in." He grinned, the same feral grimace that had bared his teeth earlier. They were so white, pristine.

But they weren't fangs. Not now.

"Nope." I beat Graves to the punch, just in case he didn't know that was a really bad idea and decided to say something.

"I'm not like a *nosferat*, you know." Christophe moved forward smoothly, his feet still not denting the snow. *How did it get all over him if he can do that?* "I don't need an invitation to step over your threshold."

*Yeah, you came right in past the wards* and *the threshold.* "I bet you say that to all the girls," my mouth replied, with no real direction from me. Graves sniggered weakly. I got him up on the porch and kept moving back. It felt uncomfortably like Christophe was herding us.

Blue Eyes grinned, still examining us both. He moved like he had all the time in the world, gliding like oil over the snow. "He's going to fall asleep soon. That *was* his first change, wasn't it? How long ago was he bitten? And by what strain?"

My breath made a cloud in front of me. Graves slumped against my shoulder. It was hard to believe he had just been running around growling like an Alsatian moments ago. "I'll ask the questions, *Chris.* You just give answers. What the hell are you? And if you didn't kill my father, who did?"

"You really don't listen, do you? I'm *djamphir.* Called a half-breed, but technically more like a sixteenth. We're the product of unions between women and *nosferatu.* Surely you've heard of *that.*"

My stomach turned over hard. *Holy shit.* "Actually, no. Not really." *Only in movies. Really bad movies.*

"Well, where have you been hiding, Miss Dru?" He was up the steps in one bound, his feet touching lightly, like ballet slippers. It was like watching a cat levitate. "I suppose you don't know what *you* are, either."

I could not get the thought of apple pie out of my head. Gran always served hers with a slab of cheese; Dad liked it that way. "I know what I am. I'm cold and hungry and pissed off. Thanks." I reached blindly for the knob, meaning to sweep the door closed and shut him out on the front porch, and hesitated.

The door hadn't done a fat lot of good five minutes ago. Still, the way he was grinning through his mask of blood wasn't encouraging.

I backed up. The gun was on the floor, too far back for me to kick the door closed and get to it. "If you're evil, you're barred from my house." My throat was dry. Graves picked that moment to go completely limp against me, and instead of being ready to kick ass, I was suddenly in danger of going down into yet another inglorious heap. My back ran with hot pain, and my shoulder wasn't too happy.

Christophe stepped over the threshold, swept the door closed, and caught Graves's other arm. In one efficient trice, he had taken all of the weight and was maneuvering Graves with dancerlike grace. It looked like Gene Kelly hauling around a doll full of sand. "Where do you want him?"

"Upstairs." I scooped the gun up. "And move slowly."

One blue eye sparkled at me. The blood was already drying. The heater was on—God, the bill was going to be sky-high this month. "If I wanted either of you dead, I'd just leave you to the wolves. 'Tis their season, after all."

*Yeah. Sure. Whatever.* "I'll keep the gun just in case. What are you doing here?"

"I thought I'd pay you a visit, my dear. Since you're so interesting."

My mouth shifted into high gear, leaving my brain behind. "You know, you're the second guy in a few days to call me that. You should be more creative."

*Good one, Dru.*

"I do hate to be imitated." He was hauling Graves up the stairs like the kid weighed nothing. "He'll be fine, if you're wondering. He'll sleep for a couple hours and wake up disoriented and hungry. I hope you have meat in the house."

*Does bologna count?* "Um, okay. Are you a hunter?" I trailed along behind him, suddenly wishing I could see Graves's face. And unless I was going nuts—which was a distinct possibility—this kid smelled just exactly like a fresh-baked pie. It was a good smell, and it made me hungry.

"Among other things." He reached the top of the stairs, sniffed, and carried Graves into my room. "My, isn't this cozy. I'll bet he sleeps *here*." He dumped the kid on the cot and covered him up with a few quick yanks on an Army blanket. Scratchy but warm, and it would forgive the snow melting from Graves's clothes.

His face looked less wary when he was asleep, and the unibrow wasn't that noticeable. His mouth gapped open a little, like a toddler's, and I pointed the gun at Christophe.

"Okay. Slowly. Back away from him."

He spread his hands, a flash of irritation crossing his blood-smeared face. "Why do you make me repeat myself? I just told you I don't want to hurt either of you. You're a babe in the woods. Who is this kid, your pet?"

I could barely believe it, but I outright bristled. If I had hackles, they would have gone straight up. "He's my *friend*." *And you're not.* "I think we need to have a little chat."

"I agree." His shoulders slumped a little, as if he was tired. "Do you have a washcloth? I'd like to get the blood off my face."

It was a pretty reasonable request, I decided. "Downstairs. Kitchen." But I covered him with the gun the entire way.

I'd hit him once, after all. And here in the house I'd already shot a zombie. Maybe this smartmouth blue-eyed apple-pie boy would be next.

# CHAPTER 21

**Without the blood** on his face, and in full light, Christophe turned out to be not just sharp-nosed but sharply handsome, too. The sweater, snowmelt weighing it down, clung to his torso. He was in good shape, and strong—I was going to have a bruise above my knee where he'd plugged me.

I kept him covered with the gun from one side of the breakfast bar while he wiped himself off, rubbing at his hands and passing the washcloth over his face. His chin was a little sharp, but he had great cheekbones. "That isn't necessary," he said, his back to me, glancing up out the window to the backyard. He didn't say a damn thing about the plywood-and-blanket baffle over the destroyed door. I wondered if he could smell the zombie.

"You'd better start talking," I informed him the third time he rinsed his hands. "I don't have all day."

"You might have all day, but you certainly don't have all night." He turned and leaned against the counter, his hair lying down a bit more now but still artistically mussed. Those blue eyes scored holes of brilliance in his face, and his elegant mouth made a small movement as if he tasted something on the borderline of bad. "Are you expecting visitors?"

*What?* "No." *I was going to re-ward the doors and windows, and I think I'd better as soon as I get you out of here.* "But you're not asking the questions, bucko. *I* am. Why don't you explain how you know my father and what *exactly* you are?"

He shrugged, and the heater shut off. I almost jumped out of my skin. "I'm *djamphir*. I hunt *nosferatu*. I suppose human hunters don't know much about us—at least, the amateurs probably don't." He grinned, and I found myself disliking him intensely. "And I know your father because he set me back months. I had almost finished preparing a trap for Sergej, but then your father had to come blundering in with his vendetta and ruin the whole thing. He's dead, then? I thought as much when I saw them take him."

"You saw it? What happened? And who the hell is Sergej?" I couldn't pronounce the name the way he could, like it was in another language. It sent the same glass dagger through my head, and the house creaked sharply as it settled on itself.

He rolled his eyes, a very teenage movement, but oddly strained. "Sergej, the Princeps. He's old, and nasty. He's the *nosferat* Dwight Anderson's been hunting these twelve years."

Hearing him say Dad's name was bad. Hearing him say *that* was . . . well, it was worse.

*Dad was hunting a sucker? No way. He always told me that was bad, bad news. That you couldn't pay him enough.* "Dad's been hunting other things." My heart gave a single hurting leap, like a spike driven through my chest. "I don't think he ever went after a sucker." *But . . . I could be wrong. There was that town north of*

*Miami. Dad got the heebies really bad on that one.*

And then there was that month I spent with August. I had a thought about that, something I should really do, but what Christophe said next knocked it right out of my head.

"Your father was a gifted amateur. It was your mother who was the real hunter." He was still looking at me steadily, as if weighing my reaction. A slant of winter light through the window brought out all the sharp detail on his face, the nap of his sweater, the glow in his eyes. "What do you remember about her?"

*We're going to play the game, Dru.*

I swallowed drily. My mouth was watering. The cinnamon and spice smell was downright distracting, especially since it covered up the faint omnipresent tang of zombie." Not much. She died when I was five."

"She was *murdered* when you were five." He folded his arms and watched my face like something was growing there. "You didn't know?"

My palms were sweating, my heart going a mile a minute. *What the hell do you think you know about me?* "How the hell do *you* know? You're as old as I am."

He seemed to find that funny. At any rate, a pained little smile crossed his sharp face. "I've got my own ways and methods, Miss Dru. And I'm going to be hanging around for a little bit. I'm your guardian angel. You *really* don't know what you are, do you?"

Irrational, nameless anger welled up behind my breastbone. Who did this guy think he was, anyway? *I said I'd be asking the questions here. Why do I feel more like he's questioning me?* "Yeah, guardian angel. Riiiight." I didn't think I could get any more sarcastic, but I gave it a try. "I told you, I'm hungry, tired, and pissed off. That about covers it. I don't get what you're hinting at."

"Do you know what *svetocha* is? No, of course not." His hand turned into a fist around the bloody washcloth. It was weird to see the difference between the white-knuckle clutch and his interested, bland expression. "I'd give a lot to know how your father thought he was going to handle you once you reached maturity. Or how he hid you. But if I know what you are, chances are someone else does too. They'll want to capture you—or kill you. Either way, you won't be running around loose for long. And if Sergej catches you, you might wish you were dead."

Oooh, was that supposed to be a threat? I summoned up my best *I don't give a shit* attitude, the one I used when in a Real World bar with Dad. "Why, because I know about the Real World? Whatever." I was getting tired of standing behind the breakfast bar. I wanted something to eat and I wanted to take a very hot shower, and I wanted my skin to stop running with chill prickles of foreboding. "I think it's time you left."

Not to mention I wanted a chance to sit down and think about this. He could just be shining me on, true. But . . .

Yeah, *but*. The most horrible little word in the English language. I hate that word. It just means something else is going to go wrong, or the shit is going to get deeper.

And it was deep enough already.

"You don't listen very well. You're in danger, Dru. Whatever you've seen up to now is a cakewalk compared to what's just around the bend. Word is out that Anderson's dead, and Sergej's looking for anyone he left behind—which means they're starting to suspect there *was* someone left behind. A secret your mother kept." His knuckles were still white around the bloody washcloth, and he was staring somewhere over my left shoulder so intently I almost looked to see what was looming behind me. "And here you are, running around with a *loup-garou* and ignoring all kinds of good advice."

*Loup-garou*, another word for werwulf. I stored the term away. I could find something out about that; it was time to hit the books like it was going out of style. "So this Sergej guy. He's a sucker, and he killed my father?" It was kind of hard to talk through all the rushing noise in my head.

The same noise I heard when I woke up a few mornings ago and found the world had twisted off its course and deposited me in a nightmare. The noise that was behind the word *gone*. Another little word I hate.

"I don't know if *killed* is the precise term. He likes to break them before he sends them into the afterlife. Your father might even be alive, for all we know." A millimeter's worth of change went through his face, those perfectly carved lips compressing slightly, and I was suddenly, instinctively aware he didn't even believe it himself.

*So you don't know. You're guessing just as much as I am.* It was a relief to start thinking logically again. I blinked hard, twice, trying to put everything together inside my head. "So what the hell are you doing here?"

"I suppose you could say I represent those who think you're precious. I told you, I'm your new guardian angel. Aren't you glad?" A wide, sunny smile broke out over his face. It would have been attractive if it hadn't been so downright freakish. Like a Halloween mask.

*Some angel. Yeah, I'm just warm all the way through.* "Precious? For what?"

"*Djamphir* are always male. If they breed with human women, they rarely have female offspring. When they do, those females are *svetocha*. The *svetocha* are fertile sometimes; their sons are strong, but their daughters—doubly rare as they are—are stronger. They always breed true when they throw a female." He paused, cocked his head, and took a good deep sniff. I wondered if he could smell pies too. "I'm good, yes. I'm strong by virtue of my blood. But with the proper training, Dru, you can become toxic to *nosferat*. You can become capable of killing them just by breathing in their vicinity. Once you bloom."

*Yeah, and I'll put on a cape and spandex, and fly to the moon, too.* "Wait. Hold on just one cotton-pickin' minute. You're telling me I'm part *sucker*?" I shook my head hard, my hair actually flying. "Sure. Tell me another fairy tale." *My mom was my mom. She wasn't a sucker, goddamn you. I know she wasn't.*

"You know better than most how true some fairy tales are." He scanned the kitchen slowly. His eyes were so blue, and they roved over every surface like he owned the place. "Can I have a glass of water? Rolling in the snow with a new *loup-garou* is thirsty work."

*Yeah, it's water you want? I saw your fangs, buddy boy.* I pointed with my free hand, kept the gun trained on him. "Glasses are up there. How do I know you're what you say you are?" *Or that anything you're telling me is anything close to the truth?*

See, that was the thing. None of this could be true.

So why was I still listening to him?

He half-shrugged, a single graceful lift of one shoulder. "I'm out during the day. You shot me the other night—that hurt, by the way—and I bleed red, as you verified not ten minutes ago. I can smell the difference on you and on your pet upstairs—and I saved your life. Aren't those enough reasons, or do you need more?" He got a glass down, moving silently except for the squeak of the cupboard. "I could have killed you both, you know. You're laughably untrained."

*I've been doing this all my life.* Still, it might be worth it to find out how he did a few things. Like standing on snow without leaving footprints. That would be a good skill to have.

What if his spiel about *djamphir* was true? I strained my memory, but couldn't drag up anything. Nothing but the movies, and while they might be better training than you'd think, they're also not as specific or thorough as a good book.

*But what really happened to Mom?* —I shut that thought down in a hurry. I didn't want to think it.

I didn't want to think about it *at all*. There was too much else to get out of the way before I could even begin.

It sounded like this Christophe knew more about the Real World than I did. His number had been in Dad's book—but without the mark that meant he was safe. He was still a contact, and—here was the magic thing—he might actually be useful.

I hated thinking about it that way. Just like I hated thinking about how useless Graves was, though to give him credit, he'd tried.

What did I want? Was it worth keeping this guy around?

Did I even have a choice? I had the gun now, but I had the sneaking suspicion Christophe was *letting* me keep it. I had another suspicion, too—if he could smell something on Graves, or something on me, he could probably smell the zombie stain in the living room. Why wasn't he saying anything about *that*, friends and neighbors?

The rushing in my head was really bad. It covered up other sounds I didn't want to hear—tapping on a window, the soft *wump!* of flames sprouting along a broad hairy back, or the terrible howls of a streak-headed werwulf. This was getting to be too much for me.

I was pretty much at the mercy of whatever this guy decided to do anyway. Wasn't it just this morning I'd been resigning myself to him killing me?

"So what's it going to be?" Christophe asked, as if he could read my mind. The spaces between his words were odd, as if he had some sort of weird American accent. I've heard just about everything on the continent, but I couldn't place it. "You're going to have to trust someone, Dru."

*I'm thinking I trust Graves, even if he is seriously wigging me out with this growling and leaping around thing. I'm thinking you're lying about my mother.*

Why bring her up at all, though? Dad didn't talk about her, even to August. He just never mentioned it. How could this guy know anything about her?

I had other things to worry about. *I'm thinking I don't trust you until I know why you want to be so helpful.*

But it was, I had to admit it, comforting. He was a professional. He'd taken care of the streak-headed werwulf and chased it off, and could obviously handle himself. Having someone else in my corner, someone more experienced who knew more than I did, wasn't something to be sneezed at.

Wasn't that what I'd been wishing for? And now here he was in my kitchen. Smelling like apple pies and looking at me with a direct seriousness that made him even cuter. The bruising spreading up the side of his face had halted, and under it he was very pretty. Not jock-pretty, or the hurtful kind of pretty that tells you a guy is too busy taking care of his royal self to think about you.

No, his face just worked. Everything in proportion, the artist in me noted. Except the sharpness of his chin and that shadow in his eyes. Like he knew more than he was telling.

*Way to judge him on his looks, Dru. Come on.* The rushing noise in my head drained away. I swallowed drily. "All right." I clicked the safety on and set the gun aside. "What do you suggest?"

"That's a good girl." He grinned. It wasn't the feral grimace he'd used before, but a genuine smile that lit up his cold eyes. There was blood drying in his hair, and he was dripping on the kitchen floor, but that smile more than made up for it. "First, Miss Dru, we take stock of your weapons and I bring some of my own. Then, before dark, we ward your house again. We may well have visitors tonight."

* * *

"I don't like it," Graves whispered. All in all, he was taking this pretty calmly. He touched the cookie jar, running his finger over the cow's belly, and took his hand back when I gave him a raised-eyebrow Look.

I closed the dishwasher, twisted the knob to turn it on. My hair was drying into frizz, but I felt a lot more human after a hot shower and some honest-to-God lunch. "I don't either. But he knows things Like about you." I caught myself whispering too, as if Christophe hadn't left to go "pick up a few things, be back before dark."

"I thought *you* knew things." Graves picked up an empty pizza box—I'd sprung for delivery, since the road was clear and we'd pretty much eaten the house clean. Groceries were in order. If there was no more snow tomorrow I'd go to the store.

It was like having Dad in the house again. Only not really. Dad would have been watching cable or quizzing me on tactics. Graves was just following me around and half-jumping nervously every time something creaked.

"I do know things. He knows *more* things." I eyed the stack of plates left over and popped the drain stopper in, reached for the dish soap. "You're taking this awfully calmly."

His face twisted up wryly. "It was amazing. It was like I could smell everything. Like the world was slow but I was moving at regular speed." He set the empty box aside, opened up one that still held two pieces of pepperoni with extra cheese. "God. I never thought I could be this hungry."

"There's cereal, too, when you're finished with that." I stared at the bubbles rising in the sink, white froth. Stole a sideways glance at him from under my lashes, looked hurriedly back at the soap foam. "Graves? Thank you."

He hastily swallowed. "For what?" Took another ginormous bite. His hair was a mess and his eyes glowed feverishly. The brighter green looked really nice on him.

"For everything. I mean . . . you didn't have to." *You didn't have to get me a cheeseburger. You didn't have to hide me. You didn't have to stick around or get me out of school today. You didn't have to be . . . trustworthy.*

"Hey." He shrugged and grinned, cheese hanging from the corner of his mouth before he hooked it in with his tongue. "It's not like I have anyone else, Dru. I figure we're both in the same boat."

*Yeah. And it's sinking fast.* I paddled my fingers in the water. "So what happened to your parents?"

He tossed the half-eaten slice back into the box. "They didn't want me. I bounced around in foster homes for a while, had some bad times. Almost got stuck in juvie because they didn't know what to do with me. Then I figured, I'm smart enough to take care of myself. So I did some lying and some moving around, and made myself a plan for getting all grown up and never being helpless again. *Ever.*" His eyes narrowed and he shrugged, as if there wasn't a world of pain hiding behind the words. "I've done pretty good, too. Mostly it's arranging things so people just assume someone's responsible for me."

"Yeah." I knew all about *that.*

*There's a fifty on the counter, Dru. And do your katas.* But Dad loved me, and there was never any question that he wanted me. He would never have just dropped me off somewhere and abandoned me, would he? He'd always come back.

But I'd always worried. *Always.* And this time he hadn't come back at all, had he?

"So what are we going to do before he comes back?" Graves eyed me, and I put the first three plates in the soapy water. Flipped the water off.

*We.* It sounded so simple when he said it like that. "We do the dishes. Then I show you how to ward the house—" I caught his wide-eyed almost-panic, and an unwilling laugh bubbled up in my throat. "Don't worry. All it takes is imagining—it's simple. We'll go over it before Christophe comes back. He helped close up the house before he left, but it doesn't hurt to do it again—and it doesn't hurt to have you know how to. My grandmother said you should do it every couple of days anyway to keep it fresh." It hurt a little to talk about Gran. Not nearly as much as it hurt to think about Dad, but close.

My brain returned to Mom, playing with the idea like a cat pawing a mouse. It couldn't be true. Mom wasn't a sucker, and neither was I. It was impossible. I went out in the sun like everyone else.

*Including Christophe. He was out by day, too. Jesus.*

"And then?" Graves asked, picking up a towel. I rinsed off the first plate and handed it to him. It was nice having him around; Dad couldn't be bothered to dry dishes.

"Then we look in a few books and figure out if everything Christophe told me before he left is true." *Especially about loup-garou.*

"Okay." He stared at the plate, polished it in circles with the towel. "Dru?" He opened up the right cabinet, set the plate gently away.

"Hm?" I swirled my fingers in slippery soap-water. The patterns almost made sense if I unfocused my eyes. The touch was getting stronger. Gran had told me it might happen, but she hadn't been too specific, and I hadn't really thought much about what that might mean.

The lump in my throat wasn't quite disgust and it wasn't quite fear. I couldn't figure out *what* it was. Svetocha. *Part* nosferat. *Is he serious?*

Well, we were going to find out. Funny how having something solid to work on gave me the sense of things being on track again. Not *right*—it wouldn't be right again, not ever. But on track. Better.

Right enough.

"Am I still human?" Graves took the next plate after I rinsed it off, swiped at it with the towel. Scrubbed at it a little harder as color mounted in his golden cheeks.

*Am I?* "Yeah, sure. Of course you are."

He shrugged. "I dunno. I felt like I wanted to kill him."

*You're not the only one.* I suppressed a shudder. "I'm not surprised. If he is what he says he is, you guys are pretty much enemies. Wulfen don't like suckers. Or even anything that smells like suckers."

That managed to prick his interest. "Is it like a big war between them?"

"Not exactly. They're just . . . well, they're like jocks and nerds. Or hyenas and lions. They coexist, right, but they're different breeds and they don't mix. And they're always on the lookout for each other." I paused. "A group of wulfen might help another group of wulfen or something else they don't like against a sucker, and suckers sometimes kill stray wulfen, of whatever type. There are lots of types, like tribes, and the suckers are organized into tribes, too. Their allegiances shift, but the suckers never band together to take out wulfen, and the wulfen don't really go after suckers unless it's to avenge one of their own. So they have this kind of agreement:

Each group doesn't really hang out with the other." I handed him a dripping glass and was kind of surprised. *Guess I knew a little more than I thought. That's a relief.*

"Okay." He nodded, dried the glass with finicky care, and put it up. "So. Warding the house. That some sort of witchcraft?"

*What do you know about witchcraft?* "More like folk magic. My Gran was a tooth-curer and hex-lifter out in the sticks back East. A wisewoman. You start throwing the W-word around and people get a little tense." *They still burn people in some places. Even here in the good ol' US of A. There was that one town —*

"I guess so. So what's involved in this?" He looked far more interested than I'd ever seen him in school, and it did wonders for him. His face looked leaner, more defined and less babyish. Maybe it was the light through the kitchen window, since Christophe had looked pretty nice under it, too.

God help me, I'd just dumbed down everything Gran taught me into folk cures. She would have just said, *A little bit o' this and a little bit o' that, and never you mind what I call it if'n it works,* while fixing him with that beady-eyed stare that had made more than one grown adult quail.

They hadn't called Gran a witch, but nobody wanted to cross her. And they would come to her door at dusk or in the middle of the night, for cures or other things. Payment was in eggs or salt pork, or herbs, or a bolt of material Gran would make dresses or quilts from. Those quilts sold for a good price, too, since rumor had it that Gran Anderson's quilts would keep lightning from the house or help make for an easy pregnancy.

I'd thought that was normal until she sent me down to the schoolhouse in the valley. And then later, after she died and Dad came to collect me, I'd found out other people didn't take spitting in someone's shadow as a deadly insult, didn't wash their floors with yarrow, and had no idea how dark and inimical the night could be.

"Dru?" Graves looked a little worried. I came back to myself with a jolt and finished washing the spaghetti pot from a couple nights ago. All shiny-clean. "Some salt water. I've got my Gran's rowan wand, too. And we've got a bunch of white candles. One of those should do fine."

# CHAPTER 22

**T**hey smell like dust, paper, old leather, and each one of them costs a pretty penny. There's Aberforth's *Creatures of Shadow*, Belt-Norsen's *Demoniaca*, Pretton's *Encyclopedia of the Darkness*, and Coilfer's weird but totally readable *Collection of True Folktales*. Which I've scared myself with a number of times, because Patton Coilfer could *write*. Dad told me that he came to a bad end, something involving an African curse and a bunch of masks, one of which had belonged to the semi-famous Sir Edwin Colin Wilson.

*That's* enough to give anyone who's read *True Folktales* nightmares, let me tell you.

We had other books, but those were the first I pulled out. After a few seconds of thought, I pulled out another prize possession—Haly Yolden's *Ars Lupica*, with its tooled leather cover and worn gilt-edged pages. Graves was making coffee—probably too weak, of course—while I spread them out in the living room and started flipping through indexes.

It's funny, a lot of books that would be otherwise useful don't have indexes. You have to kind of shoot by guess, and that's never fun. Especially when you start sneezing uncontrollably at the dust, or when you have to find something in a hurry. The only thing more annoying is having to go through microfiche. *Real* microfiche, not just the electronic captures of 'fiche they've been doing whenever they have funding lately. Nothing like scanning ancient newspapers on a 'fiche reader to make you feel old and dry. And give you a headache like a mule kicking in your skull.

I had to go through a couple of different spellings (*dhampire, dhamphir, dhampyr*) before I found *djamphir* and figured out they were all basically the same thing, and when I did, I settled down for some scanning. True to form, Coilfer was the best written and most useful of the four.

The *djamphir*—he spelled it the way Christophe had pronounced it—was a half-human vampire killer. Some had a thirst for blood; most were rumored to have bone problems. Lots of them were twins, but girl twins were never mentioned. Just boys, like a lot of other things in the books about the Real World. It's like girls are invisible.

Anyway, they were supposed to be often born without bones, and most of the legends were from the Balkans. If *djamphir* survived to adolescence or adulthood, they hunted *wampyr* or *upir*—suckers. Suckers had the hots for human women in a big way, and often bred with them. The result of those unions were *djamphir*, and once there was a taint of sucker in the bloodline, there were always *djamphir*, no matter how many generations passed.

The half or quarter or whatever bit of *wampyr* in them made *djamphir* good vampire hunters. They were always paid whatever they asked for, in cattle, clothes, or "even women."

Yeah. The Real World isn't big on feminism.

*Djamphir* were long-lived, possibly immortal—*if* the suckers didn't hunt back. But a lot of the suckers did. A lot of them killed their own part-human progeny, too. With a vengeance.

I had to sit back and think about that for a moment. *Ugh. That's* awful.

"Coffee," Graves said, and stopped in the door, looking at me a little weird. "You okay?"

*We're going to play a game, Dru.*

I shook my head, pushing the memory away. "This is gruesome stuff."

"Figures. So, is he telling the truth?" He handed me my cow mug, the one that matched the cookie jar.

"Haven't figured that out yet." I pushed the Aberforth and the Pretton over to him. "Look in those for *loup-garou,* but don't lose the pages I've marked, okay? And that one right there, *Ars Lupica.* Check that too."

"*Loup-garou.*" He looked down at the scrap of paper I'd written it on. "Okay. You got it."

"You're probably really good at this research thing." I blew across the top of my coffee, took a small sip, and was pleasantly surprised. It was getting better.

"This doesn't seem like math." He spread his free hand, looked at it. Tendons stood out on the back, his fingers blunt and nail-bitten, his knuckles chapped a bit but getting better. "And a lot of this is a direct violation of physics. Conservation of energy should make some of this stuff impossible."

"I don't know about that. I just know what I see." I took another sip. I'm not one for a lot of caffeine, but I felt fuzzy-headed. Slow and stupid.

"Yeah. That's the trouble with theories; the real world is always kicking the shit out of them." He settled down, stripping his hair back from his face. "Doesn't this sort of shit, well, *bother* you?"

I thought about it. "You mean, like it shouldn't exist?" I couldn't express it better than that.

But he understood, or I'd understood him. "Yeah. Exactly. It's . . . well, it's kind of obscene."

*That's one way of putting it.* "So's a lot of other stuff we take for granted. Burning down rain forests. Serial killers. Rush-hour traffic. Life is pretty obscene whatever way you slice it, Graves." I looked back down at the Coilfer. *Having your dad turned into a zombie kind of takes a cake, though. I'm not sure which cake it takes, but it definitely takes one of them.* "This sort of stuff is just icing, you know. On the cake."

"Some icing." He flipped immediately to the indexes, I noticed. "Wow."

"Yeah." I took a deep breath, another sip, and pulled my attention back to the page.

*The* djamphir *can use a variety of means to kill a* wampyr, *of which the most popular in folklore is a hawthorn stake. . . .*

* * *

It was a productive afternoon, even though I took down enough coffee to feel jittery by four o'clock. I closed the last book with a sigh. We were as ready as our small collection of texts could make us.

"So we're fairly sure?" Graves kept repeating "fairly" as if it were an exotic foreign word. "I'm not going to get all hairy, like that thing we saw?"

"Nope. According to this, the *loup-garou*'s a skinchanger, not actually a werwulf. Congratulations, you bucked the odds. About all you'll have is a hunger for raw meat." I shuddered. "Which you might even be able to eat, with the boost to your immune system."

The way he squinched up his face made me smile.

"Yeah, I'll get right on that dietary change. But nothing about girl . . . *djamphir*?" He tasted the word, rolling it around on his tongue, and bolted the last swallow of his coffee. It had to be cold by now.

I looked out the front window at the mess of the front yard, bits of brown grass showing through like mange wherever he and Christophe had scuffed the snow all the way down. The sky was lowering, threatening still more as sundown approached, and the radio gave faint squawks about a weather advisory. Why they would bother *now*, after days of this stuff, was beyond me.

Bits of wood were thrown in an arc, the porch railing completely shattered and flung out in an oddly perfect line. They'd hit it *hard*.

"Nope. Nothing on that." I didn't mention anything about my mother. It was nobody's business, even with Christophe's dark hints. I always thought I'd got the touch from Gran, along the Anderson side.

Now that I thought about it, nobody ever mentioned Mom's family. It just wasn't talked about. I didn't even know her maiden name, though I could probably dig up their marriage certificate. It was probably in the fireproof box.

But I wondered, and it wasn't a comfortable wondering. It was like having one of the legs your world rests on whomped away, and I wasn't too steady already.

All the legs of the table were getting chopped out from under me. Mom. *Whomp*. Gran. *Whomp*. Dad. *Whomp*.

If this was a cartoon, I'd be teetering on just one leg with my face twisted up in a picture of dismay.

It was late. Evening was gathering in the bluish shadows, even the reflection of light off the snow fading. Under the coffee jitter, exhaustion and sleeplessness plucked at my eyelids. My arms and legs were heavy, my shoulder hurt, and I knew I should probably take something for the way my back was twitching and sore.

"You hungry?" Graves asked, and I came back from staring at the front yard and realized I was. But given the choice between going to the store and getting some information under my belt, the information was probably the better bet. You had to be alive to eat, after all. I could always go tomorrow.

Which reminded me, there was the money situation to think about. And—

There was a flurry of taps at the door. Light, mocking taps.

I jumped, letting out a thin little cry, and Graves flinched, knocking over his empty coffee cup. The door swept open, and I dove for a gun, my right leg prickling because it had gone to sleep. I rolled, my aching back fetching up against the ammo crate, and clicked the safety off.

I didn't even think about it. Graves stupidly crouched right where he was, his eyes as big and green as a kid's, flicking nervously between me and the doorway. The air around him shimmered faintly, stilled.

"Easy, little birdie," Christophe called down the hall. "I can smell your adrenaline, you know. Come help me carry this in. I hope there's some coffee left."

Graves looked at me. We hadn't even seen him approach, I'd just been staring out at the front yard. You could see the walk and the driveway, for Christ's sake. Did he just show up out of thin air? Even in the *daytime*?

*Yeah. Pretty obscene.* I clicked the safety back on and let out a breath I hadn't been aware of holding. Dad would have kicked my ass for it, of course—holding your breath while under fire is a bad idea. You can pass out or just not think clearly if you're starving your brain of oxygen. There were even stories about people passing out because they were holding their breath in combat.

I was lying there on the floor, feeling a cold draft tiptoe down the hall and into the living room, and all of a sudden I felt very, very lonely.

"Come on out, little rabbits," Christophe called cheerfully. I could just see him grinning. "Come see what *Dyado Koleda* brought you, eh?"

*What the hell is he talking about?*

Graves pushed himself up. "Jesus," he whispered. He edged through the doorway into the hall, and I realized that he was trying to stay out of my field of fire.

Smart kid.

"There you are." There was the crinkle of plastic bags. "Help me with this. I stopped at the grocery store. The air smells of snow again, and not just a little bit, either."

"How'd you come up to the door without us seeing you?" Graves wanted to know. I swallowed drily and put the gun back on top of the ammo crate, pushed myself to my feet. My leg ran with waking-up tingles, like fork tines jammed into the muscles.

"I'm very sly." Christophe sounded in a hell of a jolly mood. "Now come on, beast of burden. Carry some of this. Where's *Księżniczka*? The princess?"

"Dru's finishing her coffee," Graves informed him, sarcasm dripping from every word. He came stumping down the hall with his hands loaded with shopping bags. I saw something green poking out of one. "We've been doing research."

"Oh, good. Stretching your minds like good little children. Your guardian angel is pleased." The front door closed, and there was more plastic rustling. "And?"

Graves didn't reply, just stamped past the stairs and into the kitchen. I stepped out into the hall and was greeted with the sight of Christophe in a fresh sweater, navy blue this time, with white stripes on the sleeves. It made his shoulders look a little broader, and his jeans were clean and dry. His hair all but glowed with blond streaks, and his eyes burned with sheer good cheer.

The smell of fresh apple pies filled the hall. I felt even more frizzy and hopeless.

"I brought weapons. But you can help carry these." He indicated the six shopping bags clustered around his booted feet. A backpack dangled off his shoulder, and a wide leather band crossed his chest. The blunt end of a shotgun poked up over his shoulder.

"You went grocery shopping with a shotgun?" I folded my arms, my stomach twisting with hunger.

He spread his hands, still grinning, teeth white in the shadow of the hall. "People see what they want to see, Dru. You know that. I brought canned soup. Bread. Some of the things I saw in your kitchen, and some others."

*What do you want in return?* I stayed where I was. "What do I owe you?"

That made his smile even wider, if it were possible. "Nothing at all, little bird. Nothing at all. May I come in?"

*What is it with these boys buying me food?* I shrugged. "Doesn't look like I can stop you. There's nothing in the books about girl *djamphir.*"

"Books." He shrugged. "And anyway, the books your father was likely to find wouldn't have such secrets in them."

*I don't like the way he talks about Dad.* But I just took a few steps forward, grabbed three of the bags, and turned on my heels.

"Dru." Short and sharp, he said my name like a challenge. All the good humor had drained from Christophe's voice.

I looked back over my shoulder. He stood with his back to the door, his teeth and hair glimmering. He looked impossibly finished for a seventeen-year-old.

God. Kids with guns. I had enough hardware to start an insurrection in my living room, and this kid was wandering around with a shotgun, for Chrissake. And Graves could probably wreak some serious havoc if he was angry enough and the change had him. Where were the adults who were supposed to handle this thing?

*All dead like Dad, maybe?* It was a nasty thought. "What?"

After a short, searching pause, he shrugged. "Nothing. I hope I brought what you needed."

*I hope so, too. But I don't have any clue what I need now. Although that shotgun is a good start.* "Thanks for stopping by the store. I don't know how much longer I can stay in this house, though."

"Oh?"

*You're not my first visitor, Blue Eyes.* I just swept on down the hall and let him chew on that.

# CHAPTER 23

**I** **woke up out** of a sound, dead sleep, a dream I couldn't quite remember about the dark hole in the closet receding as soon as I opened my eyes. The window was full of the weird directionless nighttime shine of streetlamps reflecting off fresh snow, and Gran's white owl fluffed its feathers and stared at me.

I was nice and warm, and Graves was breathing quietly on his cot. There was a faint sound—the television, downstairs. The soundless sound of someone breathing there, too.

Comforting. And a little bit scary.

I'd thought I wouldn't sleep with Christophe in the house. But as soon as my head touched the pillow, I'd gone out like a light.

The owl stared back at me. The smell of moonlight chased the fading tang of oranges across my tongue.

I slid out of bed, quietly, hissing in a soft breath as the temperature differential touched my skin. Even with the heater on, it was colder outside the warm nest of my bed. I stepped into sweatpants and pulled them up over the thermal bottoms I'd been sleeping in, yanked my tank top down, and fisted crusties out of my eyes with the other hand. I slipped past Graves, who made a slight sound as if he was dreaming, and ghosted down the hall, avoiding the squeaks. The stairs unreeled under my feet, and I was a shadow in the hall. Blue television flickers painted the wall; as I passed the door to the living room, I saw Christophe in Dad's camp chair, a shotgun—probably the same one I'd seen before—across his knees, his head dipped forward as if he slept. The television was turned way down, a black-and-white war movie I was sure I'd seen before unreeling between bursts of static.

*That's not right. It shouldn't be static. We have cable.* The thought was slow, moving through pudding.

Carpet, the boxes still piled in the hall, and a bullet hole shining with television light. They all looked very sad and quiet, refugees from a former life.

The front door was glowing. Thin threads of bright, cheery, summer-sky blue outlined it and scribed a complex pattern across its face, like tribal tattoos. I watched, fascinated, as they swirled like oil on water. Everything was dead silent now, the world wrapped in cotton.

I eased forward. Step by step, bare feet floating an inch above the cheap carpeting. There was a little slip-slide to each footstep, as if I was in a cartoon and someone had tied pats of butter to my feet. The door loomed larger and larger. I was on a conveyor belt sliding toward it, and my hand came up without my volition, stroked the locks. The two deadbolts moved silently, and my hand closed around the knob.

*Don't do it, Dru. Don't go out there.*

I wasn't planning on going anywhere, was I? Oranges ran in

rivulets across my tongue, fresh instead of waxed, and the shock of tasting them made my head hurt faintly, as if something had slid a thin metal tube through my skull. The knob hissed and slid like water on a hot griddle under my touch, and the blue lines on the door drew together, swirling uneasily.

The door opened silently, swinging wide, curtains of blue parting just slightly to let me through. I stepped out gingerly, still floating. Funny, but it didn't seem so cold anymore. The porch was bare, a section of railing torn loose, dead plants in plastic pots under a light scrim of frost, icicles clustered from one end near a gutter's drainpipe. They shivered, those swords of water, as my gaze blew across them.

The stairs unreeled under my feet. It was snowing again, big fat flakes whirling down in patterns I didn't have time to study; they looked like the tribal tattoos on the door, rivers of frozen stars. A humming had begun in my middle, like an electrical cord plugged into my belly button. The line of force was almost visible, snaking away across the humped drifts in the front yard, beginning to lose their peaks and valleys under a blanket of fresh white.

*Where am I going?*

There was a soft explosion of sound overhead, wings flapping frantically, and Gran's owl glided past, the eerie snowlight picking out faint dappling on its feathers. It circled, cutting a tight little figure eight with its wingtips, and slowed, floating down the street.

The line attached to my belly snapped taut and began to pull me faster. I leaned back, my heels lower than my toes as if I was waterskiing, and the sense of motion was weird—but not weirder than my hair hanging down, no breeze touching my cheeks or skin.

*I'm the Girl in the Bubble. Wow.* A dreamy giggle boiled up inside my throat, died away. The world twisted like dribbles of paint on a spinning paper plate, darkness and snow-reflection whirling together, and the owl banked again, wings outstretched and the pattern of eyes on its underside glaring through me for a moment. It dipped, then brushed past my head. I felt the wind of its passing kiss my cheeks and forehead, my hair stirring slightly before dead air returned.

It was weird, skating through the streets, the line at my belly unreeling, sometimes snapping me left or right, dragging me up over hillocks of piled snow and dropping me on their slopes, each landing curiously cushioned so it didn't jar me. Across streets, through alleys, once up and over the curve of a snowed-in car—the thought of someone waking up in the morning to find footprints running up over their car was hilarious, in a slow, disconnected way.

*But I'm not walking. I'm surfing. Snow-surfing. Wow.*

The owl made a soft passionless *who? who?* sound, and the tugging at my belly slackened. The line kept humming, but it didn't pull me. Instead, I found myself looking at a two-story frame house. Old and dilapidated, it had once been yellow. A massive, naked, gnarled oak tree stood in front, its twisted limbs reaching for the sky.

*Why does that look familiar?* I studied it for a long moment, cocked my head. The owl settled on the tiny strip of broken roof over the porch. The snow was deep, drifting up against the steps and swallowing them.

But I knew what those steps would look like. I knew what the porch would say if I stepped on its old groaning wood, and the screen door—busted off its hinges, plastic yellow crime-scene tape old and faded and fluttering over the yawning cavern leading into a front hall—I knew what sound it would make if it had still been whole. The hinges had squeaked one long, long note, a *heehaw!* Like an amused donkey.

There would be stairs inside, right off the narrow foyer. Up those stairs and to the left, there would be four doors: a bathroom, probably mildewed by now since the door was all busted open, a main bedroom and a smaller bedroom, and a closet.

*I know this house. Somehow I know this house.* I stared as the owl mantled, then tilted its head and made its soft call again. Its yellow eyes were old and terribly, terribly sad.

I moved forward, each footstep slip-sliding worse than before, as if butter was melting under my feet. It was hard—the air grew darker and darker the closer I got. And there, at the bottom of the oak tree, was a scorched place where the snow lay discolored and sunken. A moon-silvered figure lay under the darkness, terribly still, crushed under the running shadow.

*What is that?*

The owl called a third time, a new note of urgency in the soft tones. I put out my hands as the buzzing in my belly got worse, a hornet's nest in my gut, rattling and scraping.

*Wait. I know something. I know this house—*

The world shivered. I looked down at my hands and realized I could see right through them. Faint snowlight shone through my translucence, the curve of my forearm like glass full of solid smoke.

I was a ghost.

The owl spoke one final time, only that wasn't right, because it wasn't a soft hoot. It was a bell. A loud, rasping, heavy sound; the hornets had broken out of my belly and were swarming. Stinging needles rammed through my fingers as I reached the shadow of the oak tree, its branches buzzing like a rattlesnake's tail right before it decides *to hell with this* and launches itself to bite.

"What the *hell?*" someone said, and I thrashed up out of unconsciousness, snapped free of wherever I'd been like a rubber band popped off expert fingers, and came out swinging.

* * *

The window was open. Cold air drenched the room. Christophe twisted my wrist, deflecting the punch; Graves let out a high-pitched cry and the room was full of the sound of beating wings for a moment. But not soft, feather-baffled wings—no, this sound was leathery, rasping against the air.

Christophe and I tumbled to the floor while Graves wrenched the window closed. "Jesus *Christ!*" Graves kept repeating, in that same high-squeaky voice. It would have been funny if my entire body hadn't been pinned-and-needled, every square inch of skin stinging. "What the *hell* was that? What was that thing?"

I froze. Here I was in my own room, it was cold, and I was still in my thermal bottoms and tank top. My bed was thrashed out of all recognition, Graves's cot was overturned, and the room was full of a dry rotting scent, like molding feathers.

"*Revelle,*" Christophe said, grimly. His eyes burned blue, and he kept his hands clamped around my wrists, lying on top of me as if it was the most natural thing in the world. His skin was warm, and he was heavier than he should have been. All the breath left my lungs in a huff. "Dreamstealer. Hush, little bird, just a snake in the nest." This was whispered into my hair, a hot circle of breath against my shivering scalp before he raised his head. "Is it clear or snowing?"

"Snowing." Graves locked the window and shuddered again, wrapping his arms around himself so his elbows and shoulder blades made sharp-shadowed angles. "Jesus. It just came in, and Dru—"

The hollow between Christophe's throat and shoulder moved slightly, and the tingling heat coming off him drowned me. "Shush. Dru? Talk to me. Are you all right?"

I suppose he was asking because his face was in my hair, his legs twisted with mine, and he was holding onto my wrists so hard it hurt, like he had steel bands in his fingers. "Get *off* me!" I managed, before I was well on my way to suffocating.

"Yeah, she's okay." Graves cocked his head, looking at us both.

"Perhaps." Christophe let go of me—not fast enough, I might add. The pins and needles running through my skin peaked, and I curled into a ball on the floor, whooping in a gigantic, never-ending breath flavored with the ghost of apples fighting through the moldy feather-scent. The hall light was on, a rectangle of warm yellow on the floor, and I began to dry-retch.

It didn't feel good.

"*Damn* it." Christophe made it to his feet in a single curling, fluid motion. His hair was slicked down against his head, dark and sleek. "God and Hell both *damn* it. I didn't think he'd send *that*."

"Who? Who would send—someone *sent* that?" Graves's knees were all but knocking together. It sounded like his teeth were chattering, too, but his eyes burned feverish-green. "Holy shit. What the hell was it?"

"A wingéd serpent, come to rob the nest." Christophe shouldered him aside and checked the window. "She must have let it in, thinking it was someone else. Or . . . What I wouldn't give to know—" He halted, staring at the glass and the river of snow whirling down, some of it brushing the pane with little spidery sounds. "He must think she's close to blooming. But I didn't know he had access to a dreamstealer—only the Maharaja breed them." Frustration pulled his tone taut, edged each word with steel.

*Can I die now?* I dry-retched again. It felt like all my innards were trying to crawl out the hard way. *I thought I was outside. I know that house. That was where we lived Before.*

*Before the world changed. Before Mom—*

Could I find it again? I probably could. The memory wasn't fading like other dreams. Instead, it was sharp-etched, each individual owl feather shaded just so, every twist of the oak's branches easily remembered, burned into the space behind my eyelids. But my body folded up on itself in revolt, each muscle locking down. *God, what's happening to me?*

Christophe drummed his fingers on the window. The sound went straight through my head and I curled into a tighter ball. "If it was clear, I could track it. Especially now that it's wounded." He cast one bright glance over his shoulder. "That was a smart move, skinchanger, to hit between them."

"Thanks." Graves didn't sound like he accepted the compliment.

I coughed, swallowed, and hoped I wouldn't throw up for real. *Would someone mind cluing me in?* But it seemed pretty obvious— something hinky had come up to the window, and I'd mistaken it for Granmama's owl.

Or had I? I'd been gone, not here at all. I *knew* Gran's owl, and I knew that house. "It was from Before," I managed, through teeth tight-locking together. I was cold as if I'd been wandering out in the snow.

Hadn't I been?

"Get water." Christophe grabbed Graves, shoved him toward the door, and shook his hands like they had something icky on them as soon as he let go. "Get a glass of water. *Hurry.*"

Graves bolted, his curlywild hair all but standing up. I heard him bouncing down the stairs far too quickly, careering off the walls.

Christophe turned away from the window and dropped to his knees beside me. "Stupid," he hissed. His eyes were burning, and when I managed to tilt my head and look up there were dimples in his lower lip—where the fangs slid out from under the top lip and touched, ever so gently.

I couldn't even care. I was too busy.

*What, me? What did I do?* My heart gave an amazing leap and settled into pounding in my chest. It was getting harder to get air in through the retching, little sips of apples mixing with the fading cloy of rotting feathers. It was funny, it didn't seem like my body was rejecting dinner. It was more like a full-body spasm forcing a dry little sound up through the pipe of my throat and out of my mouth.

Christophe leaned down. His hands cupped my face, twisting my neck awkwardly. "You will breathe," he said calmly. Those eyes glared blue at me, colder than a thin winter sky. Snow hissed against the window, and Graves cursed downstairs. A cupboard slammed shut. "You will breathe, and you will *live*. I'm not having it any other way, *milna*. Breathe."

I tried. My eyes rolled back into my head. Darkness descended, a deep star-spangled night. My head pounded, excruciating pressure building behind my nose and eyeballs. Little spackles of light squeezed down as even my eyelids spasmed. Pain like a silver spike went through me, from the crown of my head to my soles, running down each branching nerve channel.

Graves galloped back into the room, cursing under his breath. Christophe's hands left my face, and my head thumped onto the floor a second before he shouted and threw the glass of water straight into my face.

The seizure stopped. Spluttering and choking, I twitched like a landed fish on the floor and drew in another deep heaving breath, hitched, and let it out with a torrent of cussing that would have done Dad proud, even during truck-fixing sessions.

"Yeah," Graves said, breathing heavily, when I ran out of air enough to curse and just sputtered. "I'd say she's okay."

"Idiot." Christophe handed him the glass as I tried to wipe water off myself. My muscles were weak as overcooked noodles. "That was too close. Get a towel."

"How about *you* get one? I already ran downstairs, and you're the one who threw water all over her." Graves leaned forward, eyeing me. "Hey, Dru. You were French-kissing a winged snake. Creeptastic."

"It was *stealing* her *breath*, imbecile. Go get a towel." Christophe shoved him, and Graves shoved back. The floor groaned sharply as their weight shifted. If I could have gotten in a smell through my nose it would have been the slightly oily dryness of pure macho.

Graves's lip lifted, and his teeth were just as white as Christophe's. "Don't order me around, asshole. I was here before you."

*Jesus. Boys.* I found my voice. "Goddammit, fuck you *both*. Get out of here." It was hard to sound forceful with my tank top soaked and every muscle in my body loose as wet spaghetti, but I tried my damnedest. "Go downstairs and make me some hot chocolate. Unload the dishwasher. Do something useful instead of getting in a testosterone match in *my* bedroom."

For a long, exotic moment they both stared at me, green eyes and blue burning. I managed to push myself up on weak arms, got my behind under me, and leaned against my mattresses, shivering. The heater puffed into life, but the not-sound of snow against the windowpane made me feel cold all over. *I was gone. I was out of here, and someone did something to my body. Oh, Gran, I wish you were here for real and not just sending your owl. You could tell me what the hell to do now.*

Tension snapped in the room, the air relaxing as they stepped away from each other. Christophe glanced at the window again, his profile still sharp and fanged, his hair sticking close to his head as if he'd gotten water dumped on him, too. His lips firmed up, sharp teeth retreating, and he looked like a new idea had struck him.

Graves, holding an empty glass from the kitchen, finally grinned at me. His eyes glowed, too, but green instead of blue. He looked as relieved as it was possible to get under his hair and beaky nose. "Sure you're okay?"

*No, I'm not. I'm freaked out, and you guys aren't making it any easier.* But my voice was steady. I was a master at putting on a steady voice. "Make me some hot chocolate. I'm cold. And both of you get out of here." I hugged myself as hard as I could. *I could be an actress. A talent for creative lying just has so many applications.* "Or I'll shoot you."

Christophe didn't look convinced. He blinked, as if just returning to the room, folding his arms and giving me a sideways glance. I expected his eyes to send little blue flashlight beams through the dimness. "What do you think—"

"Chris. Shut up." Much to my surprise, he did. "Go unload the dishwasher. Graves can show you where everything goes. When I get downstairs, you can tell me what that *thing* was."

They trooped obediently out of my room, and I rested my forehead on my knees. Regular aches and pains—my back twinging, my shoulder unhappy—returned like old friends, crawling back under my skin. This just kept getting more and more complex, and I wasn't sure what was real and what was the Real World anymore. Where were the grown-ups who could handle this?

An idea quivered on the tip of my brain, but I was too weirded out to follow it. Instead, I breathed deep the way Gran had taught me, and tried not to think. It was pretty useless, though, because the same thought kept coming back, circling like Gran's owl on soft soundless wings.

*I could find that house again. I know I could. It's from Before. And it's in this city.*

*Why didn't Dad tell me we used to live here?*

# CHAPTER 24

"**Sergej.**" **Christophe handed** me a mug of Swiss Miss. We didn't have any marshmallows, and I couldn't seem to warm up, even with a wool sweater on and Mom's quilt around my shoulders. "He's very old. You could call him the oldest we know of in North America and probably South America, too. He came from Europe after the war."

"Which war?" Graves wanted to know. He leaned against the breakfast bar next to me. Christophe set another mug down on the counter and gave him a withering look.

"The *Great* War, of course. Not the genocide masquerading as war from that horrid little Austrian corporal. Sergej drank his fill on the battlefields of Łódź and Gorlice-Tarnów. Before, he was merely one of the petty lordlings among the blood-drinkers. Something in the War changed him, and he came to America. Since then, he's been spreading the disease here. Killing for fun and food, and contaminating the proud and the petty to swell the ranks of his legions. We've been trying to kill him for so long."

That perked my ears right up. "We? We *who?*"

"The Order. Your mother was one of us." He said it like he would say, *That television show is on tonight,* or, *I'm going to pick up some milk at the store.*

"The *what?*" I stared at him. "What the hell?" *First she was a vampire hunter, now this. What does he really know about Mom?* "She's dead."

"Indeed. The only *svetocha* in sixty years. Sergej himself came out of hiding to kill her. She was rusty and weak, and she must have hurt him badly, but he managed."

Something horrible and buried rose briefly. *We're going to play the game, Dru.* And that ticking, like a heartbeat, faster and faster, closer and closer. I shoved it down—it was only a dream, wasn't it? I had other problems now.

*Hold on just one red-hot second. First questions first, then we'll get into this "order" thing.* "So why would Dad be calling *you?*"

Christophe's face changed. For the life of me I couldn't say how. "I think he had finally found out he needed the Order. He blamed us for your mother's death, thought a mere human could do what we couldn't. He went out to hunt alone."

I stared into the hot chocolate. It made a type of sense. Dad went wack after Mom died, and I never thought that much about it. It was just *there*. I didn't remember Mom dying.

Did I?

I remembered Dad's face, set and white, and him fighting with Gran. It was the only time I ever heard them disagree. Most of the time Gran just said *mmmh* or did whatever the hell she wanted to without bothering to give Dad the benefit of her opinion.

But that one time, when we'd arrived at the cabin in the middle of the night, they'd fought. We'd been driving with the windows down, the sharp cold smell of the mountains at night flooding through the car along with the purr and rattle of the engine. When we stopped, it had smelled like dust and new-cut grass, cold clear air and nighttime. I'd been so tired, curled up and sucking my thumb even though I was a big girl.

It was my sharpest memory of childhood, the first rock to loom up solidly in a fog of conflicting impressions before the time I actually started paying attention to everything around me. I guess you could say that's when I started growing up, smelling the sharpness of winter leaves, hearing the ticking of Gran's stove, the smell of frying eggs because Gran was cooking them just as we rolled up the rutted, potholed dirt road dipping and swinging up to her place.

Gran had actually *yelled*.

*What you gwun do, Dwight? That chile ain't old enough to know what's happenin'!*

Dad's voice, hoarse with something that might have been tears, though it was funny to think of Dad ever crying. *Damn straight she's not. Which is why we're here. Nothing can get to her here. You may hate me, old woman, but I'm doing the best I can.*

And every time I would beg and plead to go with Dad, he would just smile and ruffle my hair. *Not now, princess. When you're older.*

Gran would snort and set her false teeth together, and after Dad left she would keep me busy for days. There was no shortage of work up at her cabin, and maybe she thought it wouldn't give me time to think.

But a lot of waiting for your dad to come back and collect you gives you plenty of time to think, whether you're pitchforking hay or gathering berries or helping make salt pork.

None of that was going to help me now. I had to concentrate on what was in front of me. *Think, Dru. What would Dad ask?* "Who is this Order?"

"*The* Order," Christophe said, like I would say, *Duh, breathing!* "Professional hunters, mostly *djamphir*—the *Kouroi*. Though there are some of *his* kind." He waved a languid hand over his shoulder at Graves, whose face was set and almost white. "They do help."

"He's *loup-garou*," I supplied helpfully. "A half-imprinted werwulf. Stronger and faster than human, but not as strong as the furry type. We know that. We're not totally stupid."

Graves gave me a single, extraordinary glance. I don't know whether he understood that I didn't like Christophe's dismissive tone. But we'd been over it in the books just that afternoon, for God's sake, and we had a better idea of what had happened to him.

Graves was luckier than either of us had guessed. Not every kid who gets bit is a virgin—or gets bit by a wulf old enough and *strong* enough to half-imprint through that.

And more importantly, I didn't want Sucker Boy here thinking Graves was a second-class citizen or something because I'd gotten him bit.

"Exactly. There are full werwulfen as well as *loup-garou* in the Order." Christophe poured more milk into the saucepan and kept it moving. His own mug stood at attention right next to the stove. "The skinchangers are the princes of their type."

*Well, isn't that special.* "So you're saying I'm part sucker." I touched my mug with a finger. It was scorching hot.

"The *upir* can't stay away from human women. Sergej is . . . Well, the more powerful they are, the more mating allures them. He's always been careful to kill the offspring as well as the mother, though, lest they become a threat. All *djamphir* are survivors, or descendants of survivors." He took a deep breath, his shoulders stiffening. "They would kill us on sight if they could. And we return the favor. Just one big happy family."

*And I thought Dad and me put the "fun" in "dysfunctional."* "So this Order, they've been trying to kill this Sergej guy?" *The one you say killed my mother?*

It wasn't that I didn't believe him. It was just that my dad didn't raise an idiot. Sure, this guy had a good story and had saved my life, but good stories are as common as sneezes in the Real World. So he was *djamphir*, so what? It didn't mean he had my best interests at heart.

Or that everything he told me was the strictest truth.

On the other hand, what reason did he have to lie to me? *Or keep me alive?*

"Since 1918. He's canny, and he doesn't come out of hiding. Instead, he sends his minions, and he's old and glutted enough to have plenty of *those*. Like the wulf you saw the other night, the one with the pale patch on his temple? That's Ash."

Graves shivered, and so did I. I pulled the quilt closer around my shoulders, leaned into the counter. "How did a werwulf end up working for a sucker? Aren't they enemies?"

"Sergej," Christophe said quietly, "is an expert at breaking things to his will. Even wulfen. Ash has been his for a long, long time." The silence following this was only broken by the sound of the saucepan moving, and the chuckling hiss of snow against the window, until Christophe shook his head and continued. "If we could catch Sergej in the open, we could probably kill him. Especially if we had a *svetocha*. A fully trained daughter of one of our best." The milk sloshed back and forth in the pan. "I don't think you realize just how rare you are, Dru."

*Sends his minions. Would they happen to include a burning dog, too? Or was that something else?* "What about the burning dog?"

"Burning dog?" Christophe sounded thoughtful. "Tall and black, before it ignited?"

I thought of its glassy darkness before it inhaled and lit up like a burning Christmas tree. "Yeah. Big teeth. And it was huge."

"Big as a horse," Graves said.

"Ah." Christophe said nothing more.

"That's where the streak-headed wulf—Ash—first showed up. Following the burning thing."

Christophe nodded thoughtfully. "Ash and a tracker. How did you—"

"We drowned it in a fountain," Graves supplied helpfully. He actually sounded proud. "Then Dru shot that wulf-guy. After he bit me."

Christophe was very still for a long moment. "Ash and his trackers have been the death of many a good soldier of the Order. And two raw, untrained—"

"Yeah, we kicked his ass." *And nearly died.* But I kept that part of it to myself. My ribs twinged a little as I moved. "Wait a minute. How many of you guys—Order guys—are there?"

Christophe drew himself up, unconsciously straightening. "A few thousand *Kouroi* here in the States. More in Europe. Quite a few in Asia. We're all over."

*You are, huh?* "How come I've never heard of you? Dad and I have been pretty much all over the continent and I've never heard a single thing about you guys."

"If you know how to listen, you probably have. Your father's friend August Dobroslaw in New York, for example. He's one of us." A dismissive half-wave with his hand, and Christophe went back to keeping the milk moving as if it was the most interesting thing in the world.

I felt like I'd been pinched somewhere numb. *August. I've been thinking about him lately, too.* I nodded. "Then I can call him and he'll verify your story." My hair fell in my face. I lifted the hot chocolate and sipped it gingerly. My tongue got burned. I had to suck in a long breath. Snow spattered against the windows, and I shivered. I was *still* cold. The wind had a hungry sound again tonight, and I wasn't feeling safe even with Graves next to me.

Even with Christophe standing in the kitchen fiddling with the saucepan. "Do it and find out." His shoulders dropped. "If he does verify my story, as you put it, you think you could be a little nicer?"

"I'll try." It was my turn to sound sarcastic. Graves made a restless movement next to me, and I bumped him with my shoulder. Letting him know I was with him.

It helped me, too. The pressure of his arm against mine was comforting.

Graves drew in a deep, dissatisfied breath. "I want to know something. How are these things finding Dru?"

Silence, broken only by the sound of small snow pellets hitting the window. It was a hell of a good question.

The zombie found me because Dad knew where I lived. The streak-headed werwulf might have been watching the truck, and in any case he'd gotten a good noseful of me at the mall—which didn't explain how he'd arrived *at* the mall. If the burning dog was a tracker, as Christophe said, that explained some things—but not where it had picked up my trail in the first place.

And what about whoever was knocking on the door before dawn? I hated to admit it, but that bothered me the most. Why hadn't whatever-it-was tried to get in? Unless the warding had kept it out, which meant it *could* have been a sucker. Maybe even this Sergej.

The name sent cold little fingers sliding up my back. I had more to think about. Like how exactly had Christophe found me?

And the thing, whatever it was, that had opened up my bedroom window and sucked my breath out? *A snake with wings*, Graves had said.

*Dreamstealer*, Christophe called it. *Revelle*.

I was still cold, gooseflesh spilling up my arms and down my back. Had it been a dream, or had I been outside my own *body*? That was a creeptastic idea, and something all too likely—it was just the way the touch could work. Gran would have known what to say about it. Hell, even Dad might have had a clue. I could have asked him some questions.

"Have strange things been happening to you lately, Dru?" Christophe poured hot milk into his mug, picked up the spoon, and stirred it. The saucepan was set aside, every drop of fluid gone. He'd gauged the amount just right. "Things you didn't know you could do? Strange things, strong things, things you shouldn't know suddenly clear as day to you?" He turned and leaned against the counter, his eyes glowing slightly. The kitchen was dark but the dining room light was on, and his hair still looked sleeker, lying close to his head without all the highlights reflecting.

"Other than hexing my teacher and having the world stop like a movie on pause?" I shrugged. "I've always been weird. My grandmother called it "the touch". It's gotten stronger. But all of this is weird, even for me."

"*That's* saying something." Graves took a huge slurp, made a low half-swallowed belching sound, and I was surprised into laughing. He gave his own peculiar painful laugh, too, and I felt a lot better.

Christophe studied us, his face shut like a book. "Then you're close to blooming, Dru. Becoming a full *svetocha*." He blew across the top of his mug. "I wish I knew. . . ."

*Blooming?* I let Mom's quilt slip down a little. My hands were warmer now. "You wish you knew what? We're in a sharing space right now; you might as well ask." Graves bumped me back with his thin shoulder, and the urge to laugh hit me again. You know how it can just suddenly bubble up at the most inappropriate times? Like you're just sitting there, and a thought hits you sideways, or the absurdity of the world just smacks you out of nowhere and you have to swallow a giggle?

Yeah. Like that. I swallowed the sound; it stuck in my throat and threatened to turn into a belch. My shoulder burned dully, and my back was stiff. Getting knocked around and having someone lying on top of you doesn't do much for back pain.

"I wish I knew how your father thought he was going to train you *or* hide you long enough for you to survive into adulthood. Among other things." Christophe sighed, and set down his mug with a click. "I'll be in the living room."

And just like that, he walked away. He moved down the hall like he knew the house better than I did, and a few seconds later the formless mutter of the television blurred through the hiss of snow.

"I don't like him," Graves half-whispered.

"You already said that." I took another scalding gulp of hot milk and sugar. *There isn't even any real cocoa in this. It's all just artificial flavor.* For a moment I thought about Gran's hot chocolate and I wished, suddenly and fiercely, that I was five years old and safe again. And then I thought of Gran always washing the floors with herb mixes meant to keep evil away, and I wondered how safe I'd really been. "I'll call August tomorrow."

"Then what?"

*How the hell should I know?* But I did. I finished swallowing and leaned against the counter, watching the pattern of whirling white outside the window. "Then I'm going to find out everything I can about this Sergej guy. If Chris is right, and he killed my dad . . ." I swallowed the sudden lump in my throat.

Graves didn't think much of the notion, even half-formed and unstated. "Then what? If he's right and they've been chasing him for so long, what the hell are *we* going to do?"

*We?* But I suppose it never occurred to Graves that he might want to sit out whatever was going to happen next.

No. Of *course* it hadn't occurred to him. I'd thought of ditching him more times than I could count, and I suddenly felt like a complete asshole for it.

My chest felt funny, tight and warm at the same time. "My dad wasn't a dumbass. He taught me a lot. Maybe he taught me something these guys don't know." *Dru, you're lying.*

But what else could I do? If Christophe was telling the truth, this Sergej guy—those cold insect feet walked up my back again—turned my dad into a zombie. You don't just *forgive* something like that, do you?

But I was just a kid, and I was seriously out of my depth here. I'd shot a werwulf, yeah, and done a lot of running away. And I'd found the truck, but that was more Gran's owl than me.

If this was a game, I was losing pretty badly. I should probably get the hell out of the stadium while I was still alive.

"Oh." Graves's shoulder bumped mine again, hot milk slopping inside my cup. Warmth stole back into my fingers and toes, finally.

Still . . . "But maybe these Order guys could teach me something too. And you. There's got to be something good in being stuck on superhero, right?"

He sighed heavily. "If it makes me fall asleep and then wake up craving two whole greasy pepperoni pizzas, man, I don't know."

I actually laughed, cupping my mouth in my hand to keep it down.

"I noticed something, too." Graves didn't even crack a smile, and motioned toward the living room. "He's not answering your questions, really. I mean, not completely. Not like he doesn't have something to hide, you dig?"

*I guess not.* "If he is who he says he is, he's got reasons not to." But I met Graves's eyes, and we stared at each other for ten seconds or so, the meaningful type of stare that can happen when you know someone and eye-talk is more efficient than spending a half-hour stumbling with words. Snow slid against the window, and a thread of cool draft touched my cheek. I was going to have to put a real back door on soon, even with the almost-enclosed porch out there.

Graves shrugged. "If you say so." *I still don't trust him,* his green eyes said. There was hardly any hazel left, and the contrast was startling against caramel skin. Seen in profile, his nose looked proud instead of just too damn big for his face. When he shivered a little and hunched his shoulders, I had the sudden urge to put my arm and Mom's quilt around him, and just stay there for a while.

The thought made me feel warmer, but I didn't do it. Instead, I finished my hot chocolate. It was still too hot, but it didn't feel like liquid lava going down. "I'm going back to bed."

"Why don't you call this August guy now?" Graves hunched his shoulders even further.

"Because it's nighttime in New York, and if it's night, he's out hunting." I shuffled around the breakfast bar and put my mug in the sink. "Hey, Graves?"

"What?" Cautious, his shoulders still hunched.

*He must be used to people trying to get rid of him,* I thought, and the sharp jab of pain that ran through me twisted all the way down.

"Thanks. You got that thing off me, right?"

He stared into his hot chocolate like it held the secret to the universe. "Yeah, well, the window was open and it was really cold."

*What does that have to do with the price of tea in China?* But then I realized what he meant. It even called a creaking, half-painful smile to my face, and the last of the cold and goose bumps flushed away on a wave of welcome heat.

*No problem, Dru. First one's free.*

# CHAPTER 25

As soon as I woke up the next morning, grainy-eyed and feeling like I'd been beaten with a lead pipe, I stumbled downstairs and ate some cereal standing up. Graves got up while I was doing that, took one long look at me, and headed for the living room. I heard him say something to Christophe, and they both went out the front door.

The smell of apple pies didn't quite fill the house, but it was there, a thread under everything else. It was kind of hard to take Christophe seriously when he smelled like baked goods. I wondered if other *djamphir* smelled like Hostess Twinkies and sniggered to myself.

Then I remembered Christophe kneeling in the snow with a shotgun to his shoulder, facing down a streak-headed wulf and all but laughing, and the sniggers dried up.

I yawned and padded to the chipped yellow plastic phone attached to the wall. There was one number, at least, that I had memorized, because it was so easy. And, well, you don't forget a guy who can snap a flame off his fingers while other guys could only flick boogers. Especially not when you spend a month in his apartment while he's out with your dad, dealing with a demonic rat infestation.

And another month while your dad is off doing who-knows-what, coming back all beat-up and scary looking. August liked my omelets, and I must've cooked hundreds of them for him.

The phone rang five times before he picked up and cursed. August's voice was nasal through the line, laden with Brooklyn wheeze, every vowel cut short like it personally offended him. "This better be good."

"Hi, Augie." I tried to sound cheerful. "It's Dru."

"Holy . . ." There was a sound of sliding cloth, paper, and a clatter like he'd just dropped a knife. It didn't take him long to recover. "Hi, sweetheart. I miss your omelets."

*I'll bet you do. You ate two of them a day because you wouldn't bring home anything but eggs and vodka. It was an adventure getting you to buy some bread.* "I miss your coffee. Hey, August—"

He was quick on the uptake. Something probably didn't sound right to him. *I* probably didn't sound right to him. I didn't even sound right to myself, with a dry stone trying to lodge itself in the back of my throat.

"Dru, honey, where's your dad?" *And why isn't he the one on the phone,* was probably what he wanted to say.

"He came down with a bad case of reanimation." I tried to sound flip and offhand, but I think I succeeded only in sounding scared. And tired. And like I just got up.

August actually choked, and I heard a metallic sound as if he'd dropped something else. "*What?* Holy fu—uh, I mean, *damn.* Where are you now, kid?"

*Oh, no you don't.* "I want to ask you a few questions. First, are you part of the Order?"

A long ticking silence crackled in my ear. Finally, I heard the click of a lighter and a long inhale. I could see his apartment, the full ashtray on the spindly kitchen table, the window that looked at a blank brick wall, the walls loaded with protective items from different cultures— African masks, *ojos de Dios*, a heavy silver crucifix. I could almost hear the traffic outside his building, but that could have been because it was clearly audible through the phone. "Holy shit. Where are you?"

*Like I'm going to tell you until I know what's really going on.* "Are you a part of the Order, August? Yes or no." *My dad didn't raise an idiot. You know that.*

"Of course I am, what did you think? Where are you, honey?"

I told him, and he sucked in a long harsh breath.

I knew that sound. It was an adult getting ready to Deal With Me. I never in a zillion years thought I'd be relieved to hear it.

August didn't mess around. "Where's Reynard? He should be there. Put him on the line."

*Oh wow.* "Christophe? He's out on the porch having a cigarette and bonding with my friends." *In other words, Graves is keeping him occupied so I can make this little phone call.* "You know him?"

"He's only one of the best the Order has. Dru, you have to get *out* of there. Tell Christophe it's a red zone and you *have* to be gotten out of there."

I'd never heard August sound frightened before. "Because of Sergej?" The name stung my tongue, and I wondered if it was because of the touch or because I knew it was a sucker.

It was the first sucker's name I'd ever known. Some people who know about the Real World won't say them. They'll use initials or code words.

August almost choked. "Goddammit, Dru, this is serious business. Get Reynard and *put him on the line.*"

Finally, someone was going to deal with this. An *adult*. A real adult. "Fine, you don't have to yell. Hang on." I dropped the phone on the counter and stamped down the hall to the front door, jerked it open.

Graves's head swung around—he had a cigarette halfway to his mouth and looked pale under his perpetual tan. He was wearing *my* gloves, though they were a little too small for him, and the edge of his long black coat flapped as the wind cut across the porch, rattling the bits of dead plants that hadn't been iced down. His hair was a wind-lifted mess, but Christophe, calm and immaculate, wore the same sweater and jeans. He stood near the hole in the porch railing, his head up as if he was testing the wind. Blond highlights streaked through his hair again, and they almost seemed to move.

The cold cut right through me, and I wondered if he could teach me how to walk around in the middle of it so easily. "August wants to talk to you." It was like carrying messages for Dad, and I didn't have to name the feeling swelling behind my heart.

It was relief, getting stronger with every second. Here was someone more experienced than I was, even if he was my age. Just what I'd wanted, right? Someone who could tell me what to do now that the lines that kept my life on track had vanished. Between August and this guy, things would get Under Control. It would be Handled. It would be Dealt With.

Chris gave me an odd look as he passed, his blue eyes darkening and apple spice drifting in his wake, and I shivered. Graves pitched his butt out into the snow, the glow of the cherry vanishing in a gray glare caught between cloud-hazed sky and white-shrouded ground. "He checks out?"

I nodded. Something dry and hot caught in my throat. "Yeah, he checks out all right. Come in, it's freezing."

Graves pushed past me, and I glanced out over the street. It was so quiet, a blanket of white over everything. The snow had come down hard and pebbled, a moaning wind flinging it everywhere, and the radio said ice was coming. The morning had dawned clear and sunny, but now the sky was overcast and lowering, striations of darker cloud like ink just dropped into water billowing under the higher cloud-cover.

*Huh.* I stepped out onto the porch, cupping my elbows in my palms. Hugging myself. It was dead quiet except for the uneasy sound of air moving, the porch posts and the corner of the house like a ship's prow, slicing the waves and producing a low hum of torn air.

We could have been on the moon, I realized. The house set away from the other houses like that one kid at school who's always dressed just a little bit wrong.

No wonder nobody'd come to greet us when we moved in, or heard the gunshots and screaming.

The street was an evenly frosted expanse of white. The two driveways that didn't lead into a garage had car-sized lumps of unbroken snow, the paint jobs peeping out from underneath—the blue minivan at the corner, the green, wallowing Ford across the street. And in front of the garages were wide, pristine ribbons of snow leading down to the street.

*Why doesn't this feel right?* I had to look a little harder before the assumptions I made started crumbling and the wrong note in the orchestra jangled hard enough for me to catch it.

No tire tracks. There wasn't a single break in the snow. The street looked as deserted as a Western town right before the bad guy rides in for the ultimate battle.

The sunlight dimmed, and a chill fiercer than the wind walked down my back. I was shivering, though I didn't feel it, and Graves's curly head popped out of the doorway. "What the hell are you doing, trying to freeze to death? You're not even wearing a coat."

I took my time, watching the street. Nothing felt hinky at all.

It just felt quiet. Empty.

Dead.

*The snow must've cleared up sometime this morning when the sun rose, because we were all up having our hot chocolate and funny snakes with wings before dawn, and it was coming down hard then. What, everyone just decided to stay home today? Maybe. But. . .*

The last piece of the puzzle slotted into place as Graves made a spitting sound of annoyance. "What the hell? Dru?"

I stepped back, shifting my weight uneasily, as if the porch might decide to fall apart at any second. "The porch lights." I sounded queer even to myself. "They're all on, and it's the middle of the day." *It's eleven, and it gets dark early this time of year. Real dark, real early.*

"Yeah," he said. "Christophe said that, too. What are you—"

"We have to go." My teeth chopped the words into little bits, and I made it inside, pushing him down the hall and sweeping the door shut. Warmth closed around me. I locked the deadbolts and leaned against the door. *How long until sundown? I don't know, have to check.* "Pack your stuff, okay? And help me with the ammo boxes, and—"

"Dru?" Christophe, from the kitchen. I didn't know him at all, but I knew that tone.

The *Oh shit there is serious trouble, honey, pack everything up again and let's get movin'* tone. He appeared at the end of the hall, his sharp face suddenly graven with frowning lines that made him look a lot older.

"I know," I said. "I've got to get the ammo packed." He halted, regarding me, and I swallowed crow and a few lumps of my pride, too. "Will you . . . I mean, would you help us get the truck loaded?"

I had to keep leaning against the door because my knees were deciding again that they weren't knees, they were actually noodles. Fully cooked noodles at that. And what I was really asking was something more like, *Will you help me? Please?*

Christophe's blue, blue eyes flicked to Graves, and I was suddenly positive he was going to say, *Sure I can, but we can't take him. He'll drag us down.*

Oh, Christ. What was I going to do if he said that? Graves tensed, a movement I could feel even though all the starch had gone out of me, as Gran would have said. And I reached over, grabbed Goth Boy's thin shoulder, and dug my fingers in.

Dad would never have left me behind. Not willingly. I was damned if I would leave someone else in the dust.

*He bought me a cheeseburger.* It was a ludicrous, laughable thought. But it was just the surface over a truckload of other things. I hadn't heard a single word of complaint from Graves, not even over getting bit or having a gun held to his head. He'd done the best he could to help me, and that was something strangers rarely ever do. I was shipwrecked, and he'd been the only thing I could hang on to.

And he hadn't let me down. Not once.

He was all I had. I wasn't going to leave him here.

Christophe's eyes fastened on my hand. He really did look old before his face smoothed out and he nodded, as if finishing a long conversation with himself. His shoulders went back and his chin came up. "You probably have a system," he said, folding his arms. "What goes in first?"

"My bed—the mattresses. Everything else gets folded up and—" I stopped dead, as the next problem rose up and crashed into me.

"Where are we going?"

"Don't worry." Christophe dropped his hands. "I'll handle that. Start your packing, Dru. You, wulf-boy. Come with me."

* * *

What does it say about your life when two hours of three teenagers working folds all of it up in the back of a Chevy half-ton's camper?

I put Mom's cookie jar in the top of the bathroom box and bit the packing tape, tore it deftly, and taped it down. "This one's important," I told Graves. "Pack the blankets around it." *Next to the fireproof box. The one with the ashes in it. God, Daddy, I wish you were here.*

*If wishes were fishes, even beggars would eat.* Gran was fond of that saying, too.

"Got it." Graves tramped out of the kitchen and toed open the door to the garage. Christophe had manhandled the garage door open, metal squealing in protest—the broken spring rubbing against itself with a sound like a lost tortured soul.

Well, maybe not *exactly* like that, but pretty damn close. Dad and I had both tried to get the garage open, knowing it was going to get cold, but in the end it was a lost cause.

But not, I guess, for a half-sucker. *Djamphir.*

Would I be as strong as that once I did that thing Christophe was talking about? Blooming? Would I smell like a bakery item? Or was that just him? Did he use pie filling for cologne?

But Mom had only smelled of fresh perfume and goodness.

Mom.

Too many questions. Not enough time to answer any of them.

"I *know*," Christophe said into the phone. "Just send a pickup;

I'll get her to the rendezvous. Don't worry about that." A long pause while someone yakked on the other end. It sounded dire, especially with the way the wind was moaning a counterpoint; he'd been on the phone for ten minutes while I finished the last boxes and Graves carried them out to the truck.

He laughed, a sound twice as bitter as Graves's little unamused bark. "Do you have to repeat yourself? She's no good to us dead, and I'm the one who found her." Another pause. "They can court-martial me later. Right now I need a pickup. I don't care what the weather report— All right. Fine. *Ciao*." He hung up, stared at the phone for a few moments, and turned sharply on his heel.

I was still on my knees, a roll of packing tape in my hands, watching him.

He took two steps to the sink, peered out the window. Eerie yellow-gray light slid through, touched his hair, and made the highlights livid. "Daylight's going to fail before we're out of town."

I could only see a slice of sky through the window, cut off by an overhang and icicle-festooned gutters. It looked like the thunderstorm weather I'd seen a million times, only without the gasping-thick humidity you get below the Mason-Dixon. "It's only—"

"Do you think this is natural weather, even for here?" He shrugged. "I should have made contact earlier. I was banking on being able to distract him. And I was banking on Sergej being certain your father wouldn't be stupid enough to bring you here."

*You just shut up about my father.* "Dad wasn't stupid." It came out a lot wearier and less sharp than I thought it would. "He had reasons for everything."

"I don't suppose you'd know how good those reasons were, would you? Never mind." He waved his hand as if brushing away a fly. "We've got to get you out of here. I've got an extraction point.

They'll dock me for it later." A tight, feral smile pulled up the corners of his lips, his blue eyes burning, and I watched an ink stain of sleek darkness slide through his hair and vanish, the highlights popping out like shafts of sun on a faraway horizon. "But bringing in a *svetocha* might balance that out." He shrugged. "I'll drive."

*Oh you will, will you?* "Do you have your license?" *I don't know if I like the idea of you driving Dad's truck. Or if I like how I'm suddenly some sort of good grade for you.*

"What are you, a cop?" He held out his hand, and I automatically went to give him the packing tape.

Instead, Christophe's fingers closed around my wrist, warm and hard. His eyes met mine, and I didn't know what to think about what I saw burning in their depths. His smell *shifted*, somehow. Like the wind veering and bringing you a breath of honeysuckle on a summer's day.

I stared up at him.

The garage door opened and Graves hopped in. "It's getting colder," he announced. "And I've got the last boxes in. Have to hand it to you, Dru, it's packed tighter than Bletch's . . ." The words died.

Christophe pulled. I came up in a rush—he was *strong*. Not regular wiry-strong, or even as thoughtlessly twitchy-strong as Graves had been with the werwulf imprint burning in him. He pulled me up as if I was a piece of paper, and the only thing scarier than the strength was the sense of restraint, like he could crush my wrist if he chose to. I ended up too close to him, and he pulled again, as if he wanted me even closer.

I stepped away and twisted my hand, breaking toward his thumb. That's the weakest part of any grip. My shoulder protested, and so did my back. I was going to have to find some aspirin or something.

He did let me go—but I wasn't sure, suddenly, that I could have pulled away if he hadn't let me.

*He wasn't that strong before. Or was he, and just not showing it?*

Graves stood stock-still, watching us both.

"Keys, Dru." Christophe's teeth gleamed in the weird stormlight, one of his wide feral smiles. "The sun's fading, and if I can feel it, we can bet Sergej can too."

I struggled with this, briefly. I drove when Dad got tired, so I knew the truck better than anyone else right now. I knew how it shimmied when it hit a certain number of miles per hour and how to tap the brakes in snow; I knew how it was likely to wriggle its butt when it was packed to the gills and a whole host of other little things. I also *really* didn't like the idea of handing over my keys to this kid, no matter how much August vouched for him.

But August *had*. And I'd wanted someone to take care of me, hadn't I?

I just hadn't thought it would be some kid my own age, no matter how mature he seemed. If this was the "best" the Order had . . .

And I didn't trust him enough. He was just too . . . *dangerous.* "Where are we going?" I finally said.

"The extraction point's in the southeast section of town. Burke and 72nd. If you'd have come down there when I invited you, before Sergej knew for certain you even existed, I could have gotten you out of town and safe in the Schola in a trice." Another easy shrug. "But we have to work with what we've got, now. Give me the keys, Dru."

My bag lay on the counter. I dug in it for a moment, and my keychain jangled as I finally fished it out. "It handles weird when it's loaded. I should drive."

"Dru." Christophe's tone was icy. "If you want to get out of this alive, you'd best do as I say."

*Well, gee, when you put it like that . . .*

"Wait a second." Graves took two long swinging steps forward. His hair all but snapped and crackled with electricity. "She's driven the thing before, all the way across town in a whiteout. And it's *her* truck."

"I didn't ask you to yap, dog-boy." Christophe made a sudden swift movement, but I saw him coming and yanked the keys back.

It was a close thing—his fingers grazed mine and I skipped nervously to the side, clearing the breakfast bar and dragging my bag with me. It fell, the strap fetching up against my free hand, and everything inside it shifted. That put me between the two of them, and right in the cold draft from the garage.

*Get the situation under control, Dru.* "Let's get this straight." I had to clear my throat, because the look on Christophe's face—eyebrows drawn together a fraction, eyes burning, mouth in a tight line with no hint of a smile—made him look twice as dangerous.

And, I had to admit, very pretty, especially with his hair shifting back and forth. That smell of his should have been ludicrous, but it just made me hungry.

I wet my lips with my tongue, a quick nervous flick. "It's *my* truck, *I'll* drive. You'll stop making nasty comments to my friend. We'll all get along until we get out of town, and when we do that you can go back to your Order and Graves and I will be on our way." The wind shifted again outside, its moan veering toward a crescendo. The yellow-green light made everything look bruised, and a queer ringing under the sound of the wind threatened to fill my ears.

I tasted wax oranges, and my vision wavered for a bare half-second.

*Not now, dammit. This is important.* I pushed it aside and kept my gaze locked with Christophe's, daring him.

Once, in this little podunk outside St. Petersburg, we'd run across a huge beast of a dog guarding a place we *really needed* to get into. Dad didn't have the touch, but he showed me something else that day. He called it "starin' down, before the *throwin*' down, honey." It meant just looking at the thing in your way as if it was no bigger than a pea, making up your mind that it wasn't going to scare you or move you.

Dogs can smell fear, and sometimes people—or things from the Real World—are the same way. But ninety-nine times out of a hundred, a dog can also smell when you're the alpha. It takes the same kind of flat look and decision to be fearless as facing down a bunch of jocks bent on harassing someone.

Shoulders square. Heart thumping, but not too hard. Eyes glazed with dust and buzzing with what I hoped was power. I gave him the look I'd practiced in the mirror so many times, and pretended I was Dad, grinning easily in a bar frequented by the Real World, hands loose and easy, one of them resting on a gun butt and the other just touching a shot glass, while I sipped at a Coke and pretended not to notice.

It should have been Dad there. He would have sorted Christophe right out.

"Where do you think you're going to go that Sergej can't find you?" He made another grab for the keys, but the world slowed down and I was quicker again—just by a fraction, but still. Graves sucked in a breath and I skipped backward again, hoping he had the sense to move.

"I'm not so sure he's the problem, Chris." I ducked through my bag's strap and backed up again. Another few steps would get me to the door to the garage, and if I took my eyes off him I wasn't so sure he would stay put, either.

There were a whole lot of things I wasn't sure of anymore.

The *djamphir*'s hand made another swift move; my eyes darted instinctively, and things got very confused. I heard a snarl and a clatter, my feet shot out from under me, and the keys were ripped out of my hand. Something very warm and hard clamped around my throat, and Graves let out a high, yipping yell. Glass shattered.

Christophe's hand tightened just a little, and I choked, staring up at his three-quarter profile as he looked toward the other window, the one that looked at the bit of greenbelt running at an angle beside the house.

The window he'd just thrown Graves against. Right over the spindly little kitchen table that had been here when we moved in.

He looked down at me, fangs sliding beneath his upper lip, his eyes burning. The highlights had bled out of his hair, slicking it back against his head, and his eyes were actually *glowing* in the bruised, ugly light slanting through the kitchen.

"I'm being patient," he hissed, the *t*'s lisping slightly because of the fangs. "I'll get you and your pet through this alive, but you have to do *what I say*. Got me?"

*How did he do that?* And the other thought, so loud I could have sworn I said it out loud. *Could he teach me that?*

"Sonofa*bitch*," Graves growled, and the obscenity shaded into a low sound that rattled broken glass as cold wind spilled into the room, laden with the flat iron tang of snow and violence. "Dru? *Dru?*"

He didn't even sound human, though it was recognizably my name.

"As soon as the sun fails out here, all your neighbors will wake up." Christophe's fingers weren't cutting off my air, but there wasn't any space to wriggle, either. "I only wounded the dreamstealer; it probably crept through every window on the block and laid eggs in their sleeping bodies before dawn rose. When those young hatch, they'll be hungry, and here you are. Such a nice little morsel." He cocked his head slightly. "On the good side, Sergej probably doesn't know you're alive, but he's suspecting, since his expensive little assassin didn't come back, and as soon as the sun fails he'll— *Stay* where you are, dog-boy!" He lifted his free hand and pointed, probably at Graves. The growling subsided a little, but it was the sound of a wolf getting ready to spring, not a teenage kid who had just been thrown into a window. "Are you going to behave, little bird?"

I might have even agreed with him, at least long enough to get his hands off my throat, but the wind rose to a shriek and I realized two things.

The light was really bleeding away fast, no longer bruised but dying, my ears popping under a sudden shift in air pressure.

And the growling wasn't just coming from Graves.

The werwulf barreled through the door like a freight train and hit Christophe squarely in the chest.

There was a horrible crushing half-second as his fingers tightened on my windpipe before they were ripped away. I only found out I was screaming after I'd scrambled backward on palms and sneakered feet like an enthusiastic crab-walker at a drunken frat party, and spilled down the two steps onto chill garage concrete. I barked my elbow a good one on the doorframe, didn't care, hit so hard my teeth clicked together and I almost lost a piece of my tongue.

Another furry leaping shape sailed over me, melting and reforming as it flew, and I flinched, running out of breath and hitching in more to scream again.

"*DRU!*" someone yelled, and Graves leaped out the door, narrowly missing landing on me by twisting in midair, with a kind of breathtaking, unthinking grace. He had something glittering in his right hand—my keychain, I realized, just as he skidded to a stop and the noise from inside the house began to crash instead of just roar. Wood splintered, something thrown against the wall hard enough to punch the drywall out toward me, splinters from the studs ramming through, and there was a massive wrecked yowl of pain.

I made it to my feet and hesitated for a split second, long enough to hear other crashes and howls. It sounded like more of them had arrived—shadows flitted across the open mouth of the garage, and the howling began.

If you've ever heard that sound, you don't need it described, but here goes. It's like a spiral of glass on the coldest night you've ever known, naked outside in the deep woods. Just *hearing* it is enough to give you nightmares about hunching near a fire and praying the wood holds out until dawn.

But what's even worse—what makes it *so* much worse—is how the howling drills into your head and starts pulling on deep, secret things in the brain.

The blind, hungry thing on four legs that lives in all of us.

I clapped my hands over my ears. Graves grabbed my arm, his fingers sinking in so hard it almost went numb, and hauled me toward the truck—still parked crosswise, but it had started up just fine earlier. Thank God for the engine-block heater.

*Maybe I shouldn't have stopped to pack.*

Another long lean bullet-streak of fur bolted into the garage, its padded feet slithering on smooth concrete starred with oil droplets from a car long since vanished. Graves let out a smothered yell. I clutched at him like a girl at a scary movie hanging onto her jock boyfriend, and the thing actually lifted its lip and snarled at us before plunging past.

"They're going to *kill* him!" I yelled.

"Better him than us!" Graves screamed back, and yanked me

toward the truck.

The sky had gone livid. Little pinpricks of ice were showering down, lifting and massing on random eddies and swirls as the wind, confused, keened and turned in circles. Graves yanked the driver's-side door open and clambered in, and I followed.

*It's not right to leave him there.* It wasn't. But Jesus, what else were we supposed to do? Because the werwulfen were even climbing on the *roof*, lean humanoid shapes running with fur, orange-yellow eyes like lamps. There were at least six of them, and one landed with a thump right in front of the truck and spread its lean, muscle-ropy arms, its black-gummed upper lip lifting and the thrum of its growl making the dashboard groan sharply.

Graves and I both screamed, high, oddly harmonized cries that would have been funny if the situation hadn't been so deadly serious.

I jammed the key in the ignition and twisted so hard I almost bent it. The Chevy roused, its engine sound pale compared to the thunder rumbling around my house.

*OhGodohGod*—I smacked the lever into reverse and didn't want to turn around to see where I was going. As if I could have anyway with the camper stuffed full of my life. The truck slewed and jolted back as the werwulf loped forward, tongue lolling and teeth gleaming. The cord for the engine-block heater popped free like a cable in a high wind.

Graves grabbed the dash as we plowed through the weak spot in the mountain of snowplow-piled ick. It was a lucky thing I hit right where I'd run into it coming home a few nights ago. The back end bore down, chains rasping, and I cut the wheel a little too hard. The truck groaned, shook itself like a dog coming out of water, and decided to settle.

I jammed it into "drive" and hesitated again. Christophe was in there. August had said he was all right, and—

"DRU!" Graves yelled, and I hit the gas. The chains bit and we lurched forward, but he was pointing out the windshield, as something long and sinuous, with thin membrane wings, landed on the hood and bonked itself a good one on the glass.

I screamed again, a short little bark because I'd lost all the air I ever breathed, and for one blinding second I remembered what had happened last night after my unconscious, sleepwalking body opened the window. How the thing's tongue had pressed against mine, cold and nauseatingly slimy, tasting of spice and dead rotten ooze, like a Thanksgiving candle gone horribly wrong.

Like Christophe's good smell, turned to badness.

Christophe, back in the house with the werwulfen. I was too busy to think about it.

I hit the windshield wipers. They smacked the mini-dreamstealer's small wet snout, and for good measure I pushed the lever back and hoped the washer fluid wasn't frozen. For some reason, it wasn't, and it gushed up, spraying the thing.

It screeched, the sound scraping against the inside of my brain, and was flung aside as the wind crested again, the truck's springs groaning as fingers of cold air pushed against its side. My breath came in short sharp puffs of white.

"Holy shit," Graves whispered. "It had babies."

*That's what Christophe said. Christophe.* "OhGod," I whispered back. "They're going to kill him."

"I thought he was going to kill *you*." His teeth were chattering. Tiny round pellets of ice caught in his curls sparkled in the dimness; I flicked the headlights on. The street unreeled, and I saw the stop sign on the corner. Houses clustered around us, each of them with their porch lights on. Windows broke with sweet, sharp tinkling sounds, darkness crawling out from behind the blinds and oozing over jagged glass. The wind was suddenly full of thin wriggling things, diaphanous wings ragged and beating frantically as they dove for the truck.

"Hold on—" Snow slipped and slid under the wheels. I gave it some more gas. We were achieving a scorching twenty miles an hour—faster than it sounds with the wind howling like a lost soul, a sky the color of rotten grapes overhead, and winged snakes with dull gummy poisoned fangs trying to splat themselves through the windows.

*I'm glad we're not trying this in summer.* The lunacy of the thought jerked a giggle out of me, a high-pitched, crazy little sound.

I goosed the gas pedal again; the stop sign was coming up fast, and I had to pick a direction.

*Right or left?*

Not much time. I racked my brain for geography, but the goddamn things wouldn't stop splatting against the glass so I could *think.* Right or left? *Rightorleftrightorleftrightorleft—*

I jerked the wheel to the left, tapped the brake a little, and we started to slide. There was a smaller pile of snow, a hillock where the plow had scraped the slightly bigger road and blocked off the entrance to this one, and I had a mad moment of wondering if someone would get a stern talking-to once the neighbors called in and complained about not being able to get off their own street.

One of the winged snakes hissed, a sound clearly audible through the windshield, and I suddenly knew without a doubt, the knowledge springing whole and complete and awful into my head, that there wouldn't be any irate calls from anyone on my street. Ever. All the pretty houses that turned the cold shoulder to my house were only full of death and broken bodies, the little winged snakes tearing at flesh as they hatched. The mama snake might be dead or dying somewhere, but the babies were very much alive—and they were hungry.

*Dru. What have you done?*

Graves yelled something, but I had my hands full. The truck, unhappy with what I was asking it to do, fishtailed to see if I was paying attention. I got it back on track, bumping through the piled-high drift and feeling the front end bounce a bit. The chains bit again, the back end wallowing, and we pulled through onto the sanded road, traction suddenly giving me a whole new set of problems.

There was no traffic. The winged things shriek-hissed, battering themselves against metal and glass—I wondered if their gummy little teeth would do any damage to a tire and had to let off the brake as a skid developed, steered *into* it, the wheel twisting like a live thing in my hands.

*Good one, Dru!* Dad's voice echoed in my head, as if he was sitting right next to me, teaching me what he called defensive driving. *Physics is a bitch, ennit!*

"It is." I barely recognized my own voice, high and breathy. The skid eased, and the crunching sound was the bodies of the winged snakes. They were falling rapidly now, flopping on the icy road surface before we rolled right over them, at a whopping twenty-five miles an hour now. "It certainly is."

"What?" Graves had both hands braced on the dash. The back was packed too solid to move much, but something rolled under the bench seat and I hoped it wasn't the first aid kit. *Or* the field box. All we needed now was random gunfire.

*Oh, please God, no. Christophe.* Why was I worrying about him? Why was it okay to leave him behind, but not okay to leave Graves?

*That's not the right question, Dru.* A slight hill sloped downward and the truck picked up speed, the horrible crunching noises reaching a peak as the wind moaned. I turned the wipers off—they weren't doing anything and the snakes were falling like dead flies now. Tiny pellets of ice hit the windshield and bounced away.

*The right question is where the werwulfen came from, and why they're after Christophe. Work on that.* But I had too much to deal with already.

Then, amazingly, a stoplight reared up ahead of us, and there was actual traffic on the cross-street. Not much, just a couple of cars, but the people inside probably didn't know what to make of the things festooning the truck as we rolled through the green light. I let out a choked sound, realizing my cheeks were wet, and the streets snapped into a recognizable pattern behind my eyes. I was taking the bus route to school, probably because it was familiar.

*Holy shit. Goddamn.*

"Graves." I had to cough to get my throat clear. The crunching under the wheels began to fade, serpent bodies running with thin black moisture as they melted off the car, decaying rapidly. "There's a city map in here somewhere. It was on the seat. Find it and navigate me."

"Yeah." His voice broke. He sniffed, and I realized we were both crying—me steadily and messily, and him as quietly as he could. "Sure. Right. Fantastic. Where the hell are we *going*?"

*Oh Lord, I don't know.* "Burke and 72nd, out near the suburbs."

"Okay. Sure. Why are we going there?" But he peeled his fingers off the dash and swiped at his eyes with his coat sleeve. I couldn't take my white-knuckled hands off the wheel, but I wanted to. I wanted to reach over and comfort him.

I wanted someone to comfort me, too. "Because we won't get out of town alive at this rate. Not on our own." *During the day. It's still supposed to be day.* The headlights cut a cone of brightness, and the streetlamps were on. The taste of oranges bloomed again in my mouth, terribly, wax coating my tongue. "That's where we'll find Christophe's backup and an extraction point. We need backup. Backup is good. Getting out of town is even better." *God. Christophe.* My throat hurt and my arm pulsed. I'd probably have finger marks all over me by tomorrow—if I saw tomorrow, that was.

"Great." Paper crackled. Graves let out a hoarse sound, and I pretended not to notice. My own sobs shook everything about me but my eyes and my hands, stiffly clutching the wheel as if it was a life preserver. "What the hell was that all about?"

"I don't know." *I can't even guess.*

# CHAPTER 26

**As if to** add yet another layer of unreality, halfway there the sky lightened to depthless iron-gray in the space of a mile, as if we'd driven through some sort of porous wall and into normality again. Instead of little pinpricks of ice, dime-size snowflakes started whirling down, dancing to their own beat. The heater began to blow something other than freezer-draft, slowly warming up. My fingers were numb and I wished one of us had thought to throw a box of tissues in the car—wiping my nose was getting to be a necessity instead of just a nice thing to do.

Graves had finished crying and slumped against the seat, his hands loose and open in his lap. Driving actually wasn't so bad if we stuck to the main streets, everything scraped and sanded, slippery but passable. I deliberately didn't look at him.

I know that much about boys. They don't like it when you watch them cry. Even if you're still leaking yourself.

"What's going on?" he said, finally. "Why didn't they try to kill us? Those were the same things that bit me. Werwulf things."

*But the one that bit you belonged to a sucker, and we don't know if these did.* I nodded slightly, kept my eyes on the road. We still had three-quarters of a tank and the engine was warm now. "It was like they were driving us away." I coasted to a stop at a red light, my fingers gripping the wheel so hard they ached. My head was still ringing, full of the peculiar clarity that follows a crying fit. "We're going to get to the extraction point. Someone will be there. We'll have to tell them what happened to Christophe. And they'll be able to tell us what to do and get us out of here." I *hope*.

The light turned green. I checked—the cross-street was deserted. There was a coffee shop on the corner, warm yellow shining through its windows but nobody moving inside. Streetlights burned, even though it was daylight. The snow was beginning to pick up. Our tire tracks stretched black behind us. I eased down on the gas.

"This is weird," Graves said softly. "It's like we're the last people left on earth."

*I could have done without that thought.* But it wasn't like I hadn't been thinking it myself. "Is it usually busier around here?"

"Yeah. That's Marshall Street right there; it's *always* hopping. Maybe . . ."

"Maybe what?"

"Maybe we should stop there. Where I've got friends." He wiped at his face. "I don't trust whatever Christophe told you. Even if he checked out through your friend."

I weighed the options. My head hurt with all the thinking I was asking it to do, and the tears clotting up my throat and threatening my eyes weren't helping. "Anyone we find is just going to be in danger. We're going to *put* them in danger. I might not trust Chris, but I trust August. He wouldn't steer me wrong."

"So what were the werwulfs doing?"

"Werwulfen," I corrected. *How the hell should I know?*

"Whatever. What were they *doing*? And those snake-things—"

"The snake-things were trying to get at us. But the werwulfen . . . I just don't know. Maybe they were after Christophe, but the one that bit you, he wasn't—I just don't know, Graves. I'm sorry." *I got you into this. I'm sorrier than you'll ever know.*

"I thought he was going to kill you." He stared out the windshield as I stole a corner-of-the-eye glance at him. "I wanted to tear his throat out."

*I don't think he was going to kill me. But he certainly wasn't playing nice.* Graves sounded like he was having a hard time with the idea of anyone killing anything—I knew exactly how that felt. So I decided to change the subject. "How did you get my keys?"

"He dropped them." Silence wrapped around us both. Empty streets in the middle of the day, not a soul to be seen—even wrapped up and picking their way along the sidewalks. "God, this is weird."

*You bet it is. Can a sucker do this? Change the outside world? Is that possible? Or are people just feeling the bad outside and wanting to stay in?* The tires crunched. Snow kept falling, getting thicker by the minute. "Dig under the seat. There're a few metal boxes. One's blue, that's first aid. The second one's red, you don't want that either. The one under me is gray, and it's got a gun. We want that one."

He waited for a few seconds. "I suppose that would be a good idea. I don't want to mess with it, though."

"Just get it out." I probably didn't want him messing with it either, if he wasn't used to firearms. "I'll handle the shooting, I guess. You just turn up the superhero."

He didn't find it at all funny. "I'm serious, Dru. I saw him hurting you, and I just—"

*I know.* "Did he hurt you?"

"Nah. I broke the window, though." A jagged, bitter little laugh. He fiddled with the seat belt, and I thought of telling him to buckle up. "I was really worried about that, too. Go figure. I saw him hurting you and it was like . . . something inside me woke up, and I wanted to kill him. Really kill him, not just like saying you want to kill someone. You know? Like I wasn't even myself anymore."

"Oh." What did you say to something like that? My heart gave a funny little skip. "I'm glad you're here. This would be horrible on my own."

I expected a flip answer and a flash of humor, but he just slumped further into the seat, bent down, and started digging underneath. "Yeah, well."

*Well, you can't expect him to be very happy about this, Dru.* My eyes flicked to the driver's-side mirror for a second, catching . . . something. I kept looking, but it was gone and didn't come back. Just a shadow. The ringing in my head wouldn't go away. My shoulder hurt, and my arm wasn't too happy either. "Are we close?"

"Turn south on 72$^{nd}$; it's two streets up. Then just follow that until we hit the suburbs." He curled himself up to half-lay on the seat, peering underneath and digging for the field box. "How often does something like this happen to you?"

"Not very," I admitted. I swiped at my burning cheek with the back of my hand. Tears rose again. I pushed them down, wished I had a hankie or something. Dad always had a hankie. Most of them had his initials embroidered on them in Gran's neat, careful stitches. "More like never. Dad was always around."

"I'm sorry about your dad, Dru." He peered up awkwardly, his head almost in my lap. His eyes were very green, and since he wasn't a white boy, he missed out on the blotchy part of crying.

I attempted a half-smile, ended up with a weird grimace. "I'm sorry you got bit." I rubbed at my eyes again. The snow hissed under the tires, clumped on the windshield wipers.

"We're sure I'm not going to get all hairy like those other things, right?" He tried a smile that looked like it hurt and fished out the field box.

Another shadow flickered in the mirror. Was it nerves, or was there really something back there? I risked going a little faster. "Absolutely. Even Christophe said so, and it was in the *Ars Lupica*, too." *Dad paid good money for that book and never found a chance to use it. I wish he was here to see it useful now.*

I flinched. Dad. Christophe. Both gone. There had to have been at least a dozen werwulfen.

Why hadn't they attacked *us*?

Graves sat back up. "Jesus," he said quietly.

I heartily agreed. And the snow began to fall in rivers.

# CHAPTER 27

**W**ay out in suburbia, the streets had naked trees clutching at the sky, their cold limbs grasping at soft white ribbons and sometimes festooned with icicles. Some actually had Christmas lights up, though it wasn't even Thanksgiving yet. Or maybe they just hadn't taken them down from last year.

The streets were scraped and sanded out here too, but they were fast blurring under the onslaught of snow. 72nd Street had turned into McGill Road briefly, then jagged and become 72nd Avenue, narrowing, winding, and branching off like an artery getting further and further from the heart. The houses got a little bigger, the sidewalks broad and scraped clean. I saw flashes of fields, too—weird blank expanses of flatland, scarred only by the lines of ditches and more naked, shivering trees. The wind howled. Graves played with his half-empty pack of Winstons, glancing longingly at the window every now and again. If the wind wouldn't have torn a cigarette out of his hand, he could have had all the smokes he wanted. I might have even joined him, no matter how bad it smelled.

And, you know, if I could have forgotten the slithering, thumping sounds of the little winged snakes hitting the truck. I suspected that might make me nervous about rolling the windows down for a good long while.

The shadows kept flitting behind us. Whatever it was could have overtaken us if it was really serious about it. We were barely crawling, and I'd started to shake, hungry and sick from adrenaline all at once.

I would have given a lot for another cheeseburger just about then. Or a strawberry shake. Or anything, really. Even some stale granola.

But not apple pie. The thought made me feel even sicker.

"There's Compass Avenue." Graves shivered, though it was warm enough with the heater blasting. "Next comes Wendell Road, and then Burke. If the map's right."

I eased off the gas, ready for the truck to misbehave at any moment. The dashboard clock was still set to Florida time, an hour ahead. I was getting sick of this polar bear shit. "How do people live up here? This is insane."

"They dress up a lot. Do their hair. And drink. Beat their kids." Graves shifted nervously. "They beat their kids a *lot*." We rolled through two more intersections, then slowed to a creepy-crawl, the engine turning over smoothly, wipers muffled. "Why the hell are we coming out here again?"

"Because we won't make it out of town before dark on our own. It's already two in the afternoon." I peered at the sky, squinted out the windshield again.

"We could make it. I've got money. We could just get the hell out of here. We could take a bus if the truck won't—"

"A bus. Like we wouldn't get caught at the station waiting for the next one when the sun goes down. For God's sake, Graves, we need *help*." I wondered if I should tell him that I was seeing little darting things in the mirror. He didn't need that to worry about. "Huh."

We slowed down.

Burke and 72$^{nd}$ was actually a three-way intersection. Directly in front of us, where the two roads split to make a Y, a stone wall rose. There was nothing else around; the houses had petered out half a block ago and open space—weedy lots or fields, who could tell—ran away on both sides. Just over the wall on the right, a red-tiled roof peeked, little bits of color peeping out under the snow.

"Burke and 72$^{nd}$. It's got to be that place." I goosed the gas, pointed us toward the right fork. "Jesus. Talk about conspicuous."

"I've never been out this way." Graves drummed his fingers on the door. "It smells bad."

*Well, you're the one with the super nose now.* "Bad how?"

"Rust again. And something rotting. Like a dumpster in summer."

I sniffed deeply but didn't smell anything. The ringing in my head was a constant; I was used to thinking through it now. I didn't taste anything other than hunger and the thin metal tang of exhaustion. My back hurt, my throat hurt, my arm wasn't too happy—I was just bad all over, and ready to hand over this whole problem to someone older and more experienced.

Why hadn't I just given the keys to Christophe? He might still be alive if I had.

"I wish I'd just given him the keys." My voice broke on the last word. I snuffled up another sob, pushed it down. It was time to stop being a whiner and focus on getting us out of town.

"I don't." Graves's fingers drummed, paused. "What are we going to do, drive up to the house and walk in, announce we're vampire hunters, and ask them pretty-please to—"

"We're going in to find whoever Christophe had coming to pick us up. If I'm valuable to them, they'll help us get out of town." *Then I'm going to sleep for a week, and after that . . .*

After that, what?

"What if they . . ." He didn't go any further, but I knew what he was thinking.

"Graves." I swallowed, tried to sound hard and sure. "We're leaving town *together*. Period. End of story. You got that?"

He didn't say anything else. I didn't dare look at him.

We crept along, snow now coming sideways and the truck's springs making little sounds as the wind tried to push us into the wall. In a little while there was a driveway—obviously recently cleared— and the truck struggled through the turn as if I wasn't controlling it. An ornate iron gate was open, swept back to either side, its curlicues heavily frosted with ice. In the middle of a vast expanse of circular driveway, a fountain lifted—some kind of shell shape with a big spike coming out of the middle. Drifts piled against the wall and the edges, but the driveway itself was clean.

The house was three stories of massive overdoneness, a pile of pseudo-adobe. Why anyone would build a hacienda up here among the Eskimos was beyond me.

The truck obediently turned, following the unrolling driveway. I eased it to a stop and let out a sigh. "Okay. Let's—"

"Holy shit." Graves was staring past my nose, out the driver's-side window. "Um, Dru?"

My neck protested when I turned my head. All of a sudden every bone and muscle I owned was tired, and I had to pee like nobody's business. Driving in a snowstorm is like pulling a sled; you work muscles you never knew you had.

The big black gate had shaken itself free and was closing, little driblets of snow falling off like flaking skin. Ice crackled, and the sky overhead was a sheet of painted aluminum. The gate latched itself with a muffled clang, and a fresh wave of cold wind rattled it, moaning through the metal gingerbread.

*That's either very good or very bad.* I peered up at the slice of the house I could see. Warm electric lights through every window, no shadow of movement, no sense of someone home.

It *couldn't* be empty.

"Dru?" Graves sounded very young. It occurred to me that as much as I wanted someone older and more experienced, he must want it twice as much. And I was all he had.

The weight settled on me, heavier than ever. "I guess we go in." *If this is Christophe's extraction point. It kind of makes sense, close to the edge of town and everything, but still . . .*

It felt hinky. Super extra hinky with a side of bad sauce.

The engine kept running along. I could probably take out the gate with this piece of heavy metal. But if I killed the truck, we'd be out in the snow with no way to escape.

*This is where Christophe said. So why are you stalling?* I put the car in park, eyed the front of the house again. The front door was a huge thing of wet black wood. *They certainly like everything super-sized out here. All hail Middle America.*

I made up my mind and reached for the field box. "Stay in here. I'm going to check it out."

"No way. Are you *crazy?*" Graves shook his head like he was dislodging a bad thought. "Don't leave me out *here!*"

"Look, if I don't come out, you drive the truck through those gates and get the hell out of here. I'll go inside and make sure it's safe. No reason for us both—" *To get killed,* I was about to say, because it was what Dad often said. "—to go in," I amended hastily, "because someone needs to stay out here and keep the truck running in case we need to leave in a hurry. I'm trained for this." *At least, I'm better trained than you are.* "I'll do it."

"Jesus." Graves stared at me. His eyes were very, very green. "You've got a death wish."

*Right now I have a bathroom-and-sleep-somewhere-safe wish, kid.* "No, I don't. I want to get out of this alive and I want to get *you* out of this alive. Look, just stay here and keep the motor running. You know how to drive?"

"Are you kidding?" The look he gave me qualified as shocked. "I ride the *bus*."

*Oh yeah, this just keeps getting better.* "Don't worry. It's a piece of cake." I opened the field box, checked the gun. The clicks of the clip sliding out and back in, the safety checked, were very loud in the snowy silence, the wind suddenly hushing to a damp not-sound.

"Oh yeah? What if the door's locked, Dru?"

I actually smiled. At least, the corners of my mouth pulled up. "Places like this are never locked," I said quietly, and unlocked my door.

As soon as I slammed the door shut the wind came back, random curls flying into my eyes, driving snow against my cheeks, white flakes sticking to them. I went around the front, not looking through the windshield—if I did, I would only see Graves looking pale and scared, and I didn't need that.

I was scared enough for both of us.

There were only three steps leading up to the door. Big concrete urns that might have held plants were now only mounded with snow.

*There's nothing growing in here. It's all concrete.* I shivered—it wasn't as cold as you'd think, but snow tickled me with little wet fingers, clinging to my eyelashes and soaking through my sneakers.

I touched the door, closed my hand around the knob. It turned easily, and I heard a soft, passionless sound—an owl's throaty *who? who?*

I looked back over my shoulder. No sign of Gran's owl, but the call came again, muffled like feathered wings. The truck kept running, smooth as silk. The door opened silently, snow blowing in past me.

Through the door, then, into a foyer floored with little pieces of varnished wood all smushed together and waxed to a high gloss. I stood shivering and looking at a flight of stairs going up, a chandelier dripping warm waxen light. The gun was a heavy weight pointed at the floor. I snicked the safety lever off and wished miserably that Dad was here.

*How do you know he wasn't?* a little voice said in the very back of my head, and a cool bath of dread began at the base of my skull, sliding down my back with soft wet flabby fingers.

*I know*, I told that horrible little voice. *I saw where he died, I think. He left the truck right outside, and he went down a hall in an abandoned warehouse. And someone was waiting for him.*

The lights were on, but it was cold in here. Cold as a crypt. I took another two steps into the foyer, saw a hallway, and the light changed imperceptibly.

I whirled. The door slid closed, the slight sound of its catch just like the sound of the safety clicking off. The taste of rust ran over my tongue in a river, followed by the wet rotten smell of oranges gone bad, fuzzy and leaking in a blind wet corner. The ringing got worse, filling my head with cotton wool.

Something glinted on the floor, past a little square of rounded darkness that my eyes refused to see properly for a moment.

*Oh shit.* My sneakers made small wet sounds. Little tracers of steam lifted off my skin, it was so cold. My breath made a cloud, vanishing as soon as I inhaled. I moved as if in a dream, or as if it was last night, something pulling my unresisting body forward. It hurt to bend myself over to pick up the familiar black leather billfold.

It was thick with cash, and I flipped it open, saw Dad's ID, him staring into the camera like he dared it to take a bad shot of him. The picture of Mom was gone, but the mark where my thumb rubbed the plastic every time was still there, like an old friend. I straightened, automatically stuffing the billfold in my pocket, and was compelled to step forward, looking at the other little thing, glittering patiently on the waxed floor.

It was silver, and as I bent my aching knees to take a look at it my body knew, chilling all over, gooseflesh prickling across my back and down my arms.

It was a heavy locket, almost as long as my thumb. Scrollwork on its front I knew better than my own name, even, and a silver chain, now broken, that I'd seen all my life. The scrollwork made a heart with a cross inside it, and on the back there would be little foreign symbols sketched, where they could rest against the skin.

I touched it with my index finger, letting out a clouded breath that ended on a short sound as if I'd been punched and lost all my air. My fist closed over it and I pushed myself up, dry-eyed.

And all of a sudden I knew something else. I wasn't alone in here.

Someone spoke from the hall beyond the foyer. It was a boy's voice, more tenor-sweet than Graves's and harsher than Christophe's, with the same queer space between words and sounds as the *djamphir's*.

"Come into my parlor, said the spider." A light, happy giggle, as if someone was having a hell of a good time. "And obediently, she walks in and picks up the bait."

I raised my head. Strings of damp curling hair fell in my face.

There was a shape in the door to the hallway, a cloak of more-than-physical darkness clinging to it. I suddenly knew who had been on my front porch that night. He hadn't had an invitation, so my threshold was a barrier to him. But here I was, and here he was, and why had Christophe sent me *here*?

A cool bath of dread slid down my back.

"Sergej." I sounded normal, not terrified. As a matter of fact, I sounded pretty good.

He stepped into the wash of gold from the chandelier, and I understood why it was so cold. The cold was coming from him, breathing out from his poreless skin with its faint tint of swarthiness. And here was another shock.

He looked about eighteen—a little older than Graves, a little older than me. Broad-shouldered as if he worked out, and with a face chipped from an old coin—a long narrow nose, a chiseled mouth, a mess of artfully disheveled honey-brown curls. But his dark eyes were wrong. They were dusty, and far more adult than they should be. The closest I'd ever seen to eyes like that was on some city streets, where kids melted out of the shadows as cars cruised slowly past, their bodies young but something ancient shining from their faces. Kids who had seen a lot of things no kid should have to see, kids I shivered when I thought about always making me scoot closer to Dad on the truck's seat.

Only they were still human, those kids. And this thing wasn't. It looked young, and I suppose if you weren't in the habit of looking closely at things you'd just think he was lucky to have such great skin and killer lips.

If you looked any closer, the thing looking out of those dark sparkling eyes would leer at you. Right before it ate you alive.

He wore a thin black sweater and jeans, like Christophe. A pair of high-end black Nikes and a gold wristwatch too huge and ostentatious to be anything but real. Probably a Rolex. He looked like the Rolex type.

I stood there staring at him, my mouth fallen open a little. I heard something through the ringing in my head. A steady thumping, like a clock ticking against the head of a giant drum, echoing. Faster and faster, a sound that made me think of a small dark space, stuffed animals, and my own stale breathing as I listened before falling asleep. I'd been so tired.

*I love you, baby. I love you so much. . . . We're going to play a game.*

The knowledge rammed through me like a baseball bat swung by a player coming all the way up from his heels. That ticking beat was the sound of his heart. I was here in a huge pile of fake adobe with a snowstorm and Graves outside, and I was facing down a sucker all by my lonesome. A sucker who had turned my father into a zombie—and murdered my mother, back Before.

My left hand was still a fist around the locket. The pumping, thumping sound was very close, and the boy smiled at me. A very sweet smile, if you didn't mind looking at the needle-sharp fangs, much sharper and more grotesque than Christophe's. But white, so blinding white. And those eyes, like pools of mud just waiting to drag you down and fill your mouth and nose with cold, cold dirt Jell-O.

I heard something else, too. The muffled beating of wings.

He took a step forward. "Ripe," he said, the word contorted because of the way his teeth were now shaped. A trickle of something black slid down his chin, right below where the tip of one of his fangs scraped the perfect matte skin. "And coming so willingly to the slaughter. I've drunk from the veins of a thousand *djamphir*, but the sweetest are always the little birds, just before they flower." A low chuckle, like gas burping and bubbling up from oozing slime.

I raised the gun and his dark winged eyebrows flew up in mock astonishment. He looked just like a psychotic clown, and a red spark lit in the back of his weirdly shaped pupils. They were hourglass-shaped, darker slits against the black velvet of his irises, thin threads of black in the whites turning them gray. He looked almost blind.

The owl hooted nearby, the sound slicing sharp through a sudden howling outside, the door rattling behind me, and the sucker's eyes widened just a fraction before I squeezed the trigger and a neat half-dollar sized hole opened up in his forehead.

It was a perfect shot.

*Good girl, Dru!* I heard Dad cry, and a gout of thin blackness gushed down the sucker's face, his head snapping back like he'd just been kicked in the teeth. I heard someone screaming, thinly, and knew it was me.

Because his head jerked back down again, sharply, and he grinned at me through the mask of rotting black ichor, his teeth saw-edged except for the fangs. His entire body coiled, compressing itself. I knew he was going to jump me and knew I had no hope of getting out of the way. The blackness ate his eyes, turning them into singularity holes under the scrim of foulness, and he leaped, hanging in the air for a long moment as everything slowed down around me and the ringing in my ears turned to an agonized shriek.

The world stopped again, but only for a bare second. I dropped, one knee giving way and the gun fighting its way up through air gone clear and hard as a diamond. Pale feathers puffed as the owl swooped, razor claws raking the sucker's back, and it banked away, black goo dripping from its feet—and I knew it had missed, it hadn't hit where it wanted to, and as soon as the world snapped back up to speed the sucker was going to fall on me and bury its fangs in my neck, and I wouldn't feel a thing until it was too late.

Time popped hard, like a rubber band pulled back and let loose, careening across a classroom. A burst of warm air traveled across my skin, and there was a hideous wrenching sound.

The front door exploded inward. A streak of black and denim-blue leaped off the truck's hood, flung with sharp lances of broken, splintered wood. He flew like Superman and they collided like planets flung into each other.

*Get out of the way!* Dad's voice yelled in my ear, and I rolled, one fist full of the locket, the other weighted down with a loaded gun. Snow flew into the hole in the side of the house, the shattered door falling in bits and pieces. The headlights were on, and through the cracked windshield I could see Graves, his nose bleeding and his eyes running with green flame, clutching at the wheel like a life preserver. He must have bonked himself a good one when they hit.

Around the truck, flowing like a creek in spring, the lean long forms of werwulfen leaped. My gaze snapped back toward the roaring bloodlust, and I saw Christophe go down, red blood flying in a perfect arc before splashing onto a blank white wall.

*That's what's wrong in here*, I thought hazily. *No pictures. No furniture. Nothing living. It's an empty house.*

The sound was hideous. The wulfen were making that chilling glass-at-midnight noise again, and they flung themselves at the sucker like water running over rocks. The sucker was making a low inhuman growling, and Christophe . . .

He twisted to the side, avoiding Sergej's hand, suddenly freighted with claws that looked sharp enough to rip air. Two quick steps, Christophe's feet blurring, and he leaped, one boot cracking across the sucker's terrible-beautiful face. The kick was used to propel him *up* and *over*; it looked like he was on wires, landing lightly as a butterfly. His entire face was covered with blood, his sweater was sopping, but his eyes blazed winter-freeze blue and his lip lifted, snarling back at Sergej even as the wulfen descended.

It was the funniest thing. He *did* look like an angel, back from the dead. I choked on a sob, stared in wonderment.

The truck whined, chain-clad tires clattering, and heaved back. Thin light fell through the hole in the door, the walls on either side busted too. The engine died and Graves was scrabbling out of the truck. I was only barely aware of this, because the fight was still going on, and I was beginning to get the idea that it was more than a little one-sided.

And our side wasn't the winning one.

Sergej knocked down the wulfen like they were bowling pins and Christophe moved in again. He was shouting, but my ears were ringing too badly to hear it. He feinted, reversing to claw at the sucker's face as they closed, and I suddenly knew how the next few moments were going to play out. Christophe was slow and wounded, even though he was moving faster than anything human had a right to, and Sergej . . . He jerked a hand in a careless sweep and a wulf went flying, hitting the wall with a crunch of bones snapping and sliding down.

Cold air swarmed across my face, full of the smell of snow and coppery blood. Sergej spread his arms, inhaling as I did, a cloud of darkness crawling down from his eyes to bleed into his mouth, sliding down his throat in thin rivulets. The air popped and prickled with ice; the world slowed down again as Graves's hand closed around my arm and what he was shouting roared into my ears.

"*Come on, Dru, let's go!*"

My chest expanded, ribs popping as I took in the deepest breath of my life. Christophe crouched, fingers tented on the blood-slick floor, and his sides heaved. He looked very tired, and the blood coating him dripped, droplets hanging in the air as he gathered himself.

The wulfen didn't pause. They were still circling the sucker, clawing at him, but something invisible parried their strikes. The one who had hit the wall was just lying there, the fur running off him and the face—a young boy's face—rising out from under its sliding textures.

The ringing came again as I shook free of Graves's clutching fingers. My hands snapped out, hard, as if I was throwing a dodgeball, and something flinty and hot hit me in the stomach, boiling like water just after you throw macaroni in. The locket burned against my palm, silver scorching.

Gran's owl, glittering snowy white, arrowed over my head like a bullet, a streak of feathers and a cruel curved beak. Black claws extended, and this time it didn't miss. It caught Sergej right in the face, raking hard and sharp as the second hex I'd ever thrown in my life smashed into him with a sound like a huge Chinese gong I'd seen on a game show once. Glass broke, tinkling, the chandelier overhead veering drunkenly, lightbulbs popping. Christophe hit him at the same time, a leaping roundhouse kick that came all the way up from the floor and cracked against the sucker's jaw as the owl sheared away, its wings snapping once as it turned on a dime and shot away like a pinball.

"Come *on!*" Graves yelled, hauling me as the sucker flew backward. The wulfen followed, and the one knocked into the wall shook himself and leaped to his feet, the fur flowing back down over him, bones crackling as he changed once again.

I stared, my mouth hanging open like I was some sort of idiot.

"Get her *out* of here!" Christophe roared, and Graves pulled me along as a massive sound—like a pipe organ being smacked with the world's biggest feedback squeal and pumped through every amplifier, from every crappy garage band ever put together—tore the air into shivering bits.

I didn't resist as Graves dragged me. The gun was still in my hand, dangling, and I had locked my fingers outside the trigger guard the way Dad always told me to. Crashing sounds deeper in the house and high yapping howls from outside told me we weren't alone. Shadows filled the door, and Graves had to put up his arm, elbow out, like the prow of a ship. I crowded behind him, clinging to his waist with my free arm as the wulfen poured past. Their eyes flamed with yellow and their fur touched me, sandpaper-rasping, thin iron-gray winter light falling around us as the wulfen somehow twisted and ran like ink on wet paper. They poured past us, unlikely saviors, and I began to think we might have a chance.

It ended, my arm fell away from him, and Graves dragged me down the steps, his fingers digging into my arm right where I had a bruise. The pain jolted up through my neck, exploding in my head, and I found out my cheeks were wet. I was making little hitching sounds and my throat burned. Snow whirled down, blanketing the world. The wide expanse of driveway was starred with paw prints fast blurring under the onslaught. There would be no proof of them in a few minutes.

*They didn't even touch us. And Christophe . . .*

He was right. Dad and I were amateurs. There was no way we could have fought something like that.

And my mother . . .

Graves was swearing steadily, in a high breathy voice. He opened the driver's door and shoved me in, hopped up after me. It was still warm, and I collapsed against the passenger window, glass cold against my fevered forehead. I stuffed Mom's locket in my pocket, shoving it deep like a secret. My fingers were numb, and my palm burned.

"Jesus Christ," Graves said. "Are you okay?"

No. No way was I okay. I licked my lips with a dry tongue. "Christophe?" I whispered.

"Scared the hell out of me," he whispered back. "Showed up with those wulfen things; guess they're on his side after all. Told me to drive right through the wall, that you'd die if I didn't. Got up on the fucking hood and flew. Far out." His arm snaked over my shoulder. "Far fucking out. Dru?"

I peeled myself away from the nice cold glass and collapsed against him, burying my nose in the soft warm spot between his shoulder and his throat. He hugged me, resting his chin on my wet hair, and this time it was okay that we were both crying. We clung together like shipwreck survivors, and snow covered the cracked windshield with soft, deadly kisses.

# CHAPTER 28

**had my face** in Graves's narrow chest, and I was okay with that. He smelled good, and he was warm. The tears had trickled away, and his chin still rested on the top of my head. The windows were screened with breath-fog and with snow clinging to every surface it could find.

I could hear Graves's heart, too, ticking away. Just like a clock, but without the eerie meanness of the sucker's pulse. It was a clean sound, and it meant I wasn't alone. I hadn't been this close to anyone in a while.

Except him.

The door opened and a blast of chilly air scoured the inside of the truck cab. Someone climbed into the driver's side. It was a bit of a crowd, but the truck was big and the bench seat was long.

There was a long silence, a jingling sound as someone touched the keys in the ignition. Graves said nothing, so I figured it was okay.

And really, I didn't care. The whole world could have gone up in flames at that point and I wouldn't have given a rat's patootie.

A breath of apples touched the cold stillness. "Please tell me she's all right," Christophe finally said.

"She's okay." Graves didn't move. His chin settled more firmly atop my head and his arms tightened a fraction, that was all. "A bit beat up, but still breathing. She seems okay."

"Thank God." The *djamphir* let out a long, shaky breath. There was a scraping sound, and the engine turned over. The truck settled into running again, and the heater came on. Cool air poured through the vents. "Thank God again."

"What happens now?" Graves wanted to know. I did too, but I didn't feel like picking my head up and looking at either of them.

A slight sound of wet material as Christophe shrugged. "I take you out in the field and you get extracted. She'll go to the Schola. I'm going to vanish."

"Because there's a traitor," Graves supplied, and I was glad he was talking so I didn't have to.

"Yes." Christophe laughed, another bitter little sound. "This was my safe zone. There was no way Sergej could have known about this place, or that she would be coming here, unless someone in the Order told him. And someone in the Order sent the directive to set the wulfen on me back at her house. They didn't realize I wasn't *him*." He sighed. "If I *had* been him, you two would have been dead by the time they got there. Juan—the yellow-eyed wulf you met—is fit to be tied. He was just following orders, but the directive's disappeared. Someone's covering their tracks." He shifted a little on the seat. I wondered if he was still bleeding. "We've got to get her out of here."

"So you're sending us somewhere you know there's a traitor." Graves's chin dipped even further, resting harder on the top of my head.

I thought about all this, felt nothing but a faint weary surprise.

"I've got friends at the Schola; they'll watch over her just as I would. She'll be perfectly safe. And while she's there, she can help me find whoever's feeding information to Sergej. She's been drafted."

Graves tensed. "What if she doesn't want to?"

"Then you won't last a week out there on your own. If Ash doesn't find you, someone else will. The secret's out. If Sergej knows, *other* suckers know there's another *svetocha*. They'll hunt her down and rip her heart out." The windshield wipers flicked on. "Dru? Do you hear me? I'm sending you somewhere safe, and I'll be in touch."

"I think she hears you." Graves sighed. "What about her truck? And all her stuff?"

"I'll make sure they get to the Schola too. The important thing is to get her out of here before the sun goes down and Sergej can rise renewed. He's not dead, just driven into a dark hole and *very* angry."

"How are we going to—"

"Shut up." He didn't say it harshly or unkindly, but Graves did shut up. "Dru? You're listening."

*Oh, God, leave me alone.* But I raised my head, looked at the dash. There really was no option. Hair fell in my face, the curls slicked down with damp, behaving for once. "Yeah." It sounded like I had something caught in my throat. The word was just a husk of itself. "I heard."

"You were lucky. You ever put yourself in danger like that again and I'll make you regret it. Clear?"

He sounded just like Dad. The familiarity was a ragged spike in my chest. "Clear," I managed around it. My entire body ached, even my hair. I was wet and cold and the memory of the sucker's dead eyes and oddly wrong, melodious voice burrowed into my brain. It wouldn't let go.

*That thing killed my father. Turned him into a zombie. And Mom
. . .* "My mother." The same flat, husky tone. Shock. Maybe I was in
shock. I'd heard a lot about shock from Dad.

Silence crackled, but then Christophe took pity on me. Maybe.
Or maybe he figured I had a right to know, and that I'd listen to
him now.

When he spoke, his voice was husky too, whether with pain or
with the cold I couldn't guess. "She was *svetocha*. Decided to give
it all up, stop hunting, married a nice jarhead from the sticks and
had a kid. But the *nosferatu* don't forget, and they don't stop playing
the game because we pick up our marbles and go home. She got
rusty and she got caught away from sanctuary, drawing a *nosferat*
away from her home and her baby." He put the truck in gear. The
windshield was clearing rapidly. "I'm . . . sorry."

"What else do you know?" I pulled away from Graves, his
arm falling back down to his side. He slumped, looking acutely
uncomfortable, a raccoon-mask of bruising beginning to puff up
around his eyes. His nose was definitely broken.

"Go to the Schola and find out. They'll train you, show you
how to do things you've only dreamed of. God knows you're so close
to fully blooming, and once you do . . ." Christophe stared out the
windshield, his profile as clean and severe as ever. His eyes were bright
enough to glow even through the gray daylight. Drying blood coated
his face, a trickle of fresh red sliding from a cut along his hairline. He
was absolutely soaked in the stuff, but it didn't seem to matter to him.
"And when you hear from me, I'll set you a challenge worthy of your
talents. Like finding out who almost got you killed here."

The truck was still running like a dream. Good old American
steel. Dad's billfold sat in my jacket pocket, a heavy, accusing lump.

Christophe measured off a space on the wheel between two

fingertips, looked intently at it. "So what about it, Dru? Be a good girl and go back to school?"

Why was he even asking? Like I had anywhere else to go. But there was another question. "What about Graves?"

The kid in question glanced at me. I couldn't tell if he was grateful or not. But I meant it. I wasn't going anywhere without him.

He really was all I had. That and a locket, and Dad's billfold, and a truck full of stuff.

A shadow crossed Christophe's face. The pause was just long enough for me to figure out what he thought of me even asking that question, and how hard he was weighing the likelihood that I might be difficult. Or just letting me know I didn't have anywhere else to go. "He can go with you. There are wulfen there, one or two other *loup-garou*. He'll be an aristocrat. They'll teach him too."

*That's all right then.* I nodded. My neck ached with the movement. "Then I'll go."

"Good." Christophe took his foot off the brake. "And for the record, next time I ask for the keys, hand them over."

I didn't think that merited a response. Graves scooched a little closer to me, and I didn't even think about it. I put my arms around him and hugged. I didn't care if it hurt my arm and my ribs and my neck and pretty much every other part of me, my heart most of all.

When you're wrecked, that's the only thing to do, right? Hold on to whatever you can.

Hold on *hard*.

* * *

We bounced out through the gingerbread gates, which were knocked inward, the wrought iron curling like it had been in a fire. Christophe turned left, tapped the gas, and we bumped out onto the road. The stone wall continued to our left, snow falling thick and fast. The sky, however, was brighter. You could finally tell there was sunlight up there, instead of just a flat pan of aluminum.

"It looks different now," I said, stupidly.

"Sergej." It was all Christophe needed to say, and I shut my mouth. What else could a sucker do?

Had Dad been chasing him all along? Because he'd killed Mom?

What else was I going to find out at this Schola? How to walk on snow without leaving a track, how to float while I fought?

Too bad I wouldn't learn what I really wanted to know. I had a sneaking feeling I wouldn't *ever* learn what I really wanted to know.

As soon as the stone wall ended to our left, he cut the wheel. I braced myself—there were ditches out here, and *deep* ones, running alongside the roads—but the truck merely bumped a little, up and over, and we were swimming through a wheel-deep sea of snow. The truck jounced and whined, and the cracked windshield was still a little foggy with all of us breathing hard.

We jolted and swam for a long time; then Christophe made a quick inquiring movement with his head. The blond highlights had slid back through his hair, little bits of them visible through clotted, drying blood. He didn't seem too bruised, though. "Ah." He let off the gas, and the truck rolled to a stop. "That should be transport now. Get out and wait for them."

"Here?" Graves didn't think much of the idea. "You're going to leave us in the middle of a snowstorm?"

*Oh God, don't argue.* I pulled at his coat. "Yeah. Sure." I reached for the door handle, pulled it. The door swung open with a protesting creak, and snow puffed in on an arctic breath. The temperature was dropping. My nose was full, but I didn't want to think of *what*. "Whatever you say, Christophe."

I didn't mean it to sound snarky. Really, I didn't.

And besides, I could hear what Christophe could. A thwopping, thudding sound I've heard on a lot of TV shows late at night.

"Dru." Christophe leaned over the seat, his mouth twisting down. I couldn't smell apple pie now, and part of me was vaguely glad about that. "I'm sorry. I—"

I didn't want to hear it. He hadn't told me everything, but I'd left him for dead. I guess we were about even, especially after he took on something so old and so powerful. Something that wanted to kill me.

Something that *would* have killed me.

What do you say when someone takes on a really badass, murdering sucker for you? There just aren't words for that.

"See you around, Chris." I pulled at Graves; he slid out behind me without protesting. It was like agony to stand upright again, my hamstrings and glutes singing in pain, my neck like a solid bar of crying steel. I grabbed my bag, too. Half my body groaned in protest when our feet sank into knee-high snow, and I slammed the truck door on whatever Christophe wanted to say next.

The truck idled, and the thopping sound got closer. It hovered into view—a red-and-white helicopter, the only blot of color in the wasteland around us. The stone wall was in the distance, swallowed up in white, and the snow was coming down so heavily even the city in the distance, or the houses a few blocks away, wasn't visible. Fierce cold swallowed my sneakers and stung my calves.

White spray fumed up as the helicopter hovered for about twenty seconds, its downdraft scraping snow away before it touched down. I gingerly ducked through my bag's strap, held up an arm to shield my eyes, and almost missed it when a hatch opened on the side and a figure leaped down, bent over, and scuttled for us.

The truck pulled away. I still had the gun in one hand. For the life of me I couldn't remember if I'd clicked the safety on. I looked down to check, found it *was* on, and the scuttling figure reached us.

It was a brown-eyed kid in an orange parka, a thatch of curly brown hair filling up with snow because he'd shoved the fleecy hood back. "Holy shit!" he yelled over the sound of the 'copter. "You'd better give me that."

*Whatever you say.* I handed the gun over. He checked it expertly and made it vanish under his parka. "Don't worry, I'll give it back. Come on, we don't have much time." He waved, way up over his head, at the retreating truck, and then reached out to grab my arm.

I twitched, Graves stiffened, and Orange Parka's hand stopped in midair. He turned it into a beckoning motion, like a mama duck trying to pull recalcitrant ducklings along.

"Sorry about that. We just got scrambled half an hour ago; I'm all excited. Come on." His voice broke, reedy against the onslaught of the helicopter's noise, and we trudged through the snow after him, bending almost double when he did. My hair tried to lift up and strangle me in the downdraft, and the hatch on the side of the 'copter opened again. There was a step. I put my foot on it, grabbed the handles, and Graves boosted me. I almost creamed my head a good one against the top of the hatch, and wondered if the rotor blades would grab my hair.

The space was cramped and full of weird angles, but it was warmer than outside. I wedged myself in a part-bench seat that looked like it was made for a third-grader, and Graves piled in, wedging his taller frame beside me. The pilot didn't even look at us, and the hands on the controls were bigger and thicker than mine, though they looked young and smooth-skinned.

*Jesus, how many teenagers are doing this sort of thing?* I strangled a tired, half-hysterical snort-giggle—my nose was still full. Graves reached over and grabbed my hand, and the curly-headed kid hopped in and closed the hatch. The noise dropped, but not by much. He reached up and whapped the pilot twice on the shoulder, and the helicopter immediately lifted, whining.

My stomach turned over, hard.

"Hi," the curly-headed kid called, dropping into the little jump seat behind the pilot's chair. His hands moved with ease and familiarity, buckling himself in like it was the most natural thing in the world. He had a snub nose, freckles, and a wide innocent grin. "I'm Cory. Welcome to the Order. You must be Dru Anderson. We're really excited to meet you."

I closed my eyes, collapsed against a porthole showing the white earth receding like a bad dream, and cried. Graves clutched at my hand, his palm sweating, and he didn't let go.

*finis*

# BETRAYALS

A **STRANGE ANGELS** NOVEL

LILI ST. CROW

*For Gates. Keep holding the line.*

## Acknowledgments

*Without Miriam, this book would not be. Without Jessica, this book would not be any good. Without you, dear Reader, this book would be lost. Thank you all.*

*Love is whatever you can still betray.*

—John le Carré

**W**indshield wipers struggled back and forth, clumped with snow. The mingled breath of three teenagers fought with the defroster. Thank God the truck was still running, even after they'd driven it through a wall.

"So you're sending us somewhere you know there's a traitor." Graves's chin dipped even further, resting harder on the top of my head.

I thought about all this, felt nothing but a faint, weary surprise.

Christophe sighed, "I've got friends at the Schola—they'll watch over her just as I would. She'll be perfectly safe. And while she's there, she can help me find whoever's feeding information to Sergej. She's been drafted."

Graves tensed. "What if she doesn't want to?"

"Then you won't last a week out there on your own. If Ash doesn't find you, someone else will. The secret's out. If Sergej knows, other suckers know there's another svetocha. They'll hunt her down and rip her heart out." The windshield wipers flicked on. "Dru? Do you hear *me? I'm sending you somewhere safe, and I'll be in touch."*

"I think she hears you." Graves sighed. "What about her truck? And all her stuff?"

"I'll make sure they get to the Schola too. The important thing is to get her out of here before the sun goes down and Sergej can rise renewed. He's not dead, just driven into a dark hole and very angry."

"How are we going to—"

"Shut up." He didn't say it harshly or unkindly, but Graves did shut up. "Dru? You're listening."

*Oh God, leave me alone.* But I raised my head, looked at the dash. There really was no option. Hair fell in my face, the curls slicked down with damp, behaving for once. "Yeah." It sounded like I had something caught in my throat. The word was just a husk of itself. "I heard."

"You were lucky. You ever put yourself in danger like that again and I'll make you regret it. Clear?"

He sounded just like Dad. The familiarity was like a spike in my chest. "Clear," I managed around it. My entire body ached, even my hair. I was wet and cold, and the memory of the sucker's dead eyes and oddly wrong, melodious voice burrowed into my brain. It wouldn't let go.

That thing killed my father. Turned him into a zombie. And Mom . . . "My mother." The same husky, flat tone. Shock. Maybe I was in shock. I heard a lot about shock from Dad.

Silence crackled, but then Christophe took pity on me. Maybe. Or maybe he figured I had a right to know, and that I'd listen to him now.

When he spoke, his voice was harsh, whether with pain or with the cold I couldn't guess. "She was svetocha. Decided to give it all up, stop hunting, married a nice jarhead from the sticks and had a kid. But the nosferatu don't forget, and they don't stop playing the game because we pick up our marbles and go home. She got rusty and she got caught *away from sanctuary, drawing a* nosferat *away from her home and her baby."* Christophe put the truck in gear. The windshield was clearing rapidly. "I'm . . . sorry."

"What else do you know?" I pulled away from Graves, his arm falling back down to his side. He slumped, looking acutely uncomfortable, a raccoon mask of bruising beginning to puff up around his eyes. His nose was definitely broken.

"Go to the Schola and find out. They'll train you, show you how to do things you've only dreamed of. God knows you're so close to blooming. . . ." Christophe stared out the windshield, his profile as clean and severe as ever. His eyes were bright enough to glow even through the gray daylight. Drying blood coated his face, a trickle of fresh red sliding from a cut along his hairline. He was absolutely soaked in the stuff, but it didn't seem to matter to him. "And when you hear from me, I'll set you a challenge worthy of your talents. Like finding out who almost got you killed here."

The truck was still running like a dream. Good old American steel. Dad's billfold sat in my jacket pocket, a heavy, accusing lump.

Christophe measured off a space on the wheel between two fingertips, looked intently at it. "So what about it, Dru? Be a good girl and go back to school?"

Why was he even asking? Like I had anywhere else to go. But there was another question. "What about Graves?"

The kid in question glanced at me. I couldn't tell if he was grateful or not. But I meant it. I wasn't going anywhere without him.

He really was all I had. That and a locket, and Dad's billfold, and a truck full of stuff.

A shadow crossed Christophe's face. The pause was just long enough for me to figure out what he thought of me even asking that question, and that he was weighing my likelihood to be difficult. Or *just letting me know I didn't have anywhere else to go.* "He can go with you. There are wulfen there, one or two other loup-garou. He'll be an aristocrat. They'll teach him too."

That's all right then. *I nodded. My neck ached with the movement.* "Then I'll go."

"Good." *Christophe took his foot off the brake.* "And for the record, next time I ask for the keys, hand them over."

*I didn't think that merited a response. Graves scooched a little closer to me, and I didn't even think about it. I put my arms around him and hugged. I didn't care if it hurt my arm and my ribs and my neck and pretty much every other part of me, my heart most of all.*

*When you're wrecked, that's the only thing to do, right? Hold on to whatever you can.*

*Hold on hard.*

***

Ten hours later the black van pulled around in a neat half-circle. "End of the line," the dark-haired boy said. "Let's go."

Darkness crouched around the huge building. I had a confused impression of cold, high-piled gray stone. Towers and two wings going off to the sides, the whole thing raked back like a Gothic spaceship. Two big smooth concrete lions on pedestals faced out from the long circular driveway, glaring down the thin ribbon of blacktop that had peeled off the county highway and brought us here. Weird ropy ivy crawled over the walls, like long bony fingers. Morning fog was a thick gray blanket, and the trees dripped silently on all sides, pushing against the building's frigid personal space.

Graves held my hand, still, so hard my fingers had long ago gone numb. The driver and the dark-haired boy in the passenger seat hopped out neat as you please, taking the shotgun and the AK-47 with them.

"You okay?" Graves asked for the hundredth time.

I coughed a little, cleared my throat. The motion of the van had almost lulled me to sleep, especially since it was warm and I was exhausted. My back ran with pain and I'd stiffened up, moving like a creaky old lady when I moved at all. Plus I had to pee something fierce.

Horror movies never tell you that—about how most of the time when you're faced with the unspeakable, the biggest thing you take away from the experience is the need to find some indoor plumbing. My hair was greasy, frizzing out because it had air-dried after being drenched with snow. The wild mass of curls unraveled on my shoulders and I really, really wanted to wash it. Not to mention the rest of me. If I scrubbed hard enough, maybe I could rinse all the fear off. The thick, cloying fear that coated me like chocolate—only not so sweet or warm.

I clutched my bag with my free hand—everything I had in the world, since Christophe had the truck keys and my truck to go with it.

I was now completely at their mercy, and I wouldn't have minded so much if they would just give me a bed and let me *sleep* for a little while. Then they could do whatever they wanted. Up to and including killing me.

*Not really, Dru. Don't even joke about that.*

"One of them's going up to the door," Graves muttered. He'd done that all along, giving me a play-by-play as if I didn't have eyes. It was academic—I kept said eyes shut most of the time. I just didn't care. "The guy with the big gun is near the front of the van."

*Of course.* "Standing guard." My throat was scraped raw. I wanted a drink of water almost as much as I wanted to pee. It was ironic. "Just in case."

"How you doing?" Graves turned away from the tinted window

to peer anxiously at me, green eyes firing in the gloom, just like the silver skull and crossbones dangling from his left ear. His hair was a tangled mass of dyed black. It was predawn, gray and hushed, and now that the van had stopped you could tell it was cold outside.

A warm car never stays warm for long. Heat is like love. It drains away.

I searched for something witty to say, settled for bare honesty. "I want to pee."

Amazingly, he laughed. It was his usual bitter little bark, but heavier and deeper now. He sounded tired, and his proud, beaklike nose lifted a little. Under his half-Asian coloring, he looked so exhausted he was almost gray. There was very little left of the baby-faced Goth Boy he'd been.

Getting your life yanked out from under you will do that, I suppose.

Graves's laughter petered away. He sobered. "Yeah, me too. We haven't been left alone since they picked us up in that chopper, either. Do you think—"

Whatever he was going to ask me was lost as the kid with the AK-47 opened the van door. "It's clear." He gave me a smile that looked like it was trying to be reassuring. He was even sharply handsome, with a button nose and dark flyaway hair, an engaging smile, and light brown, almost yellowish eyes. But the gun and the way he glanced back over his shoulder, checking the space between the van and the front door of the big pile of stone, was something I'd seen a few times following Dad around while he hunted the things from the Real Word, the world of stuff that goes bump and crunch and yowl in the night.

Professionalism. It sat uncomfortably on his young face.

Every single person from the Order looked like a teenager—except my dad's friend August, who looked about twenty-five. I wasn't sure what to think of that, and just sat there staring at the rapidly strengthening foggy daylight outside the van for a moment.

"Miss Anderson?" He leaned forward a little, the mouth of the gun pointed carefully down and away. "It's okay. We're at a Schola; it's safe."

*Nowhere's safe. Not anymore.* But I moved a little, and Graves took that as a signal to slide across the seat, letting go of my hand, and hop down. He turned, awkwardly, as if he wanted to help me.

But the dark-haired kid shouldered Graves aside and offered *his* free hand. "Here. Really, everything's all right." Another one of those smiles, and his eyes glittered at me.

I made it down out of the van, ignoring his hand. As soon as my feet touched down, he slammed the door behind me. "Let's get you inside." He made little waving movements with his hands, like he was trying to herd chickens or something.

It was the crowning absurdity. Cold air pressed against my cheeks; I smelled ice and damp leaves and the particular rot of a forest in a cold winter. The fog pressed close, deadened every sound. I scrubbed at my face, surprised to find my cheeks were still wet. Had I been crying?

The steps were huge and granite, and the massive iron-bound oak door atop them opened slowly. Mr. AK-47 herded us up toward it, and my fingers fished around blindly until they hooked on Graves's and squeezed. Both of Goth Boy's eyes were puffed up with bruising, and the bridge of his nose was a little flattened, but the swelling had gone down remarkably quickly. He made the stairs easily. I had to stop on each one because my back felt like it was going to shred itself. My knees creaked. I glanced up at the sky—featureless iron. It didn't look like snow, and I was happy about that. I've had enough snow to last me a long time.

But it was *cold*, and it smelled like early morning. Like metal against the tongue, and like sodden, frozen plants. And the flat white heaviness of fog. My chin dropped toward my chest. The soft muffled wingbeats of an owl echoed inside my head.

Gran's owl, the warning of danger. I should have told Dad I'd seen it that week and a half ago. Maybe he would have stayed home, and he'd still be alive.

Jeez. Just over a week was all it took for my life to implode. It was some kind of record.

"Jesus," a boy said softly, up ahead of us. "It's really true."

I didn't even look up. We reached the top of the stairs, and Graves squeezed my hand before we were separated and I was whisked off by three boys who didn't seem as young as their unlined faces would have me believe. They were murmuring over my head, various cryptic things, and I paid no attention. They took me through halls, and I heard whispers as kids clustered in doorways. It was like running a gauntlet or something, and I pulled into myself, concentrating on one foot in front of the other.

There was a long flight of stairs at last, and then a room with blue carpet. "You look pretty tired," someone said. "Are you hungry? Thirsty? Anything we can—"

I saw an empty bed-shaped object and let out a sigh. "No thanks. No. I just want to sleep." *I just want to lay down and die.*

"All right." He was a faceless blur, I was so tired. I couldn't even ask where Graves was. "You just try to rest, then. The bathroom's through there, and—"

I didn't hear whatever he said after that. I made it to the bed and sank down in a cloud of softness. The coverlet was blue too, I figured out that much. I didn't even think about warding the walls. Gran and Dad would have been on me about that.

The thought was a pinch in a numb place. Gran and Dad. Both gone.

*I should get up and pee,* I thought, and then darkness swallowed me.

I dreamed of Gran's owl, moonlight edging its feathers as it winged through blackness. A fuzzy sense of danger enfolded me, but I was too tired to care.

And that was how I arrived at the Schola.

# CHAPTER 1

**A** **week later I** was already in trouble.

The thing with a school full of boys being taught to kill suckers is that sparring gets to be a group event. It's like a fight in a regular school, only here the teachers don't intervene—or at least, they hadn't in any of the other four fights I'd seen since I arrived. You get a mob of onlookers, all shouting, and it can turn into a melee easily enough. Things don't stop until someone's bleeding. Or worse. Being able to heal just makes the boys more likely to hurt themselves.

I couldn't heal like they could yet, because I hadn't "bloomed." So much for being special. Here I was just as fragile as a civilian. But when you've spent most of your spare time learning how to make the best of what you have against things that go bump in the night, you don't give up easy.

I came up from the floor with a punch, getting my feet under me, and Irving grabbed my wrist. He used my momentum to whip me past him, but I'd expected that, hooked my other fingers, and got a handful of his face. That's what Dad would have called "dirty fightin'," something he approved of in a girl.

Hey, there are no rules in a *fight*. Thinking there are "rules" can get you killed. Dad drilled it into my head over and over again—you fight to win, to survive. Not to look good or give the other guy a chance.

*Stop thinking about Dad, Dru.* I had other problems.

Irving had bet he could best me in under two minutes. We were at ninety seconds and counting, and I was winning.

A bet like that doesn't go unchallenged. Not when your former Marine dad's been teaching you how to kick ass for years. Not when there's a hot boiling bubble of acid right behind your breastbone all the time. Not when you're practically alone in a school full of teenage boys.

Not just any teenage boys, either. Boys who can turn into fur rugs with bad attitudes at the drop of a hat. *Djamphir* boys who are born with the eerie stuttering speed of suckers, blurring through the slow stupid daytime world like a cheesy special effect at the drop of a hat. Boy *djamphir* don't have to wait to "bloom," oh no. They're stronger and faster from the start, and they only get better once their voices break and they "hit the drift" in puberty. Some of them hit it later, in their mid-twenties. But even before they hit the drift they're more than a match for any human.

I twisted, my sneakers digging into the frayed mats, and kicked back. That caught him in the knee, and I heard bones popping and loud growling. I hit the dirt, the mats scraping against my elbow because I was only in a tank top and jeans.

I'm not stupid. When you hear the distinctive noise of werwulfen changing into the furry shape that makes them almost impossible to kill, that's the reasonable thing to do.

Except Irving wasn't wulf. He was *djamphir*, and he was already committed to his leap. So where was the sound coming from?

I rolled over just in time to see Irving hanging in the air over me, pale face alight, golden highlights slipping through his chestnut curls as the aspect took him. The world slowed down, moving through syrup just long enough for me to scramble, the clear heavy weight of physicality straining against every muscle in my body. The *snap!* like a rubber band popped off expert fingers rang through my head as time sped back up again and he rammed down into the mats a good three feet away from where I was now but exactly where I'd been. His knee hit too hard—without my face to cushion it—and he let out a short, sharp cry. The lines across his cheek from my fingernails flushed an angry red, and his hair stood up, writhing.

Now he wasn't just a teenage boy needing to save face in front of the crowd. Now he was *serious*. And we were at twenty seconds left. *Good.*

I gained my feet in a rush and skipped back twice. The mass of onlookers exploded away, giving us enough room to move. Irving bounced up like he was full of helium, his curls moving just like in a shampoo commercial, and he threw himself across the intervening space with the weird blurring speed I wasn't even close to getting accustomed to.

The speed I couldn't use—yet.

So instinct took over. It wasn't precisely a bad instinct—brace yourself and punch the guy straight in the face. But Dad would have yelled at me for being stupid, since Irving was so ungodly fast, and straight-on force, like in karate, doesn't work so much for me. I'm built too thin and rangy. I don't even have moderately big breasticles. They just look like—well, never mind what they look like. At least they stay strapped down when I worm into a sports bra.

It doesn't quite suck being a girl, but sometimes it's close.

I *should* have grabbed Irving's arm, twisted, and slid him past me, using his own momentum to help him right into the stone wall across the room. Instead, I hit him. There was a crunch as my fist met his nose, and he collided with me like a freight train. We were heading for the wall, and the thought *this is going to hurt* flashed through me like electricity popping through a lightbulb filament.

And it would have, too, if something hadn't hit us both from the side, roaring. I got an elbow in the face and went tumbling, slapping the frayed, stained mats and wrenching my back a good one. I just lay there for a second, bells ringing inside my skull and the entire world seeming very far away.

It took a long time for me to blink, looking up at the arched, ribbed vault of the ceiling. This part of the complex had been a chapel, but now it was the armory and a sparring space unfolding with mats that had seen better days and the smell of healthy young boysweat. Underneath was the ghost of incense, and if it were daytime, shafts of weak sunlight might slip between the bars and pierce dusty dimness.

During the day, though, the Schola sleeps. Right now it was just past midnight, and I was in deep shit.

"Dru?" Someone was bending over, shaking me. I tried to push them off, but my hands wouldn't quite work right. A dreamy sort of panic slid through me then, and I heaved back into my body with another elastic *snap*!

I was doing a lot of that lately. The air was full of rumbling and muttering, and there was a lot of shouting going on.

*Oh God. This might've been a bad idea.* I grabbed at a waiting pair of hands and hauled myself up. My head was ringing and my back hurt something awful.

"What the bloody blue *hell* is going on here?" The words sliced through the hubbub, except for that deep thrumming growl. I shook my head, a sliver of warm wetness threading down from my nose, and pushed between two *djamphir* boys—Clarence, his straight black bowl-cut damp with sweat and excitement, and Tor, his aspect on and thick streaks of buttery yellow sliding through his hair. Both of them were taller than me, but I shouldered them aside and found myself in the front row.

Graves had Irving down, his long, tanned-looking fingers closed on the *djamphir*'s throat. His eyes were chips of green flame, and the growl was so thick it blurred the air around him, the sound of a very pissed-off skinchanger. He probably couldn't talk, either— his jaw was subtly modified, accommodating fiercer, longer teeth. The crackle of bone had been *him*. He wouldn't get furry—he was *loup-garou*, not wulfen, only half-imprinted with the thing that made them able to shift—but he was pretty motivated to do some serious harm, and angry enough not to care about hurting someone.

It had happened three or four times by now. Twice back in the Dakotas, each time when we were in danger—or when he *thought* we were in danger, since Christophe had turned out to be on our side after all. And on the first evening I'd woken up at the Schola, I'd almost walked right into a shoving match between him and a *djamphir* in the cafeteria. From what I heard, the *djamphir* had asked him something about me, and Graves had turned on him. The result was shove, shove, growl, shove some more, yell, and me wading in to make them cut it out.

I didn't think I'd gotten the whole story, but Graves wouldn't talk about it. And now there was this.

"What the—" Dylan said again, elbowing his way through the throng.

I tuned him out and stepped forward. My right leg felt funny, and something dripped onto my upper lip. Three steps, four, my boots dragging a little against the mats. When I laid my hand on Graves's shoulder, the buzzing going through him felt like I was resting my hand on a juiced-up power transformer.

He actually snarled, his dyed-black hair curling, all but standing up and snapping with vitality. The sharp, strong bone structure of his face was subtly off-kilter now, nose less proud and cheekbones taking on the higher wolflike arc instead of the broadness of "human." Rich color flooded through his skin, making his perpetual tan deeper.

"Calm *down*," I managed. Only I sounded like Elmer Fudd, because I had a stuffed-up nose. My eyes were smarting and watering, too. "Jesus." It came out like *Jebus*, and I could have laughed. Except it wasn't funny.

"Everyone *shut up*." Dylan folded his arms, his leather jacket creaking. The noise went down. Here at the Schola, when a teacher talks, you *listen*. "And back up. Back up!"

Graves growled again, and Irving choked. He was turning an awfully deep shade of crimson. His fingers plucked weakly at Graves's hand, but with his arm twisted underneath him and an angry skinchanger on top of him, he couldn't get any leverage.

I hauled back on Graves's shoulder. A bolt of pain went down either side of my spine. "Come *on*, asshole. Calm down. This is getting ridiculous."

"Why didn't you wait for me?" Dylan addressed the air over my head. "I'm getting a little tired of—good God, girl, you're *bleeding*."

Graves let go of Irving and flowed to his feet, shaking me off. His lips were pulled back, teeth gleaming, his eyes awash with feral phosphorescence. I realized the wulfen had settled into a bloc behind him, and the tension running through them was palpable.

A few of them had gotten a little hairier, too. The tension made the wulf boys bulk up as well, shoulders straining at shirt seams. They don't take on werwulf form unless they really have to, but you can tell them from the *djamphir*. It's in the way they move—like they're shouldering fluidly through sunlit grass, instead of with the sharp hurtful grace of the half-*nosferat*.

The *djamphir* don't change, but the aspect ran through all of them—their hair moving and rippling with color changes, eyes glowing, and one or two of them showing little dimples of fangs touching their lower lips.

Boys. Jeez.

Dad had always taught me that wulfen and suckers didn't get along. I was beginning to think it was genetic. As far as I could figure, *djamphir* and wulfen were on the same side against the suckers. That was what the Order was about. But they sure as hell didn't seem to like each other much.

I pulled Graves back, and we only had a bit of a problem when I stepped in front of him and he tried to shove past me. I grabbed him by his used-to-be-bony shoulders and shook him. My fingers sank into muscle, and I didn't worry about hurting him. His head bobbled, but his gaze snapped down to mine and the snarl petered out.

I held his eyes for what seemed like a very long time. He blinked, and his shoulders relaxed a little. That's when I turned and found Dylan, arms crossed, standing over Irving with one winged black eyebrow raised and the rest of the *djamphir* utterly still behind them both. The *djamphir*'s eyes gleamed and their fangs were out.

Oh, the testosterone. You could have cut it with a cafeteria spoon.

"We were sparring. I got stupid." I took another two steps, my heels landing harder than they should have and pain jarring up through my entire spine. "You all right?" This was directed at Irving, who was coughing, a deep rasping sound. But he didn't look almost purple now.

He glared at me, and I felt sorry. It had just been a little friendly workout, nothing big. I should have just rolled my eyes and let his posturing pass.

But instead, I'd gone off on him. And I was supposed to be so much more mature than boys at this age.

"Sorry, Irving." My back seized up again, and I breathed out through my mouth. The muttering growl behind me receded a little, and I put my hand down to help him up. "I should have grabbed you and helped you into that wall instead of trying to punch you in the nose. Go figure." It was really hard to sound conciliatory with something dripping and dribbling off my top lip. I was hoping it wasn't snot. That would be gross.

I sniffed, and the rest of the nosebleed let loose in a pattering gush.

Irving froze, staring up at me. His pupils shrank. A spatter of bright-red blood hung in the air, then splashed—

—right on his clothes, starring the mat next to him too.

"Shit," Dylan said, and leapt on him. *Get her out of here!*

Hands grabbed me, hot against the bare skin of my upper arms. I was dragged backward, and the world threatened to turn over without me attached to it. The ringing inside my head got worse, the sound of owl wings brushing the inside of my skull in frantic bursts. The wulfen hauled me out, and I heard Irving screaming as Dylan held him down, the bloodhunger turning his voice into a harpy's shriek.

*Yeah. Just another night at the Schola. The fight doesn't stop until there's blood on the floor.*

But when the blood is mine, it can send the boy *djamphir* a little crazy. It's something about me being *svetocha*. Super-happy stuff in my blood even before I "bloom," something that reaches down and wakes up the crazy in anyone with a touch of *nosferat*.

After the blooming hit, I'd have my own superhuman strength and speed. And that super-happy stuff in my blood would make me toxic to suckers just like Raid is toxic to insects.

But now it just made me vulnerable. I smelled like a really nice snack.

Dylan had been drilling it into my head for the whole week now, on and on, that I couldn't spar with the *djamphir* students. They couldn't control the bloodhunger very well, I could get seriously hurt, yadda yadda.

Christophe had never told me about that.

There were a lot of things he hadn't told me.

The wulfen dragged me out into the hall, and the rushing noise inside my head got bigger. I think I probably passed out. At least, the world got really faraway and dim, and the only thing that mattered was hearing Graves. He could talk now that the rage had passed, and he was saying the same thing over and over again, a catch in his voice right before my name.

"It's okay, Dru. I promise it's okay."

He didn't sound like he believed it either.

# CHAPTER 2

The ice pack stung, but holding it against the bridge of my nose meant less swelling and bruising. I sighed, shifted uncomfortably, and blinked away the hot welling of reflex tears. Graves had thought to grab my jacket, too, so the goose bumps on my arms were covered.

"It was my fault," I repeated stubbornly. "I should have pulled Irving past me instead of trying to paste him on the nose."

"That's not the point." Dylan sighed. Some days he sighed more than others, and some days it seems like he did nothing *but*. He had a face that could have been on a Roman coin, and I'd heard his real name was something unpronounceable and Goth. Not like black-lipstick-and-angst, but actual barbarian.

Around here, you never knew. Even the teachers looked like teenagers. The really old ones look about twenty sometimes. But they're late drifters, and they never get to looking thirty. My dad's friend August—the one I'd called to confirm Christophe's story—

must've been one of them. I wondered about it, but it didn't seem polite to ask.

Dylan pushed a hand back through his dark hair and settled more firmly in his chair. His desk was stacked with papers, and a large silver blob I stared at the first time I was in here until I realized it was a skull dipped in shiny metal. The skull had long canines and long pointed incisors, and I decided not to ask if it was a real sucker skull for the thousandth time.

Behind Dylan, shelves of dusty leather-bound books stood frowning down on me, cobwebs ghosting up near their tops. The place smelled like leather, dust, and the musky smell of teenage hormones, but it still felt like the principal's office.

I've been in principals' offices all over America. Before I figured out the best way to get by was to just keep my head down.

I've kind of been sucking at that lately.

Graves stood just behind me. Dylan didn't offer him a chair. I didn't like that, especially since Dylan had refused to talk *or* sit until I sat down. His office had windows, with the obligatory iron bars. I'd made some sort of joke when I first got here about whether the bars were to keep us in or the suckers out, and the dead silence and pained look on everyone's face had told me to shut up.

Outside the barred windows, the lawns were painted with moonlight. Trees stood guard, silvered with threads of fog, a white wall sending spectral fingers up to touch naked black branches.

The ice pack crackled as I held it to the bridge of my nose, then peeked out at Dylan.

"Look." He had that I'm-being-patient tone again. "Combat training for you is going to take a while, and it won't really get started until after you bloom. If you *must*, you should be practicing with the teachers, not the students. And Graves . . . he can't be interfering every time he thinks someone's insulted you, or whatever it is. It's not safe. For either of you."

Dylan was magnanimously leaving out the part where I drove Irving into the hunger by bleeding all over him. Nice.

I waited for Graves to say something, but he remained stubbornly silent even when I looked up at him. His eyes glowed from under a thatch of dyed-black hair, his coloring back to normal. A bruise ran up his cheekbone, turning a mottled purple as it swelled.

It would be gone by tomorrow. *Loup-garou* heal even quicker than wulfen. They get all the benefits of the change, like speed and strength, without the allergy to silver or the risk of losing control.

Go figure. I'd learned more about wulfen in one week here than from all the painstaking work Dad and I did with moldering leather-bound books and years of hunting weird stuff.

Graves's mouth was set, pulled down at the corners, and he looked mulishly defiant. Only his earring sparkled a bit, peeking out from all that hair. He stood behind my chair and glared at Dylan.

No help from that quarter. It was all on me.

"It was *my* fault," I finally repeated. "None of the teachers have time to spar with me. They treat me like I'm glass, and the classes you have me in are remedial shit I could get in any normal high school. I'm not going to get any better if they keep putting me through kindergarten work."

"You're *svetocha*, Dru. You're precious. You have no idea what you're worth—dead for the *nosferat*, or alive to us." Dylan rested his elbows on his desk. Paper crackled. "Should I say it again? You haven't bloomed yet. Once you do, you'll be able to handle harder sparring, but until then—"

"Until then I'm just supposed to sit around and look pretty? No thanks." I could feel my chin jutting forward, a sure sign that I was Being

Difficult. "I want to *help*. I was out hunting with my dad when most of these kids were probably taking basic how-to-ID-a-sucker classes. Keeping me in kindergarten isn't going to *work*." Why couldn't he get that through his head? I wasn't some nine-to-fiver, some Kmart shopper.

I was a hunter too. I'd been Dad's helper, hadn't I?

"Oh Lord. Not this argument again." Dylan sighed. His eyes were bloodshot and dark-circled with fatigue. He always looked tired and stressed out. It didn't make him ugly, though. "You have bad habits from your time as an amateur, Dru. It's time for you to unlearn them from the bottom up, and that means low-level classes just like everyone else. That's what the control directive said. My hands are tied." He gave me an odd look, his dark eyes unreadable, then continued. "Irving will heal completely in less than twelve hours, your *loup-garou* friend there in under eighteen. You're stuck with longer healing time and less speed, strength, and stamina. You're not even ready for a practice run, let alone some of the junior cleaning expeditions. Not to mention the fact that any *nosferat* who gets wind of your existence will try to drain you to fuel their own hunger, or take you to—" He stopped dead, swallowed hard.

"Sergej." I said the name. It burned my tongue, made the air tighten. Here they didn't talk about it. Naming a sucker is bad luck, and who knows if they can hear? Even hunters like Dad wouldn't say a sucker's name out loud. They'll use initials, or code words.

But I'd said it before.

Dylan didn't flinch. He did, however, sigh. Again. "Dru. You have not bloomed. You can't hold a candle to even the prefects or the senior students, and there's nobody with enough control if something— God forbid—happens and you start *really* bleeding. If—" He caught himself just in time.

"If Christophe was here, things would be different." I made the words a singsong. "Come on, Dylan. I'm not stupid. Christophe isn't here, and nobody else is going to be allowed to train me, even though he's disappeared and nobody will talk about him. Even though he saved my life. What's the deal?"

"It's very complex." He looked at the silver-dipped skull on his desk, and his jaw set. Every boy at the Schola had good skin, bright eyes, sparkling teeth. It was like being trapped in a goddamn sitcom. You could only tell the teachers from the students by seeing them actually teaching. Or by the way certain older ones had of stopping and tilting their heads, becoming absolutely motionless.

They didn't even seem to breathe when they did that, and it was usually a sign of Restriction. Which meant being sent to my room while everyone else manned battle stations. Twice in the past week, and I heard there were regular Restriction drills, too. Just like fire drills out in the stupid daylight world.

Yeah. My favorite thing ever, being stuffed in a room while someone else goes out and fights. The ice crackled again as I shifted my weight. Somehow I'd bruised one of my ass cheeks, it felt like. "Well, I'm a smart girl. Try me."

"It's not a question of your brains, Dru. It's a question of what is safe for you, since Christophe feels there's a mole in the Order. You're the only *svetocha* we've been able to save for a good thirty years—you're rare, and any other *svetocha* we manage to locate are killed before we can bring them in. We want to make sure you don't come to any harm, and part of that is making sure you're properly trained from the beginning. Though why they've sent you out here and given us such a confusing directive . . ." Maddeningly, he stopped again.

A conversation with Dylan is like that. He stops in the middle of sentences, refuses to go any further, just stares down at his desk with a mournful look. You could almost feel sorry for him.

I dropped the ice pack into my lap. A thin trickle of wetness kissed the knee of my jeans, soaked in. "Why don't the teachers have any time to train me if I'm so goddamn important? Why are we waiting for Christophe when this Council of yours has such a problem with him? And why—"

"The Council doesn't have a problem with him. A *significant minority* of the Council does. It's not the same thing, and it's not anything you should be worrying about. You have enough to deal with." He eyed me. "That's going to swell more. You should go take some ibuprofen and a turn in the bath."

In other words, *la di da*, I was dismissed. "You're not answering my questions." I hauled myself upright, clapped the ice pack to my face again. "Thanks for nothing."

"You're welcome. At least I'm not putting your friend there in detention for interfering and making things worse." He probably regretted it as soon as he said it, because I wheeled around and caught him closing his mouth with a snap. But Graves finally did something—he grabbed my shoulder and hauled me out of Dylan's office suite, past the twin suits of rusting, cobwebbed armor glowering at the door, and into the quiet hall.

"Let it go, Dru." Graves finally spoke up when we got to the end of the hall, and the stairway loomed in a cochlear spiral. "He's just threatening."

*Oh, so you finally open your mouth?* "Thanks a *million*. I know that."

"You're welcome. Come on, let's get you down to the bath." He let go of me and dug in the pockets of his long dark coat until he came up with a battered pack of Winstons.

*He* got to go off-campus to get smokes almost every day. He got to hang around with the wulfen without a tide of whispers following him everywhere. He got to spar and go to classes with them, and he was starting to catch their jokes and make a few friends.

Me? I was the only girl in a boys' school, and I was kept inside like a goddamn hamster while everyone went out and had fun. Not that I wanted to go anywhere for a while, after being plucked out of snow and insanity and deposited here. The food was okay, they'd ordered jeans and T-shirts for me, and there was no shortage of drawing paper or anything else I might want. All I had to do was let Dylan or another "advisor" know and then, wham-bam, it would show up at my door the next morning. Or evening.

It was creepy. Especially since every time I wanted to take a walk, even outside on the quad of cracked pavement and dead winter garden squares, an "advisor" would show up as well. Usually Dylan, who didn't even pretend to be looking something over or just walking around.

No, he stared right at me with a mixture of worry and weirdness on his face. And that was thought-provoking too.

I just didn't know what thought it was supposed to provoke.

"How long have we been here?" I peered at him around the ice pack. "About a week, right?"

He got that prissy precision look on his face again, just like every time he corrected me. "Nine days, give or take. Yeah." He hunched his thin shoulders. Between that and the beak nose he looked bird-like. But there was something else in the set of his face now. Graves was looking more worried and adult than ever. "Seriously, you should get into the baths. That's puffing up and looking pretty bad."

The ice pack was leaking. Cold water slid a questing tendril down my wrist, soaking into my jacket sleeve — or Dad's jacket sleeve, since it was his spare army-surplus green one.

His billfold was under my bed. It wasn't the safest place in the world, but . . .

That thought hurt my chest too. The unsteady ball of fury and something else behind my ribs got a little bigger. I grabbed my temper with both hands, shoved it down. Let out a gusty sigh. "Fine, I'll go to the bath. Jesus. By the way, why did you jump on him?"

As if I didn't know. But maybe this time he'd say it.

But he didn't. He just looked away down the hall, hunched down even further, his long, clever fingers fiddling with the cigarette pack. "You were bleeding."

I opened my mouth to tell him that I hadn't been. But then I sniffed again, my skin crusted with copper-smelling dried blood, and thought that if a wulfen's nose was sensitive enough to tell right before a bloody nose started, a *loup-garou's* would be too. "Well, thanks." I tried to sound gracious, and the ice crackled again. More cold water from the leaking bag slid down my sleeve.

*Great.*

"No problem, Dru. We're going out for burgers tonight. Want me to bring you some?" He sounded hopeful.

My chest squeezed down on itself. "No." I hated to rain on his parade. "They'll be cold by the time you get back. I'll just grab something in the caf."

And all the way down the stairs, listening to his silence behind me as I stamped away, I kicked myself for not saying yes.

※ ※ ※

On the boys' side of the sparring chapel there was a long room with a ton of individual stone-lipped tubs sunk in the floor. They had lot of partitions and community tubs too, and I'd heard there was always someone in there.

On the girls' side, the long room was just as big. There were four tubs large enough to drown a couple girls apiece in. Six bathroom stalls. Granite flooring, all kept pretty spic and span. Except for the grotty corners that meant it had been damp in here for a long time. Even chlorine won't work that funk out.

Still, it was warm and steamy, and the tubs were always bubbling. But there was never anyone in here but me.

I lowered myself into the tub on the farthest side from the door. My clothes lay tangled a few steps from the rim. I'd hurled the ice pack halfheartedly at the shiny new garbage bin set by the sinks, and it hung over the edge, melting water dribbling onto the floor.

I couldn't even care.

The cloudy not-really-water bubbled. It smells like minerals, a flat palate-coating tang, and it doesn't feel like regular water. It's too jelly-thick. For a few seconds it's so hot it stings. Then it coats the skin, and the bubbles turn sheer instead of translucent. Time spent in the tubs speeds the healing process up like crazy. Which is a good thing, because the combat training here is full-contact.

If you're a boy.

I'd felt kind of weird about walking around in the locker room by myself. It was like having a whole suite to myself while the boys slept in dorms. And none of them had empty bookshelves, or a CD player of their own, or a personal advisor watching over their every sneeze. Or a computer all to themselves, with Internet shopping sites already bookmarked and a credit card registered to "Sunrise LLC" lying in a neat paper sleeve next to it on a rosewood desk, plus an info sheet telling me where to get stuff delivered to—PO box and mail stop.

Creepy. Dad never used credit cards. Not his own, anyway. Liquid resources for hunting were best. But these guys were the Order. They were big—it took money to run a place like this.

Still, it didn't seem as big as Christophe had made it sound. Which was something else to think about. And I never went to any useful website, like a GPS ping to find out exactly where I was or county records to find out who owned this chunk of land—not to mention going hunting to find out if there were any news reports about my disappearance or Graves's. That kind of information would have been useful, but there was no point in leaving tracks on a machine I knew wasn't private.

So, no shopping and nothing useful about the computer. It might as well have been a mute hunk of plastic.

A class schedule—Aspect Mastery, History, Algebra, Civics— had been tacked to my door two days after I'd gotten here, but after the first day of stupid boring remedial crap I'd wadded it up in a ball and started bugging Dylan to give me something challenging. Even the Aspect Mastery class was nothing special, just a social hour for a group of five boy *djamphir* who spent the time telling nasty jokes and watching me in their peripheral vision. History was run by some blond teacher who stared at me very hard between sentences, as if he was willing me to disappear.

I hadn't stayed in any classroom for very long. Hanging out near the armory seemed like a better deal.

Graves was always on me about it. *You shouldn't skip, Dru. It's important.*

Yeah. Like I needed a civics class, for God's sake. Like anyone cared what I did as long as I stayed inside. Like *I* cared, now that my whole world was upside down.

Now that Dad was gone.

*Don't think about that.*

The stone was slick and gritty at the same time. I found a bench and coughed, cupped some of the heavy not-really-water in my palms and smoothed it over my face. It crackled, soothing heat working its way past the ache of a pair of developing black eyes, and I let out a sound that was half-sigh, half-sob. Echoes fell flat against every clean, hard surface. The mirrors were fogged, as usual, but sound bounced off them nevertheless.

I wondered, like I did every time I sat here, if my mother had ever chosen this tub. If she'd ever sat here and heard her own voice bouncing off the stone and glass and metal. If she'd ever felt lonely.

She'd been a part of the Order, or so Christophe and Dylan had told me. But nobody would really talk about her, as if she were an embarrassment. And I didn't know if she'd ever even been here; this complex was big enough but still tiny in the scheme of things.

Small school, about four hundred students. It wasn't the kind of place that could scramble helicopters on short notice. But I could have been confused, since Christophe hadn't exactly been giving out information left and right.

I was just avoiding thinking about it for as long as I could. It wasn't working.

My eyes flew open, not-water cracking and falling away in little shards of white. Wet hair hung in strings, the curls struggling to spring up. I touched the smooth curve of metal at my throat and winced as if I'd poked at a bruise.

The locket lay just below the notch between my collarbones. Heavy silver, as long as my thumb, the heart and cross etched on the front and spidery, foreign-looking symbols on the back, their edges resting against my skin. I'd gotten so used to seeing the silver gleam on Dad. He never went anywhere without it.

Now whenever I caught sight of it in the mirror or brushed it with my hand, a shock would go through me. Like I'd stuck my finger in a light socket. It was just *wrong* to be wearing it.

The next hurtful thought arrived right on schedule. I couldn't put it off any longer.

Dad.

*He walked down the hall, and the buzzing got so bad it shook everything out of me, the dream running like colored ink on wet paper, and as it receded I struggled to say something, anything, to warn him.*

*He didn't even look up. He just kept walking toward that door, and the dream closed down like a camera lens, darkness eating through its edges.*

*I was still trying to scream when Dad reached out his free hand, like a man in a dream, and turned the knob. And the darkness behind it laughed and laughed and laughed. . . .*

I shut my eyes again. Loosened my legs and slid under the un-water's surface. It closed over me like a dream, like a balm, and the heat worked in toward my bones. Only there was a coldness inside me, too deep for it to reach. A freeze that wasn't physical.

*He's dead, Dru. You know who did it. You know why.*

Or did I? I knew Dad had been expecting to come back. He *had* to have been—there was no way he would leave me in a house all alone for good. He'd always come back for me, sooner or later.

Well, he *had* come back. Just not alive. I'd shot a zombie in my living room, and it had been my father.

Christ. Of all the things that will fuck a kid up, that has got to have a category all its own.

I knew who had killed him and turned him into a zombie. The same person Christophe and Dylan and everyone else said killed my mother.

*Sergej.* The *nosferat* who looked like yet another teenager, with oily black curls and eyes that could swallow you whole. The same sucker who had tried to kill me. The reason why I was stuck inside the complex that was the Schola, barely even going outside to walk in the barren leafless winter gardens. I *could* go outside, but not without someone showing up to stare at me.

Standing guard. Because Sergej—or another *nosferat* like him—might come back. He was a big wheel among the suckers, the closest thing to a king that they had, and he knew I was alive.

I shuddered all over. My lungs burned. The not-water fizzed around me, heat burrowing in through my muscles, soothing and healing. My face gave one last heave of red pain and subsided. The shuddering got worse as I floated, and for a moment I thought of opening my mouth and letting the stuff in the tubs rush in, coating everything down to the back of my tongue and—

I surfaced in a rushing splash. The stuff dribbled away from my hair, slicked my face, crackled as it hit open air, and instantly formed a weird, wax-white coating over every inch of my exposed skin. Rinsing it out of my hair would take ten minutes in the shower.

I blinked away the clinging on my eyelashes and inhaled, mouth gaping open to take in a deep wallop of steamy air.

White light hit my eyes, scoured through the mishmash inside my head. My breathing deepened, evened out, with a hitching at the end of each exhale.

Underneath the weird white paraffinlike coating of whatever was in the baths, the tears were hot and oily. They slicked my cheeks, but there was nobody around to see. Or to hear.

I settled back onto the stone seat, drew my knees up so I could hug them, and sobbed. Then I went up to my stupid room and cried some more, until dawn came up through a pall of cloud and I finally fell into a thin, troubled sleep.

# CHAPTER 3

**The cafeteria was** a long, narrow space, every railing and molding made of dark wood. The walls were stone and half-paneled with heavy, age-varnished oak, but the floor was garish blue linoleum. Both were chipped and worn from hard use. The tables and the squeaking plastic chairs could have been in any high school in America.

I sat alone near the exit to the halls leading to the west class wing instead of the other branch going to the infirmary and library. The trays were red plastic, bunged-up and warped. The plates were white industrial china, the silverware stamped steel.

I missed my kitchen. I missed my dishes, even the mismatched ones, and Mom's black-and-white cow-shaped cookie jar. I missed my mattress, my clothes, and my CDs, and all Dad's weapons. I'd spent all morning—evening, whatever—hanging out in front of the armory, making excuses to stand in front of the counter and breathe in the smell of metal and gun oil. I missed the boxes and my truck and everything.

I even missed cooking, and god*damn*, I never thought that would happen. The food here wasn't bad, but it was job-lot industrial, and I could never see anyone in the kitchen. Just indistinct shapes through a cloud bank, like the fog that rose out of the forest every night. It said something about my life lately, that a screen of shifting steam that dispensed food was only moderately weird to me.

The food was set out on steam tables right in front of the weird wall of vapor. Pasta and salads and desserts. Burgers and pizza and fries for the younger ones, or the ones who liked to eat like real teenagers. Raw and rare meat for the wulfen, including livers and other stuff I didn't look too closely at. There were also boxes and mini bottles of wine, but I stayed away from those.

Today it was bow-tie pasta in a cream sauce, with prosciutto and peas. Salad with fresh tomatoes and your choice of dressing. Garlic bread that wasn't half-bad. Only it just sat there on the plate, congealing. There was a carton of chocolate milk, and an energy drink in a blue can. The blue of the can against the red of the tray, the white of the plate, the green specks of peas—if I had my colored pencils, I'd draw the whole shebang and call it *Still Life with MSG*.

I ached to draw something, anything, but as soon as I settled down with a pad of paper the urge left me. It was the first time in my life I hadn't been sketching furiously. My dreams were Technicolor weird, but they didn't push me to scribble. I just felt itchy, like I was waiting for something to happen.

It was loud. The walls reflected a hundred conversations going on, and the occasional hijinks. A bunch of teenage boys in a lunchroom is a recipe for trouble most of the time. The wulfen had their tables, the *djamphir* theirs—usually in prime spots, like right off the end of the line or near the exit to the infirmary. Even here there were cliques.

Nobody sat at my table. A few of them tried, but I wasn't really interested in talking and they drifted away. It was like being the new girl all over again every damn day. Irving had tried to say something to me earlier, but I'd just put my head down and walked off. I still felt bad over making him lose his shit in front of everyone. It was embarrassing. What on earth could I say?

I wasn't used to being such a failure at everything. And Jesus, I wasn't looking to make new bosom buddies. Why bother? I mean, something was bound to come up. It always did.

I'd never been at any school longer than three months. Not since Gran died.

Dylan kept saying I was important, but none of the teachers would make any time for anything useful, like combat training. The only time I did my katas in the sparring chapel there was a whispering audience, and that was horrible. I was used to Dad just watching quietly, maybe offering a suggestion when I finished. Now a tide of whispers followed me everywhere.

So I did my tai chi in my room once or twice, but even that didn't help. The calm and grace that always used to wait for me if I just did the movements long enough was gone. Everything that used to make it okay enough to cope with was just not working.

I just sat there, feeling the eyes on me. I hate that feeling.

Irving was sitting two tables away. He kept glancing over, and he finally put his palms on the table and made as if to stand up. But then he dropped back down and looked at his tray.

Graves pulled out the chair next to me. "Hey, kid."

"Hey." I dropped Mom's locket against my chest as if it had stung me, looked up and grinned. It felt strange on my face, but then the happiness caught up with me and it turned more natural. Relief burst behind my breastbone like a mortar shell. "How was your morning? Evening? Whatever."

He set his tray down, dropped into the chair. "Full of new information. You know some brain-damaged vampires can't cross running water or major interstates? And the most common type of poltergeist feeds almost exclusively on the bioelectricity of teenage girls." He wagged his unibrow at me—nobody had held him down and plucked at the caterpillar crossing his forehead yet. I thought about saying something about it, decided not to for the hundredth time. His green eyes burned, and it wasn't just my imagination. His face *was* different. Less baby, more sharpness.

He was looking more like a wulfen now.

"Yeah, I knew about that. The poltergeist, I mean. There was this one time, in backwoods Louisiana . . ." The sentence died. I didn't want to think about that. Dad had held the girl down while I did the taking-apart-the-poltergeist thing, with salt water and Gran's rowan wand. The thing had hurled all sorts of small household items at both of us, clipping Dad a good one on the head with a teacup before I'd remembered to circle the bed the girl was tied to, cutting off the poltergeist's access to her. Weakening it enough for me to tear it apart.

Dad hadn't said a single thing about that—he didn't need to. I kicked myself all over for *that* one. And here they were wanting to put me in boring, normal, *remedial* classes. Jesus.

Graves snapped his fingers. He had two lattes in paper cups, and handed me one of them. "Earth to Dru. You wanna tell me about it?"

"Not really." I hunched my shoulders. "I didn't know that about *nosferatu*. Brain damage?"

"We did this experiment with holy water today and slides of tissue—big fun. If I get a good grade in the basics, I can start doing computer modeling for vampire migrations. Put my math mojo to good use." His eyes lit up, and he sucked at his latte before casting a shrewd glance over my tray. "Want a burger?"

He got to do real classwork while I was stuck in civics. I shrugged. "Not that hungry. I wish I could see who's doing all the cooking."

He nodded, in that way that told me he understood completely. "Yeah, I can't even smell anything through that cloud stuff. It's why I try to stick to fried instead of baked or boiled. Can't quite handle the raw meat yet. But I found out something interesting." The corner of his mouth curled up into one of his bitter little smiles. "Come on. Ask me."

The unwilling grin on my face just wouldn't go away. "Okay, I'm asking. What did you find out?"

"The kids here are troublemakers from wulfen families. Mommy and Daddy Wulfen pack the boys off to Scholas. The girls stay home and are taught to fight by their parents. Isn't that interesting?"

*Wulfen girls get to stay home. So there is more than one Schola.* That answered those questions, at least. "Why are the troublemakers sent here? Is this, like, a reform school?"

He brightened again, like I'd handed him exactly the right question. "Yeah, sort of. Tight discipline, tough love, all that. But there's something else. It's not just the troublemakers, but all boys get sent to Scholas. It's the treaty. An agreement between the ruling wulfen packs and the *djamphir* running the Order. The Order's not the only ones out there fighting, but they are the *official* ones, and they've a big infrastructure in place to keep the kids safe while they're being trained, *and* they promise to support the ruling wulfen families as long as they send a quota of their boys every year. They call it the Tithe."

*Well, that answers that.* "Are there *djamphir* families?"

"Some *djamphir* marry or shack up with normal girls. Most of them live incognito because of the vampire-hunting teams, and a lot of them only stick around long enough to find out if the girl breeds more *djamphir*. Sometimes they don't. You really *should* come to class, Dru."

*Eww. There's a word for guys like that.* "Uh-huh. When they put me into classes that are as cool as yours, I will." I took a cautious sip of the latte. It was a little too hot, but okay. It wasn't like Dad's coffee.

I almost flinched. There it was again.

"So how are you doing?" Graves picked up a burger and took a massive bite. Settled into chewing. It was the same thing he asked me every mealtime.

Every mealtime he was here instead of off running with his new friends, that is.

Across the room, a shoving match erupted between a dark-haired *djamphir* and a tall, skinny wulf. The noise changed for a minute, growls and yips running under the surface of the crowd roar, and a wulf teacher—leather pants, a Kiss T-shirt, and muttonchop whiskers that looked odd on his unlined face—stepped in, sending the wulfen one direction and the *djamphir* boy another. The *djamphir* boy waited until the wulf teacher's back was turned, then made a nasty gesture to all and sundry.

I'd kind of expected that kids who knew about the Real World wouldn't act like jock dipwads. Guess I was wrong.

I let out a sharp breath I hadn't been aware of holding. "Fine." I set the paper cup down. "Wanna go for a walk?"

Graves swallowed hastily. "I've got sparring after this. It's hell. I never knew I could get so sore."

"Sparring practice, huh?" They would teach *him* to fight. No problem. But nobody had time for me. "What are they teaching you?"

He shrugged. "Shanks is teaching me some basic stuff. He says I've got to get over that afraid-of-getting-hit thing. He also says I'd better train hard, because when I go all loco it's going to be training that saves me."

"Shanks?"

His hair flopped over his face as he nodded. "Bobby. That's his nickname—he's tall, especially when he changes. Grasshopper legs."

"Oh." *Aren't you just making friends all over.* "You going out again after classes?"

"Yeah, we're going running. There's going to be a full moon in a couple weeks; some of the kids are going to do their first Change. If I do my parkour practice right—"

"Parkour. That's a funny word." I said it for the hundredth time, and watched him grin for the hundredth time.

His eyes really lit up. He actually looked happy. "You'd really like it. Freerunning is *awesome*. And once they teach you how to fall and leap and stuff, it's super easy."

"But just for wulfen?"

Another shrug. "You could come along. Some of the *djamphir* do it too. The practice, not the actual runs."

"Graves! Hey, Graves!" someone shouted, and he looked up. A curly-headed wulf yelled something across the lunchroom, and Graves whipped him the bird almost faster than the eye could follow. A tide of growling swirled through the room, but it subsided as Graves looked steadily at the wulf in question, his green eyes narrowing.

Back in the Dakotas, Goth Boy would never have done that. He'd been on the bottom of the food chain, same as me. But now, he was actually, sort of, kind of . . . well, popular. Or at least getting there. It helped that he was *loup-garou*—all of the benefits of being wulfen without the crazy part. He didn't get seven feet tall and hairy like an overgrown toupee. Christophe had said it would make him a "prince" here.

And Graves was all over it in a big way.

I stared back down at my tray. Nothing on it looked even remotely edible anymore, so I took another gulp of my latte. It splashed in my stomach, gurgled a bit, and subsided. "What was that?"

He shrugged. "Nothing. They like to tease."

"About . . .?" *About you sitting next to the Typhoid Female?*

"Nothing, Dru. Here." He scooted my tray away and slid a small plate off his, setting it in front of me. A burger, a mound of fries. "It's hot. Eat."

I picked up a fry. He had packets of ketchup, too, and squeezed one out on his plate. We lapsed into silence, a bubble of companionable quiet almost deep enough to swallow the empty chairs ranked along the sides of our table.

Maybe I had some sort of social plague. Besides, I didn't want to talk. Except to Graves, and there was really nothing to say.

I found out I was hungry after all. He'd even dumped pickles on the burger and left off the onions. He must've been sure I'd eat. "Thanks."

"Hey, no problem. First one's free."

I dredged up another unwilling smile. "This isn't the first burger you've gotten me."

"Won't be the last, either. It's the first one I've gotten you today, so just eat, all right? I've got a half hour before I have to be down to get my ass beat up. So talk to me. You get anything ordered to your room finally?"

"Nope." The clothes I was wearing now had shown up in packages with a post office box number on them, a number different than the mail stop on the info sheet in my room. I'd written it down and stashed it in my bag—information like that might be useful later. Someone had guessed at my sizes and done a handy job of it. And the wulfen had taken Graves "into town"—there was something close by, even though this place sat on a few acres of Sticksville—to get kitted out.

But not me. They couldn't have anyone knowing about a *girl* up here at this school.

I wondered where all the money came from, then decided maybe I didn't want to know. I had a roll of cash in my battered black canvas bag, and it's usually no big trick to get more.

But still. I'd never had to get more on my own before. I knew *how*, sure. But Dad had always been there, and—

"Hello? Earth to Dru?" Graves waved a broad, long-fingered hand in front of my face. "Whatcha thinking? It must be deep."

I shrugged. Took another french fry. "I was just wondering where all the money comes from. This isn't a cheap operation they've got going. I wonder if the other schools are bigger. Which still leaves the question of how they pay for this."

Graves studied me sideways for a moment. That adult look was back, as if he was listening to a song I couldn't quite hear. "That's true. I thought about that too. Want me to see if I can find out?"

"Sure." Another fry, and another bite of burger and sip of latte. "Can I come with you? To sparring?"

His pause was long enough that I knew what he'd say. *Probably not a good idea, Dru.*

I wanted to hear him say it, anyway. The bubbling ball of acid inside my chest swelled another few notches. "Why?"

He hunched his shoulders. It was no good—he wasn't as bird-like-thin as he'd been a couple of weeks ago, before he'd gotten bit. He couldn't look small anymore. "No offense, but you like to pick fights too much. And I hate having a chick see me get my ass handed to me. It's a guy thing."

My face felt funny, so I let my hair fall down between us, curtaining my expression. Long hair is good for some things. And since we weren't in Midwest Podunk anymore, my hair had actually been behaving. Go figure. "*This* chick could hand your ass to you, you know."

"One of the teachers would jump me or throw me out of here if we got into it, Dru. Let's not."

"They wouldn't throw you out. I'd leave too." *I'd go just about anywhere to get out of here.* But I couldn't, could I. Not with the vampire king looking for me, right?

"We'd both end up dead." He sounded uncharacteristically serious, and his free hand came up, touched his opposite shoulder. Right where he'd been bitten. He rubbed at it a little, as if it still hurt. "Please, Dru. Let's not do this, okay?"

I dropped the burger. It splatted down on the plate and I pushed my chair back. My lips were greasy. Chewed food sat in my stomach like a bowling ball. "Fine. Let's not. Have fun at sparring."

"Dru—"

But I got up, shoved my chair back under the table, and fled. When he came by my room later, I kept the door closed and locked. He knocked for a while, but then he went away. And I sat there on the bed, fingering my mother's locket and wondering how much longer I was going to be trapped here.

# CHAPTER 4

**T**ap. Taptap. Tap.

I turned over restlessly. Sleep retreated like a cat, on soft little feet. I didn't want it to go, clutched at it with dreaming fingers. I had been dreaming of something important, a warning, owl wings brushing the air around me.

The bed was wide and deep and soft, a maple four-poster with filmy, dusty blue curtains drawn back. The whole room was blue, from the indigo velvet quilt cover to the pale-sky wallpaper figured with gold crosses, to the tinted varnish on the seven bookcases and the heavy cobalt velvet drapes. The rug was sapphire, and thick enough to lose dimes in even though it was older than me. The window behind it didn't have iron bars, because it opened onto a little private garden completely enclosed by high, blank walls—three stories down, with a barred door I could reach only by going out my door, making three turns, and going down two flights of stairs.

A lot of effort to spend if I wanted to walk outside into a raw, blustery little plot of ground with gravel paths and leafless, pinched-looking things that might have been rosebushes—in spring, that is. If I really, truly wanted to wander around thorny stabbing vines under a gray sky.

Instead of bars, there were heavy iron shutters, with little hearts and crosses punched out in even rows marching down their lengths.

I left those open. When they were closed, the entire room got still and, well, dead.

My eyes opened slowly. The warning retreated. Had it been Gran? Whoever it was was trying to tell me something very important.

*Taptaptap. Tap. Taptap.*

A cool bath of dread started at my scalp and slid down the rest of me. The sound was familiar—fingers drumming impatiently on glass. Memory mixed with dreaming, conspired to pull me under as the pillow turned hard and hot against my cheek.

*There was a zombie at my back door. Its eyes swung up, and they were blue, the whites already clouding with the egg-rot of death. Its jaw was a mess of meat and frozen blood; something had eaten half its face. Its fingertips, already worn down to bony nubs, scraped against the window. Flesh hung in strips from its hand, and my stomach turned over hard. Black mist rose at the corners of my vision, and the funny rushing sound in my head sounded like a jet plane taking off.*

*I'd know that zombie anywhere. Even if he was dead and mangled, his eyes were the same. Blue as winter ice, fringed with pale lashes.*

*The zombie's gaze locked with mine. It cocked its head like it had just heard a faraway noise.*

*I let out a dry barking sound and my back hit the wall next to the hallway, smacking my hip against a stack of boxes.*

*Dad bunched up his rotting fist, the meat chewed away from finger bones by something I didn't want to imagine or even think about, and punched his way through the window.*

I sat straight up, gasping for air, fighting free of the heavy blankets. Threadbare sateen sheets slid sweat-slick against my skin, turned into wet fingers clutching me at hip and ankle. My fists balled up and I hit nothing but air, the scream dying in my throat. The soft brush of feather-muffled wings filled the room for a moment, but Gran's owl—the bird that had sat on her windowsill while she died, the bird that had warned me of danger and led me to Dad's truck a week and a half ago—didn't show up.

*Something is very wrong here, Dru. You should beware.* But the voice receded as soon as I lunged into wakefulness, and I found I was clutching my mother's locket in one damp hand.

I blinked again, trying to separate dream from reality.

*Tap. Taptap.* The sound was real. And it was coming from my bedroom window.

I rolled out of the bed, hit the floor hard. Teeth clicking together—lucky I didn't have my tongue between them. My hands were too clumsy and slow, patting the top of the nightstand for a weapon. At home I'd have a gun. But here, there was nothing but the silver-loaded stiletto—all the weapons were signed into the sparring chapel or the armory, including the gun I'd had when they rescued me. Except for the switchblade that had been forgotten in my pocket, the one I didn't tell anyone about.

It just seemed like a good idea not to, that's all.

I pressed the button for the suicide spring. The blade snicked free and the tapping stopped.

I blinked, fisted sleep-crusties away with my free hand. Thin swords of pale winter daylight shifted position as whatever was outside my window moved.

Daytime. Of course it was—that's when the Schola sleeps, because that's when it's safe. Or at least, safe from *nosferatu*. Some of the older werwulfen students haunt the grounds during the day, running patrols in human and not-so-human form. I thought maybe a few of the *djamphir* teachers did too, but I hadn't bothered to ask. It had seemed enough just to sleep during the day and be up all night, even when my body clock had a little trouble adjusting.

My breath turned stale in my throat. I crouched beside my bed, weighing my options.

*Click.* The window catch snicked up. The stiletto turned itself in my hand, blade flat against my wrist and forearm. Silver loaded along the blade would hurt just about anything evil, and I would at least give a good lick or two in any fight. I took in a deep lungful of still, dusty air, my heart crawling up into my throat but a strange sense of calm descending on me.

Everything else in this place left me at sea. But something weird threatening to crawl into my bedroom window?

I knew how to deal with this. It was *familiar.* Once in Louisiana we'd tangled with a voodoo king, and we'd had a hex climb in through the window carrying roach spirits. But I'd seen Gran's owl before and told Dad, so when the window had broken with a silvery tinkling sound and the first huge roaches spilled through, we were ready.

When whatever-it-was came through the window, *I* was going to be ready.

This was what I'd been waiting for, without even realizing it. Everything else was just treading water. This, with my heart in my throat and my entire body suddenly awake and tingling with fear, was real.

And I didn't have to think about being alone or lonely when I was afraid.

I was still crouching there, my tank top twisted and the boxers I'd been sleeping in crawling up my crack, when I realized the thin blue lines of energy running through the walls weren't sparking and crackling. It had been a job to do the warding without Gran's rowan wand, but I'd managed. The wand was, after all, only a symbol—as Gran had endlessly reminded me. *Ain't nearly as good as the will behind it, Dru. You just remember that.*

She was always saying something like that. *You just remember, Dru. Just remember.*

That was the trouble. I was starting to get stuff I'd rather forget stuck in my head on repeat. Stuff like a zombie at my kitchen door, or a small dark space full of stuffed animals and the smell of drowsy little-girl fear.

What would wards not react to? There was a short list of things. I began running through them frantically.

The window opened. A breath of chill, rain-laden air puffed past the curtains, and they separated just enough for him to shimmy through. His boots landed on the carpet, the window closed with a slight squeak, and he turned around. Weak gray daylight touched his sleek dark hair, the blond highlights slipping through and retreating like fingers combing the silk-heavy strands.

His eyes swept the room once, then settled on me. Burning winter-blue eyes, glowing in the half-dark. He was in a hip-length, rock-star leather jacket, and he passed one hand back through his hair, shaking it down as water flung itself free. That cold blue gaze came to rest on me, and I suddenly smelled apple pies baking.

"Hello, Dru." His mouth curled up in a grin. I had forgotten how the planes and angles of his face all worked together, making him not handsome but just . . . *right*. How his eyebrows slanted up a little, and how his shaggy haircut looked expensive and relaxed all at once. "Have you been a good girl? Your guardian angel wants to know."

I stared at Christophe, my mouth open slightly, and realized how ridiculous I probably looked just as he slid the curtains closed and the room turned dark.

"Jesus," I whispered. "Where have you *been*?" It was about the most useless question in the world, and it came straight out of my mouth.

"Out and around, around and about." He paced across the room with long, springing strides, stopped at the door, and touched the chain lock, the deadbolt, and the bolt I'd shot home before lying down to sleep. "Very good, barring your door and warding your walls. You're not such a careless little bird now."

*I wasn't ever careless!* But there were more important things to open my mouth about. Every single question I hadn't been able to get answered in the past week and a half fought for place in the line, but they lost out to two inconsequentials. "Where's my truck? And all my clothes?"

Well, maybe not *inconsequential*, but I could've asked something else. Like, *Why didn't you tell me about the bloodhunger? Or, Was this my mother's room? Or even, Why does it seem like they were waiting for me here? What did you tell them? Why won't they teach me anything real?*

Christophe turned on one heel, surveyed the rest of the room, and finally looked back down at me again. I still crouched right by my bed, the knife ready in my fist. "I have taken good care of everything of yours, little bird. The truck is in a storage facility downstate under another name, safe and sound." He raised one elegant eyebrow, slightly. "They didn't give you any clothes? Or an expense account?"

My cheeks turned so hot I'm surprised they didn't glow. I straightened, suppressing the urge to pick at my boxers. Fixing a wedgie is *so* not the way to look competent. "Of course they did. But I was *sleeping*."

"All safe in a little blue nest. I wonder why they put you here?" He shook himself again, water spattering. He was soaked. "Did you miss me?"

*Oh, for chrissake.* I set the knife down on the elegant little night-stand and pulled the hem of my tank top down. "I'm going to get you a towel, and I'm going to get some clothes on. Then we can—"

One very blue glance, before he pushed his hair back with stiff fingers and gave the rest of the room a once-over. "A towel would be nice, but you don't need to bother getting dressed. You're not going anywhere."

Silence filled the room. He looked steadily at me, I looked back, and the flush died on my cheeks. The smell of apple pies filled up the space between us, and I suddenly was pretty glad I wasn't bleeding anywhere, or even scabbed up. I knew how strong and fast Christophe was. If he decided to go all bloodhungry on me, what chance did I have?

Which all of a sudden made me think of something else. What if Irving had been taking it easy on me? Or if he hadn't, and Christophe was stronger, why the hell *was* he that way?

How old was this *djamphir* who'd rescued me? He was pretty obviously an "advisor," and they tend to be older.

Like, *way* older.

"There's a lot of things you didn't tell me." I tried not to sound accusing. I was suddenly very aware of the tank top clinging to me and cool air touching exposed skin. My legs felt very long, very skinny, and pretty unshaved.

Hey, I wear jeans all the time. You couldn't pay me to wax, and who has time to drag a razor over everything every day? When we'd lived below the Mason-Dixon I'd kept up with it, but moving up with the polar bears and finding out I was a lot deeper in the Real

World than I'd ever guessed didn't leave me with a lot of time for hair removal.

I thought I might make some time from now on, though. My cheeks were so hot I was amazed steam wasn't rising off the skin.

"Dru." He took two steps toward me, his boots crushing the carpet. "I didn't have time for a lot of niceties. You realize that, right?"

I crossed my arms over my chest. Jeez, it was cold in here all of a sudden. And had he always smelled this good? Was it a cologne? *Eau de Christmas Pie?* "I guess," I said finally. There hadn't exactly been time for a lot of note taking, but he still could have told me a few things.

Would I have believed him? All I had to do now was look around this pretty little room and think of the bars on the other windows. Or of the first Restriction, when the bell jangled and everyone leapt for their stations, and Dylan dragged me up to this room and told me to lock the door.

*But why?* I'd wanted to know, and Dylan had showed his teeth, fangs curving down as his aspect slid over him.

*Because this isn't a drill,* he'd said. *And you are what we're going to die for if they break through the outer defenses. Now lock your door.*

Christophe shook his head again. Water flew like jewels. "A towel *would* be nice, Dru."

"Yeah, sure. Fine." I stamped barefoot toward the door between two bookshelves. I had my own bathroom, while the boys in the dorms had to make do with communal ones. And I still couldn't figure out who cleaned it, though it wasn't as old-grungy as the caves downstairs. And I don't make much of a mess, either.

Living with Dad taught me that much, at least.

The towels were blue too, and a little threadbare. Bright blue like a summer sky. The color of our truck, the color of Dad's eyes—

warmer than Christophe's, even when bloodshot after a night of sipping Beam, or when he was in what he called a "damn bad mood."

I had to stop and take a deep breath. Right next to the squirrelly panic-feeling of being left behind again was a hot wash of relief, as vivid as oil paint. It was a familiar feeling—the relief I felt each time Dad showed back up to collect me.

What did I have to be relieved about? Nothing except the fact that *someone* had come back for me. When you've spent your life waiting to be collected like a library book or a piece of luggage, the intensity of that relief gets a little ridiculous.

But at least Christophe hadn't forgotten about me.

I grabbed a bath sheet and stamped back out. Christophe hadn't moved. He was staring at the empty bookcases with a peculiar look on his face. I'd tried to make them look a little *less* empty by arranging some of the knickknacks—including a blue glass elephant with its trunk lifted—on different shelves. My books, my CDs, my mattresses—everything was in the truck. Nothing here was mine. It didn't even smell right—when a place hasn't been lived in for a while, you can tell. The air itself gets stale. Moving into a place where nobody's been breathing for a while is like trying on shoes that don't fit quite right and hoping they'll wear in.

Shoes never do. I've never spent long enough in a house that felt this unfriendly, I don't know if they ever relax.

Still, I was beginning to call a truce with some of the knickknacks. They'd stopped looking like prissy little disapproving things and started to look a little easier with the idea of me. And when I came back after going down to the caf, at least it smelled a little bit more like a hotel each time instead of a crypt.

"Here." I tossed the towel at Christophe, who caught it with a clean, economical motion. "Start talking."

"What if I just came to see you?" He scrubbed at his hair, wiped his face and hands. The jacket squeaked a little. His hands were wet, and I saw deep red, dripping lines crisscrossing his palms and scoring his knuckles before he shook his fingers out. They were pale and perfect again when he held one up and examined it critically, exhaling.

My heart made a funny flipping movement. "Oh, please. You wouldn't have waited if you really wanted to see me that bad." *And you wouldn't be sneaking in through my window if everything was all right.* I found a big plaid flannel shirt Graves had gotten on one of his shopping runs and shrugged into it, my fingers fumbling with the buttons. It smelled vaguely of cigarette smoke, boy, and harsh deodorant soap. Another odd flush of relief spilled through me. "Where have you really been? Driving here? Are you okay?"

"I'm fine. Touched that you care." He rubbed behind his ear and grinned like a cat. The blond highlights sliding through his hair were darkened by the wet, but still visible. He shucked out of the jacket, too, and looked for a place to put it. I pointed at the creaking office chair in front of the computer and he hung it up, muscle moving under his thin black V-neck sweater.

I looked away at the drapes pulled closed over the window. It was pretty dark in here, and I was kind of happy about that.

But there was plenty not to be happy about in the dark, too. I flicked the bedside lamp on—an antique brass number with a blue stained-glass shade—and turned to find Christophe watching me. His eyes were even bluer than the room, but oddly bleached.

Winter eyes.

"How old are you, anyway?" I didn't cross my arms, but I did pick up the stiletto again. I did not try to push the blade back in, just held it loosely.

It made me feel better. My hair was all messed up and my boxers were on weird, but at least I felt equipped to handle this if I kept a grip on the knife.

*Why? He's not going to hurt me.* The relief burst inside my chest again, but under it was the bald edge of fear. Now I'd seen what a *djamphir* could do.

It was stupid not to be frightened of them.

Christophe kept very still. He was staring at my breastbone, where my mother's locket glistened. When I moved a little bit, pulling the top of the flannel shirt closed, he finally examined my face instead. My cheeks were hot as stove burners.

"Just a little older than you, Dru." He flicked a quick glance at the rest of the room again, like he expected there to be someone hiding in the shadows. "This reminds me of your mother's room. She was the last *svetocha* we managed to save." *There,* his tone said. *Does that answer the question you were really asking?* He shook the towel and glanced around the room again. A breath of pie scent touched my cheek. "She had books, lots of them. They're probably in a holding room. Waiting for you."

My hand made a tiny movement, wanting to touch Mom's locket. I forced it down. "They won't train me." It burst out in a cascade I tried not to make into a whine. "You said they would. No combat training or *anything*, they treat me like I'm—"

"Glass?" He tilted his head. His rain-wet skin was perfect, like damp silk. "Like you're fragile? Precious? There are worse things, *moj ptaszku*."

*Not from where I'm sitting.* "Look, I'm not going to get any better if they keep treating me like—"

I didn't even see him move. One moment he was all the way across the room, with the towel in his hands and his head cocked.

The next, he was nose to nose with me, a warm draft smelling of apples and spice pushing at my hair, kissing my cheeks.

I half-fell back, slashing up with the knife. Warm steel bands closed around my wrist and *twisted*. My arm shrieked with pain, the knife plucked from my suddenly nerveless fingers, and my knees buckled. His other hand clamped at the back of my neck, under my hair. My shoulder wrenched, screaming as it twisted in a way it wasn't built for.

*Move it, Dru!* Dad's voice, filling my head. There was only one way out, and I took it—bending forward, kicking up to roll, my shoulder giving a high, hard pop of pain as Christophe's fingers loosened. My bare foot hit his knee, heel grinding in. It was a good kick, and he let out a short, sharp sound like a laugh.

I hit the floor and rolled, came up in a crouch. The knife was nowhere to be seen, and Christophe bent his leg a little, shaking it out. He should have looked ridiculous on one leg, but instead he looked like a cat flicking one paw, the rest of him perfectly poised.

*Stay down. If he comes at you, you've got a better chance of shaking him off.* I flicked a glance at the door. No help there—it would cost me too many precious seconds to unlock, unbar, unchain it.

"Good," he said. "Looking for escape, since I'm too fast. Very good. But I'm already here and you have no weapons, *moj mały ptaszku*. What do you do?"

*No weapons my ass. There's always a weapon.* I cast around, found nothing but knickknacks for throwing, and heard the muffled beat of feathered wings again. They brushed the air of the room. My hair lifted on a faint breeze that seemed to come from nowhere, and I went very still.

I half-expected to see Gran's owl. But nothing happened. I watched Christophe carefully.

"There it is." He nodded. His hair had gone slick and dark as his aspect rose to the surface. You could either have a weak aspect or a strong one, and the ones that came out "externalized" in another form—usually an animal nobody normal could see—were the strongest of all.

It was also the part the bloodhunger came from. A deep, dark place that drove you crazy when you smelled the red stuff.

Christophe sank down, slowly, until he was crouching. One hand was tented on the carpet for balance, and his gaze never left mine. "You're very close to blooming, Dru. You have a certain natural facility, especially when you're in a high emotional state. But you can't count on that. It could be that you haven't been allowed into sparring sessions because they're designing a program for you, or importing teachers. Or there could be other reasons."

Something told me he was more in the "other reasons" camp. Still not telling me what he knew, or what he guessed. "Dylan said it was because you weren't back yet." I didn't relax. Neither did he. The tension was a rope between us, a nameless heat through my bones.

"Ah, Dylan. How is he?" The smile that spread over Christophe's face wasn't nice at all. It was the grin of a cat in front of a mouse hole. "Did he tell you he was in love with her?"

*Huh?* "What?"

"We all were. She was a moment of light, your mother. Sergej stole her away, though not before she left us of her own will. We were all . . ." He straightened slowly. The stiletto spun around his fingers, silver-loaded blade blurring in a complex series of half-arcs as his hand flicked. "That's enough for today, Dru. You can stand up."

I stayed where I was. This was more than I'd gotten out of anyone, and besides, I didn't trust that he wouldn't jump me again just to prove a point.

I should have been more scared. But I wasn't, despite the fact that my heart was pounding hard enough to force its way out through my throat-pulse. My breath came in short, sharp little puffs, and all of me tingled with adrenaline.

It was the first time since I'd gotten here that I felt actually awake and reasonably alive, instead of numb and terrified.

"Stubborn as usual." He sighed, tossed the knife back on the nightstand. It clattered against the lamp's base. "I have about a half hour until I can leave. I won't waste it tossing you around the room."

"Gee, thanks." I couldn't sound more sarcastic, but I was willing to give it a try. My breathing evened out. "What are you here for, then? Tea and cookies?" My mouth wanted to water. He smelled like cookies. Cinnamon ones, with dabs of apple-pie filling.

But my stomach had shrunk to the size of a dime. Climbing in through the window plus "a half hour until I can leave" didn't equal anything good. I had that much figured out, at least.

Every speck of amusement was gone. He looked a lot older, suddenly, even though his face hadn't changed. "To find you and make sure you're safe."

*Well, isn't that nice of you.* My heart gave another pounding leap. I made my knees work, pushing the rest of me slowly up. My shoulder ached fiercely. "They won't even let me go outside alone."

"It's not outside that worries me. Much." Christophe let out a sigh. The sweater clung to him, and his jeans were soaked through, especially the knees. Which brought up another question.

"How the hell did you get in the window, anyway? And what are you worried about in here?"

"A traitor." He looked at the bed, visibly decided he'd better not sit on it, and stretched his hands in a curiously helpless motion. "Someone who gave away the location of an Order-approved safe house, one even I wasn't supposed to know about, to Sergej. Which, incidentally, made it possible for him to lie in wait for both of us."

I tried not to shiver at the thought. Christophe flying through the wreckage of the wall on the truck's hood, just like Superman. Graves behind the wheel, terrified and hanging on. And me, almost drowning in Sergej's dark, oily eyes. "But we kicked his ass, right? Even though someone gave that away. And—"

Christophe shook his head, and for a moment he looked sad. He moved and I flinched, but it was just to walk over to the computer chair and drop down as it squawked slightly. "It was a draw, Dru. Barely that. If it hadn't been daytime, if Juan and the others hadn't believed me rather than a control directive, if your friend hadn't trusted me, if you hadn't already fought Sergej with more skill and power than anyone expected, if, if, *if*. You would have died." The snarl that crossed his face was there and gone in an instant, so fast I might have imagined it. "I would have lost you."

He said it like it had just occurred to him.

Another uncomfortable silence filled the room up, pushed against the curtains and made the rain-filtered light seem dimmer. I stared at him.

"And you're not supposed to be here." He took a deep breath. "I assumed you'd be sent to the main Schola. I don't know how you ended up in this satellite, among . . . well, this type."

Well, we'd already answered that question—this wasn't the only Schola. But what was he going on about? "What type? Wulfen? There are *djamphir* here, too, you know."

"Never mind. Maybe . . . they . . . decided you'd be safer at a smaller school. And it does make things easier for me."

"What kind of things?" I sounded suspicious even to myself. My cheeks were on fire again, and my knees didn't feel too steady.

"Things like watching over my careless little bird until she blooms. This Schola is fairly well known to me. No, your mother was never here."

*Thanks, Christophe. I didn't ask.* But it felt sneakingly good to *know*. Another one of those uncomfortable quiet spaces between us. I tried not to hunch my shoulders. "What else haven't you told me?"

"Nothing important. Nothing critical. But you want me to talk?" His chin tipped down and he stared at me. "So, *skowroneczko moja*, come sit at my feet and listen. We don't have much time. And I have something to give you."

# CHAPTER 5

**sat on my** bed, my arms wrapped around my knees. Sometimes I moved so my legs didn't fall asleep. Most of the time, though, I just sat and stared at the thin gray daylight coating the window, sleet beating in waves now. He'd gone out through the window and just . . . vanished, even though I ran across the room and stuck my head out like an idiot, peering after him.

Christophe left behind the fading smell of baking apple pies, wet footprints on the carpet, a soaking towel with spots of rust, a sodden computer chair . . . and the two wooden things.

*Practice swords?* I touched one handle. It was warm, the wood worn down and oiled, dark with use. Fine-grained, and very hard.

No. Christophe had touched one of them, just the way I was touching it now, running his fingers gently over the curves. *These are* malaika, *made of hawthorn. They are not made for practice. These are for killing things that walk the night, and they were made for a svetocha's hands. Very few djam-phir are skilled in the use of the Kouroi's traditional blade anymore.*

*But what good are wooden swords?* Long, slightly curving, oddly leaf-shaped blades. They looked like they belonged in a high-budget chop-saki movie, the kind I'd seen a hundred times on late-late-night cable while waiting for Dad to come back.

I winced at the thought. It was much easier and nicer to think of Christophe's measured, even voice.

*Hawthorn is deadly to* nosferatu, *and even deadlier when wielded by a Kouroi. How much more deadly, then, when wielded by you? Be good, and you'll learn to use them. When it's safer, and I come back.*

And he'd left them here. Weapons. They might have been wood, but their edges were bastard sharp. To prove it, Christophe had sliced off a little bit of his hair. The small lock of blond-streaked brown lay on the nightstand next to the stiletto. A *keepsake*, he'd said. *So you know I'll return.*

And I'd blushed, again, like an idiot. It was absurdly comforting to know that *someone* would be coming back for me. Now that I'd lost everything—every*one*—else.

I stared down at the swords, the hot flush dying in my cheeks, sliding back down my throat to settle in my chest next to the acid bubble. The locket was a warm spot on my breastbone.

Pale gray light ran over every curve. They looked like they belonged here on the bed, against the rucked-up velvet of the quilt cover. More than I did, at least. There was a fresh scab on my unshaved knee, a rash of red rug burn on my other leg.

As the afternoon wended toward evening, I got up. My legs were a little unsteady from sitting curled up on the bed for so long. I carried one of the wooden swords into the bathroom. There was a mirror over the sink, a nice big one. The light in here was good too, warm gold from the dusty bulbs. It ran over my tangled hair and the hollows under my eyes.

Just one average teenage girl, rangy and awkward. Cheekbones too big for her face, blue eyes a different shade than Christophe's. My eyes were all Dad's, right down to the faint lavender lines in the irises. My hair was Mom's, but without the sleek glossiness of her ringlets. The curls tangled every which way, but they weren't the halo of frizz they used to be.

I wasn't breaking out anymore. The bath, I guess. I couldn't even feel good about that. I was too dead-pale. Between the rings under my eyes and the two fever spots on my cheeks, I looked like a ghost.

And I should know. I've seen a few.

I lifted the sword, tipped its curve down, back up. "*Malaika*," I whispered. It *did* look like it belonged here. With the velvet and the satin and the chipped stone.

But not me. The circles under my eyes were the remains of bruises. My upper lip was too thin, lower lip too fat, my nose too long, and my hair was hopeless. The plaid shirt was a glaring mixture of red and yellow and green, and my sleeping boxers had penguins on them. They were still crawling up my ass crack.

Yeah. I'd never win any prizes.

I was tough, though. Wasn't I? I could spot Dad, no matter what he was benching. I'd gotten Graves away from a crazed wulfen and out of a deserted mall, through a snowstorm, and faced down Sergej on my own. So what if I'd had to be rescued? I'd still gone a couple rounds with him, shot him in the head, and managed to come out still breathing.

*Dad. And Gran. And Mom. All gone.*

Something too hot and sharp to be tears rose up in my throat. I was the only one left.

*If you are a good girl, go to classes no matter how boring, and keep your ears open; I'll teach you how to use these. Your mother was a master of the* malaika. *I don't know why she left hers behind.* He had touched a hilt again, his fingers oddly gentle and his mouth drawn down bitterly. *I have the pair she used in a safe place. When you're ready, they're yours.*

My breath hitched in my throat. I let myself remember my mother. It was the most painful of all, because . . . well, just because.

Her hair always smelled of warmth and fresh perfume. Her heart-shaped face and the prettiness of even her smallest gestures. Her dark eyes and Dad's picture of her kept in his wallet, with a shiny place rubbed in the plastic over her face.

That shiny place was still there, though the picture was gone. If I dug out Dad's billfold, I would find the photo missing and the place where I always ran my thumb while getting out a twenty or a fifty would glare at me. If I stared long enough, I could probably even see the curves and lines of her face from a long time ago.

*Oh God.* I pushed away the memory that wanted to rise to the surface, but not nearly quick enough. You can't ever stop thinking something quick enough. Something that hurts always gets the knife in too fast for you to slam a lid on it and shove it away.

*We're going to play the game, Dru.* She'd hidden me in a closet and gone out to fight Sergej. Dad had left me at the house and gone to face Sergej alone. Gran had tried to stay with me, but old age had taken her. Her body had failed right out from under her, and I could tell she'd hated leaving me. She'd held on all through summer, but the first cold wind coming up the valley had been too much for her, and the hospital . . .

There it was again, a hurtful thought. I let out a long, slow breath, as if I was working through a cramp. It didn't help. This cramp was on the inside, someplace no deep breathing could touch.

I wasn't as pretty as Mom, or as smart as Dad. I wasn't good at everything I touched, like either of them. I was just one scrawny punk-ass girl.

I met my own gaze in the mirror. I didn't look like I should be holding the wooden sword. I clasped it awkwardly in one hand, away from my body like a baseball bat I was afraid might bite me.

*Just me. Just Dru.*

The girl in the mirror was smiling a little, which I suppose meant I was, even though my face felt frozen. I cautiously put my hand down, let the sword dangle.

I stamped back to the bed and slid the swords underneath the dust ruffle with Dad's billfold. I wasn't supposed to let anyone know I had them. I wasn't supposed to tell anyone I'd seen Christophe—but there was one person I *had* to tell. If Graves wasn't too busy running around with his new friends, if I could get him alone, he could . . . what could he do?

Was it even fair to dump this on him too and ask him to help me figure it out and deal with it?

Most of all, I wasn't supposed to let anyone know I had a job now, one Christophe had given me. And that was trying to find out who at the Schola had wanted me dead bad enough to betray Christophe as well.

*So I'm not pretty or smart or any other hundred things. But I'm stubborn. And tough.*

It was time to start using what I had.

# CHAPTER 6

Cafeteria noise washed over me in waves. Catcalls, conversations, laughter—everyone was at breakfast. I stabbed at my scrambled eggs with a fork. The pancakes had been steaming hot and fresh; now they just sat there.

Like me, just sitting here. It was just after dusk, class started in forty-five minutes, and I was really feeling the urge to go back to bed. I mean, I've never loved school, and I was determined to start *doing* something, even if it was putting up with the stupid remedial classes.

But getting up and getting dressed, braiding my hair back, and dealing with the cafeteria was really testing that determination. My shoulder still ached from the little tango with Christophe, but not as bad as it could have. Those baths worked wonders.

A shadow fell over me. I was hard-put not to twitch. But it was just a young blond wulfen with dark eyes and a gentle face. He was pale and gripped his tray so hard his knuckles were white. He looked about ready to break something from sheer nervousness.

I seconded that emotion.

His mouth moved, but I couldn't hear whatever he was saying under the noise. The screen of steam that the food came through hissed underneath all the crowd sounds.

"What?" My fork clattered on my tray. He flinched, shoulders hunching under a blue cable-knit sweater. He was built slight and narrow-hipped for a wulfen, but long corded muscle stood out on his forearms beneath the pushed-up sweater cuffs.

"Dibs," he croaked. "Name's Dibs."

I closed my mouth with a snap. I've seen shy all over the United States, and this kid had a bad case of it. My conscience poked at me, hard.

I pushed out the chair next to me. "Hi. I'm Dru."

The way his face lit up, you'd have thought I'd just given him a winning lottery ticket. He dropped down, and his tray held a huge pile of raw meat slopping over the edge of a plate. I saw two T-bone steaks and a mess of hamburger, and my stomach turned over. I swallowed and reached for my coffee.

"Hi." He scratched at his leg through his jeans and grinned. White teeth gleamed, and his hair was a buttergloss sheen. Girls would probably love him—he had the big-eyed look of a nervous deer. "I, um. Hi."

"Hey." I took a mouthful of scrambled eggs. Tried not to look at his plate. "So what is it?"

"What?" He looked genuinely confused.

"Nobody wants to talk to me. Why are you here?" I was glad of the company, especially since Graves was nowhere in sight. But I've been the new girl in schools all over the country. You don't ever trust the first boy who wanders up to you. Or at least, you learn to look for what they might be thinking they can get out of the new kid in town.

Of course, Graves had been the first one to approach me back in the Dakotas. I wasn't sure what to think about that. It had been lucky, I guess. Maybe.

Not so lucky for him, since he'd got bitten and ended up here.

"You looked lonely." He hunched over his plate, his long fingers almost but not quite touching the meat. "And they bet I wouldn't do it, since I'm sub. Sometimes you have to show them they're wrong, even the doms."

"Sub?" *Doms? Oh boy.*

"I, um, was born that way. Born, not bitten, and born sub, too." He blinked. "You don't know about that, huh? Graves said you knew a lot, but not some stuff."

"He did, huh?" I shoved in another bite of egg. Dibs relaxed a little. "What else did Graves say?"

"That if anyone messed with you, he'd call 'em out. He got into it the first day he got here, proved he was dom. He sleeps in a top bunk." Even though he was showing his teeth, Dibs's expression was gentle. He scooped up one of the steaks and bit into it, teeth scissoring effortlessly through.

*Isn't that interesting.* "And you don't?" I played with a line of syrup on my plate, dragging fork tines through it and swirling.

"There're lots of beds, but not every wulf sleeps in one. It's complicated." He took another massive bite. The meat splorched a little, and I felt distinctly queasy.

*Deal with it, Dru.*

But I remembered a werwulf's teeth tearing through flesh and grinding down on Graves's shoulder, and the thought made me feel green all over. Not a nice springtime green, either.

"Hey, dogboy!" A yell from a passing *djamphir*—one of Irving's friends, a slim dark-haired kid in a red shirt and jeans, slouching past with that eerie gracefulness. "Put your dish on the floor!" He sneered a little as he passed, elegantly.

Dibs hunched up even further, and the ball of acid inside my chest boiled up as if something had been dropped in it. I slid my chair back, my legs tensing, but Dibs's hand came down on my wrist with surprising strength.

"Just let it go," he whispered under the crowd noise. "It doesn't mean anything."

"It *does*." I tried to pull my hand away. "It means something."

A ripple ran through the caf. I turned my head, keeping the *djamphir* in sight. He dropped down at Irving's table, one of the prime spots of cafeteria real estate, and laughed. His friends were laughing too. My braid bumped my back as I tried to pull away from Dibs again.

*Mark.* Memory served up the *djamphir's* name just as my free hand curled into a fist. *I'm pretty sure his name is Mark. He even* looks *like a Mark. Go figure.*

"Wow. You really do care." He laughed, a shaky little sound. "Just let it roll off. I'm not upset, see? You'll just make trouble if you say anything. Keep your head down."

The tension simmered down a notch, but it didn't leave me. My shoulders were a rigid bar under my T-shirt and hoodie, and I'd lost every ounce of appetite I'd had.

"You don't argue with them." He let go of me, finger by finger. "Not over a wulf. They won't make it hard for you, get it? They'll make it hard for me. But don't worry, the doms will take care of it. Sooner or later. They always do."

"Jesus." I let out a long, shaky breath. It had bothered me before, the dismissive way Christophe treated Graves; as if he was somehow tainted. Somehow *less*. It bothered me here, too—the *djamphir* were the top of the food chain.

I'd thought things would be different somehow. I'd thought the Real World didn't play petty bullshit high school games. But here, it was just the same old thing. It was depressing. Could you ever get away from it?

But picking a fight the day I'd decided to turn over a new leaf wasn't a good idea. I should start this out right.

Dibs was watching me anxiously, a vertical line between his golden eyebrows as they wrinkled together. He looked like a retriever I'd seen once, a sweet dog that lived in a trailer park outside Pensacola. The way he tilted his head and chewed at the same time reinforced the impression.

*Scratch behind his ears, who's a good boy?* I swallowed hard, disgusted at the thought. I wasn't like them, the dismissive, pretty *djamphir* boys. I'd always been an outsider.

I stabbed at my pancakes like I was stabbing at the face of stupidity. "Do they all act that way? The *djamphir?*"

"Yeah. I mean, except you. Graves said you were different. He said you—"

"Hey, Dru." Graves yanked out the chair on my other side and dropped into it. He smelled like cold air and cigarette smoke, his long black coat still carrying a chill from outside. A bloom of red up high on his cheekbones did good things for him, and his earring glittered. His eyes were sparkling, too. "Dibs. Nice to see you, man."

Dibs shut up so fast I was surprised he didn't lose a chunk of his tongue. He busied himself with tearing at the steak and chewing, with a guilty hangdog look.

"So you're a dom, huh? Nice." I stabbed my pancakes again. "Kinky."

"You're the one who ties people up, babe." Graves's gaze flicked past me, touched Dibs, and returned. "What happened?"

Dibs shrugged, took another mouthful.

My tone was hard and dismissive. "Some *djamphir* asshole just catcalling, that's all." Stab, stab, the fork hit the plate hard. "I'm about due for class."

"I'll walk you—we've got first period together. Glad you decided to show up." He looked smug. Insufferably smug. His smile was a wide V, so big a dimple came out on his left cheek. He wasn't so baby-faced anymore, and was that dark stubble spreading up from his chin? His hair was starred with little beads of moisture—it must have been raining outside.

Yeah. He got to go outside and smoke, and then come back in and—

*Jesus.* I grabbed the edge of the table with both hands. The fork mashed itself against fake wood. My teeth gritted together so hard my jaw ached. I'd been mad before, plenty of times. Kid-mad. This was a new feeling, and it swallowed me whole. I actually saw little sparkles of red around the corners of my field of vision, and my arm ached with the need to punch that fucking smile right off his face. Arm? No, my whole *body* vibrated with the urge.

"Uh-oh." Dibs's chair scraped as he pushed back. "Graves? She smells red."

I shook. The wave of trembling passed through me. What the hell was I thinking? It was Graves. He was pretty much my only friend here. Was I really going to go ballistic on him? Over *what*?

"She's fine." Graves just looked at me. His face didn't seem nearly as smug now. Just thoughtful, and familiar. "She gets a little antsy sometimes, but she's okay. Right, Dru?"

And just like that, the rage evaporated, leaving only the sour little red-hot bubble in my chest. I found my voice. "Right. Antsy." *Where did that come from? What was that?* "Jesus." It came out sounding breathy and exhausted.

The cafeteria was curiously hushed. Tension ran under the surface of that quiet before my ears popped and I relaxed a little bit more.

"You're wound pretty tight," was all Graves said. "Hey, you should eat something other than that. Want some bacon?"

*Christophe visited me. I have to talk to you.* The words died on my lips. Dibs crunched down on something next to me. It sounded like bone, and my stomach did a funny sideways jigging movement. "I, um, I'll just stick with toast." To prove it, I picked up a half-slice of sourdough covered in butter. It was cold, but I put it in my mouth and bit down. My teeth were tingling. It was a weird feeling, like they were waking up from novocaine. I mean, I've never had a cavity, but I can imagine.

Graves nodded. A shadow of relief slid through his green eyes. "'Kay. Hey, we're going out for burgers again after classes. Want me to bring you some?"

*No. It'll be cold when you get here. I don't want any grease, thanks.* "Maybe a milkshake one of these days. I haven't had a milkshake in a while."

Not since he'd handed me one in a mall food court and asked me what was wrong. The memory pushed through my head, tinted with panic, and I let out another shaky sigh.

"You got it. If you're still awake when I get in." His hair fell over his face as he nodded, the dead-black strings looking normal on him. His skin had cleared up, the caramel coloring nice and even. "Sure you don't want any bacon?"

*Yeah, if I'm still awake when you condescend to come back? No thanks.* I took another hurried bite of toast as Dibs cracked down on another bone and made a happy, humming little sound. I suppose I should have been ready for that. It was one thing to feel lonely because nobody would sit with you. It was another thing entirely to have a wulf chowing down right next door. "Nah, I'm good. Really." I made the words come out through a mouthful of cold soggy toast and congealed butter, and told myself I'd better start eating my food while it was hot.

Maybe I shouldn't tell him about Christophe at all. I mulled over this until the bell for first period rang, and was still mulling over it hours later when I fell asleep in the gray light of predawn. Graves didn't show up with that shake. But it wasn't like I was expecting him to, either.

Yeah, right.

# CHAPTER 7

**M**y second week at the Schola ended in a hard freeze. Temperatures plunged, especially at night when the stars became hard clear points in a naked inky sky. Ice dribbled over the windows, and I couldn't even feel relieved that the constant fog had drawn back. All the wulfen were complaining because this kind of weather kept them indoors. And believe me, if you've never been stuck inside a room with twenty restless young wulfen while a teenage-looking *djamphir* drones on about the anatomy of suckers, well, you've missed a real party.

A Schola classroom generally isn't like a regular classroom. They're concave, most of the time. The teacher stands in the bottom of the bowl, and the students sit on benches or couches in concentric circles. It was couches in first-period history class, which meant Graves was sitting right next to me, leaning forward with his elbows on his knees. He looked like he was paying attention, too, under the mess of dyed-black hair falling in his face. His nose jutted out, and his chin was set. The usual black coat strained at his shoulders.

The intensity in his green eyes was new, though. I'd never seen him concentrate this fiercely.

I still felt sorry for dragging him into this.

On my other side, the only other *djamphir* student in the room leaned away from me, taking notes on a yellow legal pad. It was Irving, his curly hair slicked down a little. He'd apparently forgiven me for the sparring thing. He didn't seem the type to hold a grudge.

His friend in the red shirt wasn't here, thank God.

Everyone was freshly showered and bright-eyed for the first class of the evening, and it was so cold I was in layers—T-shirt, Graves's flannel, and a blue wool sweater. I'd have preferred to be hanging out in front of the armory, but at least the lecture was something I hadn't heard before. The teacher had thrown out the textbook and was teaching something new.

"For the wulfen attacking, the primary target is usually the unprotected belly." The instructor, a pale blond *djamphir*, had stopped staring at me. He still halted every once in a while, glancing at me and going completely motionless for a few seconds. It was eerie. "This bleeds a *wampyr* out, and has the added bonus of leaving a blood trail should the thing escape."

Irving raised his hand. "Why not the throat?" He looked like a bright student giving the teacher an opening. His eyes had lit up, and he leaned forward. "Wulfen claws are more durable than plenty of weapons."

"Good question." The teacher nodded. I still hadn't figured out his name yet. "Anyone?"

A shaggy dark-haired wulf perched in one of the very back rows spoke up. "Throat's too small a target." His upper lip lifted for a moment, a gleam of teeth. "Plus, gets you too close to the thing. Arm's length is safer."

"And?" The teacher's eyebrows rose. Nobody said anything.

I tentatively raised a hand.

Immediately, every pair of eyes in the room fastened on me. "Yes?" The blond wasn't sneering now. Instead, he was looking attentively at me, eyebrows raised.

*Oh Lord. I'm going to feel stupid.* My heart was going a mile a minute. "Wulfen fight in packs?" I hazarded. "I mean, I haven't seen much, but they seemed to be pretty good at fighting as a unit. I guess *djam-djamphir—*" I stumbled nervously over the word and immediately felt like a dumb-ass. "Well, I don't see them working together a lot, not in a case like that."

"*Very* good!" The teacher beamed like I'd just handed him Christmas. "Striking for the belly is a strategy with greater returns if the creature is distracted by other team members. What are other strategies for distracting a *wampyr*?"

I felt like I'd just won a prize. And this was *real*. It wasn't like a stupid history class where they aren't telling you the truth anyway, just the regular collage of corporate-approved lies to suck all the interest out of everything.

No, this was about the Real World. How many times had I told Dad high school wouldn't prepare me for anything? We'd gone round and round over it.

The thought of Dad hurt, so I tried thinking about something else. Now I felt kind of bad about skipping all the time and fighting with him. Maybe if I hadn't—

I didn't want to think that all the way through either. I sat up a little straighter.

Graves gave me an unreadable glance. He didn't bother to raise his hand. "Blood," he said. The single word dropped into the room like a rock into a pond. "Spill enough and the animals go crazy."

A ripple ran through everyone. Irving made a single restless movement next to me. The couch creaked.

The teacher's mouth made a weird little twitch. He didn't quite dart Graves a venomous look, but it was close. "The hunger."

"More like a thirst, actually." Irving shifted again. I got the idea he was trying to get the teacher's attention. "Why do we call it hunger, anyway?"

"Putting a pretty face on it?" Graves suggested sweetly. I cottoned onto what he was doing a little too late, and the teacher actually stiffened.

*Oh Lord. Here we go.* I sighed internally and threw a question in I wouldn't have asked if I hadn't been trying to distract everyone. "What I want to know is, why don't I have it? And does it really make suckers go nuts?" I moved, and my elbow whapped into Graves's side. *Hard.*

I hoped it looked unintentional.

The room went still again. I was almost getting used to the way everyone shut up whenever I asked a stupid question. At least I'd been learning for a few days now, even if Civics and Aspect Mastery were still total wastes of time.

Maybe this wasn't so bad.

Blondie looked relieved, but he darted a little glance at Graves. Then at me, and I swear I saw a flash of anger. "Some *svetocha* have the bloodhunger, but not until blooming. And yes, even a small amount of vital fluid can drive a new *nosferat*—or an older one— into a state of severely diminished rationality. It depends on how long ago their last feeding was, and—"

*Feeding. Like, on people.* I shivered, but didn't have a chance to finish the thought. The low clear tones of a bell sliced through whatever Blondie had been meaning to say, and everyone in the room leapt to their feet.

*Shit. Restriction.* Maybe it was a drill. I grabbed Graves's arm, the decision made almost before I was aware I'd touched him. "Come with me."

"I've got to—" He tried to step away, stopped, and looked down at me.

The wulfen were jamming up at the door, some of them half-changing already, fur running up over their bodies. Irving paused just at the door to look back, his aspect sliding through his curls with golden highlights as his eyes lit up. His lower lip was dimpled, the tips of his fangs just slightly touching the flesh. The teacher was already gone, vanishing on a wind that smelled of some fancy-dancy cologne.

But *he* didn't smell like a Christmas candle. Only Christophe. Who could I ask about that?

I kept hold of Graves. "Please. I'll go nuts if I'm locked up in my room again without anyone to talk to." *And I haven't been able to get you alone, you're always hanging out with the hairy boys. I do want to tell you about Christophe. Go figure.* "Graves. *Please.*"

He shrugged, shoulders lifting and dropping. "I'm supposed to go to the armory. It's detention if I don't show up."

*What, you won't get involved unless I'm getting beat up? And since when are you worried about detention, for chrissake?* A sour taste filled my mouth. "Fine." But I didn't let go of his coat. Dylan would probably be along any second. "Go on, then."

"You don't understand—" Maddeningly, he shut his mouth and glared at me, like I was the problem. The bell rang again, urgently, and he tore himself free and headed out the door, the coat flapping around his calves.

Leaving me all alone in the empty classroom. My fingers stung, like from rug burn. My mother's locket was a cold, heavy weight under my layered shirts.

The bell finished ringing, and the weird staticky silence of the Schola under siege crawled into my head.

The boys all had jobs when that bell rang. Battle stations, some of them in the armory passing out weapons, others meeting at predetermined points and waiting. The oldest students and the teachers went out to sweep the grounds.

Last time, some of them had come back beat up pretty bad. Bleeding, even. From the suckers.

I stood there for a few seconds, my hand scraped raw from the rough cotton of Graves's coat, yanked free of my grasp. This made the fourth Restriction. Someone always showed up to take me back to my room.

Not this time. Seconds ticked by, one after another. The fluorescents buzzed, and cobwebs in the upper corners drifted like seaweed. Some of the ceiling tiles were crumbling too.

*This place is falling apart. Jeez.*

It occurred to me that this was the first time I'd been really alone outside my room since I got here. I hunched my shoulders, pulled my sweater sleeves down, and realized I was waiting for someone to show up and tell me what to do. The switchblade was a heavy weight in my ass pocket, covered up by the sweater and the edge of Graves's flannel shirt.

*Way to go, Dru.* There was probably something else I could be doing. Anything. I'd been Dad's helper since Gran died, moving from town to town, getting rid of the nasty things that go bump in the night. Just standing here wasn't going to help anything. And waiting for someone to come back and shove me into my room wasn't going to help either.

The silence took on a new quality, static draining away, replaced with breathlessness. I blinked hard, twice, and turned around sharply. My hair fanned out in an arc, I moved so fast.

Perched on the back of the couch I'd sat on, Gran's owl ruffled its white feathers, each tipped with a shadow of gray. Its black beak looked unholy sharp. Yellow eyes held mine, and I let out a sharp sigh of mingled relief and pain.

*Oh, thank God. Where have you been?*

It was the first time I'd seen Gran's owl since I got here, outside of dreaming. The usual ringing started in my ears, a high clear thin tone like a bell stroked over and over. It filled my skull like cotton wool.

The owl cocked its head, a *what's up, boss?* look. I blinked. Dust motes hung suspended in the air, and the round clock fastened up over the door had gone silent. It wasn't even ticking.

This was the space between precognition and something weird happening. Something weird or Seriously Bad. It was too soon to tell which.

*Whoosh.* The owl took wing in a flurry of feathers. It was a big bird, almost too big for the room, turning in tight circles and heading for the door. Its wings *thopped* down just as it was about to hit them on the jamb on either side; it turned, smart as a spaceship in a movie, and was gone out into the hall.

Sudden certainty filled me. I was supposed to follow it.

Gran had always told me to trust this feeling, and Dad always told me not to let the backwoods foolishness take the place of clear logic. But he also never stopped me when I got that look on my face—the look that said I was seeing something he couldn't.

Gran was famous for "the touch" for miles around, and I'd always assumed I'd gotten it from her. After all, she'd trained me, right?

But now I was wondering just what I'd gotten from where.

The owl had shown up on my windowsill the last morning I'd seen Dad alive. Last time, the owl had led me to Dad's truck—and Christophe. The streak-headed werwulf that had bitten Graves had also been there, but that was incidental.

Wasn't it?

I didn't have time to sit around. I bolted after Gran's owl, my legs full of heavy unwillingness. The world slowed down to something covered in hard goopy plastic, a clear fluid I had to force my way through to move anywhere. This was also part of the space-between, that heaviness. I didn't have time to wonder if I was moving too quickly for the world to catch up, or if I just had to reach through a little more space to reach the body I moved around in on a daily basis.

My bruised shoulder clipped the door on the way out, and a zigzag of red pain shot all the way down my ribs. My sneakers slapped the stone floor, and I got up a good head of speed even through the clinging flood of whatever slows the world down when you're following your dead grandmother's owl.

The hall receded like a mirrored passage in a fun house, the kind where everything is multiplied into infinity. The yellow-pale glare of fluorescent lighting crawled into each crack and chip in the walls. Stone floor with occasional bursts of worn industrial carpet or old linoleum blurred under my squeaking sneaker soles. The Schola receded around me, its halls warping. One sleeve of the too-big blue sweater unrolled and flapped around my left hand, but I didn't have time to pull it up. It was hard work keeping the owl in sight as I slipped and skidded, bouncing off walls and on the verge of tripping countless times. Until it banked again, zooming down another short hall, and a pair of double doors was in front of me.

*I hope they're not locked.* But the right one threw itself open as soon as I hit it, the little pump-thing on top that made it close without slamming giving a high hard pop and a clatter as bits of it rained down. The door smacked the stone wall, and its hinges gave a scream. Chill night air poured in, blowing my hair back.

I leapt the threshold at warp speed, and the cold was a hammer blow against every inch of exposed skin. It cut right through me, and my tongue stuck to the roof of my mouth. The thick clotted taste of wax and citrus poured over my palate. The owl banked in a tight circle again, then headed away at a good clip.

The taste of oranges is bad trouble; Gran would call it an *arrah*. She meant "aura," like when people with migraines get weird tastes or smells right before their heads decide to cave in. Me, I just get a mouthful of fake rotting fruit, kind of, when something *really-bad-weird* is about to happen.

Like, say, when a sucker is about to come out of nowhere and paste you a good one. I mean, I also get it—but with a different tang—when I'm about to see an old friend, or things are going to get weird but not dangerous.

I wasn't going to slow down to find out which flavor of weird this was going to be. Not with that sudden sureness in the middle of my chest pulling me forward. Urging me on.

The woods pressed close into the building's personal space, and ribbons of greasy white threaded between black naked branches. It smelled wrong—too powdery for fog, with an undertone of the ugly dry smell of a snakeskin. And the cold was more than weather—it was a weight pressing against skin and heart and bone.

I took the three stairs down with a leap and landed hard, gravel crunching underfoot. Almost slipped, but pulled up high and tight like a ballerina, and flung myself after the owl. Here there were gardens— it might be pretty once spring came. Now, however, ice rimmed the wooden boards holding long rectangular plots of winter-dead garden back and dripped in icicles from the fog-ribboned trees. It was the east side of the complex of buildings that was the Schola, and I wondered in a dreamy sort of way how the hell I'd gotten over *here*.

Right behind the panic beating like a second heart inside me. And the fear soaking through my entire body. Something bad *was* about to happen, I was sure of it now. I could only hope I'd received the warning in time, and that I would be able to get away from it fast enough.

Past the gardens the land ran downhill in a gentle slope, toward the river. A ribbon of paved path curved down toward a shack of a boathouse, crouching against the moon-silvered water. The moon was half-full, shedding her light over a gray and white landscape that looked exactly like an ice sculpture with streaks of oil-soaked cotton wool hanging from every sharp edge.

The fog was closing around the Schola in grasping, veiny fingers.

Halfway down the hill, saplings and bushes started springing up, the forest's outliers. Then the trees rose, dense and black even though they were naked and festooned with shards of ice. The owl soared, came back, circled me as I ran, and shot forward down the hill, leaving the graveled path behind and crossing the paving, heading for the inky smear of trees.

My breath came in harsh caws of effort. I ran, and the owl returned, like it was pressing me to go faster. It wheeled over my head again, and I thought I heard Gran's voice. *That's a wise animal what muffles its wings so the mouse can't hear it, Dru. And it's a wise animal what hides even when it's quiet. You never know when somethin's up over the top of you lookin' down.*

The first time I'd seen the owl was on the sill of Gran's hospital window, the night she died. I'd kept quiet about it ever since. Only Dad knew about it, and he was—

*Stop thinking and run.* This time it was Dad's voice, full of quiet urgency. The only place their voices were left was in my head. It was better than being alone but it was so, so lonely.

I tried to speed up, but the thick clear goop over the world was hardening. My heart rammed against the walls of my chest, pulsing in my throat and wrists and eyes so hard, like it wanted to escape.

The world popped back up to speed like a rubber band, and I was flung forward as if a huge warm hand had reached down and tapped me like a pool ball. Almost fell, caught myself, and leapt over the last garden box, clearing it with feet to spare.

Sound rushed back in. Ice crackling, gravel flying, my own footsteps a hard tattoo against frozen ground, the harsh rhythm of my breathing—

—and behind me, padded footsteps and a high, chilling howl, queerly diluted through the odd, gleaming fog. The taste of oranges ran over my tongue again; I couldn't spit to clear my mouth and wouldn't have anyway, since it wasn't just waxen oranges. I knew for sure now it meant something totally and completely bad was going down.

I ran for the trees like my life depended on it. Because I knew, deep down, that it did.

# CHAPTER 8

**B**ranches slapped at my face and hands. I leapt over a fallen log, crunched down in a pile of leaves, and fell. Scudgy leafmuck splorched up through my fingers. The darkness scored itself with little diamond holes of moonlight, sharp frozen reflections. I scrambled to my feet and took off again, dodging a creeping streamer of fog. The locket was a lump of ice on my chest.

Behind me, another howl lifted to the cold sky. This one was edged with broken glass and razors. It burrowed into my head, scraping against the inside of my skull.

*They've found my trail.* I didn't know who *they* were, or even why I was so sure they'd run across my scent. I just . . . knew, the way you know how to breathe or to pull your hand back from a hot stove. The way I knew to avoid the creeping little fingers of vapor rising from the ground.

The same way I knew to keep running. No matter how many times I fell.

I scrambled and floundered on. The owl's soft passionless *who? who?* slid through the woods, bouncing off the steel-hard bole of each frozen tree. There was a kind of halfass trail running along the leaf-strewn floor; I broke through the hard shell of a deep puddle and gasped as icy water grabbed at my ankles. Leapt and landed badly, my ankle almost rolling, stumbled on. The owl called again—*hurry up, Dru.*

Another inhuman scream lit the night, digging into the meat behind my eyes with razor claws. I let out a miserable, thin, gasping cry and stumbled forward, my hands coming up to clasp my head until the pain was cut off in mid-howl, just like a flipped switch.

*What the hell was that?* But I had no time to figure it out. I pulled myself into a fist inside my skull, just like Gran taught me. When another scream lifted out of the night, somewhere off to my left and a good ways away, it didn't scrape along the inside of my head. It just ran hard over my skin like a wire brush dripping with acid, and if I hadn't been throwing myself forward so hard, I probably would have yelled, too, in miserable surprise and pain.

That's the trouble with getting involved in the Real World. Once you're in, you can't shut it out and go back to daylight nine-to-five. You're stuck running through the woods at night, risking a broken leg and even worse, while something horrible chases you.

The thin track petered out, the way false trails in the woods do. One minute you think you're following the road back to somewhere you know; the next you leap sideways to avoid fog that shouldn't be moving like that, tip into a bunch of friendly thorn bushes, and wonder what the hell happened.

Except when you're running for your life, those bushes aren't friends. They spear through your clothes and rip at your skin, and by the time you thrash almost free, the footsteps behind you have drawn much nearer. So near you can hear every shift of weight and crackle of twigs breaking, each splutch of muck on the forest floor as they leap, higher and faster than a human ever could.

Gran's owl was now nowhere in sight. I froze, tangled in a bunch of thorny vines, and tried to control my gasping. My lungs were on fire; my heart was just about ready to bust out through my ribs and go sailing.

But I tried to be still and quiet. The bushes crackled, thorns scraping. One of them touched my cheek, a cold pinprick. I wanted to shut my eyes, lying tangled on my side, but the idea of being in the dark woods with my eyes closed just didn't work.

Even the fog was making a sound now. A small rasping, like scales against glass.

My hip, pressed against the cold ground, turned almost numb. Wetness seeped into my sweater and jeans. A cloud hung in front of my face—my own breath, gauzy and translucent.

The footsteps slid around me. There seemed to be two sets, circling each other. I squeezed my eyes shut, lost the battle with myself again, opened them. A line of thorns pressed into my sweater's back. My sneakers were soaked and my feet were so cold they had vanished into numbness.

Crashing. Snapping branches. Moonlight trickled in, spots of false color whirling in front of my light-starved eyes. The greasy white vapor pulled close, questing through tree branches and reaching down to puddle against frozen leaves with that tiny, horrible sound.

Soft, stealthy movement under the crashing. I couldn't tell where it was coming from, and locked my teeth over a helpless noise. Swallowed hard. The fog was creeping closer, closer, little drablets of it touching under leaves. It looked like claw-tipped fingers plucking at the fabric of the forest floor.

Something moved in my field of vision. Once I saw it, everything resolved into sharp focus. Anything moving is easier to see at night. The trouble comes when whatever it is stops and goes motionless, but this figure had a patch of shaggy white up near the top. It moved like a wulfen, with thoughtless grace, the fur blurring its outlines as it sidestepped a long white rope of seeking fog.

There was only one streak-headed werwulf I knew of, and I'd already tangled with him before. I'd shot him in the jaw, but not before he bit Graves. Christophe had shot him, too, right in front of Dad's truck. Sergej's pet, a wulfen broken to his will.

I didn't think he was here to offer me cookies.

*Ohshit. It's Ash.* I pulled in a soft breath. My lungs were starving, crying out for air. I lay still, and a cough tickled at the back of my throat. It always happens when you're hiding— a cough, a sneeze, something. It's stupid. The body decides to screw around with you, even though it knows being quiet is the only way it's going to go on living.

Ash stopped, head upflung, and sniffed. The tickle got worse. His head ducked a little, lean muzzle dipping, testing the air. He stepped sideways, utterly silent, and stopped again. The fog cringed away from him.

*Keep moving. Oh God, let him keep moving.*

Another soft call from Gran's owl marred the sudden silence, but I couldn't see it. The crashing and snapping had stopped. Everything was still, even the spots and shafts of moonlight holding their breath, trapped in reflective veils of white vapor.

Too late I remembered the stiletto in my ass pocket. If I'd thought to get it out, I could be armed now, instead of lying helpless in a tangle of thorns.

The streak-headed werwulf took another three steps, quick and eerily graceful, to the side. His head turned, and the mad gleam of his eyes seemed to pierce the darkness and burn into my skin.

*Did he see me? God, oh God. Did he?* My hand twitched, wanting to get at the knife. But if I did, I'd have to roll over and make noise. And good luck getting it out of my jeans in time to do anything about the werwulf.

God, how I wished for a gun. *Any* gun, even a .22. A nine-millimeter would be better. A .45 or an assault rifle would be the best. And someone to work it who had a bead on this thing would be awful nice too.

*And while I'm dreaming, I'd really like a pony.* My heart hammered, thudded, and basically tried to make me gasp again. I couldn't even start moving my hand toward my pocket—if I could see movement at night, a wulfen damn sure could. If he couldn't already *smell* me.

Why was he hesitating?

The tension stretched, unbearable second after unbearable second, and the taste of wax and dead oranges burst on my tongue, so hard I almost gagged.

I *hate* that. My eyes rolled as I tried not to swallow it, my mouth was full of spit—Jesus Christ, I was going to start *drooling* now. I know that taste isn't real, I know there's nothing in my mouth, but fuck if I'm ever going to swallow it.

The streak-headed werwulf folded down like a toy, a slow fluid movement. His shape rippled, becoming more slump-shouldered animal than vaguely human. The white streak got more vivid, or maybe it was a spot of moonlight pulsing on his pelt. A slight wheezing, chuffing noise came out of him. He was facing away from me, and I wondered if some of the teachers from the Schola were in the woods now.

*Ohplease. Please, God. Help me out a little here, come on. Please.*

Another shape resolved out of the moon-and-tree chiaroscuro, fog melding around it in a cloak of greasy cotton. Vaguely humanoid, tall and broad-shouldered. The moonlight picked out a white blur of face and two white blurs of hands, the rest just a shadow.

"Isn't this *nice*," the newcomer hissed, an affront to the silence filling the woods. The rasp underneath the words ran over my skin like a wire brush, again. I tried not to flinch. "Where is the little bitch? I can smell her."

Ash growled. The growl held not even the approximation of words, but it was chock-full of warning. Fur rippled, and the white streak on his head glowed.

"Shut up and *find* her!" The words held a slight lisp, and I knew why.

Because the tongue didn't work right around fangs. This was a sucker, a *nosferat*. I could tell by the way his voice sucked at the world around it, oily and cold.

And it sounded like he was after me.

*Well, duh, Dru. Big deal. Stay still.* The maddening tickle got worse. It was like a sharp stick digging into the back of my throat. Reflex tears built up in my eyes, hot and aching. A thin finger of fog was creeping closer and closer to my feet, and I *knew* that it would touch me, and when it did the sucker would know I was here, and—

The werwulf's growl changed pitch and tone.

"Don't presume to bark at me, beast. The Master wants—"

I didn't get to find out what the Master wanted, because the werwulf sprang—*away* from me.

He collided with the sucker like a runaway freight train, a crunch that echoed between the fog-hung trees. The sucker let out an amazing, blood-chilling howl. They rolled over and over, hitting and splintering trees, bones and teeth snapping.

*Move move move!* Dad's bark in my head, as if I was on the heavy bag again, popping punches and sweating, wanting to make him proud. Or as if we were dealing with those roach spirits again, me passing ammo through the window with shaking hands and—

I scrambled to my feet, thorns raking every exposed edge and pulling at my sweater like they were trying to tell me to stay down, and bolted. Leapt over the fingers of vapor crawling over the ground like I was doing football tryouts or something, skipping too fast to really keep my balance. It didn't matter where I was heading, as long as it was *away*.

The woods got deeper and denser, and I tore through them. Trees whipped past, some of them clutching at me like they were on the sucker's side, trying to slow me down. More thorny vines snaked across my path, but the fog had retreated. I floundered through, making a hell of a lot of noise, and heard a high, chilling howl behind me.

I thought wulfen howls were bad when I heard them in my own garage. Hearing the high, glassy cry in the middle of the woods at night is infinitely worse, because the howl sounds like it could be words if you just listen hard enough. The horrible thing is that it pulls on that deep hidden part in every person—the blind animal part.

The part that knows you're the prey.

But the worst thing about it?

Is when it sounds *right behind you*, and something hits from behind, tumbling you into another thorn-spiked mess of vines and branches, leaf mold and dirt filling your nose, and a huge, hot, hairy hand winds in your hair.

# CHAPTER 9

**I tried to scream,** but the other paw-hand had clamped over my mouth just before I could get enough air in. Hot breath touched the top of my head as we both lay for a second, me with the sense knocked out of me, stunned and scraped all over.

*Goddammit, girl, that ain't gonna cut it!* Dad's voice yelled in my head. *Let's see some action here!*

It's what he used to yell when I was working the heavy bag, so tired my arms were about to fall off. It meant I was going to have to do more, be more, in order to help him. He needed his helper, and that was me, and death doesn't wait for when you're rested and ready. It sneaks up on you when you're exhausted and hungry and cold and so scared you can't even see straight.

I thrashed, flung my head back and clipped a wet, cold nose with my skull. It hurt and the wulf made a little pained yowl, like a puppy running into something. My elbow sank into his midriff, and he huffed out another sound with a whine at the end. His hand loosened from my hair, but that was only so he could grab me by the waist as I struggled and he braced himself.

His arms clamped down like steel bands, and he growled. Terror short-circuited everything inside my head, and I still don't know how I got free, rolling away along a slippery, gucky strip of rotting leaves.

He growled again and scrambled fluidly to his feet. I scooted backward, my filthy palms skidding in muck and dirt, and hitched in a breath to scream, as the wulf gathered himself, the white streak glowing at his temple like a neon sign, and leapt—

—straight *over* me, colliding with a shape in midair and both of them falling less than three feet from me with a jarring thud, squirts and puffs of fog evaporating. Hissing, tearing, bone-ripping sounds filled my head as I lunged away from this new madness. They rolled, the white streak bobbing, and an unutterably final crunching sound was followed by a hot black gush that splattered the trees in every direction. Sucker blood smoked where it landed, and some of it whizzed past my face, speckling my sweater and sending a stripe of thick warmth up the left leg of my jeans. I cried out, a small sound of disgust lost in the larger noise as the streak-headed wulfen threw back his head and growled, a shattering thunderous noise.

I was still trying to get away, scooting backward in wet jeans, the smoking vampire blood puffing into that same greasy mist once it had finished eating through denim. I was going so fast, in fact, that I ran smack into a tree for the first time that night. Which was pretty miraculous, you know, it being only the first time instead of the fourth or fifth.

A keg of dynamite went off inside my head, and my ribs screamed in pain. I was pretty much full of agony all over, and pretty goddamn sure I'd pulled something in my back again, too. God, if I lived to be an old lady I would probably have so many back problems—but it looked like I wouldn't be around that long.

The streak-headed werwulf hitched himself up and jerked across the space between us. Furrows of dead wet leaves exploded up, and he dug his claws in and stopped, his snout in my face and his breath touching my wet skin. The fog retreated behind him, pulling back like singed fingers.

I let out another small sound, this one cut in half as my breath hitched, every aching muscle tensing in preparation. His breath chuffed in, chuffed out, and it smelled oddly like peppermint and copper.

His eyes were inches from mine, his longer, sleek nose almost touching the tip of my just-human one. A long, long inhale, and I leaned back into the trunk as far as I could. The gleam in his dark eyes was horribly human, and just as terribly hurt and insane. The white streak glowed at me, so bright I thought another random beam of moonlight had gotten caught in his fur.

He sniffed me again and made a low, painful sound. His mouth couldn't shape a human word, so I had no idea what he was saying, whether he was threatening me or . . .

Or what? Why was he just *crouching* there, staring into my eyes? The tree behind me was an icy wall of rough steel, and my legs were still twitching, trying to push me right through it. The werwulf leaned forward again, making that queer, horrible noise, and I smelled hot copper.

Blood. Someone was bleeding. Was it me? Had I just not felt it when he clawed me open?

A rushing noise filled my head, and I heard the beat of muffle-feathered wings just before the werwulf dipped forward, his cold nose-tip pressing my cheek for a moment. Then he melted away. He ran across the small clearing, hitching and favoring his front left paw-hand, and vanished into the trees just as I heard someone yelling my name.

"*Dru! Dru! Goddamn you Dru where are you?*" It was Graves,

screaming-hoarse, and I was faintly surprised. I was even more surprised not to be dead. There was no fog now. The trees were silvered only by moonlight and festooning ice.

I sagged against the tree, vampire blood smoking all over my ruined, filthy clothes, and I did the single most inappropriate thing I could.

I began to laugh. High-pitched, whistling laughter as insane as the broken thing peering out through Ash's eyes.

# CHAPTER 10

"**et me get** this straight." Dylan's hair was wildly mussed, his aspect shining through as he struggled to retain his composure. The way his fangs kept popping out and retreating was not happy or helpful. "Three dead *nosferatu* on your trail, you're beat up and covered in their blood, and you can't remember what happened?"

I couldn't stop shivering. I just nodded. My hair dripped muddy water, and I smelled like I'd been dipped in death.

Graves had his arm around the blanket he'd wrapped me in, and he made a restless movement. "Come on. Let's get you somewhere warm." He gave Dylan a green-eyed glare and started up the hill, half holding me up.

"Wait a goddamn second." Dylan didn't think much of this. "The Schola was broken into. They went right for her classroom. She somehow escaped a trio of hunters—none of whom we can identify yet, all three of them eviscerated out here in the damn woods. She needs to tell us what happened so we can—"

"Have her die of hypothermia? Good plan. Jesus Christ, you guys are jackasses." The hem of Graves's coat flapped as he sped up. "Look at her, dammit. Her lips are blue and she's covered in crap. Is she bleeding? Do you even care? No wonder there's no girls around."

I wondered what that had to do with anything, couldn't figure it out, and hiccupped out another long string of half-hysterical, muffled laughter. I kept glancing around and flinching whenever I saw white moonlight.

Dylan's eyes glittered in the dimness. "Shut *up*, dogboy. Just because you're a prince among your kind doesn't mean you can—"

That hot pocket of rage bubbled up inside me. This was getting ridiculous—but I welcomed the heat, because it was anything other than the dazed, panicked numbness. "Dylan," I heard myself say, between two choked giggles and a coughing snort, since there was mud in my nose. "You call him a nasty name again and I'm going to knock your teeth out." I found that my wet feet could still grip the ground, and— even better—my weak shivering legs could still carry me. "Graves . . ." The word died in a spate of deep bronchial almost-retches.

"Just relax, kiddo," Graves muttered. His arm was tense over my shoulder, pulling me closer to his warmth. The food around here was bulking him up big-time. Or maybe I just felt so small, the way I hardly ever do. "Christ."

Yeah, I felt small. And vulnerable. And very, very terrified.

Dylan shook his head like I hadn't even said anything. "Why did you leave the Schola, Dru?"

*Because something was coming to kill me, duh. When Gran's owl shows up, I follow. It's that simple.* I was too tired to even begin explaining.

A running mass of shapes clustered at the top of the hill. Some had thought to bring flashlights, and golden beams scoured the darkness. It was useless—*djamphir* and wulfen could both see way better than the average human after sunset. But those swords of light were a welcome sight, because they weren't greasefog or moonlight on a crazy wulfen's pelt, and I let out a half-sob. Graves's arm tightened again over my shoulders. "It's okay," he called. "We found her!"

Dylan cursed. They started down, a mass of boyshapes. The wulfen leapt ahead, some of them blurring between fur and skin in that clay-under-water way they do, and I swallowed another harsh sound. It's always weird to see them change and to hear the crackle of bone shifting, flesh running, and fur sprouting. . . .

Yeah. It about makes your lunch want to escape, even if you haven't had any. And even if you were used to Bigtime Weird.

"Goddammit." Dylan made a short, sharp movement, and his voice dropped into a hurt-angry whisper. "I can't help you if you don't talk to me, Dru."

*Yeah, I don't think you could help me even if I did talk to you. There's just not enough words in the world.* My brain hurt, and the rest of me was clumsy and cold.

I couldn't stop coughing. Or laughing, little hitching noises that spilled out of my throat between the harsh rasping. Graves just pulled me along, and the wulfen reached us in a tide of fur and bright eyes. They flowed around me, some of them clapping Graves on the shoulder, most of them sliding between human form and furry, loping kind-of-quadruped. The sudden babble, after the silence and terror of the woods, broke over us both.

"Is she okay?"

"She all right?"

"Dru?" Dibs stepped close, was pushed aside, but not before his fingers brushed my wrist—a fleeting, warm touch. I let out another choking sound.

"Is she all right?"

Behind them, the *djamphir* came crowding. Irving was pale, his curls springing as his aspect slid over him and retreated. They started asking if I was okay, too, but Graves just dragged me through, the wulfen moving with him and somehow everyone getting out of his way, until we got to the doors on the east side of the Schola.

The doors were blown outward, shards of wood lying over the steps, and I blinked. *I didn't do that.*

But maybe something behind me *had*. Once more, Gran's owl had led me out of danger. Or into it, depending.

And oh God but another memory was rising up, the owl on my window ledge the last morning I ever saw Dad alive. I started coughing in earnest.

I didn't want to think about that. I'd rather cough my lungs out.

The hall I'd run down was a mess, splattered with smoking black sucker blood, the carpet torn up and the waist-high paneling gouged. Paler wood in the deep furrows glared at me. "J-j-j-j—" I was trying to express my dismay, but Graves just kept going at a good clip, his arm a steel bar over my shoulders. My feet dragged uselessly most of the time. He actually shouldered a few kids out of the way, a snarl running just under the surface of the babble of voices.

I gathered there had been two teams of suckers, one that had burst in near the sparring chapel and made a lot of ruckus, and a trio of "hunters" who had quietly infiltrated the west wing of the Schola—the one I'd had my first class of the evening in. I must have just escaped them.

*That* was an uncomfortable thought. My feet dragged along the floor. I left dirty clumps wherever I tried to step, but Graves was doing all the work of moving us along. As long as he was doing such a handy job of it, I didn't care.

The sparring chapel was a long way away, and it seemed awful cold. My teeth were still chattering, and everything seemed very far away, even the noise as some kind of scuffle and yelling started.

We reached the deserted chapel, every footfall echoing. Graves palmed open the door on the girls' side, and a gasp went up behind us. He just kept going, dragging me through, and the door whooshed shut. Thick, silky steam billowed, and I coughed again.

"Goddammit," he said quietly, and hauled me across the tiled floor. The word bounced back at us through the vapor in the air. "What the fuck is going on?"

"I d-d-d—" I was about to say I didn't know, gave up. He looked down at me, his face sallow in the steam-filled light, and his jaw set. When he looked like that, serious and determined, you could see where he would be handsome. The girls would go for him big-time, especially in any urban place where they don't value cookie-cutter looks as much. A bolt of shameful, nameless heat went through me at the thought.

"You want me to help with your clothes?" The blanket fell with a sodden plop, and he shucked his coat, almost tearing the sleeve because he couldn't get out of it and hold me upright at the same time very well. "Or, um, I can just stay at the door. In case."

"H-h-h-help. M-me." The shivers were making it hard to think or breathe. I grabbed at the hem of my sweater with clumsy-cold swollen fingers. Graves pulled it up as he braced me; I got lost in it for a second and finally struggled out of the heavy, wet wool. It landed with a splutching sound, and I wondered how much water I'd been lying in out in the woods, and why it wasn't more frozen when ice was everywhere.

Ribbons of steam in the air were white and heavy. I didn't want to think about it.

The entire world went glaring white for a minute, and the next thing I knew Graves was holding me up and awkwardly peeling the sleeves of the flannel shirt off my goose bump–covered arms. I struggled out of my T-shirt, swaying as he held me up. My teeth clicked like castanets, and he went for my jeans while looking grimly up over my shoulder. My bra was wet too, but thankfully not dirty.

My fingers were like wet sausages, too clumsy to do much. The jeans were loose, and he let out a low whistle when he saw the bruises ringing my shoulder, my ribs, and the fresh ones beginning on my arms and the side of my right leg. My socks were filthy, and I'd lost a sneaker somewhere. I honestly didn't remember *where*. I hadn't even noticed it was gone.

His hands were scorching hot; he dragged me to the lip of the closest tub and paused for only half a second, looking up at the ceiling like he was gathering himself. His beat-up black nylon wallet landed on the floor three feet away, and he pitched down the steps and into the huge tub with me, fully clothed, his shoes giving one forlorn underwater squeak before I lost my footing and cried out miserably. It felt like being dipped in hot lava, but he held onto me, guiding me down.

I'd never been in the baths in my underwear. The feeling was weird, like sitting in a hot tub full of Jell-O while wearing a swimsuit that definitely wasn't made for this sort of thing.

"Dru?" For the first time that evening, he sounded scared. "Come on. Say something."

The chattering had stopped, but I was still shivering. Somehow my arm had ended up around his waist, and he settled onto the seat right next to me. The surface of the bath crackled against his sweater. I gasped again, my skin pain-peeled like after a sunburn, and tipped my head back. Bubbling not-water turned gray, dirt swirling through it before it was whisked away by the current. A leaf fell out of my hair, hit the turbulent surface, and was pulled under. The not-water was neck-deep on me, and only chest-deep on him.

"Dru?" Now he sounded close to panic, and I realized I was making another low, keening sound. My throat was full of something too hot and nasty to be tears. "Say something, dammit."

I swallowed the weird moaning sound I was making. My mouth opened. "S-s-s-something." I paused. "D-d-dam-mmit."

He snorted. The laugh caught him sideways, his usual bitter, sarcastic little bark, and I was too grateful to still be alive to really think about the fact of being half-naked in a tub with a boy.

Besides, it was *Graves*. And his arm was still around me. I put my head down on his shoulder and forgot about everything other than the stinging heat pushing its pins and needles into my flesh.

I hadn't been this close to him since we'd both squeezed onto a helicopter lifting out of a Midwest snowstorm. I'd been crying then, too.

Now I wondered about all sorts of things. Especially about him having to fight the first night he got here. Getting Dibs alone and having him explain a few things seemed like a good idea. I wondered why I hadn't thought of it before. My head was so heavy, and Graves's shoulder was bony but comfortable.

"Talk to me," he pressed. "Don't pass out on me, Dru. Hey, I got a question."

"Huh." An affirmative noise was about all I could come up with. *So do I. Why didn't Ash kill me? And how in God's name do I start telling you about all this when it doesn't make any sense even to me?*

"What's Dru short for?"

*Jesus.* It was my turn to half-snort a laugh. "D-don't ask."

"Too late. I been wondering all this time."

The shivers started easing up. My jaw was sore when it finally unclenched. "Tell you l-later."

"Mh. So you wanna tell me what happened?" Gently, carefully, like he was lifting up a Band-Aid and checking underneath it.

"I—" The water bubbled. The door banged a little, like someone was leaning on it. The sound echoed through the locker room. I blinked, waking up inside my own head. "Oh jeez. You're in *here*."

"Uh, yeah." He didn't sound surprised. "Was thinking you might fall and hurt yourself or something. Drown. If you're okay, or—"

I kept my head on his shoulder. Pressed it down a little and made my arm tense up. "Don't. Don't leave." My teeth ached. Even my *hair* ached. "There was . . . I saw . . . okay, it was my grandmother's owl." A brief flare of panic worked up inside me—I'd never really *wanted* to tell anyone about it, and the habit of the secret was hard to break.

But this was Graves. And he didn't disappoint me. He just accepted it. "Owl." Nodded, his sharp chin dipping. "Okay."

"And it led me outside, and I ran. I think it was trying to get me away from the suckers. I ended up in some bushes and I saw . . ." The rest of it spilled out in an incoherent jumble, but he nodded every once in a while. I liked that about him. He was so smart you didn't have to hold his hand and walk him through everything. He could fill in the blanks on his own.

"You're sure it was the same one?" His eyes had half-lidded. The not-water began to calm down, bubbling and fizzing. It stung my scratched hands and spread up my shoulder in little waxy dollops, heat sinking in.

I suddenly wanted to wash my hair. My scalp crawled. My heart had finished its pounding and finally settled down. "I guess. How many werwulfen with white streaks on their heads have we seen?"

"Point." His head dipped in another nod. His hair, getting damp from the steam, fell in his eyes. He tossed it out with a shaking, sudden motion.

I let out a sigh. I couldn't keep it in any longer. It came out in a whisper. "I saw Christophe. During the day." It was more like three or four days ago, but I didn't want to tell him *that*.

Graves stiffened. A full thirty seconds ticked by, him staring at the mirrored wall through veils of steam. "Jesus, Dru."

Like it was *my* fault. "I couldn't get you alone to tell you."

"So you tried *this*?" But he was joking. He shifted uneasily, moving as if his arm was cramping, but he left it where it was, his fingers no longer burning my other shoulder. "Where did you see him?"

"He came in through my window. You can't tell anyone."

He rolled his eyes. I couldn't see it, but I could *feel* the movement. And the rolling of teenage eyes has a noiseless noise all its own. "Duh. But what was he doing coming through your *window*?"

*Hell if I know, kid.* "Giving me some things. Stuff like my mother owned. And telling me some things."

"How the hell did he have things that belonged to your mother?"

Trust Graves to boil everything down to its essentials. "They aren't; they're just *like* hers. And, well, I guess he knew her." I hadn't thought about it just that way before. He'd certainly *sounded* like he knew her. And now that I thought about it, he'd said specifically that the wooden swords weren't hers. I opened my mouth to go on with explanations.

But he asked the other sixty-four-thousand-dollar question before I could. "Just how old is he, anyway? And *who* is he?"

"I dunno." I slid down a little further into the not-water's embrace, and another cloud of dirt from my wet hair went through the bubbling jelly. *Jeez. How much guck did I get rolled in?* "I'm more worried about Ash not killing me. He had the chance. He got rid of those other suckers, and—"

"You saw that?"

"I saw one. Stands to reason he did the other two." A tremor went through the center of my bones. "Jesus." *I could have died. There's no way out of that classroom, and three suckers . . .*" He was right nose to nose with me, Graves. Nose to nose." My brain kept making a funny hitching stop when it got to the memory, replaying it, throwing up its hands in horror, and stalling like an engine. "And the fog . . ."

But I didn't want to think about the fog ever again. Thank God it hadn't touched me. If it had . . . I didn't know quite what would have happened, but it would have been bad. I *knew* that much, all the way down to my quivering, aching bones.

It's hard to argue with certainty like that.

Graves was more worried about essentials. "A wulf working alone did that? And he just . . . what, ran away?"

"Guess he heard the rest of you coming." The shaking intensified. It wasn't shivering. It was my body rebelling against everything. I wanted a cheeseburger, and I wanted to curl up and sleep, and I wanted things I couldn't even name. Most of all, I wanted to just shut my eyes and make all this madness go away.

My head was still on his shoulder. He was still holding me. He was still fully clothed and hadn't said a word about it. A long silence passed between us, full of steam and the funny burpchuckle bubbling of the not-water. It hissed a little bit as I slid down some more, more of the dirt in my hair getting whisked free.

"I don't know what to do," I whispered finally. It scared me more than I wanted to admit. I was used to knowing what the procedure was in every situation; I was used to Dad knowing what I didn't and giving me orders when I was out of my depth.

I mean, Dad never let me flounder. Not like some parents, who will just sit there and watch you flail around. I've seen that a lot, and it always looks to me like the adults *want* the kid to fail.

Maybe it makes them feel better when we do, or something.

Graves sighed. "Okay." His shoulders came up, the one I'd propped my head on, digging into my cheekbone. "We should get you cleaned up. And Dylan's going to have a cow."

"Why wasn't he there?" As soon as I said it out loud, I regretted it. "Someone always came to get me when the bell rang before. This time, nobody."

"Yeah." Not-water splashed as he moved. "I was thinking that too. Let's get you cleaned up." He untangled himself from me, and I had to lift my head. The burning had settled into a more soothing heat, soaking in. My back hurt, but not as much as it could have.

"Graves?"

"Huh?" He swung back, and for the second time that night I was face-to-face with a shapechanger. But this one had bright green eyes, and his dyed-black hair hung in damp strings, and he was the same half-ugly kid who had been the only person I could depend on since a zombie smashed its way through my kitchen door.

Less than a month, and my entire life was in the kind of mess only the Real World could make. I had no idea how to start fixing it, but he was here, and he hadn't let me down yet.

We stared at each other for a long moment. My throat was dry. I was pretty sure dirt was smeared all over my face and my hair was sticking up like Medusa's. But I leaned forward just a little, and if he hadn't turned his head a little bit, my lips wouldn't have landed on his cheek.

His skin was softer than I'd have thought under the stubble showing up, and I had to sniff because my nose was full. But I pressed my lips against his cheek and felt like an idiot. What had I been about to do?

*Okay, Dru. Time to play this cool.* "Thanks. I mean, for getting me in here, and all." I retreated, suddenly very aware I was just in panties and a bra that were probably now ruined, and that he had dumped himself into the tub without even taking his shirt off. And I probably had dirt all over my stupid face. "You're always, you know, around. When I need you. Thanks."

Of all the things to say.

*OhmyfuckingGOD, Dru, how stupid can you be?* I made it over to the other side of the tub and hoped the heat would hide the red marching up my neck to plant itself in my cheeks.

Graves actually coughed. It was kind of decent of him. "No problem." He headed for the stairs out of the tub, awkwardly swilling a lot of crackling wax around. He floundered up and out, almost slipped, grabbed the edge of the tub. "First one's. Yeah. Free."

He was probably just as embarrassed as I was. I sank back into the tub, reached out, and held onto the edge myself. I was feeling kind of like my arms and legs might fail me at any moment.

I hunched in the bath for a long while, shivering and shaking, and the only thing that got me out of there was the thought that one of the teachers might think I was drowning and come in to "rescue" me.

Or, you know, kill me. Because it seemed pretty obvious that the Schola, where Christophe had promised me I'd be safe, was a pretty damn dangerous place.

# CHAPTER 11

**W**hen you're up all night all the time, midnight is the middle of the day. It's not late enough to be lunch yet, but it's too late for breakfast, and when you've been chased and have rolled around in muck, are you hungry anyway?

I was. I was *starving*. But instead of being in the caf, I was sitting in Dylan's office again. Looking at the shelves of leather-bound books and waiting. It *was* just like the principal's office, and Graves had vanished after handing me a fistful of dry clothes brought from my own room through the door of the girls' locker room.

I didn't like that. It was just numbers one and two on a list of things I didn't like. Someone—maybe even Graves himself—would have had to go through the rosewood dresser in my room, and whoever it was even brought panties, for God's sake. It was creepy. Thank God I hadn't hidden anything in there. I mean, the panty drawer has *got* to be the first place anyone's going to look, right?

And where was Graves? I had a funny squirrelly feeling in my chest when I thought about him not being here. I wanted to see him.

I wanted to see any friendly face. Nobody else here qualified except maybe Christophe, and he was nowhere around. I didn't have any clue *where* he was.

Dylan was off doing whatever it was he did when he wasn't sighing at me, or preparing to come in and sigh at me. Which left me all alone, my hair washed clean and dripping and my teeth clenched together. Not to mention with my head full of questions, and arms and legs that didn't feel too steady. I slumped in the usual high-backed, carved chair, staring at the books. They were a treasure trove of titles about the Real World, from demographic surveys on werwulfen to a whole section on witchcraft and black hexes, their spines lettered with crimson foil.

I bit on my right index fingernail, chewing along until it was nonexistent. Moved to the next nail. *What I wouldn't have given to have a crack at some of those while Dad was alive. He might've liked it too.* I wouldn't have minded a peek at the hex books. Dad preferred human intel—asking questions in occult shops and bars where the Real World congregated. I'd been in and out of those places ever since Gran died and Dad came to pick me up, and I was beginning to think it had been a lot more dangerous than even he had thought. Every time he took me into another place to get the lay of the land, he got really tense.

Now I wondered if it was because I was with him, or because a misstep could have meant both of us ending up dead. And I wondered why he never told me about Mom being *svetocha*. Why hadn't he said something? Anything? Was he planning on telling me when I was old enough? How old was "old enough"? What the hell had he been waiting for?

Or had he not known? Had it been my mother's secret?

How *could* it have been?

I started chewing on my right ring fingernail. Then again, Dad never was a touchy-feely say-everything kind of guy. We could spend whole days not talking, just getting things done. I was always proud of knowing exactly what to do without him having to tell me every time. Gran hadn't been a big one for talking either, preferring to teach by example, but next to Dad she was positively chatty.

And how would Dad have told me, anyway? *Dru, honey, your mother was part vampire, which means you are too. Sorry about that.*

My heart hurt. I squeezed my eyes shut, tried not to think about it.

The door opened. I stayed slumped in the chair, even though my heart leapt nastily and I had to swallow a gasp. I grabbed at the chair's arms, and my feet slid in a little bit in case I had to stand up in a hurry.

Almost dying will make you a little jumpy.

"Here she is." Dylan sounded tired. "*Entrez-vous*, my space is yours."

I heard a light step and a swish of something. A spicy, pretty smell filled the air, and I craned my neck, opening my mouth to ask Dylan where the hell Graves was.

The words died in my throat as the advisor stepped to one side, closing the door and standing at attention right in front of it. A shadow slid past him and glided toward me.

She was tall for a girl, and her hair was a glory of reddish curls. Narrow shoulders, wide blue eyes, a pointed chin, and a long, old-timey dress of red silk. That hair was perfect, held back from her heart-shaped face with two black-velvet bows. She half-turned, leaned back, and hopped up to perch on Dylan's desk, shoving paper back with her skirt.

I stared. Her boots were pointed and heeled, and rows of tiny buttons marched up her shins. She crossed her ankles and looked at me. Her eyes turned a little lighter as dark streaks slid through her hair, the curls becoming looser and longer as her aspect flooded her. The twin points of delicate little fangs touched her pink-glossed lower lip.

*Holy shit.* I stared some more.

"Dru," Dylan said, calmly enough. "This is Lady Anna. Milady, this is Dru Anderson."

"Hello, Dru." She had a sweet, chiming voice. I stayed where I was, nailed in place, my mouth half-open. "Is that a nickname? What is it short for?"

I was *so* not going to answer that. But my mouth opened anyway. "You're *svetocha*." The words just fell out. "Jesus Christ. I thought I was—" I sounded accusing, and Dylan straightened self-consciously, his jacket creaking. "Holy *shit*."

Her smile faltered for a moment. "I'm a well-kept secret. If the *nosferatu* suspected, they would attack every place we own, even this small satellite of the Order, with far more frequency. Already, with you here for such a short period of time, we've had several students injured and a marked increase in the number of . . . incidents."

*So that's my fault? Jesus.* A hot ugly feeling welled up inside me. I closed my mouth with a snap. We looked at each other for a few minutes, her fangs retreating and the curls in her hair tightening up, until she looked just like a storybook impression of a princess.

"We are hoping that the attack on this Schola was merely routine, a matter of them probing our defenses. Though it seems unlikely, doesn't it?" She tilted her perfect head. "Hopefully none of them escaped to carry tales."

I finally dug up something to say that wasn't a cussword. "Where's Graves?" This was all very well, but he was the one person I wanted to talk to. I needed him here for this.

Dylan shifted uneasily. "He's in the dorms." His fangs were out, and he looked unhappy. It was just a subtle downward tilt to the corners of his mouth, but it was such a change from his generally irritated expression, it was pretty shocking. "Milady wanted to meet you, Dru. It's a high honor for a first-year student."

*Color me all impressed and shit.* "Why? I mean, why did she want to come here? If I'm such a problem."

"You're not a problem—" Dylan began, but the girl glanced at him mildly, and he shut up so fast I was surprised he didn't lose a chunk of his tongue.

"May I?" She cocked her head, and Dylan spread his hands helplessly. She smiled a little bit. Those teensy little fangs were creepy as hell, especially when she tilted her head and looked cat-content. "You are unruly, Miss Anderson. You have been here barely two weeks and have already pressured a Kouroi into sparring with you, with unpleasant results. You seem to have no pride in your heritage—which isn't your fault, given your upbringing, but it is distressing. You have so much potential, but you seem content to waste it on pointless intransigence." She was solemn now, her mouth turning down like she tasted something a little unpleasant but was too polite to spit it out. "That's our fault. We have not expressed to you the reasons why we do things as we do, and I confess I have been very busy making arrangements for your continued safety, as well as other . . . arrangements for the safety of others in the Order. The work has taken up so much of my time that I have been unable to meet with you before now. And . . . well, I suppose the best way to say it is just to *say* it."

*I don't like the sound of that.* My "wrong" chimes were ringing like mad. I shifted uncomfortably. The chair had gotten really hard all of a sudden. Dylan made a soft coughing noise, clearing his throat. His dark eyes flashed, but whether it was a warning or an allergy attack, I couldn't tell.

Anna lifted one narrow hand, and her nails were lacquered pink too. *My God. All she needs is a muff and a cute little pink cell phone all covered in rhinestones. Ugh.* The smell of her—spice and goodness and warm perfume—reminded me of something, but I didn't know just what. I was too busy staring at her flawless face, the blush rising in her matte cheeks, the arc of her eyelashes.

My next thought was sudden and chilling. *I could never in a million years look like that. I'm not sure I'd want to, either.*

"We don't know why Reynard saved you from Sergej." Her tone dropped to confidential instead of just worried and hoity-toity. "Did he tell you anything at all?"

*Reynard? Oh yeah.* She meant Christophe. "He said he was part of the Order, and—"

"He said that?" Her gaze sharpened over my shoulder, and I knew she and Dylan were exchanging a Look that could have been Parental. Or at least Teacherlike. How old was this girl? She looked about eighteen, which could have meant anything here. "Would it surprise you to know Christophe Reynard hasn't been an *official* part of the Order for a good seventeen years or so? The negotiations to bring him back to us have been . . . difficult."

"Nobody trusts him." Next to her careful, polite, well-modulated tone, my voice was harsh. I'd scraped my throat raw with coughing. "Dylan said when he came back he'd train me, because—"

"Dylan is of Christophe's camp. He's been his supporter for a long time, and indeed was Reynard's sponsor. He argued and pressed and cajoled to have Reynard accorded the honor of membership in our ranks, despite his . . . unfortunate ancestry."

"His what? Slow down and speak English." I pushed myself upright in the chair. I was tired and hungry, and I wanted to see Graves. And oh yeah, I wanted to curl up in bed and shake. I wanted to lock my door and the shutters over my window and spend a little time just trembling. It sure as hell sounded good.

There was a slow, uncomfortable silence. "You might as well tell her," Dylan said. "If you're going to."

"I suppose so." She fixed me with her limpid look, and I felt every pimple I'd ever had fighting toward the surface again. "Did Christophe tell you anything about his family?"

"Just that his mom was dead too, I think." It was hard to remember when I was thinking through soup. Come to think of it, he hadn't told me much at all. "Other than that, nothing. What's this all about? He didn't tell me a goddamn thing, and nobody's told me really anything since I *got* here."

"It would surprise you, then, to know that Christophe's given name was Krystof Gogol?" A significant pause while I shook my head, mute, wondering where the hell she was going. "And the *nosferat* you escaped from two months ago, the acknowledged king of those who hunt the night, was born Sergej Gogol?"

"Huh?" I was exhausted. That's the only reason why it took ten full seconds for what she was really saying to trickle through the fog in my head. "You what?"

Anna's shoulders slumped. For the first time, she looked a little tired too. But it was just a gloss over her prettiness. "You didn't know. Christophe is Sergej's son. The eldest and, for a time, the most proud and wicked of his progeny. He saved you from his father and disappeared. But even before that, Reynard was interfering in your family."

My heart was beating very loudly. All the breath had whooshed out of me. "Say *what*?" It was a tiny little squeak from a dry throat.

Anna hopped off the desk and faced me squarely, her hands clasped in front of her. She said what I was afraid she'd say. "We have reason to believe, Miss Anderson, that it was Reynard who gave away your mother's location to Sergej. And we need your help to find out if he did."

\* \* \*

She laid the manila folder on the desk's cluttered surface. Her pink-lacquered fingernails scraped slightly. "This is what we think happened. Your mother was in a safe location." The folder flipped open, and the world skidded to a halt underneath me.

My teeth ground together behind the frozen lake of my face. They were tingling again, and the red sparkles at the corners of my vision were back. I swallowed harshly, tasting danger and rage.

It was an eight-by-ten glossy in full color, and it showed a yellow house with an oak tree growing by the front steps. I stared at the picture and my skin went cold, then hot, then cold again. Every muscle ache twinged once, then hardened into nausea.

Have you ever felt so sick your entire body feels like throwing up? Like that.

The last time I'd seen that house was in a dream.

Or was it a dream? Something I'd woken up from with Christophe and Graves both in the room, fighting off a dreamstealer—a winged serpent sucking at my breath, a thing that slunk away to lay eggs in my neighbors. Those eggs had hatched the next morning, and driving through a bunch of young wiggling dreamstealers to escape the wulfen attack on my house had been a nightmare.

I'd thought maybe it was a hallucination, the impossibly clear and detailed vision of my mother hiding me in the middle of the night.

*It wasn't a dream.* A chill hard voice spoke up in the very middle of my head. *It was memory. That was what happened when Mom died. This is the house she died in. She hid me in the closet and went out to fight. And she got killed.*

The *svetocha* next to me flipped the photo aside. Next was another glossy eight-by-ten. This time, the oak was in full summer leaf—except for the huge scorched half of it, twisted and blackened by some horrible thing still vibrating in the branches. The screen door was busted off its hinges, and the steps were shattered.

There was something terrible caught in the tree's clutching fingers. Something human-shaped, but agonizingly distorted. The image seared itself on my eyes, burrowed into my brain.

"We think she died on the steps," Anna said softly, "but Sergej hung her in the tree and . . . well. We didn't get there in time. Your father was long gone, too, with you. We didn't even know about you until years later."

*He hung her in the tree. Oh God.* "You didn't know about me?" I sounded breathless even to myself.

When she answered, there was a faint tinge of something—bitterness? Anger? I couldn't decide and didn't care. "No. Your mother . . . left the Order for her own reasons. Nobody knows what those reasons were."

*I don't either.* I blinked hard. Cleared my throat. "I thought *svetocha* were toxic to suckers. That's what—" *That's what Christophe said.*

"We are. We poison them just by breathing, just by existing in their vicinity. But some—a very few—*nosferatu* are powerful enough to endure that toxicity for a short amount of time. And a short amount of time was all Sergej needed." Her perfect eyebrows drew together. "There is a reason he is their leader."

It was weird. Nobody else would say his name. They said *he* or *you-know-who*. But Christophe, and this chick, said it quietly. Like they were talking about someone they knew.

I didn't want to think about it. My entire body, and everything inside my head, felt like throwing up, passing out, or just sinking down on the floor and trembling for a bit. "What does this have to do with Christophe?"

She flipped that photo over too. The back of it had a scribble in blue pen, a streak like someone had slashed at it. More papers. "This is a transcript of a call between an unidentified member of the Order and a *nosferat* of Sergej's line. In it, the unidentified Kouroi gives your mother's location. Christophe is the only person who might have known—he trained your mother personally, and they were close."

*He trained her?* "Close? How old *is* he?"

"Old enough to remember the last half of the First World War, Miss Anderson. We have no more proof—the recording is gone and the person who transcribed it died in battle. Rather suspiciously, I might add." She was watching me very carefully, I realized. There's a certain way people look when they're not focusing forward, when they're tracking you in their peripheral vision. "It is very likely Christophe will seek further contact with you. If and when he does, it is imperative that you notify an advisor and stand by for debriefing. Is that clear?"

The tone of command was something new. I got the idea that when this lady said *jump*, everyone around her made like a basketball player going up for a dunk.

The words hovered right on the tip of my tongue. *He's already been to see me.* A few simple words, and I could stop feeling like there was a weight pressing against my heart. I could lay the problem in someone else's lap and stop worrying about it. I could hand it over to an adult and be done.

But I heard the sound of soft wings again, and feathers brushed my face. I almost flinched, the feeling was so real.

*Look what happened last time you tried to dump the problem in someone else's lap, Dru. You called Augustine, and things seemed like they were going to get better—and now look at where you are.*

It was a warning, delivered just like all of Gran's lessons. Simple and without a lot of bullshit messing it up. "Crystal," I heard myself say. It was the first time I'd ever sounded as weary and adult as Graves sometimes did. Did he ever feel this weight pressing on him too?

He probably did. I wanted to see him so bad my hands almost shook.

"Then I shall be on my way." She scooped the file together, and I glanced up. Dylan looked worried, as usual, and he was staring straight at me. It was like he was willing me to figure something out, his lips pressed together and his dark eyes beaming a message I couldn't decode.

"The transcript. Do I get to look at it?" I didn't mean to sound stubborn, but I guess I did. Dylan actually flinched, and Anna drew herself up.

I finally figured out what bothered me about her face. She looked Popular. She'd never been an outcast; we all just existed to throw her own reflection back at her. There was the same unfinished, greedy kind of prettiness I'd seen on cheerleaders and female boa constrictors all over America. If she wasn't *djamphir*, she'd probably have ended up as an obese, lacquered middle-aged woman with a turned-down, bitter mouth. The kind that makes a huge fuss in a grocery store over an expired coupon, or a can of corn costing fifteen cents more than she'd thought.

The kind that always gets her way, because she's shameless when it comes to wearing you down over it. Like that.

"It's classified, Miss Anderson. When Christophe contacts you, listen to what he has to say. Remember it, and be ready to repeat it."

She nodded brusquely and tucked the manila folder under her arm. Her silk swished as she headed for the door. "My bodyguard will see me out, Dylan. Thank you."

"Milady." How he managed to say the word without choking, I don't know. She swept away, her heels tapping with little sharp sounds.

The door swung shut. Cobwebs up at the top of the tall bookcases made little shushing movements. The ceiling tiles in here were rotting too.

This place was really falling apart in more ways than one.

Dylan tilted his head, one eyebrow raised. I stood there, aching and wet with sweat. I didn't realize I was shaking until I sat back down in the chair, hard. Every part of me was quivering like electrified Jell-O. Her smell left reluctantly, heaviness coating the back of my throat—especially that place on the palate normal people don't have, the place where I taste danger.

It's like the pickled ginger you get with sushi. That always tastes like perfume to me. This was heavy, oily perfume too.

*What does that remind me of? I swear to God it reminds me of something.* But the little spring that wheels memories out of their slots and throws them into the soup of your brain was busted in my head. I just couldn't come up with anything coherent.

Climbing up the stairs to my room seemed like an awfully huge task. But the thought of hiding under the bed with the dust kitties, the *malaika*, and Dad's billfold more than made up for it. I was glad, for no reason that I could name, that Mom's locket was tucked safely under my T-shirt. The idea of Anna seeing it made my heart feel cold.

Dylan's shoulders slumped. "They're gone," he said quietly. "Are you all right?"

*What a question.* "Yeah." I cleared my throat. "Peachy. Perfect. *Not.*"

"I'm sorry." He really did sound sorry. But then, he always did. "She insisted on seeing you, and . . ."

*And what? What the fuck was that?* I stared at the space on his cluttered desk where the file had rested. I knew it existed now. I'd seen where my mother died.

*He hung her in the tree.* Her sweet little voice, saying it like it was nothing when it wasn't. It wasn't nothing. It was *my mother*, and she—

"Have you seen Christophe, Dru?" His jacket creaked as he leaned away from the wall. "I don't think I have to tell you he's in deep shit. And it's getting deeper."

I was trying to think, but he was making it harder by talking to me. "I want to go to my room." I sounded about five years old. "Please."

"All right." But he just couldn't let it be. "Dru—"

"Who was supposed to be watching me?" The space where the file had been was a hole in the world, and I wasn't sure I liked the way the wind was whistling over it. I hate that empty sound, like a storm rasping against the edges of an empty house while you're waiting for your dad to come home and collect you. That low, impatient moaning. "Who was supposed to take me up to my room when the bell went off? It's the only time someone hasn't come to get me."

"I don't know, I didn't get a chance to check the schedule. And now the duty roster's disappeared." He moved again, restlessly, leather creaking. I coughed once more, a deep hacking sound. "I was called to greet Anna's transport. We never receive any warnings for her visits, so—"

"She doesn't live here?" But I didn't care. My legs felt like they would work now. Kind of. Something else he said seemed important, but I couldn't make my brain work.

"No, she doesn't." He stopped short again, and I was getting really tired of the feeling that he wasn't telling me everything. Or even anything.

I braced myself on the chair, pushed. Failed the first time. Dylan stepped forward like he wanted to help.

I leapt up as if burned, put the chair between us, and stared at him.

"Dru—" He stopped dead. We watched each other over a couple yards of traitorous air. There didn't seem to be enough of it to breathe, but there was sure enough to press down on me from all sides. Had anyone ever drowned on *air*?

I sidled toward the door. He kept very still, like he wasn't sure which way I was going to jump. The aspect folded over him, retreated, his fangs sliding under his lips.

"I'm on your side," he said, when I was almost at the door. "I wish—"

"I don't have a side," I informed him, found the doorknob with one numb hand and fled. All the halls were empty, and I managed to make it to my room without anything *else* happening.

It was a completely unexpected gift. I half-expected there to be a fire, or another attack, or some other damn thing.

I locked the door, put my back against it, and held up my hand. It was shaking like a windblown leaf. The room was dead silent, the curtains askew just a little bit, and a square of white paper against the blue of the quilt cover.

Hot and cold swept over me in alternating waves. I set out across the acres of blue carpet. My socks whispered, and could anyone else see the faint marks where Christophe's wet feet had rested?

Even though I was jolting from the fading adrenaline overload and seriously busted up, I am not stupid. It was too wrong. Two photos of the house I'd lived in Before—before Mom died and the world changed—didn't make a case against Christophe. If the information was so secret and classified, Anna shouldn't have brought the file out at all. And ordering me around is exactly the wrong way to make me do what you want.

Yeah, I mean, I understand about obeying orders when you're under fire. That's totally different. But Dad hadn't raised a blindly obedient idiot. I don't think he was capable of it.

The paper was crisp, heavy, and expensive. The writing was careful copperplate script.

> *Svetocha,*
> *Be careful. Nothing here is what it appears to be.*
> *Meet me at the boathouse.*
> *Your Friend.*

I collapsed on the bed. If it was a code, the message was lost on me. *What the fuck?*

And what was someone—maybe Christophe—doing leaving messages on my pillow when vampires were trying to kill me? While Ash, of all people (was *people* even the right word for a werwulf?) was rescuing me?

*Had* Ash been trying to rescue me?

My brain finally kicked in, far too late. *And now the duty roster's gone.* Which meant whoever was supposed to be watching me had taken it, because they knew I'd be attacked.

*Killed. Not just attacked, but killed. Call it what it is, Dru.*

I let out a long, shuddering breath. Christophe. Sergej's son. He was right—someone was trying to kill him. But he wasn't telling the whole truth either. All these lies, crowding all around me, hemming me in. Dangerous lies.

*Deadly* lies. What happened tonight could have easily ended with me murdered out in the woods.

I could end up dead tomorrow. In my sleep, even. I shivered, hugging myself for warmth. The room was cold, and it wasn't mine.

The one person I could have talked to, the one person who could have helped me make sense of this madness, was down in the dorms. I didn't feel up to going down there. Not now.

I huddled on the bed. Outside, it was night, and the Schola was awake and alive. The not-noise of people living in a space, filling it up with their breathing and heartbeats, quivered in the air. I still felt completely, utterly alone. More alone than I'd ever felt in a house waiting for Dad to come back, and that's saying something.

# CHAPTER 12

**The cold front** coming down from Canada finally broke two days later. Ice melted, the river became a supple silver snake instead of a flat gray ribbon. Everything turned soggy instead of hard-frozen. Thundering storms blew in, dumped a load of rain every night, and blew out. The daylight came through a filter of overcast and dry white fog. It was like being in a glass globe, because I only saw the weather through barred windows.

I couldn't stay cooped up in the room. It was like sitting in a prison cell. So I would go to class.

Classes were a special kind of hell. I'd sit there and think, *He lied to me.* Or even better, *Someone here wants to kill me.* It would knock every other thought out of my head, stamp on it a few times, and I'd lose track of everything the teacher was saying. Dibs hung out with me at breakfast and lunch, but he didn't say much. He had all he could handle just sitting still and sometimes forcing out a *hello*. The kid's shyness was just short of terminal.

Nobody else talked to me except Graves. And he hardly talked at all. At least, not about anything important. It was all, *We went running through the park* this or *Shanks took us shopping* that or *I heard about this guy in sparring, guess what he did?* the other.

I made noises, nodded, and tried to look interested. Then the gong would go off inside my head.

*He lied to me.* Or *Someone here wants to kill me. Maybe in this very room.* And I would stare off into the distance, because I was afraid to start examining everyone around for signs of murderous intent. It wasn't like I could even tell how old any of them were. They could have all been ancient and I wouldn't know, would I?

I don't know why I felt so betrayed, really. Christophe was part vampire, after all. Like everyone else here who might want me dead.

Like me.

The taint doesn't wash out. I found out that much in the increasingly useful two-hour span that was history class. No matter how far back in the family tree the sucker is, it still makes the kids *djamphir*. They get the aspect, the speed, the strength—and the hunger. And they're all boys, except for the one-in-a-thousand girl. Who rarely ever reaches adulthood, because the suckers find them before they bloom and drink them dry, getting a big old jolt of power from it.

Nice, huh? I was just special all over the place. Me and Anna. Were there more? There could be. I might not be so special.

It also occurred to me that the wulfen were probably my best bet of surviving. They couldn't want me dead, really. Right? Because I didn't matter either way to them unless they were working for Sergej too.

There was no way of knowing for sure. Which meant the wulfen weren't that great of a bet after all.

I had no way of getting out of here. Not for a while.

Graves didn't want to hang out that much, and what could I do?

Just follow the werewolves around until they took pity on me? What if some of them had a reason, God only knew what, for hating me?

And did I even dare to figure out how to sneak down to the boathouse?

I was in history class, again, sitting on one end of the couch. The doors had been replaced and the halls repaired, but you could still see the white gouges in the paneling and the carpet was a glaring mismatch, the only patches of new flooring in the whole school. The renovated bits smelled like formaldehyde, and I pulled my knees up, resting the pad of paper on them. The doodle unreeled under my pencil, long narrow arches and stone walls. I shaded in each block of rock, the grass forcing up through flagstones, and worked all around a huge blank spot in the middle of the page.

Graves perched next to me, and the kid he called Shanks—dark emo-boy hair brushed sideways across his forehead and hanging in his chocolate eyes, bony wrists sticking out from under his sleeves, en-gineer boots, and a sideways smile—leaned forward on his other side, elbows braced on his knees. Irving had settled himself on the floor, knees up and arms circling them. Other than that, everyone gave me a wide berth. Even Dibs acted like he didn't know me in class.

I caught Graves and the Shanks kid exchanging pointed looks, usually every time Irving opened his mouth.

Right now Blondie the teacher was droning on about basic rules for interaction between *djamphir* and wulfen. I filled in another block of shading.

"*Djamphir* are trained for tactics and wulfen are trained for lo-gistics. This plays to the particular strength of both. Wulfen lack a *djamphir*'s sensitivity to *nosferat* infestation, and *djamphir* lack the peculiar qualities of consensus and cooperation that come naturally to wulfen. Each is half of a balanced equation, and it was only when we started cooperating that we began to be able to clear entire territories and hold them."

"What happened before?" Graves wanted to know.

Blondie's teeth peeped out from behind his lips. Very white, but his aspect was nowhere to be found. "Before? We died. We were very close to being eradicated completely, and it was war on wulfen whenever the *nosferatu* felt like it. Those who weren't taken were killed, or they lived by the leave of the Blood Princes only. As the Broken."

That perked my ears up. *Broken to his will*, Christophe whispered inside my head.

I looked up from the paper. "Broken? What does that mean?"

I immediately felt stupid. It was probably not the best thing to ask in a room full of wulfen. They might be, you know, offended.

*Oh jeez.* A slight rustle went through the room. Shanks hunched his shoulders and settled back on the couch.

"Anyone want to answer that?" Blondie turned in a full circle, taking in the faces all around him. "No? Well, I'll go ahead then. 'Breaking' a human being, even a *djamphir*, is easy. Sleep deprivation, temporary lack of protein, a constant stream of propaganda— it's called brainwashing, and it's very simple to do. Doing it to a werwulf—or a skinchanger like Mr. Graves here—is harder, because of their resistance to both physical damage and persuasion."

"They're stubborn," Irving said, *sotto voce*, and another ripple ran through the room. It might've sounded like laughter if you weren't listening too closely.

"They are *resistant*," Blondie corrected, in the snootiest possible voice. "Nevertheless, it can be done. The most popular method was chaining in a *tatra*. This is a stone cube just big enough to allow the victim to stand upright, but not enough to turn around, bend over, or sit. The chain is fastened to a spiked collar—the spikes are turned inward, like so." His manicured hands sketched the air. "So the victim must move carefully even in that confined space. Then, raw meat is thrown onto the floor or placed just outside. The food scent torments until the meat begins to rot, and every day water is flung in through an aperture above the head. It cascades down, and the danger of inhaling it and developing pneumonia is very real. Then there are the *Revelle*, the dreamstealers, creatures bred by the Maharaja."

That got my attention all over again. Graves tensed next to me.

"The dreamstealer is brought in close proximity to the wulfen, fed carrion, and allowed to sing. Does anyone here know what a dreamstealer's song can do?"

"I know what happens when they stick their tongues in someone's mouth and start drinking," Graves muttered. "It *was* singing. I remember that much."

I didn't remember that. I still hadn't decided if I'd been out of my body or just having a really vivid dream that was my unconscious putting things together and presenting me with memory. But I did remember what happened *after* Graves tore the dreamstealer off me and Christophe stopped me retching and seizing.

*Christophe. He lied. He didn't tell me. Bastard. And someone else. Maybe that Anna chick. But she's svetocha too. It doesn't make sense. The vampires are the enemy, right? Why would anyone work with them?*

*His son. Sergej's son.*

Blondie paused, visibly deciding not to respond. "A dreamstealer's song takes hope away and drives its victim to the brink of insanity. Exposure for more than a few hours breaks down the barriers between a werwulf's conscious mind and the Other — the thing inside them that encloses and permits the change. Leaving the werwulf both psychotic and unable to reclaim his or her human form."

"They did this to *girls*, too?" Someone behind me sounded horrified. I guess chivalry isn't completely dead.

But I was thinking of the maddened, insane thing in Ash's eyes. He'd once been a werwulf like the kids in the classroom with me, all of them shifting uneasily in their seats. And Sergej had done that— chained him in a stone box and turned him into something that couldn't change back into a boy.

Blondie now looked pained. I was liking him more and more over the past couple of days, until I remembered he'd disappeared out the door and left me alone to be attacked. But right now, he was the teacher I was getting the most out of. "Sometimes," he said, quietly, "a psychotic female werwulf is nearly unstoppable. However, it is more difficult to break down a female's resistance and turn her into a Broken. Other methods were employed to force female wulfen's compliance. Anyway, once the wulf can no longer shift back into even a simulacrum of humanity, it is collared by its master and becomes an automaton with no free will of its own. It becomes merely appetite and obedience."

*Wait a second.* I sat up straight, the pad of paper sliding on my jeans. "Can you stop it? I mean—can you make someone like that human again?"

"Reclaim a Broken? It's possible, if you have a strong enough chain, enough time, and a compelling reason to do so. But the master of such a creature will rarely let it go, and will call it back with such intensity the wulf will often kill itself trying to escape. Wulfen have been known to break their own necks, chew through their own arms or legs—"

"There were reclamation projects, though." Shanks folded his arms. "My dad talks about them. There were whole *teams* of them in the 1920s." His entire body shouted *I don't like this*, from hunched-up shoulders to the uneasy way his fingers flicked and his knees joggled.

Of course, it was probably uncomfortable listening for a guy who could turn furry.

"There were," Blondie agreed. "Most of the projects ended in abject failure, or the death of those who tried to reclaim the Broken. However, when the wulfen and the founders of the Order made their compact, it became much more difficult for the *nosferatu* to abduct wulfen for their purposes." An odd smile tilted the corners of his mouth. "On this continent, we have the *wampyr* on the run. Most of the time, that is."

"But there *is* a way to reverse the damage, to fix it?" I persisted. "How exactly would you do it?"

He gave me a long measuring look. "That's a question for another time. Class dismissed."

Everyone started moving and shuffling, and Blondie gave me one last long look before striding out of the room. I folded up my pad and slid it into my bag, and hauled myself up from the couch with a creak and a sigh. Graves looked up at me, his unibrow peaking once over each eye. His entire face shouted, *What the hell are you thinking?*

I felt like I'd just been dunked in a cold bath, every nerve standing upright and shrieking. My next class was Aspect Mastery. I wasn't even sure who the teacher was, so I could miss it, no problem. I bet there was something in the school library—or even Dylan's office—that covered the Broken, and I am really good at finding shit like this out. Give me some research to do, and I am *all* over it.

It was a relief to find a concrete action to take.

A cool touch of dread stroked my nape. The note on my bed. My "friend." Was it the same friend who was supposed to have been getting me to my room when the vampires attacked? Was it Christophe? But what would he be doing in my room while vampires were attacking? Wouldn't he have heard the noise and—

God, if I could just stop thinking about it, I might've been able to get some sleep, or stop jumping nervously at every little sound.

Yeah. Like that was gonna happen.

"Walk you to class?" Graves said, cutting right across the noise in my head.

"Um." I blinked. *What exactly are you thinking, Dru?* But there had to be an explanation. Something wasn't jelling, and . . . well, it was crazy.

It was *nuts.*

But I was beginning to have an idea. It might even have been a good one, but I was so tired I couldn't tell.

Graves apparently took my *um* for a *yes*, I guess, because he stood up and tucked his hands in the pockets of the long black coat. He wore the goddamn thing everywhere. "All right. Come on, you don't wanna be late."

"They roast late students over fires." Shanks bounced up to his feet, collecting his notebook and a couple of textbooks covered with brown kraft paper. He gave me an odd look, and grinned, exposing very sharp white teeth. "But not *special* ones."

"Lay off," Graves said over his shoulder. "Jesus."

"I'm interested, actually. Wanna hear about how to brainwash a wulfen, Dru?" A crackling growl ran under the surface of the words. "Gonna start a breeding stable? They used to do that too. You can get pictures on the Internet."

Kids say horrible things to each other every day, in every high school in America. But this was something else. "I asked because I want to know how to fix it." I glared at him. "What's your *problem*?"

He made a mock-astonished face. "Oooh. You're going to *fix* it, like a good little *djamphir*?"

"Bobby." Graves half-turned, his coat flaring out and brushing my knees. "Lay. Off."

"Can she actually talk when she's not sucking up to the teachers?" He leaned forward on his toes, and the growl dropped a notch. "Or playing kissy-face with you? Got her own little *loup-garou* bodyguard. Why is she even *here*?"

Jesus. I'd never talked to this kid. I was kind of beginning to see why. "Come on." I pulled at Graves's sleeve. "Let's go."

He shook me off, took two steps forward. He was tall, but Shanks topped him by a good half-head. Still, Graves didn't look impressed *or* afraid in the least. "Go fuck yourself. Or get spayed. Either would be an improvement."

*Oh Christ.* Did this have to happen the instant I had an idea of something to actually *do*, instead of rattling around inside here chewing on myself? "Look—"

Fur was crawling up Bobby's thin cheeks. "Hold him back, bitch," he snarled, his shoulders hunching and hulking at once. It's always disconcerting to see muscle plumping up on a wulf when the hair pops up all over them and the jaw starts mutating. He was only halfway changed, but that's enough.

"Holy *shi*—" I didn't get to finish, because Graves hauled off and cold-cocked him. They went over the back of the couch in a tangle of fur and snapping black coat-cloth, and the other wulfen gathered around, making the weird yipping noise they sometimes did to spur each other on.

*Oh, for God's sake.* I dropped my bag and hopped over the back of the couch, then started shoving. The wulfen squeezed together, shoulder to shoulder, shouting—and I actually kicked someone behind the knee, squeezed forward, and pushed another one aside with strength I didn't know I had.

They were rolling around, Shanks half-changed and making a lot of noise, Graves growling as his eyes glowed—and then Bobby got in a knee to the nuts.

And punched him right in the face.

I heard the fist hit, the crunch of bone, and almost felt it in my own face.

*Graves!* Something inside me snapped. The red-tinted rage swelled up, coated my skin, and pushed me aside.

The world slowed down again, clear syrup hardening over every surface, and I bolted forward. This time, the weight didn't close over my arms and legs, and I had a vague idea that I was going much too fast before I *kicked*. There was a crunch, weirdly distorted and amplified, as my sneakered foot smashed into the other boy's face. He went careening back, still in that slow motion, and the fresh swell of rage that flooded me was clean and clear in its intensity.

It was a tidal wave of pure incandescent anger, turning me into a glass girl full of sparkling red fluid. I hit him twice more before he landed, both good solid shots. He crashed into a tangled knot of wulfen, their mouths open as they yelled. The entire scene was strangely soundless, and the wulfen began to scatter in slow motion.

I was on Shanks again, my hand closing around his throat and pushing him down through the syrup. His arm came up, like a sleepwalker's. I avoided the claws that would have sheared through my face and deflected the blow with one wrist, slapping it lightly away. The movement continued, my arm drawing back, and I heard Dad's voice again.

*Put your thumb outside, Dru. Tuck your thumb in and you'll break it when you punch that sad, sorry bastard. That's good. Now hit 'im hard, and hit 'im good! Good girl!*

The weird elongated noises around me drew away. Time slowed

down even further, and I knew it was going to snap and speed up soon. I had enough time to hit him but good with my cocked-back fist. I could probably break his nose, or if I punched a little lower I could crush his larynx and he'd suffocate.

*Dru, what are you doing?*

The rage still burned inside me. He'd hit Graves, and *hurt* him.

But I was seriously considering a punch that could truly disable someone, even kill them. And this was just a schoolroom brawl. Like every other schoolroom brawl I'd stayed out of, both out in the regular world and here.

Well, maybe not so much here.

*What is really going on here? Why don't the teachers intervene more?* The answer occurred to me a split second later—*they're teaching them to fight. Teaching them to hate each other, too.*

The fury was still boiling inside me. My temper frayed down to the thinnest of threads spinning over an abyss. The snap to speed everything up was coming. I could feel it, hovering on the edge of my awareness the way a sneeze tingles in your nose.

A hand closed over my shoulder, and if I was going to hit the kid I had to do it now. My fist leapt forward an inch, ducked back as the wulfen squirmed slowly, his mouth half-open, blood splattering down from his nose.

I let go of him, my fingers cramping. Someone dragged me back, fingers biting into my flesh so hard I could feel the bruising begin. I was a regular old punching bag. Jeez.

Time snapped like a thick rubber band, and this time I felt jarred all the way down to my bones. I'd just been dropped into the world again, a jolt like a car hitting a brick wall. There was shouting and screaming going on, and my hair hung in my face.

I watched, hypnotized, as blonde streaks slid through my curls.

They stretched out, longer and looser, into sleek waves instead of frizz. The golden streaks retreated, darkness eating them up, and my hair was my hair again.

*Holy shit. Was that—*

"Get *back!*" Graves yelled, dragging me back further as the wulfen closed over Shanks's still figure, lying on the floor against the bottom of a couch, the blood red and startling. Several of them had turned my direction and were advancing, fur crawling over their skin, shoulders and legs hulking up. "I'm *fucking warning you!*" It was an actual roar, his entire body vibrating. It shook through me, his voice, and I'd never heard him sound that way before.

That voice had a snap to it. A *bite*. I could almost see it shoving the clustered wulfen back. *Dominant*, I realized. *That's a loup-garou's command voice.*

They halted, all snarling. Even pale, gentle Dibs, who rarely spoke above a scared whisper. Their faces wrinkled up, teeth growing, fur sliding and rippling over their boy-forms.

Graves pulled me back another few steps. "*Stay where you are!*" he snapped, still in that shake-the-world voice. Everything actually rattled, including the inside of my head.

Then I realized I was making a weird sound too, a high keening noise with strange stops when my windpipe closed up and I had to breathe. The smell hit me—copper, hot, and good. It smashed into a place in the very back of my throat I never knew existed before, right next to the spot normal people don't have. The one that tells me when something weird is going to happen. That red coppery smell reached all the way down and ripped the world apart. I pitched forward again, fighting against Graves's hands on me, but he'd somehow gotten his arm around my waist and was hauling me away. I lunged again, almost dragging him with me, and I realized what I wanted to do.

I wanted to knock all of them out of my way and put my face in the wounded werwulf's throat.

I wanted to *drink*.

A roaring thirst crawled out from the middle of my throat, spread through my entire body. I was dry, cracking and burning, and the only thing that could quench the fire was the sweet red fluid I could smell all over. It tapped inside my head, whispered and cajoled, and my teeth turned achingly sensitive. I could almost feel them lengthening, sharp tickling crawling over the enamel. My hair tingled, and every inch of me was awake again. The persistent exhaustion of the last few sleepless days vanished, replaced with high, crackling energy.

Graves's other arm came around my throat and he choked up as I writhed, pitching back and forth. My teeth snapped together, making little clicking sounds. The wulfen snarled back, but Graves made that weird, world-shaking sound again and they stayed away.

I wish I could say I was relieved when Shanks rose up out of the middle of a knot of werwulfen, his face a mask of blood and his eyes blazing. But I wasn't. I wanted to lick the stuff off his face and put my teeth in his throat, and *I wanted to drink*.

He snarled, Graves rumbled back. And I don't know what would have happened if a flood of *djamphir* hadn't burst through the door and surrounded me. They held me down as I started screaming, shouldering Graves aside. But he stayed, holding onto my hand even when my fingers bit down and bones in both our hands crackled.

It was the first time the bloodhunger had struck me. And now, oh God, I understood so much more.

Graves didn't leave me, even though everyone was shouting. He stayed right there, making a noise over and over again, and I finally realized he was saying my name. The hunger crested, and when it finally retreated, I started crying. Graves was the one who pulled me close and hugged me. I was sobbing and shaking like a little kid, and some of them started telling him to leave, but he just shook them off and kept holding me.

I clung to him too. They couldn't pull me away.

# Chapter 13

Graves set the stack of books down on the wooden table with a thump. My teeth still ached. So did my entire body. But all in all, it was apparently no big deal at the Schola. Shanks was in the baths, and Graves was skipping whatever he was supposed to be doing, and I'd been told to "just go somewhere else and calm down."

Yeah. Calm down. Two of the most useless words in the English language. But Dylan told me the danger was past, and I wasn't going to go and bite someone. He said it was normal, because I was so close to blooming. And that I'd get used to it.

I wasn't so sure.

He also said they hadn't had a death "from student interactions" at this Schola for about sixty-two years, which wasn't as comforting as it could have been either.

The library was full of the smell of dust and old paper. Barred windows let in sharp swords of golden evening light between heavy antique wooden bookshelves—the sun had finally come out, too late in the day to do any good. Nobody was behind the circulation desk.

It was a good thing. I could still smell the blood. My teeth were still sensitive, as if I'd just gone to the dentist's. Every nerve in me was raw, and I sat with my arms cupping my elbows, hugging myself.

"It's fucking crazy. *You're* crazy," Graves said flatly. "What are you going to do, tie him up in your room? They'll kill him."

At least he was talking about something other than me growing fangs and wanting to go all *nosferat* on someone. He just plain refused to discuss *that*, and I was grateful.

Well, as grateful as I could be with my brain refusing to work right and my hair changing color and Jesus God, what the hell was happening to me?

Who was I anymore? When I looked in the mirror, would I still see myself?

It was like vanishing into a funhouse to ask yourself that ques-0tion—I mean, seriously ask yourself, in a funhouse where the horror is real and anything but fun, and see what happens. Asking yourself that sort of question makes everything inside you that's not nailed down do a funny jigging dance.

I had precious little that was nailed down anymore.

If I focused on something else, I could probably get through this. "Something just doesn't add up." At least I wasn't lisping around fangs. My teeth were normal, but I kept running my tongue over them, testing. They *felt* normal. Except for the aching in them, and the thirsty place at the back of my throat. "He was *this close* to me, Graves. And he didn't do anything but sniff me. I—"

"Shut up." He dropped down into a chair and glared at me. "What the hell is going on with you, Dru?"

*You mean, other than having my dad murdered, finding out I'm part sucker, getting chased and beaten up, and turning into a blood-craving fiend prepared to really, really hurt someone? Jeez, I'm pink. I'm perfect. I'm the picture of health.* I opened my mouth to say something smart or at least less stupid than usual, but closed it again because, well, what could I say?

It was hopeless. I looked down at the mellow glow of the wood's surface. Heat rose behind my eyes, the unsteady ball of rage caged in my ribs kicked up another notch, and I swallowed hard. Kept my temper down through sheer force of will.

Now that I knew what the bloodhunger did, would I ever be able to look at myself in the mirror? Or at any of the *djamphir* without flinching?

"Come *on.*" He was still glaring at me, I could *feel* it. "Say something, Dru. Don't just sit there and look like I've stabbed you. Christ."

The sunshine faded as dusk took hold. I slumped back in the chair, hugging myself. The whirling inside me wouldn't stop. I breathed in, breathed out, trying to make it slow down a little. If I freaked out now, what the hell *else* might happen?

Would I jump on Graves? Would my teeth get long and sharp, and would I want to put my face in his throat and *drink*?

My chest hurt. I hugged myself harder.

"Come on." His tone gentled. "What are you doing? You keep shoving everything down like this and you're going to give yourself an ulcer or something. I'm here, okay? I've taken everything this place could throw at me. I'm not going anywhere."

That just made me feel worse. He was here because of me. Great. "Do you ever want to go home?" I had to fight to keep the words steady. My chest hurt. It was the same old pain, the breathless feeling of sitting in a hospital corridor once Gran was dead, just repeating over and over, *My dad is coming, he'll take care of it. He's on his way*. And hoping it was true.

*Praying* it was true. But this time I was left behind for good. There was nobody coming to get me. Not in any good way, at least.

And the sooner I started dealing with that the better. But oh God, the thought scared me, way down deep.

He was quiet for a long few moments. "Shit no," he finally said. "Look, I don't know if you caught this, Dru, but I don't have a fireplace and picket fence to go back to. I was *homeless*, okay?"

I'd suspected, but it was a different thing altogether to hear it out loud. "You had—"

"That room at the mall? Fuck, what kind of kid lives in the mall? Here at least there's enough food. There's a bed I earned, and I'm keeping it. Nobody's trying to peddle my ass or beating me because he's drunk." He inhaled sharply, blew the air out. "At least here, there's *rules*. Werwulfen and vampires I can handle. It's the adults back in that other world I can't. They . . . At least here the evil has reasons. It's not just . . ." He searched for the word, his face twisting in on itself for a second as he struggled to articulate. "It's not just *senseless*."

*What happened to my dad was senseless*. I didn't say it. How could you say something like that to someone? "You wanted to be a physics professor." My throat had closed up; I could only whisper.

"Yeah, well, things change. Now I want to be here." Another long, seconds-ticking pause. Dust danced in one fading gleam of gold coming through a low window, following long lazy swirls down to the ground. "With you."

I stared at the motes suspended in the air, all dancing to music nobody could hear. I read somewhere once that dust could even be bits of exploded stars, falling to earth. How far does a bit of star-stuff fall and float before it gives up and just gets pulled into any planet's orbit?

Did it matter?

The sun slid below the edge of the horizon, and the Schola sighed, settling into itself.

"I don't know who I am anymore." The words were throttled halfway out, died in the library's silence. I expected the world to crack open and the sky to fall once I said it.

Nothing happened. The library still held its breath, and Graves still stood there looking at me.

"Nobody does, Dru." It was the same quiet, oddly adult tone he'd used that first evening, sitting in the mall and asking me just how bad everything was and if I needed a place to sleep. "It's called growing up."

The whirling inside me had gone down a little. I could finally unreel my arms from around my chest. I pushed my hair back. The curls felt weird—not frizzy but silky, clinging to my fingers. "I'm sorry."

"Yeah, well." Was he *blushing*? "I'm never going to live it down that a *girl* knocked Bobby on his ass defending me. Jeez."

Something tight-sprung inside me eased a little bit. The rage retreated. There was enough room to breathe, and I took in a sharp deep lungful. "Well, next time I'll let him mess with you. Happy?"

"Yeah, well. I had him handled, but still. Anyway, you wanna take half these books?"

The world was seeming manageable again. How did he *do* that? "What for?"

"Well, if you're so interested in rehabilitating Broken werwulfen, these seem like a reasonable place to start. Haven't you been in here before?"

"Once or twice." *But you're right, this is a good idea. Dad always said research is what saves you.*

Yeah, right on schedule, the most uncomfortable thought in the room was moving into my head and calling it home. I should start charging uncomfortable thoughts rent. Except what would they pay me in? Probably something even worse.

"You've been going to class more." He separated the stack into two equal piles, and it was official. He *was* blushing. High flags of color stood out on his face, so deep they were damn close to maroon. An ugly bruise was spreading up his jawbone, too.

I'd thought he was half-ugly before. Unfinished-looking. It was hard to believe. "Yeah, well, nothing else to do." I took the pile he pushed toward me. "Doesn't it bother you? That I . . . well, that I wanted to . . . suck his blood?"

His Adam's apple bobbed as he swallowed. The silver earring winked mischievously at me, catching a stray gleam of sun. "Nah. You wouldn't, you'd have stopped yourself."

I wasn't so sure, and I opened my mouth to tell him so.

"Besides," he said, flipping open the first huge leather-bound book with a thump, "it's kind of hot." A smile hovered around the corners of his mouth, fighting to stay hidden.

*What?* I stared at him for a few seconds. My jaw had officially dropped. "You're *insane.*"

"Pot calling kettle, anyone? Start reading."

I wasn't sure I'd be able to concentrate, but I did. The sensitivity in my mouth retreated, and after a little while I couldn't smell the blood anymore. After another while I could actually read the page in front of me without the tears welling up and making all the words blur. I made like I was brushing dust off my cheeks, when I was really smearing hot salt water over them.

Graves didn't say anything about me leaking. But he didn't turn a page for a long time either. When it was time to go to his last class of the night he walked me back to my room first, carrying a double armful of books that we piled on my bed. I finally fell asleep with one of them propped against the headboard, and slept all the way through until morning's faint blush against the sky.

I could have slept longer, but I had something to do.

# CHAPTER 14

**took a shower,** braided my hair back. The hall felt weird. I stood on my side of the door, my hand spread against its chill heaviness, and felt someone outside listening intently. It was the same feeling I used to get right before I told Dad a certain motel or house wasn't safe.

He'd never argued.

So that left just one option. I didn't like it, but it was better than sitting around moping.

Weak sun slid through the stamped holes in the iron shutters. I pushed them as wide as they would go, struggled with the window. I had to walk a fine line between wrenching it open and trying to be quiet about it. A drench of cold air heavy with the promise of rain flooded through, and I glanced down into the dead rose garden.

The paving-stone paths looked very hard from up here.

It was a long way to fall. I swallowed, hard. *Wish I had a rope. Jeez.*

But if Christophe had done this, I could too. The worst that could happen was a broken leg and a bunch of questions, right?

I'd never broken a bone before. And those questions had teeth. Everything here had teeth.

*This is a stupid idea, Dru.*

But I was going to do it anyway. With someone watching my door, I *had* to. I couldn't take the chance of anyone, friendly or otherwise, following me. And I had to know if it was possible to escape the Schola during the day.

I grabbed the window frame and put my foot up, made sure it was secure, and hauled myself carefully up to stand on the sill. Told myself not to look down, instead studying the stone wall and the roof overhang. It looked like slate tile and the angle would make it tricky. No gutter, either. That was both good—gutters could tear away from the roof—and bad, because I wouldn't have anything to curl my fingers around but the roof's edge.

I turned my back on the dead garden, bracing myself on the sill. Reached up and back with one hand.

*This is a bad idea. Figure something else out.*

The trouble was, there was nothing else. And Christophe had done this. I'd be damned if I didn't at least try. Not to mention that if I pulled this off, I would have an escape route already scoped. And it would be the last path anyone would expect me to take.

Less speed, less strength, less stamina since I hadn't "bloomed." But I'd bet I was outweighing everyone around me in the brain category. It was all I had.

*Then why are you going to do something this stupid?*

I told that voice of reason to take a hike and wrapped my fingers around the edge of the overhang. The angle wasn't really bad, just kind of bad. I shut my eyes and breathed in, out, slate gritty and cold under my hands. The red crisscross slashes on Christophe's hands suddenly made sense now, as I'd known they would.

My other hand found the roof edge too. I played the action over and over in my head, the way Dad taught me to practice rifle shots. *Half of it's in getting it clear inside your noggin, Dru girl, and the body will know what to do when the time comes. See it behind your eyes, feel yourself doing it.*

I'd only have one shot at it. My arms tensed, relaxed, practicing. I stilled the movement of myself inside my skin, focusing inward. Listening.

My heartbeat thudded, a comforting rhythm. My breathing evened out, soft and deep. The wet braid touched my back, moving as my body balanced itself on the sill, weight forward on the ball of my right foot. Heels hung out in space, the cool morning breeze pushing past me into the room.

*Breathe in, breathe out.* Feeling the tingle along my skin. Little tiny muscle movements that make up balance—you never stand completely still. If you did, you'd fall over. Stillness is a constant adjustment, a series of tiny little corrections, like steering a car.

Dad taught me that.

The thought stung, whipped through me, and every muscle fiber tensed. I heard wingbeats, feathers brushing air and whispering against my face. I didn't have to lean back too far; it was almost like pulling myself out of a swimming pool.

The slate edges bit deep into the meat of my hands. I let out a sharp breath, got a knee up. Good thing I was wearing jeans. I found myself scrabbling up the slope of the roof, hunched over and thanking God I'd worn sneakers instead of boots. The soles gripped, and my fingernails splintered on the slate as I drove them in hard.

*Oh crap.* The slope was incredibly sharp, and I made it to the crest and straddled the ridgeline. The big muscles in my legs were shaking. My arms, including the deep bruises on my shoulder, throbbed heavily. I was a song of pain, and the healing capability of the baths wasn't helping as much as I wished it would. My hands cried out, palms full of hot wetness and fingertips scraped raw.

But I got myself arranged so I wouldn't fall off, and I raised my head. The wind hit my face, full of the peculiar smell of being high up, and I saw.

Today there was no fog.

The countryside folded away on all sides, trees choking-close except where two-lane blacktop ribboned in from what I knew from my trip here was a county highway. This was the highest point for a ways around. There was a blue smudge far, far to the south that I thought might be the Alleghenies, but could have been just a fog or cloud.

Down the hill a stream came meandering past, glittering dull silver in the overcast. Clouds were shredding away, and we'd have some full sun before long when they burned off. I saw the boathouse, a run-down shack that didn't look sturdy enough to hold up in a sharp breeze. The Schola turned a cold shoulder to it, its wings raked back like a bird of prey. A gray one with a sharp beak, settled and dozing in its nest.

I couldn't quite see the big circular driveway, but I saw the vine-draped pedestals at the end of it and blinked, rubbing my eyes. I could've sworn there had been stone lions there —

*No,* the voice of instinct whispered. *They were there, but they're not now. For whatever reason.*

I had a sudden, vivid mental image, playing itself inside my head the way a song will get stuck between the ear and the brain.

*Concrete-gray lion padding softly through forest-dappled sunlight, hard muscles under worn-smooth skin. The lion turned its heavy neck and lifted its head, blind stone eyes searching, and its mouth opened. Needle-sharp, slivered teeth packed close, and it exhaled, ruf-*

*fling leaves on the forest floor. It senses eyes upon it, and confusion plucks inside its cold, massive head. The eyes are of a Ruler, but far away, and the stone mane curls upon its shoulders with a sound like wet clay sliding against itself. . . .*

The image faded. I shook my head to clear it. I had to stay sharp, because the roof was steeply pitched all around me, and the slate was damp in places. I could slip and tumble for a long way before falling off the edge, and that wouldn't be any fun for anyone.

I clutched my bleeding hands to my chest and wished I'd thought of gloves. But then I'd lose out on traction. Sometimes you just have to suck up the damage.

I was doing a lot of that lately.

The wind whistled across peaks and valleys of slate tiling. Some tiles were missing, and some sagged, but all in all, the roof looked pretty solid. My hand twitched, and I kept my fingers away from the locket with an effort. I let out another sharp breath, this time in wonder. My heart banged once, twice, settled into a high, hard galloping run. It took a moment of thought before I realized I wasn't scared.

No, the feeling was actually happiness. It swelled behind my pulse and pushed my arms out, fingers spread as a huge disbelieving grin wrinkled up my face. I'm sure I looked like a moron, balancing on a ridgepole and holding my arms out like a circus performer. But here, with the wind keening past me and the trees choking up on the Schola's gray bulk, I felt . . . well, I felt free. For the first time in a long time.

Up here, there was nothing but me and the wind. And a tingling in my teeth, as a feeling I was sure was the aspect blurred through me. This time it was a warm, comforting glow, banishing the pain. My hands stopped bleeding, and when I looked down at them, the ladderlike cuts had scabbed over. The flat-copper smell of my own blood washed away on fresh rainy air, but I thought I caught a thread of warm perfume. When I fisted my hands, lightly, they didn't hurt much and the scabs didn't tear.

*Wow.* I wondered why it didn't work for the bruises and aches inside me. But they were muted now too. The aspect tingled through me, retreated with a sound like owl wings.

*Is this what blooming feels like?* I wished I could ask someone. Gran had told me about The Facts of Life pretty early, and Dad had told me in his gruff way what he thought I should know—which boiled down to *Don't be stupid* and *Don't buy cheap tampons; we've got money*.

This "blooming" thing was like having puberty questions all over again and having nowhere to go to do some, you know, research. Maybe the library had something for curious girl *djamphir*. I laughed, a short disbelieving sound, and felt more like myself than I had for weeks.

After a little while standing there like an idiot, it occurred to me that I'd better start looking for a way down. I had a plan, after all, and it didn't include hanging out up here all day. So I stopped staring at the woods and the sky and breathing in the odd cold rain-soaked happiness. It still stayed with me as I studied the lay of the rooftops, trying to see it like the hollers and ridges around Gran's house. If you could get a vantage point, you could work out your way just about anywhere—with a compass and some common sense, that is. All I'd need up here was the sense.

How much sense I had climbing around on a roof, I don't know. But I took a good look, and the fist inside my head opened up a little, sending out little bits of questing awareness. I waited for the tingle that would tell me it was safe to go, and would also tell me which road to take.

You can't ever rush something like that. It's the same reason why you can't ask a pendulum anything you really, really want to know about. The wanting makes a screen in front of the real answer, which might be something you'd prefer not to hear. So you've got to go still and quiet, as unattached from the answer as possible. It's different from really needing intuition in a pinch, when you have to just shut out the screaming all around you and listen for the still small voice of certainty.

Gran always harped on it, actually, how the pendulum would sometimes tell you just what you wanted to hear, and hang the rest. *Common sense,* she'd say over and over again. *Ha! Common as hen's teeth, maybe. Got to apply that old meat twixt your ears, honey.*

A wave of homesickness crashed into me, so sharp and hot it almost rocked me back on my heels. I longed to be back in Gran's narrow little house up in Appalachians, listening to the whirr and thump of her spinning wheel on a cold evening, smelling whatever she'd cooked for dinner and the floor and window washes she was always using. Yarrow, lavender, wild rose, constant scrubbing. But there was also that time in the evening when it was too dark to work outside, when Gran would spin and I would half-lay on the old love seat and stare at the iron stove. It was warm and safe and I never had to wait for Gran to come get me. She was always there.

The tugging tingle in my solar plexus came. I studied the roof some more and saw the way down. It didn't look like much; I'd have to zag over a couple of sharp slopes, and there was a bit of a drop onto a long, gallery-type roof. I could hop down from there in a protected angle, using a set of—were those dumpsters? Had to be, yeah, that would be right behind the kitchen. Maybe I could even peek in and see who was doing the cooking behind that screen of steam.

*What about getting back up? You're so smart, what about getting back into the Schola?*

Getting in wouldn't be a problem. I'd just bang on the front door for a while. They'd let me in, right?

I thought of the missing stone lions and wasn't too sure. But it was too late to back out now. I'd figure something out.

I checked my scabbed hands one last time and got going.

\* \* \*

It wasn't hard to get into the boathouse. A plain wooden door, a latch that had once probably held a padlock rusted wide open. I looked for any sign of habitation, didn't find it. Pushed the door gingerly with my foot, wincing at the screech of rusted locks, and stepped in. The stiletto had eased itself out of my pocket, and I wished I had a gun instead, to sweep the place.

The entire structure was completely dilapidated. One boat had sunk, rotting, under the glassine water lapping at the central well. Another hung overhead on rusting chains, looking like it hadn't been touched in easily twenty years or so. Holes glared in its sides, and the chains didn't seem too solid.

Coils of rope moldered in the corners. The place smelled like rot and mildew, and the flat iron tang of snowmelt river water. The floor sagged underneath my feet with each cautious step.

And on the other side of the bay where the rowboat wallowed at the sandy bottom under a blanket of clear heavy weight, he just *appeared*.

Christophe stepped out of the shadows, his blue eyes alight. Not a blond-highlighted, expensively cut hair was out of place. His hands dropped down to his sides, as if he'd been holding them up. What had he been planning on doing? Did he think I was an enemy?

Everything boiled up inside of me and I let out a high-pitched, girly sound. The switchblade clicked open at the same time.

*Great. Just great.* All the practicing I'd done for this moment failed me utterly, and I stood there next to a pile of slumping, damp-eaten lumber and stared at him. "You *lied* to me!" I sounded like I'd been punched, hard.

"*Hello* is usually considered a more appropriate greeting." He lifted one shoulder, dropped it. A breath of apples and cinnamon reached me, hit the back of my throat, and tickled the bloodhunger. "And what am I supposed to have lied to you about, Dru?"

Each time I saw him, it was like I'd forgotten how his face worked together, every line and plane proportionate. "A sixteenth, you said! You said you were called a half-breed, but you were technically a sixteenth!"

"What? A lecture on genetics?" But his face clouded. He obviously guessed where this was going.

For one long second I considered how satisfying it would be to hit him, to unleash the ball of rage behind my ribs and see if he could still smack me around so easily. "Sergej." The name sent a glass spike of hatred through my head. "Your *father.*"

Christophe went utterly still, his eyes burning. His thumbs were hooked in his jean pockets, but his hands were tense and his shoulders rigid under the usual black sweater. He stared at me for a little while, his head cocked like he'd just had a good idea and was running it through before he swung into motion.

Finally, he spoke. "Who told you?"

I swallowed hard, lowering the knife. Its blade winked once in the hard, thin light. *Oh God. Did you help kill my mother? Tell me. I have to know. I have to know something, anything, for sure.* "Who? Oh, nobody. Just Anna. Another *svetocha* like me. Was that something you forgot too? She said—"

"Ah. Anna. Spreading her poison." A silent snarl drifted over his face. "I didn't *ask* to be born into my bloodline, Dru. Just like you didn't *ask* to be born *svetocha*." He showed his teeth, blond highlights sliding back through his hair as the aspect folded over him. "You should be grateful, though. My father's strength passed on to me, and it's the reason you're still breathing enough to fling accusations." He straightened. "What are you doing here? Someone should be watching you during the day."

*Yeah, right. Like someone's supposed to watch me when it's Restriction. That's really been working out well.* "I got out of my room. Didn't you leave this?" I dug the note out of my pocket, suddenly wishing I could fold up the knife again. "The night I was . . . attacked?"

"Attacked? And . . . Anna." The aspect kept his hair dark, and his teeth didn't retract. "Tell me."

"I want to know—" My heart was in my throat again.

I didn't even see him move. One moment he was all the way across the boathouse. The next, the silvery screen of water over the sunken rowboat rippled, and he was right in front of me. I jerked back, my shoulders hitting the door, and his nose was inches from mine. His hands thudded onto the wood behind me, his wrists against my abused shoulders. Apple scent drifted around me.

Jesus. He was so *fast*. And his eyes were burning. The aspect retreated, blond sliding in his hair as a stray band of sunlight caressed it. "What do you think you want to know? If I wanted to betray you, *kochana*, I could have. Easily. If I wanted to hurt you, I would have already *done* it. I could have . . ." He paused. His fingers came down, wrapped around my wrist. The knife lifted, and he held it with the point just over the left side of his chest. "There. There's the spot. Between those two ribs and twist, if you can. Don't hesitate, Dru. If you honestly think *I'm* a danger to you, push the knife in. I'll help." His lips skinned back from his teeth, and his fingers tensed on mine. He jerked the knife forward, and I surprised myself by yanking back. I couldn't let go—he was holding it too hard. My scraped fingers gave a flare of red pain, subsided.

He tried again, pulling. The point touched his sweater. The same paper-thin black V-neck he always wore, whether it was hip-deep in snow in the Dakotas, or freezing here. "Go ahead." His breath touched my face. "Every *djamphir* is technically a sixteenth. Any more than that and we're *nosferatu*; any less and we're malformed things, not even human. Something about the gene pairs; I don't claim to be a scientist. It was a joke. But feel free to use your little knife, *kochana*."

I tried uncurling my fingers. He wouldn't let me. We stood like that, him tugging forward and me pulling back, until he let go of my hand. Spread his palms against the wood behind my shoulders and leaned in. "Satisfied?"

My mouth opened. The knife dropped and dangled in my nerveless hand. I couldn't find a damn thing to say. He waited, and the sound of water whispering away under half the boathouse's floor, touching its rotting pilings, was a cold silken whisper.

I dropped my eyes. Looked at his throat. His Adam's apple moved as he swallowed. When he spoke, it was the same businesslike, mocking tone he'd used when I first met him.

"Now, let's talk about something useful. Attacked? When? Tell me about that first. Then Anna." He plucked the note from my nerveless fingers, held it to his nose, and inhaled. But he didn't step back, and the note vanished into his back pocket. Just like that, it was gone. "Ah. Dylan. Sneaky old man. This was our meeting place, once."

"I—what? Jesus." What was *Dylan* doing leaving notes on my pillow? But it solved one riddle.

Christophe leaned back toward me, his hands on either side of my shoulders again. "He's reassuring me of his loyalty. Touching. As well as giving you a reason to slip your leash during the daytime, which I'm not so sure I like. Now start talking. When?"

I told him the whole thing, stealing little glances at his expression. It was a type of relief to spill it all out, like lancing an infection or popping a zit. It's also kind of hard to talk with a *djamphir* staring you in the face. Especially when the aspect keeps flickering through him, and his canines are touching his lower lip, dimpling softly. His entire body tensed when I got to the part about Ash and the sucker. I was busy thinking of what I'd do if he got angry—could I dump him in the water and run for it?

My voice faltered when I got to Ash sniffing me. Just . . . sniffing me. After he'd torn a couple of suckers apart, suckers who said the Master wanted something.

It didn't take a rocket scientist to figure out the "Master" was Sergej. Or to figure out what he wanted with "the little bitch."

"*Mój boże*," Christophe whispered. "You're certain? *Certain* it was him?"

I nodded. He was so close it was hard to breathe. It was *exactly* like being next to an oven baking a really spicy apple pie. "He bit Graves, I'd know him anywhere—"

"*Mój boże*," he repeated, then grabbed my shoulders. I was confused, but then I found myself caught in a bear hug, his arms around me and his chin atop my head. He wasn't as tall as Graves, but he was wiry-strong and very warm, burning through his clothes. "He must have killed them all, or Sergej would have sent more. It's only a matter of time now." It sounded like he was talking to himself, and I was frozen. I hadn't been this close to anyone except Graves lately, and there was a weird feeling to it.

A weird, warm feeling. Warm all over, like being dipped in oil. It was kind of like Dad's infrequent hugs when I'd done something really well. But there was something else to it. Dad hadn't smelled like apple pie and he hadn't hugged me so hard my bones creaked, and breathed into my hair. Christophe's breath was a warm spot on my head—he'd tucked his chin to the side now, and his hands spread against my back. The locket, caught between us on my breastbone, was a hard lump of warning.

"Dear God." His arms didn't tighten, but he was still tense. I was trying to figure out what exactly the feeling was.

Then it hit me. It was *safety*. Christophe wasn't about to let anyone hurt me. I don't know when I'd started believing that rather than being afraid of him, but there it was. It was like I felt when I heard Dad's truck rumbling into the driveway in a strange new house, coming back to get me. Like someone was going to Deal With Things, and I could relax a little and just go with it.

Like I knew my place in the world again.

We stood like that for a little while, Christophe and me. I breathed in the smell of apple pies and everything else fell away. The boathouse creaked a little in the thin sunlight, and I couldn't see anything because my face was buried where his neck met his shoulder, my nose in the slight hollow just above his collarbone.

I didn't mind as much as I thought I would.

"Listen to me," he finally said, as if I'd been arguing with him. "Are you listening, little bird?"

My voice wouldn't work right. I made a tiny little nod instead, because—how's this for weird—I didn't want him to let go of me. He'd pulled back a little, just with his lower half, and I was afraid the scorch in my cheeks would set fire to the rest of me, because I had an idea why.

*Wow. Oh wow.*

"I'll take you to a safe entrance. Go back up to your room—don't worry if someone sees you. At this point, it doesn't matter. I have to ask you to wait, Dru. I'll be gone for a day, perhaps as many as three or four; there are arrangements I must make for your escape. Will you trust me?"

You know, if he'd asked me this way the first time—serious instead of mocking, his voice almost breaking—I would have handed over my car keys. Or maybe I was just thinking that now, because he was so close and because he was shaking. We both were. The trembling spilled through me like wind through aspen leaves.

"Anna said you betrayed my mother. Told S-Sergej where to find—" The sentence died because he squeezed me, hard. I was almost afraid my bones would break. The breath huffed out of me, against his neck.

"I would *never*," he snarled, "have done that. Never. Do you *understand* me? God and Hell both damn it, Dru. I couldn't save her, but I'm going to save you. I *swear* it."

And you know, I believed him.

What girl wouldn't?

# CHAPTER 15

**T**wo hours later, I eased down the hall. I didn't see anyone outside my room, but I *felt* them there. I made it in and locked, barred, bolted the door. And that, apparently, was that. Christophe told me not to worry about someone seeing me come back—it was getting out without being caught that was the problem.

It reminded me of Dad. Shaking a tail or pursuit was second nature, and it was better for someone to lose you on the way out to a meet so you didn't compromise anyone else. I would have liked to be a fly on the wall when someone told Dylan I'd been spotted coming *back* to my room. It was amusing, in a grim, ironic sort of way.

*Wait,* Christophe had said. *I'll come back for you, as soon as I know . . . when I have a safe place for you. Will you trust me?*

It was just like Dad leaving me a fifty and telling me to do my katas. But scalding flushes kept going through me whenever I thought of Christophe hugging me. I would turn hot, then cold, just like alternating tap water. It lasted all the way through the rest of the sunny day and into nightfall, and I almost didn't hear the bell for wakeup. I was too busy trying to pin down where the hot and cold was coming from. My internal thermostat was way wack.

The lunchroom was a chaos of surf noise. Graves set his tray down. "I've got an idea."

"Oh God." I stared at my plate. Nothing on it looked even remotely appetizing. "What now?"

The cafeteria echoed around us, and he took a good look at my face. "Jesus. You're pale."

*Tell nobody. Not even Dylan. But if there is another attack, try to find him. Don't stay in your room.* Here Christophe had smiled grimly, just a slight curve of lips. *Or if you do, little bird, make certain you bar your door.*

"Just . . . I don't know." Now it was time for a cold flash. I shivered. The entire place was too noisy and bright. Boys kept glancing at me, though once Graves sat down they went back to what they were doing. And only snuck glances at me instead of staring openly. Except for Shanks, who stared at me from under his emo-boy swoop until I locked eyes with him, and he hurriedly looked away. He was all the way across the caf, too.

Dibs hadn't shown up yet. I actually . . . well, kind of missed him. I'd gotten used to that terminal shyness.

"You okay?"

*I saw Christophe again.* The words boiled behind my lips. "Fine." I still felt cold. Even the fact that my hair was behaving couldn't make me happy. I'd braided the whole mess back and forgot about it first thing.

It would figure, the instant I get okay hair I *also* start getting hot flashes. And keeping more secrets than I ever thought possible. Jeez.

"You sure? You look—"

"It's my room." The half-lie felt dirty and left a bad taste in my mouth. "I've been thinking about it. Someone has to have keys. Several someones *could* have the keys. I can't lock the dead bolt unless I'm in there, but someone could have the key for *that* too. There's a bolt and a chain, but they're both old and the door won't stand up to a beating. And warding won't stop *djamphir* or wulfen. It never stopped Christophe."

Saying his name was like a pinch in an already-sore place. *I saw him. He hugged me, and . . . Jesus, Graves. You don't even like me that way, but I can't tell you about Christophe, either.*

"Point." Graves stared at the paper, chewing his lower lip gently with startlingly white teeth. They hadn't been that white before. It was the wulfen dental plan—get bit and never have to worry about your canines again. "You're just frightening yourself, you know."

*Is that all it is? Well, it's working. Spectacularly.* I hunched my shoulders. Waiting for Christophe to come back and collect me was going to wear my nerves down to bare nubs.

"Really," Graves persisted. "You're pretty safe here. If the suckers were planning to kill you, they could do it easier if you were alone and on the run with nobody watching out for you."

"I don't know that anyone's watching out for me here," I mumbled to my plate. "Look at what's happened already."

"Some of *them*—the teachers—must be. And Jesus, Dru, *I'm* watching out for you too." He picked up his burger, took a huge bite. Chewed while examining me, with the air of a man who considered the matter closed.

That only managed to make me feel worse. He'd gotten bit because of me, and he was here because of me—no matter that he thought it was a better place than where he'd been. The Real World was nothing to play with, and he could get killed tomorrow or even tonight if a group of suckers attacked again.

And Christophe. The secret trembled behind my lips again, I swallowed until it sat in my stomach like a stone.

I had to say something about him. Maybe Graves would guess and I wouldn't have to say it out loud. "Why did Christophe send us here?" I picked up my fork and poked at the pile of salad on my plate. I'd dumped some blue-cheese dressing over it, but it still didn't look even remotely appetizing. What I wouldn't have given for Dad's special pancakes, or chili the way he used to make it. Or a good heaping helping of Gran's chicken and dumplings. Or fried chicken and slaw, with biscuits the way she taught me to make them.

"I been thinking about that."

Well, that was good, because I was fresh out of ideas. The secrets hemming me in fought for release, met with the bubble of heat behind my breastbone, and retreated. Even in two hours I hadn't asked Christophe half of what I wanted to. He'd been in a hurry to get me back to the Schola's walls and disappear to *make arrangements*. "And?"

"Maybe he didn't mean to send us *here* in specific. This is a small school. There's got to be others. What if we got put somewhere he didn't plan for?"

I turned it over inside my head. It would make sense, especially if Anna wanted to accuse him of killing my mother. But *why*? Why the cloak-and-dagger? Why all the bullshit?

I didn't have an answer for that one, and pulled myself back to the present with a twitch. "But he found me. Came in right through the window."

"And what if he can't get in again because of the watch the teachers set on the grounds? This place is closed up tighter than Fort Knox. And, well, Dru, he might not have your best interests at heart."

*He's in the boathouse, or he was and said he wouldn't ever . . . and if you'd been there . . .* But the idea of Graves standing there watching while Christophe hugged me made a weird unsteady guilt flood through me. I felt my chin set itself stubbornly. "He saved me from Sergej."

"But he might have done that for a thousand different reasons we don't know about. He called in the Order and said he was a part of them, but there's just as many people here who think he's some sort of traitor. And . . ." But he shut up and took another monstrous bite. He looked hungry, and his shoulders were bulking up. Now he was rangy instead of thin. Like the other wulfen boys, wide-shouldered and narrow-hipped. "Look, I've got an idea."

I hunched my shoulders even further. "You don't understand. I can't even sleep anywhere safe."

"So we steal a solid chair and put it under your doorknob. Even if they have keys, they can't get past that. And it'll brace the door, make it harder to knock down. Right?"

It was such a simple, obvious solution I felt like a moron. "Oh. Yeah." *Unless they hack the door down, but I'm sure I'd wake up for that. And get out the window again. Great.* "I guess."

"All right. So that solves that problem." He gave me a quick sideways glance. "You okay?"

*No, I'm not. Everyone's lying to me, I'm rattled, everything's screwed up all over, and now I feel stupid too. And to top it all off, I feel like I'm lying to you, even.* I flinched away from that thought. Pushed my plate away. "Fine. So what's your big idea?"

He told me, and I was even happier I hadn't eaten. We argued about it until the bell rang, and he went off to his next class.

I went to steal a chair. I was sucking at the attending-classes-every-day thing, but the chair was more important. And if several someones were trying to kill me, a chair would do better than a class would. At least I'd be able to sleep.

While I was at it, I tried to think of how to break into the armory and steal my gun back, too. Once I had a firearm, I'd feel better about a whole lot of things. If more suckers attacked or someone else came after me while Christophe was gone, a gun would do me a lot better than a chair *or* a switchblade.

I carried the chair up the long winding flights of stairs, got it into my room, and stopped two steps inside.

Someone had been in here. I knew it even though nothing was moved. Even the dust was undisturbed, but the room didn't *smell* right.

Cold and heat fought over me. Neither won. I dropped the chair on the faded carpet and reached for the switchblade. My hand stopped halfway. Nobody was in here now; the unloosed fist inside my head stroked the air with sensitive fingers and told me so. I swept the door closed and checked under the bed, pushing aside the dust ruffle.

The *malaika* were still there, oiled wood with its own mellow gleam. So was Dad's billfold. But the lock of Christophe's hair on my nightstand was gone.

My heart leapt into my throat. I stared at the edge of the blue-painted stand, the cold coming back until I had to clench my teeth to keep them from chattering.

There, delicately caught on the grain of the wood, was a single, curling, golden hair. There were a lot of curly-headed blonds at this school—Dibs, Blondie the teacher, Irving . . .

Which one of them would be in my room?

I crouched there for a long time, hugging myself. The cold had finally won, and it didn't go away.

# CHAPTER 16

**did manage to** grab a couple hours of sleep with a wooden chair propped under the doorknob. As soon as I set it there, the feeling of relief was intense, but short-lived. I stumbled over to my bed, fell into it, and only woke up when a bar of weak, cold morning light struggling through fog and the window glass touched the foot of the bed.

My internal clock was all messed up by now, so it didn't seem to matter. Besides, moving around during the day meant there would be no suckers, and most of the teachers would be asleep.

I stood in front of the bathroom mirror and ran through every curse word I knew.

*You can do this*, I told myself for the hundredth time. *Come on. It's no big deal.* Rain-soaked sunlight struggled through the window of the blue room. I checked my sneakers again, scrubbed my hands against my sweater. Paced the whole length of the room, dropped down to my knees to peer under the bed, and saw the glowing curves of wood gathering dust.

When would Christophe come back? As soon as I asked myself, I shoved the question away. There was no reason not to work on trying to find out who was after me, and to do that, I'd need allies. The *djamphir* boys weren't going to be any help. So it was the wulfen, and Graves said—

Just then, there were two taps at the door. I bounded up, raced across the carpet, and jerked it open to find Graves right outside. The hall was shadowed, so his eyes flared green under his messy hair. He shook it back and gave me a fey grin, then laid his finger against his lips.

I nodded. He gave my outfit—jeans, thermal shirt under a big gray wool sweater, sneakers, my mom's locket safely hidden—a critical once-over and shrugged.

I suppose he thought I'd be cold or something, but I knew better. If we were going to do this, I was going to sweat.

*No big deal. Come on, Dru. Buck up.*

Besides, I *was* cold, deep down where no amount of wool was going to warm me up. Who would come into my room and take Christophe's hair, and leave one of his own behind? It was pointless.

Unless it was Blondie the teacher, and he had a reason to tell someone—maybe Anna—that Christophe had been in my room. I didn't know what would happen then, but it would probably be unpleasant.

But I most likely would have been yanked out of bed and questioned by now, wouldn't I? I tried to tell myself to relax, that I'd figure something out. I didn't even buy my own pep talk by now.

And what the hell was I about to do? But I couldn't back out now. And Graves . . .

He beckoned. I stepped out and followed him down the hall. We threaded through the sunlit, sleeping Schola. Every once in a while he'd stop, holding up a hand, and we'd wait for a little bit, or he'd pick an alternate route.

It looked like he'd done a lot of exploring in the last three weeks. But that didn't surprise me. Knowing your ground is good strategic habit, and I had a good idea of the layout too. I should have had a better one, gone exploring instead of standing around in front of the armory or moping in my room.

*Woulda, coulda, shoulda, Dru. Besides, you're not going to be here much longer.* I stepped softly, breathing through my mouth, and we finally ended up in a concrete-floored corridor somewhere in the depths of the building. Graves chose lefts and rights seemingly at random, and we took a right into a dead end, one blank door set in the wall. He reached up, going on tiptoe, and did something to the little plastic box clinging to the wall over it. Wires threaded away, his fingers flicked, and he swept the door open with a grin. Midmorning sunlight burst through, and we stepped out of the Schola.

I took a deep breath. Rotting leaves, wet dirt, rain on the wind that touched the curls springing free of my ponytail. The light felt good, pouring over me. The fog would probably come back around dusk, but for right now we had a clear, pale blue sky and a sun that looked like a yellow-white faraway coin. High horsetails of white cloud brushed what little horizon I could see with the trees pulled so close.

In spring it would probably be pretty here. Too bad I wasn't sticking around to find out.

Graves closed the door with a click. "Come on, we're almost late."

"I am never going to be able to take that route again," I muttered.

"Yeah, well, next time it'll be different. They're watching you pretty close, you know. It's not so bad getting out when it's just me."

"Me being so valuable and all." *And there's another* svetocha. But I still hadn't told him about that either. It seemed like a bad idea. I was struggling with what to tell him about someone stealing Christophe's hair, too.

Two things stopped me. What could he do about it, and if he asked me what Christophe was doing leaving bits of his hair in my room, what would I say?

What *could* I say?

Secrets everywhere, pressing in on me.

I'm good at keeping them. I mean, Jesus, my whole life was nothing *but* secrets from the time Gran died. But it's a whole lot easier to keep them when you've got someone else who knows breathing in the same room. Carrying them alone is like having a huge spiky weight digging into your shoulders and chest, a weight you can't shift even while you're sleeping.

Graves let out a tired sigh. He was almost sounding like Dylan now. "Yeah, well, I'm beginning to think there's something else going on. See, you're supposed to be trained to survive, right? Everyone here is slated for grunt work, infantry. Shock troops. But the instant you show up in a class—except for Kruger's, that is—everything gets dumbed down and the kids get a day off. It's weird. It's like they're waiting for something."

*Kruger? Does he mean Blondie in history class?* It made me feel a little better—if he was honestly trying to teach me, maybe he hadn't come into my room. I ran up against the problem of who could have and threw up my mental hands in despair. "Christophe said I was supposed to be learning and he'll come back." *But he's off making arrangements to spring me from this place.* Something I hadn't considered before hit me: *And where is that going to leave Graves?*

I'd figure it out when the time came. Or so I told myself. But I felt even worse.

"Yeah, well. Christophe's not actually popular around here. Half the teachers hate him, and the wulfen say he's got a long history of being an arrogant jerk. About the only person who's neutral is Dylan, but he's got his own weird thing going on. He's always watching you. It's creepy."

"Yeah. Creep central around here. But we're in a school full of werewolves and part-suckers." I wasn't sure what to think about Dylan either. Everyone was acting weird. Which was probably to be expected in a place where the Real World was taken for granted, but . . .

I was glad to have Graves. And when Christophe came back, I'd argue him into taking Graves with us. He'd agree—he *had* to. And once we were out of here I could tell Graves everything.

As soon as I decided that, the weight on me eased a little bit.

Graves gave a bitter little laugh. "Point. Some of the teachers have something against Dylan, too. Or with him. It's like watching *Wild Kingdom* in here. Much more interesting than high school."

Trust him to put that sort of spin on it. "High school's a jungle too." I followed him up an overgrown path, almost trotting to keep up with his long strides.

He was still in his boots and coat, and there was a bounce to his walk. He was even smiling. "True."

"You're sure this is going to work?" Christ, I even sounded uncertain. Almost wistful.

"You want friends, right? They don't hate you, Dru. This is a good idea. Trust me."

I think it was the first time I ever saw Goth Boy look *happy*. Most of the time he was just kind of dealing with it. But now he looked pretty bright and sunny, his head up and his hair shaken back. The essential difference of skinchanger shone through, subtly different from a wulfen's but miles away from a *djamphir*'s sharp handsomeness.

Happy looked good on him, bringing out the strength instead of the weirdness in the architecture of his face. High cheekbones, big nose, his chin too strong too—but he was looking better these days. Or at least, not so strange.

I was looking at him so intently I almost tripped, had to watch where I was going. I hurried alongside him, brushing past scrubby bushes and trashwood. He took the left fork when the trail divided, and we ended up in a small clearing on the wooded west side of the Schola. Here the forest curved around and hugged the buildings, and there were about fifteen werwulfen gathered.

They all went still when they saw me. Dibs let out a squeak and hunched down. I tried not to stare at his hair. My heart was in my throat.

"What the *fuck* are you doing?" Shanks snarled. Even his emo-boy forehead swoop puffed up.

"She's coming with us." Graves didn't look fazed in the least.

"The Bloodkin watch her." Another boy unfolded himself from the fallen log he was perched on, rising and hopping down to the leaf-littered ground. "And she's slow and clumsy. We're not waiting for anyone."

"I got her out without anyone knowing." Graves folded his arms. "She'll keep up."

"Please. She's one of *them*." Shanks said it like I had some sort of disease.

Graves's upper lip lifted a fraction. "She's with me. You got a problem? Want a girl to kick your ass again?"

I tried to look dangerous. I probably only succeeded in looking thoughtful. Or constipated. But Dibs caught my eye and actually—go figure—*winked* at me. Sunlight ran through his buttery hair, and I caught a flash of an encouraging smile before he looked down at the ground.

Nobody noticed. And I couldn't see Dibs sneaking into my room to steal *anything*.

Shanks's lip lifted in a silent snarl. "If she gets caught out with us, she's not the one they'll punish. You like detention that much? What is *wrong* with you?"

"It's time she started knowing more about this place." Graves didn't look perturbed at all. "If she gets caught, they'll punish me. It was my idea anyway, and whining about detention is for candyasses. Now are we gonna do this, or are you gonna stand around flapping your lips all day?"

"I don't like it." This was from a rangy blond werwulf next to Dibs, one with a thick, corn-fed face and a thatch of golden hair. Straight, not curly. "She's not gonna be able to keep up."

"She'll keep up." Graves sighed and rolled his eyes. "Are we gonna run or not?"

"Let her try." A short, compact wulf with dark stubble all over his pale cheeks spoke up. "If somethin' happens, she's not going to tell on us. Not a squealer, that one."

"That's right." Dibs nodded vigorously, still staring at the ground. "Dru wouldn't squeal on us. She's nice. She's not like *them*. They wouldn't even wipe their boots on us."

Silence. They all stood around, thinking it over. That's the thing about werwulfen—it takes a while for them to do anything. They all have to agree before something happens. Once you think about the fact that they have those teeth and claws, it makes more sense. If they didn't find ways to cooperate, they'd argue each other right into extinction.

Finally, a murmur went through them. I thought about trying to look trustworthy. Considering I was holding a couple of guilty secrets, I guess it was working.

Some essential tension leaked out of Graves. He gave me a sideways look, green eyes glinting. I straightened a little.

It was apparent they'd made their decision.

"Huh. Well." Shanks shrugged. "Fine. It's your ass, anyway. Think you can keep up, little girl?"

*You know, I hate people calling me that.* "I'll do my best." I tried not to sound sarcastic, failed miserably. Graves didn't wince, but he was probably close.

As soon as the words were out of my mouth, an electric current ran through the assembled werwulfen. I glanced at Graves as everyone started getting up, dusting off their clothes, one or two of them bouncing in place. There was a lot of nervous energy in them, crackling just under their skins.

*I am so not ready for this.*

Graves cast me a single look. You know how when you know someone, sometimes all it takes is a meeting of eyes, a slight lift to the eyebrow, a tightening of the lips to speak volumes? It was like that. His green eyes said, *Are you sure?*

My face shifted. *No, I'm not,* it was saying, *but I'm gonna do it.*

He gave me a quirk of a smile, and Shanks rolled his shoulders in their sockets, tilted his head back, and inhaled for a long time, filling his lungs. A crackling, popping sound raced around the clearing, and I caught my own breathing speeding up.

*Just listen for the howl,* Graves had said. *It'll tell you all you need to know. Let it pull you along. I'll be right beside you.*

They began to growl, all of them, the sound rising like steam. Graves was a tense, hurtful silence next to me.

I was really hoping this would work. Then I thought, *Well, if I could handle Christophe hugging me so tight my bones creaked, if I could handle climbing up on the Schola's roof, and if I could handle being nose to nose with Ash, I can probably handle this too.*

*Probably.*

Shanks's head snapped back down, fur swirling up over his

cheekbones, his eyes a hurtful gleam. Seeing them change in full daylight was something else. I lost pretty much all my air as their familiar boy-forms ran like clay underwater, some of them crouched now, knees splayed and hands touching the leafy dirt.

Then, as if on some prearranged signal, they all tossed up their chins and howled.

Hearing wulfen howl is . . . well, it's horrible. The sound is glassy, hovering at the upper ranges of hearing, and it's full of paws on snow and running with the icy wind hitting the back of your throat like stars. Underneath that glassy edge is the song of flesh ripped apart, the sweetness of hot blood, and the savagery of crunching bones with sharp white teeth.

The worst part is how it climbs into your brain, pressing itself like a hard sharpness into the soft folds, and drags open the doors socialization slams shut to keep the howling ravening thing deep inside down and tame.

The thing on four clawed legs that lives in all of us.

A civilized person flinches away from that thing. At the Schola, they called it the Other. Werwulfen use it to violate the laws of thermodynamics and physics, to set the inner beast free. And Graves, a *loup-garou*, uses it in a different way—for mental dominance instead of physical change. I wondered how, and why, and wished they would actually train me instead of dumping me in kindergarten classes.

It didn't matter. I was leaving soon anyway.

Graves's fingers slid through mine, hot and hard. He squeezed my hand, and I flinched. My initial panicked reaction was to curl up more tightly inside my head, squeezing out the little stroking fingers and paws gently tapping at that door in my brain. But the place at the back of my throat where the hunger had blazed through was still raw-sensitive, and the wulfen's cry rasped against it like a cat's tongue.

The cry modulated, ending on a low lonely sound, and the wulfen moved. Graves leapt forward, and I had to go along or get my arm torn off. My feet slipped in leaves and dirt, and the fear arrived, smashing through me and laying copper against my tongue.

Graves dragged me. I had enough to do keeping my feet on the ground. The other wulfen were leaping fluid forms, and I began to get a very, very bad feeling about all this.

We crested a high wooded hill, sloping down a pile of rocks and tree roots, leafless oaks and maples standing wet and secretive, clutching at the ground so they wouldn't slide. Graves yanked me forward, and as we went over the side his fingers loosened and slipped free of mine.

I was falling. My foot hit a rock, the sneakers slipped, and I knew I was going to end up in a heap on the bottom. My heart leapt; I gave a short, blurting scream—

—and the world *snapped* again, hard. My other foot landed squarely on the top of a boulder I hadn't even known was there, and my body woke up, tingling all over. The aspect flooded me like the heat of alcohol on an empty stomach, the Beam and Cokes I used to drink while waiting for Dad to come home and collect me. The heat burst through me, my teeth turned crackling-sensitive, and even my hair tingled as the aspect slid through it. Mom's locket dilated into a point of heat, as if it were melting against my chest.

Have you ever run so hard you thought your heart would burst? There's just you and your legs and the sound of wind in your ears mixing with the pounding of your pulse. The endorphins kick in if you can do it long enough, and all of a sudden you're not thinking. Your body's doing all the thinking for you. It leaps like a gazelle, it dances like a star, and the only thought on your mind is *God, keep going, don't let this slow down, don't let it ever stop.*

Running. With werwulfen. Their shapes blurred around me, the high unearthly howls distorted because of the speed, splashes of sunlight on fur and bright eyes as we moved in a mass. They spread out around me like a cat's cradle, and if I'd had time I might've wondered who was picking the direction. But it was enough to just run. If I just *ran*, nothing else mattered, and I didn't have to think about Mom or Dad or Gran or Christophe or any other hundred things crawling through my cluttered head. I could just *be*. It was like that place in the middle of tai chi where the world faded and there was just the movement, force and reaction spilling through arms and legs, hands like birds and feet like horse's hooves.

We crested another hill. The world was spinning underneath me, I didn't even have to move forward, just put my feet down every now and again to touch it. I heard the muffled wingbeats of Gran's owl, and a fierce joy flushed through me, a cleaner feeling than the rage of the bloodhunger. I was clear. I was see-through, I was a girl made of crystal, and this was the best thing in the world.

I don't know how long it lasted, but the force bled away. It got harder and harder to keep up with the world, but I was doing my best when someone grabbed my arm and everything came to a tumbling, spinning halt.

I landed hard on my knees, jarring, and retched. Someone dropped down beside me and patted my back. A couple other kids were coughing too.

"Jesus *Christ*," someone gasped, a high boyish voice. Someone else laughed, a high, unsteady sound, and the hilarity spilled through the rest of them. It bubbled up in my own mouth between the retches, my stomach informing me that *oh holy God, you should not have done that.*

My legs were on fire. All of me was burning and my back was a solid bar of pain. But it didn't matter.

What mattered was Graves next to me, also rubbing my back and laughing like he'd just found Christmas in his pants. Dibs was on my other side, on his knees and leaning against me, coughing. His eyes were bright with the tears that trickled down his cheeks, but he didn't look sad in the least.

Then Shanks squatted easily in front of me, flushed and windswept, leaves caught in his thick dark hair. "Well. You kept up." For once, he didn't sound supercilious. "Never had *that* happen before."

"Told you." Graves was breathless. A hiccupping laugh interrupted the words. "It's in the books. *Svetocha* can keep up."

"Huh." The taller boy eyed me. I tried not to puke on him. No wonder Graves had told me not to eat anything beforehand.

*But God.* I managed to get some breath back. "When . . . can we . . . do that . . . again?"

At that, everyone burst into laughter. Some of us were still retching, but the merriment kind of canceled that out. It didn't matter how much I hurt or how my heart felt like it was trying to climb out my windpipe. It didn't matter that everything was fucked up beyond repair and I was stumbling blindly around in the middle of a game that was way too big for me.

All that mattered was the sun on my shoulders, the wulfen gathered around me, and the way every one of them suddenly looked like . . . yes. Like a friend. And Graves right beside me, his hand making little circles on my back, his face all alight. It was like standing on the Schola's roof and seeing the world spread out underneath me, but not nearly so lonely.

It was the best I'd felt since my world fell apart and a zombie smashed through my kitchen door.

Hey, you take what you can get.

# CHAPTER 17

**The disused classroom** was in the bowels of the Schola, and it had an empty chalkboard on the curved wall. When filled with wulfen, the entire room had a nervous, fidgeting feel to it.

"So they're not teaching you anything." Shanks nodded. "Yeah, we wondered about that."

What else had they wondered about me? "I, uh, just don't go. It's all remedial shit I could get in normal high school."

Graves shook his head. "Skipping isn't allowed for anyone else. It's a trip to detention, and who wants that? So why let *you* do it? I mean, you're special and all"—he ignored Shanks's snicker—"but it don't make sense, and putting you in remedial classes doesn't make sense either. Especially with the chance of you-know-who finding out you're here—they should want you trained and trained *hard*, so you have a better chance of surviving."

"And then there's Christophe." Shanks was settled on a dusty brown couch, taking up most of it with his long legs. A ripple ran through the rest of the wulfen at the name. "He hasn't been around for years, but they're scared of him."

"Wouldn't you be?" Dibs piped up. "He's *dangerous*. Just look at his kill record. He's never wanted to make himself liked, either."

"Well, people have been calling him a traitor for a long time, but never to his face." Shanks shrugged. He'd picked most of the leaves out of his hair. "And he did bring her in. I know Juan's cousin—I talked to him last week during phonetime. When Christophe was tryin' to save your asses, someone was tryin' to kill him. The battle-group got a directive to kill a *nosferat*, and he didn't realize it wasn't a *wampyr* but Christophe until the guy had held off every one of them and had plenty of chances to kill 'im but didn't, and he was *djamphir* to boot. And he fucked up *you-know-who* but good, to rescue her."

A hot flush went through me. Did they know about Christophe and Sergej? And now that I'd gotten some sleep and run until I was close to a cardiac arrest, I felt like I was thinking clearly. If Dylan thought Anna was right, why would he be telling me Christophe was going to train me? If he didn't, why did he stay quiet when she accused him?

Why did he say he was on my side? And what was Anna's whole game with the file and the pictures of the house my mother had died in front of?

I didn't remember enough about the night Mom died. I didn't *want* to remember about that night. I was five years old, for chrissake.

I tried working it out again inside my head. Christophe said Dylan was loyal. I'd carried that note between them like a message, and Dylan was supposed to find me if there was another vampire attack. But I wasn't supposed to tell anyone, even Dylan, that I'd seen Christophe.

That didn't make sense either. But I'd been so confused from the heat of Christophe's body against mine.....

*Don't think about that, Dru. Jesus.* But what else was there to think of? The single blond hair caught on my nightstand? Other secrets, other lies, all pressing down on me?

"Something's off," another wulfen said. "They just watch her. And then there was the other night."

"Yeah." Graves leaned forward next to me. He still hadn't taken his coat off, and I understood why. It was chilly in the classroom, especially with sweat drying on my skin. "Nobody came to pick her up from the classroom and get her to her room. Isn't that a little suspicious, given how they're watching her?"

I stared at the cracked chalkboard. How long had it been since I'd seen an actual *chalk*board? Most schools had whiteboards nowadays. "Dylan said he didn't know who was supposed to be watching me. The duty roster disappeared, and—" I stopped short. I could have gone on, but I was taking Dylan's word for an awful lot, and I couldn't say any more without explaining the whole Anna thing.

I was pretty sure talking about another *svetocha* wasn't a good idea, if she was supposed to be a big secret.

But it didn't look like *I* was such a big secret, maybe. Had Ash killed every sucker there? If they were from Sergej and none of them came back, he wouldn't know for sure I was here—unless the traitor, whoever it was, could manage to tell him. Or a sucker could survive the next attack and go tell him.

The pieces fit together inside my head. Christophe must have realized this—it was why he was coming back to get me out.

It was anyone's guess whether he'd get back in time. My mouth was dry and my heart was still thumping along.

"Shit." Shanks rubbed at his chin. "I didn't know that." His dark eyes rested on me for a long moment. "That true?"

I nodded. "Someone was supposed to come and get me, or the teacher's supposed to take me to my room. That's what happened every other time. But that time Blondie vanished as soon as class was out. And nobody else came."

"Blondie?" Someone chuckled. "Oh wow."

"Kruger." Shanks didn't look amused. "And his helpful lectures. So how did you get out of there?"

"I saw . . ." The usual habit of keeping the woo-woo a secret made me pause. I plunged ahead. This, at least, was one secret I could get off my chest. "I saw an owl. My grandmother's owl. Whenever there's trouble, it shows up and tells me to get out." I took a deep breath. "And so I ran. But when I was outside . . . I saw a wulfen."

"Who?" Shanks could really bore a hole in someone with those eyes. He leaned forward, tense and expectant, like I was going to produce something he could chase down and bite.

"His name's Ash. He's got a streak on his head—"

"He's a Broken," someone supplied. "The last Silverhead. You-know-who's wulf."

Shanks waved a hand. "Yeah, I know about the Silverhead. You saw him?"

"I didn't just *see* him. He killed the suckers chasing me. He was pretty beat up afterward. He sniffed me, but he didn't hurt me." It wasn't coming out right. "I mean—"

"He sniffed you?" They were peppering me with questions now, one after another.

"How did he sniff you?"

"How close was he?"

"Was he bleeding?"

Shanks held up a hand. "Slow *down*, everyone. Jesus. First things first, okay?" He looked at me speculatively for a long, tense-ticking twenty seconds. "Dru." It was the first time he'd said my name without sneering. "Do you have any idea why you're here and not at the main Schola? Or even a big Schola?"

"The main . . ." I sounded as blank as I must've looked. "Isn't this, like, *a* main Schola? A big one?"

"Shit, no." He laughed, and some of the other older boys did too. It wasn't nice laughter, but it wasn't pointed at me, either. "This is like reform school. We're the troublemakers, the retards. The actual Schola for *this* district, the first Schola ever made, is in the Big Apple. Down over the state line. I wondered why you were way the hell out here."

*Oh.* "Nobody . . ." It made sense now. And of course Anna would have been coming from a bigger city, right? It was all over her.

"Nobody said to your face that you were on the short bus?" He shrugged. "That's interesting. But you shouldn't trust what they tell you even if they open up their mouths. *Nosferatu* lie, and half-vamps are right behind them sometimes. We're just dumb muscle and they're supplying the *tactics*, they say. So they get to order us around."

"But we're surviving now," Dibs piped up. "Not like it was. My grandfather told me about the Dark Times. They aren't so far away." A murmur of assent greeted the words.

"Dark Times, man." Another dark wulfen shuddered. "At least we're not slaves now."

"Yeah, well." Shanks shrugged. "They still treat us like shit even if they don't murder and enslave us. It's not a huge step up, but I'll take it. Most of the time."

"That always bothered me," I had to tell Graves. "The way Christophe treated you." The other, more tremendous secret swelled behind my ribs. I pushed it down. *Tell nobody*, he'd said. And they didn't need to know I was leaving soon anyway, did they?

Graves shook his head, black hair falling in his glowing eyes. The restlessness in him was evident. "This really isn't getting us anywhere."

"Patience," a lean lanky wulf with broad shoulders and a blond buzz-cut said. His hair wasn't long enough for me to stare at him. "This is how consensus works."

"What exactly are we discussing here?" I wanted to know. I was tired of stumbling around and having people drop information on me. I wanted to *do* something.

Shanks held up a finger. "You're at a small satellite full of delinquents instead of the main Schola. Could be to throw people off the scent, but"—another finger—"Ash knows you're here. Which means you-know-who could know. He killed the *nosferatu* who attacked last time—but we don't know if he killed *all* of them." One more finger, the nail chewed all the way down. "They're lying to you about a whole hell of a lot, and refusing to train you."

"Christophe said there was a traitor in the Order," I said, slowly.

Shanks nodded. "Whoever signed the directive to send Juan and his pack after him, right? Okay. Huh."

Everyone thought this over. At least, I was thinking furiously, and everyone around me had a creased forehead. Graves fidgeted a little, then a little more. He opened his mouth, closed it, and stared at me.

"What?" I sounded more irritated than I really was. "What are you sitting on?"

"You're bait." The words came out flat and sharp. "Christophe wants to know who the traitor is, so he's dangling you out in front of someone. You were his bait for Sergej, too. Maybe he *did* specifically send you here."

The room went cold when he said *Sergej*, and several of the wulfen shivered. It wasn't like Christophe saying it, with the tinge of hatred instead of outright fear. It still sent a glass spike of pain through my head.

Graves didn't seem to notice. "He was all over getting you out of town once he realized the bad guy knew where you were, but before that? He was just hanging around, waiting for something before he'd make his move. Your dad had his phone number. They talked at least *once*. And the teachers here, some of them might be wanting to train you, but they've gotten orders not to, probably from . . ." He trailed off. "I don't have that part of it yet. I don't know why they wouldn't be training you even if you are supposed to be just dangled out in front of the suckers. But I'd bet my last smoke you're bait, Dru."

*Stay here, Dru. Trust me.* Everything fell into place. As hard as I tried, I couldn't find a flaw in that logic. "It would explain a lot. But what about Ash?"

"What about him? Just be grateful he didn't open your guts up." Shanks laughed, a cold sound.

"What if he needs help?" I persisted. "I've been thinking about it, and I—"

"You want to help a Broken? You want to help *Ash*? He was probably confused, or he didn't want to kill you just yet because you-know-who wants the pleasure."

"But when he was after me before he damn well wanted to kill me!" I was shouting before I realized it. My chest ached with the enormity of the confusion. "He *saved my life* the other night—there's got to be a reason!"

Graves grabbed my shoulder. "Calm down."

Calm *down*? He wanted me to calm *down*? Oh, *hell* no.

I was about ready to explode. "All this talking doesn't get anything *done*! What if we could find Ash? We could try to help him, and then we'd have a chance of finding something, *anything* else out."

"Why are you so set on this?" Shanks wanted to know. "You were poking pretty hard about saving a Broken in class the other day, too."

*Right before we got into it and I kicked your ass.* I went cold all over, goose bumps standing up on my skin. *Right before I wanted to drink blood. Just like a sucker.* "You didn't see his eyes." Almost defeated, I slumped back into the couch. "You just didn't. I want to help him."

"He's been you-know-who's wulf for a long time. Since the Dark Times, when you-know-who used him for hunting his kin. There aren't any other Silverheads left, just Ash." Dibs shivered. His tone was soft, scared, and terribly sad.

My hands were fists. I took a deep breath. "But he didn't hurt me. And he killed how many suckers? This wouldn't be a bad thing on our side."

A ripple ran through them, like ink threading into water, and I knew I'd said the wrong thing.

"Sides. You *djamphir* are all the same. Sooner or later you start talking about sides." Shanks's lip curled up. "Then it's time for wulfen to do the dirty work while you lay back and—"

The ball of fury inside my chest swelled. My teeth tingled, and I felt something sharp touching my lower lip on each side. I rocketed up to my feet. "*Fuck* you."

"Let's just calm down—" Graves began.

"Calm down my *ass*! I almost died, and this asshole's acting like everything's *my* fault!" Frustration boiled sharply under my skin, prickles and pokings. Every secret I was keeping jostling for release. "If we're gonna start the *you're just like the rest of them* shit, then how about finding someone else to pick on? I didn't ask to be born part sucker! I didn't fucking know until everyone was trying to *kill* me and my dad never came *back*!" I had to stop to take a deep breath. Everyone was staring at me. "Now nobody will tell me what the fuck is going on, and I'm sick of it! I'm sick of feeling like I've done something wrong just by *breathing*! I didn't *ask* for this!"

"Nobody's saying you—" Graves started. To give him some credit, he was trying to smooth the ruffled waters, or something. But I was done with being soothed.

"Yes they *are*!" I jabbed an accusing finger at Shanks. "That's *exactly* what he's saying! That I deserve all this shit somehow because of what I was born like!"

The air changed just as I ran out of breath, and a ripple ran through the room again. This one was cold, a breath of warning. Graves grabbed for my shoulder, but I ducked away from him. If anyone touched me right now I was going to go absolutely postal.

The bloodhunger was a roiling ball of fury inside my chest, and it was hard to push it down and lock it away. Did all the other *djamphir* feel like this? All the time, or just when the aspect came over them?

How did they stand it? How could *anyone* stand it?

"Oh Jesus." A wulfen in a crouch by the door lifted his head and sniffed. "*Djamphir* on the way. Must be a teacher."

"Crap." Shanks bounded to his feet. "We'll have to split up. If they catch us out here with *her*—"

"Don't worry about it." I had already spun on my heel and was headed for the door.

He let out a snorting laugh. "What are you gonna do, tell on us?"

"I should," I tossed over my shoulder, picking up my weary feet. "But I'm not like *you* assholes. My dad raised me right, dammit. I'm going to draw whoever it is off so you can go back to the dorms and fuck yourselves."

I hit the hall at a run and plunged into the corridor. Here in this wing it was cold, and my shoes were wet and covered in dirt. I made a lot of noise, feet slapping, yelling anything that came into my head—usually four-letter words, bouncing back eerily at me from the stone and paneling.

That, at least, would distract any teacher coming down here. The wulfen of them could go back to the dorms and play pinochle or spin the bottle or whatever, for all I cared.

I burst out into the lunchroom. Which was strangely deserted, sunlight falling from the high windows. The chairs were all stacked on the tables, and I picked one stack and pulled it down with a bouncing clatter. *That ought to bring someone out.* My heart pounded, and the sheer injustice of it all rose up to choke me. The ball of fury behind my ribs smoked and boiled so hard my eyes leaked heat and water.

"FUCK THIS PLACE!" I yelled. "I WANT SOME ANSWERS!"

"You don't need to scream," someone said behind me, and I whirled. Dylan stepped out of the shadows with a creak of leather, stopping just short of a bar of heavy yellow sunlight. "You should be more careful. If I can catch you out during the day, so can someone else."

It took a couple seconds for my heart to climb down out of my throat. "Jesus Christ!"

"Nope. Just me." A crooked smile lifted the corners of his lips. But his dark eyes were serious, and there were bruised-looking rings underneath them. "We don't have much time, Dru. Come on."

You know, any other day I probably just would have gone with him. But not today. I was tired of following people around, tired of being led by the nose. "Where? Does what's-her-face want to see me again?"

Dylan sighed, an aggravated, familiar sound. The sleepless rings under his eyes matched the tension around his mouth, and his hair was messy too. "You should hope not. Come *on*, Dru. Please. I've got something to show you."

I folded my arms and refused to budge. "Why should I hope not?"

"Because I'm not so sure Milady can be trusted." He stepped back, retreating from the sunlight. "Are you coming, or do I have to wait for another time when I'm on duty to watch you?"

"You were on duty?"

He shrugged. "Why do you think I let you out with your little friend? At least I'm sure he and his wulfen won't kill you, even if they are delinquents and thieves." Another two steps back. Dylan's eyes glittered, the aspect sliding over him and retreating in waves, sending fingers of ebony highlighting through his hair. "Dru. Believe me. You want to see this, and it's not safe to talk up here."

*Up here?* I sighed. It was what everyone said: *Trust me, Dru. Believe me, Dru. Let me do what I want, Dru.*

I was helpless, the way I'd been all along. And the idea that Christophe maybe wasn't coming back for me, that he was using me as bait, that I might be stuck here for a while—it was enough to take the fight right out of anyone.

My shoulders slumped. The dampness on my cheeks clung to my fingers as I scrubbed at it.

I followed.

# CHAPTER 18

**I** **was spending a** lot of time following boys through stone-walled halls. Dylan didn't speak for a long time, just took me into the north wing. He moved soundlessly in his heavy engineer boots, with the peculiar grace of the Kouroi. I got the idea his jacket only creaked for effect, too.

I finally had to open my mouth. "The wulfen. They're not going to get in trouble, are they?"

"Of course not. I'm not one of the proud." He unlocked a wooden door and paused for a moment, breathing in deeply. "There's so much more than you've been told. I wondered why they sent you here, and I wondered even more when the directive came that you needed 'time to recover' and shouldn't be held to a teaching schedule, and that no allotment would be made for tutors or bodyguards this quarter." His tone turned bitter. "Then Milady started meddling even further. And when Milady meddles, beware."

*Milady?* "You mean the chick who was here the other day." *The one who thinks it's really important that I hate Christophe. He called her that, too.*

"That 'chick' is the queen of the Order, Dru, and the head of the Council. *Svetocha* are precious. Milady was saved from the *nosferatu* about fifteen years before your mother was, and I think those years gave her a taste of ambition. I wonder . . ." Maddeningly, he stopped short, so I didn't get to hear what he wondered. "At the main Schola, you would be given everything your heart desired. Here we've had to make do because of funding restrictions. I thought you'd be sent downstate as soon as arrangements could be made. I *thought* you'd at least have a battery of tutors, not to mention a bodyguard or five like Milady herself. But it would draw too much attention, the directive said. You were better protected when you were less protected, because it wouldn't bring attention to your survival, and Sergej would be looking for traces."

When he said it, the name didn't make the air turn chill and unwelcoming. But it still sent a bolt of almost-pain through my head. *That doesn't make much sense.* "That doesn't make any sense at all."

He bared his white *djamphir* teeth in a wide, mirthless smile. "That's what I thought. But I've already been demoted to running a tiny little reform school for cannon fodder out here in the sticks. Mine is not to question why, Dru."

*Oh, comforting. Not.* "Wait a second—"

A shrug and a quick motion, brushing the past away. His leather jacket creaked. "When you bring in the fact that Christophe found you, there's also the question of his loyalty. And the fact that you are . . . who you are." He pushed the door open and motioned me through. "I've been stuck here for a long time. My own loyalty, to your mother and to Christophe, was professionally expensive, to say the least."

"So—" I wanted to get a word in edgewise. Unfortunately, I had no word to get in. I tried again. "Okay. Can you do me a favor and start from the beginning? What the hell *am* I doing here?" *Am I bait?*

But I felt the heat of Christophe's body against mine again, and didn't believe it. Couldn't believe it. No matter how much sense it made.

The room was long and low, windowless, and full of metal racks with boxes stacked on them. It went back for a long while, and the only light came from bulbs in thick, wire-crossed glass shields wrapped with cobwebs. It looked like an abandoned bomb shelter, and the rows of shelves receded to infinity.

"I think you're here because someone is biding their time. It's the oddest thing, but I can't get through to any of my regular contacts over the state line. This entire node is being held as a blackout zone. Now, that *could* be to protect you. But it's looking more and more like *nobody even knows you're here*. Nobody at the main Schola, nobody in the Order except Augustine and Milady, and nobody's heard from August recently. He's missed his last two call-ins with his handler—who is, incidentally, one of my friends." Dylan swung the door shut, turning back to face me as I edged nervously away. "And Christophe is unreachable too." His eyes asked a question; did he suspect I'd taken his note to Christophe?

He *had* to suspect it. Which meant he was playing a game too. Just what kind of game I couldn't guess yet.

"August is missing?" My throat was closing down to a pinhole, I had trouble getting the words out. Augie was Dad's friend from way back—and the person I'd called to verify Christophe's story. Right before everything went to hell with the dreamstealer, the sky turning dark in the middle of the day, and Sergej.

I shivered. The sweat dried on my skin itched and reeked. It was a sour scent I was pretty used to by now.

It was fear.

I didn't even remember what it was like not to be terrified anymore. Dylan examined me for a long ten seconds or so, and I was suddenly, scorchingly aware that I was down here alone. Nobody knew where I was. And he was telling me an awful lot of stuff about how I wouldn't be missed by anyone who had the power to do something about it if I just up and disappeared.

But Christophe had told me to go find Dylan if there was another attack. He'd said Dylan was loyal. He'd told me he was coming back for me, too, and if I doubted that there were all sorts of things I could doubt.

*Oh crap. I don't trust anyone anymore. Not even myself.*

"I've stolen this from the armory." Dylan's hand made a small movement, and I stared at the gun. It was reversed, the butt offered to me. It was the nine-millimeter I'd handed over when the helicopter landed in the snow, to take me to the Schola and what I thought was safety. My heart pounded high and hard in my throat. "If what I suspect is true, you're not safe here. You're not safe *anywhere*, but especially not here."

I reached out. Heavy metal, cold against my fingers. My hand closed around the gun. I popped the clip out and checked it, habitually. Still loaded with Dad's silver-coated bullets. "So what am I supposed to do now?"

"Come take a look at this. Do you have a holster for that thing?"

I shrugged. *Um, no. I can't sign weapons out in the armory; all my stuff is in the truck—which Christophe's hidden. And I have no way of contacting him.* "How about I hide it in my bra?"

I didn't mean to sound so sarcastic. But Jesus. And I felt a lot better with the gun in my hand.

Ridiculously better.

He sighed, a regular vintage Dylan sigh. "We'll figure that out in a little bit. This way."

I followed him between two rows of bookshelves, the gun kept carefully pointed at the floor. "What am I supposed to be taking a look at?"

His shoulders came up a little. "Something I've been sitting on for a while. The transcript Milady was talking about exists, but the one she showed me was heavily redacted. I have the original."

All the breath left me in a whoosh. "Whoa. You've got it?"

"See? I told you you'd want to see this. The agent who transcribed the call was a friend of mine and a good Kouroi." He hunched even further, as if the weight of the world was bearing down directly on him. "He died alone, in terrible pain. He was betrayed. I didn't believe him when he gave me the envelope and told me not to share it with anyone unless it was an emergency."

"So it's an emergency now?"

"I certainly think this qualifies, Dru." Dylan took a sharp right at the end of the row of bookcases and kept going until we ended up at a heavy wooden door set in the stone wall. "I thought I would give this to Christophe. But you'll probably see him before I do. If he's still alive." He gave me an odd look, his eyes shadowed.

The urge to tell him that I'd already seen Christophe fought with the reasonable caution to keep my mouth shut. Everyone was lying, for God's sake. Next I was going to find out that even Graves was fucking around with me.

*No. Not him. You know better.* But Graves was okay hanging out with his wulfen buddies. They didn't seem like bad kids to me, just stupid and aggressive. Hey, that's boys for you.

And if nobody was supposed to know I was here, where did that leave them?

Dylan unlocked the door with a heavy iron key. "We've got about two hours until Kruger's on duty to stand guard. I want to get you back in your room before then."

"Sounds like a plan." The weird spinning sensation had filled up my chest again. *God, I wish Dad was here. Or August. Or even Christophe. Just someone else to deal with this.*

I closed that thought away for the hundredth time, and followed Dylan through the door.

\* \* \*

I watched the sunset spill orange and gold through my bedroom window. The gun was on the bedside table, pointed carefully toward the blind corner behind the door. A copy of the transcript—three and a half pages covered in single-space typing—sat obediently near my bare feet.

The date and time were military; I could tell just by looking. Strings of numbers marched across the top and bottom of each page. The text in the middle was even and close, little black ants marching on white paper.

SFR-1: *The information is well guarded.*

SFR-2: *That's none of your concern. Where is she? We are prepared to pay for the information.*

SFR-1: *Keep your money. I just want the bitch dead.*

SFR-2: *I can arrange that.*

It was my *mother* they were talking about. Calmly discussing killing her, like her death was just one more item on a grocery list. There was a mention of Dad, too—"the husband." Nothing about me.

Of course, according to the date, I would have been about five years old. Was I my mother's secret?

I squeezed my eyes shut so hard phantom yellow fireworks

splashed in the darkness behind my lids. It was the most hurtful memory of all, even worse than Dad's eyes, the whites rotting and the blue irises clouded as his dead body chewed at the air and shambled straight for me.

This memory lay at the very bottom of a deep well inside my head, and dragging it out made my entire body shake just a little.

*"Dru," she says, softly but urgently. "Get up."*

*I rub my eyes and yawn. "Mommy?" My voice is muffled. Sometimes it's the voice of a two-year-old, sometimes it's older. But always, it's wondering and quiet, sleepy.*

*"Come on, Dru." She puts her hands down and picks me up, with a slight* oof! *as if she can't believe how much I've grown. I'm a big girl now, and I don't need her to carry me, but I'm so tired I don't protest. I cuddle into her warmth and feel the hummingbird beat of her heart. "I love you, baby," she whispers into my hair. She smells of fresh cookies and warm perfume, and it is here the dream starts to fray. Because I hear something like footsteps, or a pulse. It is quiet at first, but it gets louder and more rapid with each beat. "I love you so much."*

*"Mommy . . ." I put my head on her shoulder. I know I am heavy, but she is carrying me, and when she sets me down to open a door I protest only a little.*

*It is the closet downstairs. Just how I know it's downstairs I'm not sure. There is something in the floor she pulls up, and some of my stuffed animals have been jammed into the square hole, along with blankets and a pillow from her and Daddy's bed. She scoops me up again and settles me in the hole, and I begin to feel faintly alarmed. "Mommy?"*

*"We're going to play the game, Dru. You hide here and wait for Daddy to come home from work."*

*This is all wrong. Sometimes I hide in the closet to scare Daddy, but never in the middle of the night. And never in a hole in the floor—a hole I didn't even know was there. "I don't wanna," I say, and try to get up.*

*"Dru." She grabs my arm, and it hurts for a second before her grip gentles. "It's important, baby. This is a special game. Hide in the closet, and when Daddy comes home, he'll find you. Lie down now. Be a good girl."*

*I protest, I whine a little. "I don't wanna." But I am a good girl. I snuggle down into the hole, because it's dark and warm and I'm tired, and the shadow on Mommy's face gets deeper. Only her eyes glitter, glowing summer-blue. She covers me up with a blanket and smiles at me until I close my eyes. Sleep isn't far behind, but as I go down I hear something, and I understand she's fitted the cover over the hole, and I am in the dark. But it smells like her, and I am so tired.*

*I hear, very faint and far away, the closet door close, and a scratching sound. And just before the dream ends, I hear a long, low, chilling laugh, like someone trying to speak with a mouthful of razor blades, and I know my mother is somewhere close, and she is desperate, and something very bad is about to happen.*

My eyes flew open. Sunlight poured in a flood through the window, past the curtains.

Things don't just go wrong once. They go wrong far enough and then they explode and it's impossible to put everything back together. If I was with Dad down South right now, we'd be either getting ready to go out and deal with something—poltergeist infestation, hex trouble, cockroach or gator spirits, you name it. Or he'd be getting ready to go out and I'd be cooking dinner, moving around the kitchen while he loaded clips or filled holy-water ampoules, and sometimes played Twenty Hunter Questions with me. He'd pop the questions and I'd answer, usually correctly. Each right answer would get me a smile and a *Good girl, Dru. Now here's another one for you.*

Everything from *How do you take apart a poltergeist?* to *What are the rules in a bar full of Others?* And if it took me more than thirty seconds of thinking, he wouldn't let me flounder. He would jump right in and explain. Not like so many others who liked to call themselves teachers.

*Say it, Dru. Say it out loud.*

"No." My own voice startled me. Here I was, sitting up here in this bedroom that was kind of pretty, yeah, but it was also cold and soulless and there was no safety in it. Dylan had just brought me back and plopped me down in here with the gun and the transcript, and a warning.

*Don't trust anyone. If we're attacked again, hide. Don't let anyone know where you're hiding until the all-clear sounds. Take the gun with you, and for God's sake keep it hidden.*

And the point to this whole thing, delivered just before he closed my door.

*I'm going to try to find Christophe. He needs to know that this is a blackout zone, and that* wampyr *attacks have been increasing. We need to get you out of here.*

There I was, throwing a distraction across my own brain. *Say it, Dru. You might as well.*

"He's gone," I whispered.

Gran had pretty much raised me, until she let go and I was in free fall for that one awful night before Dad showed up to sign all the papers and collect me. I never knew how he'd known, but then again, she'd raised him, too. He hadn't put much credence to "that backwoods foolishness," but he still tossed salt over his shoulder when it spilled.

You'd be a fool not to, when you're hunting the things that go bump in the night.

And he'd still sometimes known things. He didn't laugh when people talked about intuition. He also never really doubted mine.

"He's really gone." It sounded even worse when I repeated it. It was like I had just fully realized I wasn't dreaming, that I wouldn't wake up from this and find him in the kitchen loading bullets in clips, or in his camp chair in front of the TV, or . . .

No more driving with the windows down and the atlas in my lap, navigating him to where he needed to go. No more handing ammunition in through the broken windows while things skittered and leapt for him. No more playing the guessing game, figuring out which part of the Real World we were up against this time.

No more listening to someone else breathing in the house in the middle of the night. No more seeing him slumped in his chair in front of the television, no more of his special pancakes on Sunday mornings or the immediate call when he stamped in the door. *Dru? Dru, honey, you there?*

No more chili nights or warm arms over my shoulder, no more reassurance in the middle of the night when I woke up screaming— it didn't happen often after I was about fourteen, but it was nice to know he was there, you know?

He was really, truly gone. I was all alone here, and what I thought would be a safe place was turning out to be a snakes' nest. Like that little store we'd been in before heading to the Dakotas. The one with the copperheads and cottonmouths in glass aquariums, stinking and making that awful ratcheting noise.

Cottonmouths are mean, too. They'll jump you with no warning. They hit the sides of the aquariums with dry thumps the entire time I was in there, while Dad was closeted with the owner.

Had he been getting Christophe's phone number? What else had he been doing?

I rubbed at my wet cheeks. I hate crying. It fills up your head with stupid and makes your entire face hurt. I folded up the transcript, leaving damp tear marks on the edges of the paper.

The *malaika* were still under my bed. Right next to them were Dad's billfold and a blot of darkness I grabbed and pulled out. It was my black canvas bag, still dirty from the snowy mess of the Dakotas. I'd packed it carefully while Graves and I were clearing out the house and Christophe was on the phone, arguing with someone about coming to pick me up.

That felt like a lifetime ago. Back when I'd still been thinking things could be fixed, maybe, if I just coped hard enough.

Cash, both in my wallet and in the little space under the flap at the bottom of the bag, a sort of secret compartment Dad had shown me how to sew in and use. ID, both in the wallet and under the flap. A fresh clip of nine-millimeter ammo under the flap. ChapStick, my Yoda notebook, a comb, two pens, a handkerchief, a clean pair of underwear and a bra, and a small bar of hotel soap.

Hey, you never know.

The black book with Dad's contacts, because I'd thought it would be a good idea to keep it with me. But if August had disappeared, who else could I call? And it wasn't like there was a phone here. I hadn't even seen one in Dylan's office. Shanks had talked about phonetime, but I had no idea where to even find a line to the outside world.

I was as isolated as a prisoner.

Compass, road map for Florida, and another for North and South Dakota. Neither map would do me any good, but the compass would be useful. Mini flashlight—I flicked it on and off, checked for the extra batteries. It still worked. Those were good things to have.

Travel-size bottle of ibuprofen, small bottle of holy water, bottle of salt. I slid the switchblade in one of the smaller pockets sewn along the back of the bag. It rattled against two large silver dollars and four or five iron nails. Well, they're steel, actually, but the iron content makes them a good defense against all sorts of things. Revenants, some apparitions, fairies—you name it.

I shivered, thinking of fairies. People who think they're all sweetness and wings should pray they never run across a sidhe with a bad temper and the ability to steal years from your life. And pray that they never hear silver horns in the dead of night, echoing against the hills as hoofbeats rattle on a lonely stretch of road and the Wild Hunt looks for a victim. Gran taught me about never, ever messing with fairies.

I was even scaring myself at this point, but it felt good to be doing something. To be planning, instead of just being buffeted along with what everyone else wanted me to do. This preparation was something I could have done in my sleep.

Dad's billfold went in the secret compartment under the flap. I folded the transcript one more time and slid it into Dad's little black book. Then I picked up the nine-millimeter and checked the clip once more. It was habit. I tore up a pillowcase from the blue bed and wrapped the gun, so something couldn't press against the trigger. I put the wrapped gun in the bag and wished I did indeed have a holster.

Wishing wouldn't get me one, though.

*Come on, Dru. Think. Think hard, and think fast. How would Dad put it? Think logically.*

My logic-thingy wasn't working too well lately. But I'd give it the old college try.

Anna wanted me to think Christophe had betrayed my mother. But he'd saved me, so that didn't make much sense. She *also* thought

I was stupid. Just showing me two pictures of the house we'd lived in Before wasn't going to make me not trust Christophe.

Unless . . .

Things exploded behind my eyes, my brain finally making some connections. *Oh shit.*

My hands were shaking. I held up one of them. Even my fingers were jittering. I grabbed for the locket and rubbed it with my thumb, hard, like I could polish away the fear.

Showing me two pictures was useless. Unless she wanted to find out what I remembered about that house. She'd been watching me very carefully while trying not to look directly at me.

And why the hell would she come all the way up here herself, especially since it was so dangerous for a *svetocha*? Bodyguards and tutors, and here I was locked in a room for them to decide what to do with me.

For Anna to decide? Or for Sergej to decide? Did it matter?

*Well, Dru, there're two words that apply.* Fuck that. *That about covers it.*

But what about Ash? And what about Christophe, asking me to wait? Could I depend on him to come back for me?

*It doesn't matter. You can't help either of them if you're dead. Blondie's on duty to watch you at the moment, but as soon as it's dark it'll be time for the first class of the evening and he'll be gone. You'll have a chance.*

A chance to do *what*, though? What could I do? I wasn't about to go crawling around the roofs at night.

At least I knew Christophe was alive. I could be the only person that did know that for sure—and still, anything could happen to him in the next few days.

And there was the fact that Christophe could be using me for bait. Everything inside me rose up in revolt at the notion, because every time I thought of him I felt his warmth against me and smelled a ghost of his apple-pie self. Maybe I *should* just wait around for—

*Dru, you're counting on other people to save you. That's not going to happen.* I let out a shaking breath. *This one's all about you.*

But what about Graves?

*Shit. That's the only hole in this plan.* But if I wasn't around, would he be so much in danger? And he was happy here, even if it was a reform school. Graves was just peachy hanging out with his hairy friends.

His hairy friends who liked blaming me for even being born. Jesus.

A band of shadow was moving up the window as the sun sank, the light taking on that golden-honey cast of the best hour to capture it, if you could. I'd never been much into photography, but I remembered drawing in this light while Gran spun thread or finished dinner, sometimes singing in her queer atonal way, other times muttering imprecations at chicken broth or vegetables. I missed both things—her singing, and the steady hiss-thump of the antique spinning wheel. It was probably sitting under a dust cloth in the corner near the fireplace right where she'd left it. The house, mine under the terms of the trust, was closed up nice and tight, and I had the keys right on my key ring—that was still probably with the truck Christophe had hidden.

But there was another key ring, and I knew exactly where it was. In a metal box buried under the north side of a big granite boulder, the one Gran poured fresh milk over every new moon.

She also bolted the door every new moon. They left her house alone. That's another reason why I always shiver when I think about fairies.

There's nothing like waiting for the night to make you really nervous. The plan came together inside my head, and I was really wishing I had access to a car, any car. How did the food get to the school? Who did all the laundry?

It was a fine time to wish I'd been looking around instead of moping up here in my room or skipping classes. Then again, I wouldn't have been taught anything worthwhile if I'd attended class, now would I. They were actively trying to prevent me from learning something.

So. No car, just me. There was one lonely country road dipping away from the school, hitching up with the county highway a good distance away. Far enough away that I hadn't seen it from the roof of the Schola.

Two unpainted lanes of blacktop, with a deep ditch on either side, ribboning through the woods and occasional fields. It joined up just north of the town the wulfen were always running to. I could buy a map there and . . .

*Then what? You don't know anyone around here, and anyone you contact is going to be a question mark. If August was a part of the Order, maybe some more of Dad's friends were too. And if he's vanished, what's to say the others won't as soon as you call them for help?*

My head hurt trying to think about all of it. But the absolutely essential first step was getting *out* of here. Once I was on the move, I could figure everything else out.

Graves and Christophe had both pointed out it was easier for the vampires to kill me when I was away from a Schola, even a small one.

But they'd have to *find* me first.

I got up, left the bag on the bed. What do you wear when you're running for your life? Layers, boots because your feet are your lifeline and sneakers are too flimsy, and wool. Graves's shirt had vanished in the laundry. It gave me a funny feeling to think about it.

I felt like I'd just woken up after a long winter's nap, but I couldn't stop shaking.

# CHAPTER 19

**I**t got dark early, heavy overcast coming in from the northeast. The sky turned steel-indigo, and thunder rumbled in the distance. Fog didn't rise, and that was odd. I was used to the whole place being wrapped up in cotton wool. It felt oddly naked, and I didn't like it.

I also didn't like the clouds. They just didn't *look* right, thick dark blankets boiling lower and lower until they seemed to press the tree-tops in some weird way. It reminded me of the iron-gray sheet of the sky back in the Dakotas, the day I'd come face-to-face with Sergej.

Unusual weather. Vampire weather.

I stayed at the window, rubbing at the locket and watching the shadows stretch through the ruined garden below. The Schola woke up, a subliminal buzz just under the surface of the silence. It was the same as every other night. Except this night I was cold even through three sweater-layers, jeans, and a pair of almost-new boots. I had my bag on, strap snugged diagonally across my body. After some thought, I slid the switchblade in my left ass pocket. Now if I could just remember to dig it—or the gun—out when someone was trying to kill me, I'd be all set.

I ran over it again in my head. Down the stairs once the bell for first classes rang, through the halls, and into the night. Now was my chance.

I gave the room one last glance, from the pile of clothes I'd tossed in front of the closet to the rucked-up bed. I was getting sloppy and not taking care of my space. It would have gotten me another Lecture from Dad.

Christ. I was even missing his lectures about *Cleaning Up So You Can Find What You Need When You're Under Fire, Dru, and That's Going to Save Your Ass.*

Loneliness rose in a wave that tasted like acid. I paused by the door, closed my eyes, and *listened*, unloosing the fist Gran had taught me to make inside my head. That clenched-tight feeling is necessary if you don't want to end up saying the wrong thing, or repeating people's thoughts back to them. Plus, it's hard to concentrate on your own business if you're busy listening to everyone else's, as Gran told me until she was blue in the face.

Gran was big on concentrating on your own business. I wondered what she would make of all this, and missing her was a stone in my throat.

There was definitely a sense of *presence* in the hall outside my room. I suddenly wished I'd gone up and out of the window again, but the thought of doing that so close to dark made my knees feel kind of funny. Once was enough. Besides, the whole point of this was getting out before it was an emergency.

I waited, barely breathing. The presence slowly slid away, just in time for the first bell. It tinkled sweetly all through the halls, muffled by the door. Time for breakfast. Or dinner, whatever way you wanted to look at it. The boys would be getting up, getting dressed, and getting to the caf.

I took a deep breath, twisted the knob, and stepped out into the hall. It was empty. The whole place seethed quietly. Was it just me, or was there an odd note in the seething? Something feverish?

*It's just you, Dru. Focus on what you've got in front of you.*

Still, I hesitated. What about Graves?

*The farther you get from him, the safer he probably is. The wulfen will look after him. They won't do a damn thing to help you, though, so get your ass moving.*

The door clicked shut behind me. I took two steps and froze again, because a new sound filtered through the air.

It was the Restriction bell, its high hard tones cutting through the silence like a hot knife through butter. I could tell this wasn't a drill, too. The awareness of danger prickled all over me with little diamond claws.

The Schola took a deep breath, bracing itself, and just as the tones of the bell died away I set off down the hall, my jaw firming and my hands turning into fists.

I would never have a better chance to escape.

* * *

Even the best-laid plans have holes in them. My beautiful little plan was to get downstairs and to the intersecting halls, where I could take a hard right and have a clear shot at a gallery with doors on either side. Half those doors led to a courtyard garden; the other half opened up to a crumbling playground with swings and foursquare courts, quietly rusting away. From there I had a chance to get to a belt of shrubbery, and once there—

Well, anyway, I didn't get that far. I took the hard right, and as soon as I did my head pounded with approaching footsteps. They were running, and each step landed too hard to be human. I backed up, buttonhooked around the corner back into the hall I'd just left, and cast around for cover.

Nothing. Carpeted floor, industrial lighting, bare walls. Locked, empty classrooms on either side, other halls opening up to go down to the caf, two janitors' closets.

*Janitors' closets. Great.* One was locked. The other wasn't, and I lunged in, pulled the door to, and crouched in the darkness. My hip hit something metallic; I grabbed and stopped it from falling over. It was a metal bucket. I let out a soft, wincing breath and hoped they'd be making too much noise to hear me.

The footsteps ran in lockstep, hard metal sounds like iron poles hitting frozen earth. The taste of rusty blood and wax oranges burst over my tongue in a rotten flood, and the weird places on the back of my palate both opened up like flowers. My teeth ached, even the pressure of my tongue and lips against them agonizing. Little cold prickles raced up my arms and legs.

The steps were going pretty fast, and I shivered when they echoed on the winding stair up into the tower room.

The secret was out. They knew I was here now. A wounded vampire from last time had escaped to tell Sergej so, or the traitor had managed to tell him I was here, all wrapped up in a nice little blue room like a TV dinner in foil.

*Holy shit. I . . . holy shit.* The shaking had me by my scruff like I was a puppy, pitching me back and forth. Something crumpled in my left hand, the metallic thing I'd hit on the way down into a crouch making an odd soft sound as it bent.

*They're going up to your room,* Dad's voice said inside my head, pitilessly. *Move your ass, girl!*

I slid out of the closet on noodle-soft legs, shut it as quietly as

I could, and set off down the hall as fast as my protesting muscles would allow. Everything in me wanted to go back and cower in the dark, waiting for someone to find me.

*That's rabbit talk, Dru. Move it along.*

Down the side of the hall, hard right. There was my shot at the next part of the plan, and I took it, much faster than I should have been able to. My boots made odd scuffing sounds on the short carpet as I bolted into the gallery. Now the darkness pressed against the windows and glass parts of the door, and I'd forgotten I'd be clearly visible to anyone watching from outside.

*Shit. Shitshitshit!* No help for it now, nothing to do but to go flat-out toward the door I'd chosen and hope nobody was watching. Maybe they would all be too busy with—

An enormous crashing jolt shook everything around me. The fabric of the Schola rippled like a bedsheet given a good hard shake, and the glass broke with tinkling, pretty sounds, a shower of crystalline snow. It actually knocked me off my feet, tossing me into the side of the hall, directly against the stone facing. My shoulder flared with red pain, I went down in a heap, and it was a good thing too. Because then the screaming started, and I huddled against the wall with my head in my hands, trying to shut it *out*. It went on and on, scraping against the sensitive inside of my skull without pausing for breath. I clapped my hands over my ears, uselessly, and screamed as well. Hate exploded behind my eyes, fear and pain smashing bright fireworks through the map of my nervous system.

It was a struggle to pull myself back *into* myself. A thin thread of something warm trickled down from my nose, caressing my upper lip with a tiny wet finger. I licked without thinking, and a warm copper taste coated the inside of my mouth, reached down, and woke up the hunger.

My teeth hurt, a sharp piercing pain. Two pinpricks touched my lower lip, and I pushed myself forward on hands and knees, crawling. *Outside. Get outside.*

The bloodhunger set me on fire with thirst, but it also smacked the screaming away from the inside of my head and gave me a chance to make myself a fist again. The sheer hatred in that sound tore against my skin, rubbing like a wire brush. Broken glass littered the floor. I scrambled to my feet as cold air poured up the hall, whistling.

I hit the door in a mad tangle of arms and legs and dove into a bath of frigid air. It was a clear night, the stars coming up in small hard diamond-points of useless light, and I took off for the playground as fast as I could stumble. The swings that weren't broken moved gently, back and forth, and my boot soles slapped crumbling concrete.

The scream behind me ended, and another glassy cry split the air from the other side of the Schola. It was then I realized the entire place was lit up too bright to be night, and when I snapped a look over my shoulder I found out why.

The school was burning. You wouldn't think there would be a lot in a stone building to burn, but wet orange flames with blue wires in their centers leapt and crawled through the turrets, shone out through broken windows, and turned the night into flickering shadows. Those flames were wrong, and the snapping crackling hate in them told me what I needed to know—that this was something *nosferat*-based. There was nothing natural about the flames, just like there was nothing natural about suckers.

The fire shaded into regular orange with no blue threads out toward its edges. But that didn't make it look less freaky.

*Wow.* I stared. *If that reaches the library, fat chance studying afterward. Holy crap.* Another grinding crash rocked the building, and I heard more screaming.

This time the voices were young, and human. Well, mostly. Human at the bottom, even if there was growling over the top.

*Oh no.* I skidded to a stop. *Oh, shit no. Fuck. No, no, no.*

There were kids in there. I *knew* them. Cody and Shanks and Dibs and—

And oh holy God, Graves was in there and it was *burning*.

*Stick with the plan, Dru. It's a good plan, and it'll let you live.*

I hung there for a few moments, sick with indecision, the pinpricks against my lower lip turning more definite as half of me ached to bolt for the belt of scrub brush at the edge of the playground. The other half told me in no uncertain terms to turn right back around and tear the whole place apart until I found Graves. I had a gun, an extra clip, and a knife. That had to be enough.

*But—*

*But nothing!* This time it was Gran's voice, and it spoke up loud and clear. *You get your ass in there and you find that boy! He never would leave you behind!*

He wouldn't. I knew he wouldn't. But hadn't I been planning on doing just that to him?

*He's already left you behind! He's always playing with his happy shaggy friends! Get going, Dru!*

They were fighting over me, the two voices, and I had no idea who would win. But my stupid body turned itself around and started running straight for the burning building and certain death.

I really don't know why.

# CHAPTER 20

**I** **ran along the** side of the gallery. *He'd be in the caf or the dorms; it wasn't time for class yet. So if they—*

Another big ripping sound. Jesus. Had they brought supernatural dynamite in to tear the whole place apart? Blue-flaming stuff fell, hitting the ground less than three feet away and hissing like a rattlesnake. I leapt back and found that I'd stopped shaking. I was too busy, and it was too warm. Sweat sprang up in the curve of my lower back and the hollows under my arms. It was like standing in front of an oven, heat radiating in every direction. Mom's locket was a chip of ice against my skin.

I made it around the corner of the building, skipped over more hiss-burning debris, and decided maybe I shouldn't run right next to the wall. Shapes flew like wet ink over the big lawn in front of the school, the wide circular driveway painted with leaping shadows and lurid orange light. The concrete lions watching the entrance to the driveway seemed to shift, raising their heads and baring their teeth as I skidded to a stop. My heels dug in, and I stared with a dropping jaw.

It was a war zone.

The wide circular paved expanse ran with lean hairy forms. The wulfen leapt and circled, teams of them peeling away to dash in, clustering dark forms with shining eyes and inhuman speed. There were *djamphir* there too, a line of defense in front of the massive steps I'd struggled up the day we arrived. One of them had long slender blades that didn't gleam in the light.

One of them had the wooden swords. *Malaika*. It was Blondie, his curls glistening in the flickering light as he lifted his chin and yelled something. The *djamphir* shifted their collective weight.

My knees went squooshy. I couldn't see Graves, and I swayed drunkenly for a moment. Another explosion ripped the air, and the breeze veered. Thick smoke wandered across the open space, threading between the motionless and moving forms like questing fingers.

The wulfen gave ground, falling back, and the *djamphir* on the defense line bunched up a little. It was confusing, everything moving so fast, and I hesitated, unsure what to do.

Dad never said anything about charging into a pitched battle.

I was still standing there like an idiot, staring at the chaos, when another unearthly howl split the night behind me. A breath of air touched the back of my neck under my braid, and I spun, throwing myself aside and down. The world slowed again, and this time I actually felt the muscle inside my head flexing to encase everything in clear Lucite. It hurt a little, like when you've pulled something and haven't slowed down enough to let it heal.

The wulf hung over me, firelight glittering in the white streak down one side of his head. All the breath whooshed out of me and I rolled, gravel scraping the back of my sweater. The firelight twisted in weird ways, refracting around him, and he landed in a scrabble just as I realized he hadn't been aiming for me at all.

*Oh crap.* I scrambled to my feet, right-hand fingers fumbling at the flap on my bag. It was time to get the gun out, because everyone fighting in front of the school had seen us.

Ash hunched in front of me, snarling. Little strings of spittle dripped as he snapped, twice, white teeth clicking. I let out a choked sound, my feet threatening to tangle as I backed up in a hell of a hurry.

He snapped again, and the mad gleam in his eyes was like the unearthly firelight. Another explosion shook the school, and the wall nearest me started to crumble. The noise was immense, and Ash dashed forward a couple of steps.

I half-screamed again and backed up, realized he wasn't attacking. He was just snapping at me, like a sheepdog.

*Herding* me. And when I glanced up, I could guess why.

Because every vampire who had been trying to get into the front door of the school was now looking at me. The fire lit them all in weird stasis, wulfen forms tumbling in the air, the *djamphir* on the steps—I saw Kruger, his jaw dropping—all staring at me with various horrified expressions.

"*Svetosssssssssssha!*" The cry lifted on the night wind, and their faces blurred into caricatures of hate and sharp teeth. "*Sveto-sssssssssssssha!*"

*Oh shit.*

The *nosferat* broke and wheeled at once, blurring toward me. Ash lunged again, desperately, the white stripe on his head actually leaving a blurring trail, like a sparkler waved in the dark. It shook me out of shock and I whirled, my braid flying out in an arc, and took off around the side of the burning school again.

I wasn't going to make it, I could just tell. It was pretty clear now why they were attacking the school. And now, again, I was running for my life.

Just before I reached the corner, I heard the cries behind me—the wulfen's rising chill and glassy, the *djamphir*'s a shrill piercing ululation, and the vampires' a weird deadly scream lodging in the brain like crystal splinters. They made a weird three-part harmony, and if you ever recorded that sound, you could stop someone's heart just by playing it loud enough. The locket bounced against my breastbone, trapped in a fold of cloth and so cold it stung.

My teeth filled with aching, and if I'd had enough breath I would've screamed too. There was no time for it, because the footsteps behind me shook the earth, so I did the only thing I could do.

It wasn't a great idea, but it was all I had.

I ran along the side of the school, fists pumping and bag slapping against my hip, and as soon as the gallery loomed ahead of me I jagged for the biggest hole I could find, braced myself as best I could, and hurled myself forward into the unnatural flames.

\* \* \*

Burning. Smoke choking the air. I reached the end of the hall and dropped to my hands and knees, crawled forward in a blur. Glass glittered, crunched under my jean-clad knees, and I hoped I wasn't about to flay my hands. My mouth ran with wax and rotten oranges. I spat and heard sizzling. The heat was like oil, my skin tight and shiny. The fire turned weirder—blue wires in the middle of orange flames, crawling through the stone walls like veins and spreading oven heat. Still, a circle of orange moved with me, the blue fading out of the flames as they drew closer.

Screaming behind me. If you've never heard a vampire die in battle, you can count yourself lucky. They don't just scream with their mouths—the sound goes on and on inside your head, bouncing off the inside of your skull and burrowing under your sanity until you want to scream yourself, until the edge of the world peels up and you can sense the nasty things that lie underneath regular waking consciousness. I scrambled through the burning gallery, carpet melting under and sticking to my fingers, until I spilled out another broken door into the courtyard garden. It was pure instinct, a draft of cooler air pulling me out.

Coughing, retching, I scrambled toward the middle of the garden. Smoke belched. Burning things fell like meteors, crashing to the ground.

*Well, Dru, this was not your best idea.* I almost pitched headfirst into the gravel path, snapped a terrified glance over my shoulder. There was a wall of orange flame and black smoke, but no vampires yet. Their keening soaked the air, fueling the flames. It was pure hate, rolled in agony and set alight, just like the Schola itself. I tried to shut out the noise again, failed, gasped and choked, and tried again while I crawled.

The bushes were burning out here too. I made it to the middle of the courtyard—there were stone benches with wooden slats, the paint on the wood smoking. I made myself as small as I could, knees up, my back braced against a bench's legs. I dug in my bag, got the gun out, and the tears rolling down my cheeks weren't from pain or fear. It was the smoke crawling around me, thick greasy fingers pressing behind my eyes. Coughing shook me in great racking bursts.

I'd thought I could break through the gallery and maybe find a flame-free part of the school to hide in. Now I was trapped. The vampires couldn't come in here and get me, but the fire might do their job for them. Still, I'd take being roasted alive over getting ripped to shreds by suckers any day.

Or would I? It was getting awful hard to breathe. I hunched

down further, trying for usable air close to the ground. The locket was still oddly cold and buzzing against my chest. Steam rose from my sweater, and the smoking paint on the bench wasn't too happy either, adding a weird pungent note to the thick vapor. A dead-looking rosebush in one corner of the courtyard blossomed into flame.

*Oh wow.* I stared at the thin thorny sticks, now alive with crawling orange flowers that fizzed and crackled. The gun dipped. Everything was a wall of flame, and I was beginning to feel lightheaded.

"DRUUUUUUUUUUU!" A long-drawn-out howl. I didn't recognize the voice, and it shook the streaming flames. I coughed steadily now, choking on the smoke. Everything blurred, the blue wires threading through the stone of the courtyard pressing against the circle of orange around me. The bench was getting awful hot, and I had a sudden terrible mental vision of the gun blowing up in my hand. Ammo could do that, if it got too hot. Dad had told me.

*Really not your best idea, Dru,* I thought, right before I slid over to the side, my fingers cramping on the gun. A black blot dilated in the middle of the flames. "DRUUUUU!"

I coughed again, scouring my lungs. There was nothing to breathe; it was all smoke. Haziness filled my eyes.

Someone was cursing steadily. At least, it sounded like cursing, but the words were put together funny. They sounded foreign. Fingers bit my shoulder and I was dragged up. I fought feebly, the gun loosened from my fingers. Something pressed itself against my cheek, hard little divots and something softer. Then, movement. The world fell away underneath me.

Falling. A jarring through my entire body. Splintering glass and a roar, and I was on fire, burning, flesh crisping and peeling before we burst out into cooler air and rolled, steam rising in waves, a hissing sound and a scream of pain. Then, more chaos.

*"Get the goddamn oxygen!"* someone screamed. Hands grabbed me and I fought back wildly, coughing and retching as I struck out with fists and feet.

*"Calm down!"* Another yell, this one I recognized. *"Goddammit, Dru, we're trying to help!"*

*Graves?* I tried to say his name, choked, tried again. My eyes wouldn't work right. My skin was still on fire, and I starfished again, throwing out my arms and legs as I tried to breathe. That was my last hurrah. All the fight just spilled out of me.

Something wet and cold wiped at my face. It felt good.

More coughing. They rolled me on my side, I choked up a thick mass of burning snot and spat. Someone caught my head, something was jammed in my nose, and a flood of something cool hit my burning lungs.

I collapsed again onto cold, hard ground, wet grass poking at my hands. My arms and legs refused to work properly. Someone had their arms around me, and I blinked, gritty stuff filling my eyes the tears flooded.

"Jesus Christ," Graves whispered brokenly. Someone else was coughing and cursing. There was a crash and a snarl. "Leave him alone, he dragged her *out*! Leave him *alone!*"

The last three words hit that rolling-thunder-under-the-surface tone again, and the noise subsided except for the roar of the burning.

"I'll take care of the oxygen," I heard Dibs say. "Dial it up as high as it'll go. She's almost cyanotic."

"Never seen a Burner before. I thought they died out years ago." Someone coughed, a deep racking sound.

"Well, they found one." It was Shanks. I barely recognized his voice without all the mockery. "Guess they had to, with a *svetocha* here. Jesus."

"You're in my way." Dibs had lost the squeaking, terrified tone; his voice was cool and professional. "Give me that, you're not a medic."

"Can you carry her?" Shanks sounded deathly tired. "They're going to come back as soon as they regroup."

"I'll carry her," Graves answered grimly. "You okay?"

"Had better days." Shanks coughed weakly. "I'll do. Come on."

"What about him?" someone else asked. "He's one of *them*."

"Bring him," Graves said immediately. He sounded like he was getting used to this answering-questions thing. "They'll kill him if we leave him here. Let's go."

I was dragged, then. I was too busy breathing to really care. Blessedly cool air touched my soot-stained cheeks, and my feet padded at the ground uselessly. I kept blinking, hoping my eyesight would come back. The whole world was black with smudges of gray. My head lolled drunkenly.

"Is she all right?" A hoarse rasp of a voice, one I should've recognized. "Is she?"

I choked, spat another gob of stuff. It splatted dully. *Ewwww. Gross.* The song of pain that was my entire body hitched up another notch, a choir of pulled muscles and still-burning skin. I couldn't feel Mom's locket, and it disturbed me until I retched again and had other things to worry about until the nausea retreated a little.

"She's fine. Probably a bit stunned." Graves sounded worried: I was jostled as well as dragged now, one of my arms over someone's shoulders, the other over someone else. I hung between them like a scarecrow. "She's still breathing, at least."

"Let me see. Let me *see* her." A scuffing, footsteps. The movement halted, and someone let out a sharp, pained sound. A light feathering touch along my forehead, grit scraping lightly against the skin. A gusty sigh. "God in Heaven, *dziękuję*. Thank you."

"Can we move it along?" Shanks sounded irritated. "I would really *hate* to fight another pitched battle with vampire shock troops *and* a Burner."

"They've probably set up a cordon." The husky voice was so familiar—I couldn't place it though. "Do we have any water?"

Shanks actually sighed, an aggrieved sound. "Dylan broke out to the west. They're going fast and loud to draw attention away from us. Let's go." A sloshing sound. "Drink while we run. Can you keep up?"

"The day I can't is the day I turn in my blades."

I finally placed the husky, sour voice. My heart leapt inside my chest.

I had to cough and spit again before I could rasp, "Christophe?" The word was a husk of itself, scarring my throat. *You came back.* Intense relief warred with the fact that I really, truly was not feeling very good.

The person holding up my right side stiffened just a little.

"Right here, *malutka*." He coughed again, a deep racking that ended on a choke. "Keep breathing. We'll handle the rest."

*He sounds really sure.* "I've g-g-g—" My lips refused to work right. My entire brain had seized up. There was so much to tell him. And so many questions to ask.

But he'd come back. For me.

"Later, *moj mały ptaszku*. Later. Focus on breathing for right now." There was a crackle of undergrowth. We started moving again. "Your guardian angel is here, Dru. Don't fear."

# CHAPTER 21

**M**y vision returned in fits and starts, and a little while later I could walk. The stuff jammed in my nose was clear tubing attached to an oxygen canister slung over Dibs's shoulder as he braced me on my left side. Graves was on my right, his hair wildly mussed and his coat singed. Blood painted the right side of his face, and his jaw was set.

My heart almost burst. My arm tightened, and he gave me a sideways look. "Hey," he said, quietly. "How you, kiddo?"

My mouth was full of poison. I spat again to clear it, and Dibs giggled, a high, nervous sound. "Peachy," I managed. "Wha' happen?"

"All hell broke loose." Graves barely looked where he was going. Trees pressed close, the night like a wet washcloth over the eyes. I wasn't blind; it was just *dark*. Country-dark. There was a sense of stealthy movement, and the glitters and lamps of eyes around me told me I was in the middle of a group of wulfen. "They got into the school. There was a vampire with red hair, she just looked at things and they started exploding. Shanks and Dylan—"

"Save your breath," came Christophe's harsh voice. "We're not free yet."

"Christophe?" I had to know. "Where *were* you? I thought—"

"Around and about. Be quiet now." He didn't bother sugarcoating the command, but then his tone softened. "You seem to delight in doing the worst, most dangerous thing possible. Try to restrain yourself for a day or two, hmm?"

*I'm just trying to stay alive, Christophe. Thanks.* I wished I could put my head down on Graves's shoulder, settled for putting one foot in front of the other. I was reeling, step to side-step. The oxygen felt good and cool on my burning throat. My teeth weren't aching anymore. Much.

My head dropped forward. I sighed. Coughed again, trying to do it quietly. There was a pause, all the wulfen stopping at once.

A howl lifted in the distance. *Vampire.* The hatred in it scraped inside my skull, the taste of wax oranges on my tongue over the foulness, and I found out I was shaking again. I didn't have the energy to pull myself up inside my head and block it out.

"God and Hell both *damn* it," Christophe said quietly, but with a coldness to the words that turned the darkness into danger.

"Shit." Shanks sounded like he seconded that emotion. "Let's hurry it up, people."

"What happened?" I whispered. Graves just shook his head. His arm tightened around me, like he wanted to pull me away from Dibs. The small blond werwulf was quivering too. I couldn't tell whether I was shaking him or he was as scared as I was.

"Someone just died. We can hope it was the Burner—she would be a high-priority target. Without her, the *nosferatu* are merely dangerous, not overwhelming," Christophe said softly. "Just breathe, Dru. Do we have another oxygen tank?"

"Just the one." Shanks moved away. They glided noiselessly through the forest. My eyes were doing funny things, piercing the gloom one moment and showing me moving shapes, sticks, and the texture of bark. My teeth would give a sudden burst of pain; then the darkness would return.

All the questions I couldn't ask swirled around inside my head. My right arm tightened over Graves's shoulders. "I thought you were inside." My voice was a harsh croak. "God."

"Is that why you ran into a burning building?" He sounded shocked. Go figure.

*I thought I could throw the vampires off my trail.* It was too hard to explain and I didn't have the breath. I tried anyway. "Well, yeah. That, and—"

"Quiet." Christophe was a deeper shadow, his eyes glowing weirdly blue. Most of the wulfen's eyes just glimmered dully. Shanks's were actually yellow, and I could tell whenever Graves blinked because the green gleams next to me would vanish for a moment and my heart would stop again.

The motion suddenly halted. Everyone froze. I leaned on Graves. His hand, spread against my sore ribs on my left side, tensed just a little, fingers gone hard. I tried not to breathe too loudly. The oxygen bottle made a small sound, and I winced. Dibs and I shook together, my teeth clenched to stop their chattering.

Little noises filled the woods around us. I couldn't tell if they were the regular cacophony of the woods at night—because it's rarely ever silent out in the country—or if it was *something else*. I felt very small, and very soft and pink in the middle of the wulfen.

"We need cover," Shanks mouthed. He leaned toward the shape that was Christophe, their eyes glowing at each other. "How drained are you?"

Christophe blinked, slowly, deliberately. The blue glow of his eyes came back, settled on me. "And I thought you would take convincing."

A movement that could have been a shrug. "I don't want to die. And I'm responsible for them."

"Granted." The single word had sharp edges. "I'll need to drink."

The four words fell like a stone into a glassy pool and vanished without a trace. There was a collective sharp inhale among the wulfen.

"Wait a second." Graves sounded like he was having trouble with this. I tried to hold my head up. It dipped forward. Curls had come free of my braid and bobbled in front of my face. "What are we talking about here?"

Shanks didn't even bother to listen. "You can't take it from one of mine. So it's me, or . . ."

A sliding motion. Graves sucked in a sharp breath, and Christophe was suddenly right in front of me.

"Dru," he said softly. The hurtfulness was gone from his voice. "I need your help."

I swallowed. My throat was full of smoky acid. "Yeah. Sure. What?"

Christophe moved in closer, but not as close as he had been before. Still, I could feel his heat. "Give me your hand."

"Oh *hell* no." Graves shifted his weight, like he was going to pull me back and away.

I stayed where I was, digging my feet into the ground. "What are you going to do?"

"I need to borrow something of yours. It will come back, I promise. It will save all of us." Those blue eyes held mine, glowing in the darkness. Was it just me, or were they not quite as cold as they used to be? He smelled like smoke too, and under it was the edge of apple pies—spice and goodness. Jesus. Even after all that he smelled like a bakery. "You're going to have to give me the keys this time, Dru."

It wouldn't make sense to anyone other than Graves and me. I'd refused to trust him once before, and it had ended up with Sergej almost having me for lunch. Now we were out in the middle of the woods with vampires looking for us, and there were a bunch of terrified kids here in the dark.

Kids who had done their best to save me. Kids who would be in the cafeteria or heading for their first classes right now if not for me.

*Way to go, Dru. You just get everyone in trouble, don't you?*

I licked my dry, smoke-tarnished lips. "It'll get them out of here?"

"All of us." Christophe sounded utterly sure. "I just need to borrow something of yours."

*What, the wooden swords? I left them behind, couldn't carry them.* "All right. What?" My throat was full of something. Graves shifted again, but I stayed where I was.

"You don't have to," Dibs whispered. He sounded scared to death. "Dru . . ."

"Give me your hand," Christophe repeated. "Either one."

I slid my heavy left arm free of Dibs's shoulders. Blindly stuck my left hand out in his general direction. "I don't know what you're gonna do, but do it." I leaned into Graves, who was shaking now too. I couldn't tell if it was the stress of holding me up or something else. "They're getting closer." I didn't know how I knew. The sounds in the woods drew close, nasty tittering laughter and the padding of booted feet.

Warm fingers clasped my wrist. Christophe ran his fingertips down the center of my palm, and a weird feeling shot up my arm.

I had to know. "Christophe?"

He went utterly still. "What, *skowroneczo moja?*"

"Where were you?" *Was I bait? What were you doing? You said you'd be gone, but here you are.*

"I was making arrangements to come collect my little bird." His fingers bit in, and he raised my hand, palm up. "You don't think I'd leave you, do you?" There was a gleam of teeth under the lamps of his eyes, and all of a sudden I knew what he was going to do. The knowledge sprang full-blown into my head, and if I hadn't been so scared, exhausted, lonely, pained—you name it— I might have tried to backpedal. Graves let out another strangled sound, his arm tightening as I lost all the strength left in my legs.

And Christophe drove his fangs into my wrist, just where the radial pulse beats. It was like rusty spikes spearing through my arm, the pain branching up nerves to detonate in my head, and a horrible *draining* sensation spilled through me.

It hurt. Have you ever been so sick dying seems like an okay thing because it will make the feeling *stop?* Have you ever felt something inside you—something you never noticed before, something rooted deep in your chest—getting ripped up inch by inch? Stubbornly resisting, something twined around your ribs and internal organs being torn free.

I collapsed. A wave of coldness dilated around my mother's locket, held trapped against my skin.

Graves made a soft, hurt little sound, holding me up. "Dru—" he whispered.

The drawing pull came again. This time it stretched up into my brain, a bony hand digging clawed fingers up my throat and into my skull the hard way, squeezing the tender meat I thought with. Memories splashed and whirled, draining away.

Graves was holding me up now. I was trying to scream, but I couldn't. My voice box had frozen up. Everything about me had frozen. One thought managed to escape the relentless, digging agony.

*—please don't please don't not again please don'tdon'tdon't—*

But it came one more time, and this time was the worst because the digging, awful fingers weren't pulling at anything physical. Instead they were scraping and burrowing and twisting into *me*. The part of me that wasn't anything but me, the invisible core of what I was.

I'd call it the soul, but I don't think the word fits. It's as close as I can get.

Digging scraping pulling tearing *ripping*, invisible things inside me being pulled away, and something left me in a huge gush. My head tipped back, breath locked in my throat. Graves made another small horrified sound and tried to pull me away.

Christophe jerked his head back, fangs sliding free of my flesh, and something wrapped itself tightly around my wrist, below his bruising-hard grip on my forearm. He exhaled, shuddering, and Graves tried to pull me away again. My arm stretched like Silly Putty between them, my shoulder screaming, and I couldn't make a sound.

The winter-blue of Christophe's irises clouded, dark striations like food coloring dropped in water threading through the light. They still glowed even more intensely, in a way that shouldn't have made sense. "Sweet," he hissed, and made an odd hitching movement. His chin dipped, and his fingers tightened bruising-hard on my wrist, like he was going to do that again.

I wanted to scream, couldn't. Nothing worked. My body just hung there, frozen and unresponsive.

"Christophe." Shanks sounded nervous. "Um, Christophe?"

The world trembled on a knife edge. Blackness crowded in around the corners. My head tipped further back. Graves held me up, both arms around me now. I was so tired it was work to breathe. In, out, in, out, my ribs almost refused to rise. There was air outside my face, but it was just so hard to bring it in. Instead, the sea of atmosphere pushed down on me, crushing.

"Jesus," Graves whispered. "What did you do to her?"

Another gleam of teeth below Christophe's darkened eyes. "I just *borrowed* her for a while, dogboy." The casual, hurtful edge to the words abraded the inside of my head like an ice scraper against a windshield. I flinched. "Don't worry. I'm not about to let one of *them* get their ugly fangs in *moja księżniczko*."

Pain and dragging weariness pulled on every nerve and muscle in my body. Behind us, another chilling howl lifted into the night.

"We need cover," Shanks said urgently. "And—"

"I know what you need. Shut up." Christophe touched my face, stepping close and sliding his fingertips against my dirty cheek. I flinched. Graves dragged me back, and how weird was it that he stepped silently? All around us, the woods creaked and sighed in the darkness. The snarl running under the surface of Graves's skin bounced around, echoing, inside my skull.

They faced each other, the two boys, and I was suddenly very sure something bad was about to happen. The moment hung, suspended in the cold night air.

"They're getting closer," someone whispered.

Christophe laughed. It was a bitter little sound, not unlike Graves's sarcastic, pained bark. "I'm not saving *you*," he said, very quietly. "I'm saving *her*. Remember that."

He turned and literally vanished. The air made a weird popping sound, collapsing where he'd stood, and one of the wulfen sniffed deeply. Shanks cursed, but softly. Thick white wetness boiled in the air, rising from the ground where Christophe had stood. It rose in veiny, ropy fingers, curls of it touching my legs.

The touch made my skin crawl. It was exactly the kind of greasy fog the suckers had shown up in. *Wait a minute. What did he just do?*

"Bloodfog," one of them said. "It'll cover us, and he'll hunt *them*. Let's go."

At that point everything just turned weird and soupy gray. Dibs helped Graves heft me up on his back like I was a little kid getting piggybacks. I tried to say I was sorry, but the words wouldn't come.

They started moving through the forest, everything blurring together. My head bobbled and joggled against Graves's shoulder, and I heard him cursing steadily under his breath. The places inside me where everything had been ripped up twinged and settled, throbbing like a sore tooth. It was like a headache, only not in my head. In the invisible places where I lived that weren't connected with any muscle or bone.

"Graves . . ." I whispered against his shoulder. Then the darkness swallowed me, and everything inside me still hurt. I fell down into the hole where things had been ripped free, and small chill voices laughed while I did.

# CHAPTER 22

**I came back to** myself slowly, in fits and starts. First there was gray light, coming through two horizontal cracks. A single spot of warmth against my chest, like someone had breathed on me. Voices—Shanks and Graves, mostly.

"She still out?" Grudging concern. The tall werwulf didn't sound happy.

"Like a light. I can't believe you suggested that." Graves, tired and unhappy too. The movement under me hadn't stopped. Wind touched my hair. For the first time I smelled something other than smoke. Leaf sludge, fresh air, the iron smell of very early or very, very late.

"We had to. Jesus Christ." Feet hitting the ground. "All right, everyone. Let's get moving."

The horizontal slices of light thinned and vanished. I drowned in blackness again. Something inside me felt different, but I couldn't figure out what.

A sound like feathers surrounded me. I waited for the owl, but it didn't show up. Its wings beat frantically, a muffled heartbeat. The horizontal bars of light dawned again, and I realized they were my eyelids opening a little to let in morning.

Voices, arguing. I felt like I'd been ripped apart and put back together wrong. My arms were around something, and a tree trunk was braced against my back. My feet dangled. I hitched in a breath. It was a relief to find that breathing wasn't a huge struggle anymore. My lungs and ribs had decided to work together, and the air was no longer heavy as lead.

"The *wampyr* have gone to earth—if Reynard left any alive. We have to move *now*, and get to a safe place."

"Like where? And Shanks is half-dead. We can't leave him."

"You're not in charge. We're already carrying *her*. You gonna carry him too?"

"Fuck you I'm not in charge. We're not leaving anyone behind." It was Graves, like I'd never heard him. Angry, determined—and with that growl under the edge of the words. He sounded like he knew what he was talking about, and he wasn't about to take any shit.

I realized my mouth was open, dry, and tasted like something had died in it. I closed it and tried an experimental movement. The haze of light coming in through my eyelids sharpened.

"Please. Who do you think you're kidding? The *djamphir* might think you're gonna control us, but you're not."

Movement. I was shifted to the side. A small sound escaped me, like I was caught in a nightmare.

Go figure.

"Let's get this figured out right now," Graves said, quietly. The growl turned into a sharp crackling, as if bones under plastic wrap were snapping into dust.

*Oh boy.* The thought was sharp and clear, and it was another relief. A little bit of warmth stole back into me, the locket oddly heavy under my shirt. The ripped-up places inside me quivered like scabs. With thought came being again. I *was*.

*Dru. I'm Dru. And that's Graves.*

Life, color, and sound all rushed back into me. I opened my eyes and found out I was slumped against Dibs, who had gone pale, his eyes wide. He stared at the clearing, which was ringed by wulfen in various hunching poses. Some of them even lay stretched flat on the forest floor. Oily-white, almost-glowing fog drifted cotton-packed between the trees, and birds were calling uncertainly. It even smelled like dawn—if you've ever been out when the sun comes up, you know what I mean. It's the metallic scent of sunlight hitting the atmosphere and everyone needing a good shot of caffeine.

Graves and another black-haired boy were the only ones standing up in the middle of the clearing. Beads of water touched Graves's messy hair. The fog was so thick it was like being caught in a bubble, swallowing the rest of the world.

The shape at my feet was Shanks, stretched out at full-length, dried blood in a shocking spill down the side of his face. His clothes were ripped to shreds, and more blood—black and still-smoking as well as red and human—crusted him. He looked like he was in bad shape, cheese-pale and with his sides heaving as he breathed in shallow gasps.

Graves leaned forward. The other boy—slim, black hair cut short, big dark eyes almost glowing with anger—rocked back on his heels as if he'd been punched. The invisible tension between them boiled like heat-haze above pavement on a tar-melting-hot day.

"Don't fucking mess with me right now, man." Graves said every word very slowly and very clearly, his lips moving as he enunciated. He had to, because his jaw was shifting. Still, the command-voice came out clean and clear. The other boy rocked back even further on his heels, dropping his shoulders and dipping his chin.

"We'll all die," the other kid whined, but all the starch had gone out of him. "You're not ready."

"Not ready my *ass*," Graves snapped. "I was born ready, dick-wipe. You want to test me now, you go ahead, but it'll waste valuable time. We get caught, you'll die just like the rest of us. So *stop* being an asshole and *shut* the fuck up."

Silence, as ticking-tense as the moment between stepping off a diving board and the instant you hit the water. I leaned against Dibs and looked down at Shanks. His eyes were half-closed, little gleams peeking out from under the eyelids. There was no sign of iris or pupil, just blind white.

Something was wrong. The world looked flat, oddly two-dimensional. I tilted my head back, trying to hear something, anything, with the touch. Trying to unloose the fist and send little questing fingers out to take in the world.

My pulse leapt up, hard and high in my throat. There was nothing there.

*Stop it. You're just tired.* God knew I was exhausted. But it was like being blind. I'd never realized before how the *touch* lay under every thought, bubbling and boiling and showing me the depths of things.

It was gone, and I was blind. I hated the feeling.

I found I could stand on my own two feet. Dibs still clutched at me, though. His skin was hot against mine, and he smelled just like a regular boy, without the undertone of cold fur and danger.

*Is this what it's like to be normal?* Shaking spilled through me. The trees looked dead. The fog was flat. And Graves and the rest—

No, wait. Graves looked normal. He stared at the other boy, green eyes piercing and a high blush of color on his cheekbones, the slight suggestion of epicanthic folds vanishing as his face shifted to more hawklike than half-Asian. Other than that, he looked just the same as usual, except a little more unwashed. His coat was singed and plastered with mud up the side, his hair was wildly mussed, and a bolt of something hot and hard went through my chest as the other black-haired boy dropped his eyes. Graves kept staring until the kid actually crouched, as if the green gaze was a heavy weight.

It looked like a grainy color film I'd seen on late-night cable in a weird little motel outside a teensy town named Zavalla in Texas. It was a nature special on satellite cable about wolf packs, and all about how wolves will give in and give up so the more dominant wolf keeps his position and the less dominant one doesn't get killed. There was a lot of snapping and snarling, but killing everyone who wanted to maybe get a little higher on the ladder was bad evolutionary logic.

I blinked. My eyes were full of crusty stuff. And Graves really did look like the only real 3-D human being standing there. Even with his hair in messy strings and his coat singed, he looked . . .

I don't have a word for the way he looked. Solid. Comforting. Like he was the one piece of the world that was holding the whole damn thing up. I let out a small sipping breath, trying not to taste the smoke smell rising up all around me or the stink of danger in the air. And that was another thing too—everything smelled washed out. Insipid. Not as real and true as it should have.

There was that spot of warmth against my chest, though. That was comforting.

"Now," Graves finally said, "anyone else want to piss me off? Anyone else think this is a goddamn *democracy*?"

I swallowed, hard. My throat clicked, but nobody paid any attention. He'd drawn himself up to his full height, and turned slowly in a circle, looking at everyone.

"We're a *pack*." He halted once he'd made a full circle, and looked down at the kid in front of him. It might've looked weird anywhere else, but here in the woods surrounded by fog it looked perfectly normal.

Well, not *normal*. But natural. It looked like he belonged here, splashed with mud and scorch, his eyes burning and his coat straining across shoulders that had grown broader. It was the *loup-garou* burning in him, turning him into something other than the weirdo bird-thin Goth Boy hiding in the corners of your average school.

His hands were whiteknuckle fists. "We don't leave someone behind. We've all been left behind one way or another, we ain't gonna do it to nobody else. Anyone got a *problem* with that?"

Seconds ticked away. The tension went out of the air, but Graves tilted his head. A few of the boys sat up, and the black-haired boy made a quick inquiring movement.

"You hear that?" Dibs whispered. Either his skin was burning hot or mine was ice cold. I wasn't sure which. "Choppers. Again."

"What if it's the Order?" someone wanted to know. "I mean, coming to get us?"

"Too fucking late," the black-haired boy muttered. *Peter*, my weary brain finally whispered. *That's his name.*

Graves scrubbed at his chin with long fingers. "We'll move as far as we can under the fog. We can't trust that it might be the right kind of people up there looking for us."

"Are we on our own, now? No more Order?" Dibs piped up. He was dirty and disheveled as the rest of us, his round blond face creased with worry. But he didn't look as scared as he'd always looked in the cafeteria.

"Don't know yet." Graves sighed. "We'll move as long as we have cover, then hide until nightfall. By then Christophe will be around again."

"So will the *nosferatu.*" This boy, long and brown-haired, lay on his back with an arm over his face. He wore a flannel shirt that had seen better days and a messy bandage tied around his head, a dark bloody patch over his left temple. "I got an idea."

"Shoot," Graves said immediately.

"I've got family around here—not kincousins, my aunts married into them. Maybe we should go to ground. It's a short shot from the last town we passed. We're all exhausted, the girl don't smell like herself, and if we dive now, we'll have a better chance of running at full strength tonight—or even better, tomorrow when the sun rises."

Graves half-turned and looked across the clearing, straight at me. I looked back, as steadily as I could while hanging onto Dibs and sandwiched against a tree trunk.

He was looking to me for direction, I realized. Back in his snow-piled hometown, I'd been the one who knew what to do when it all went sideways. At least, I'd known what to do when the burning dog and the streak-headed werwulf tried to kill us. I'd gotten Graves to my house. I'd been the one who had the books and the guns and the knowledge, however patchy.

We looked at each other. *What the fuck do we do now?* he was asking.

I tried to think. "What do we have?" My throat was sore, and the words didn't have the weight I was used to hearing behind them. They were made of paper. "In the way of supplies."

Because I knew how to do this. It didn't depend on the touch or the aspect or anything else. It was just doing what I'd been taught. We were in hostile territory, and we had an objective—the objective was not dying.

*First you find out what you have,* Dad would say. *Then you figure out how to make it work for what you need, 'cause you don't get what you want. You get just what you have and no more.*

It turned out to be a load of cash, my bag, the clothes on our backs, some switchblades, the oxygen tank, a medikit Dibs was carrying as well, and two packs of cigarettes. Shanks lay on the ground, breathing shallowly. He didn't look good.

It was a relief to have my brain working again. Every muscle I had hurt like hell, and the weird two-dimensionality of the world was new and awful. My head ached, but I'd done this sort of thing a lot with Dad—him throwing scenarios at me, teaching me how to plan.

"We didn't have enough time to get to the armory." Peter very carefully slid his switchblade back in his pocket. "They hit us so fast. And a Burner. Jesus."

*At least we've got money.* I leaned against the tree instead of Dibs. My left wrist was wrapped in a very capable pressure bandage. Shut my eyes, squeezing out the light, and took a deep breath. *Come on, Dru. You know how to do this.* "So our choices are to run on the money we've got and try to make the city tonight with the wounded, or hide at Andy's family's house until tomorrow." I paused. "Do we even know where to go once we get to the city limits?"

"Shanks knows." Andy had sat up, and he was looking at me like I'd grown a new head. "My aunts are loyal. They'd hide us even if it was the Dark Times."

"I'm just not sure we won't bring them trouble." I blinked again, tried to focus. The world still didn't look right, and a funny quivering feeling was pushing its way up through my chest. I didn't need a dictionary to know it was called fear. A whole new brand of being afraid, an unsteady heat like indigestion underneath the warm spot of Mom's locket. I was beginning to realize there were shades of fear just like on a color wheel, all of them slightly different but still awful. I looked up at Graves again. "You're not going to like this."

"What?" He leaned on the other side of the tree I was holding onto, his messy hair shaken down over his eyes again. Goth Boy was back on display. His earring winked once, silver shining.

"My dad trained me for this type of thing. I can hit the next town and find some transportation. I can vanish, and that means they won't have a reason to chase—"

"No." Graves shook his head. "Hell no."

"Let her finish." Peter crouched next to Shanks. His face twisted up bitterly as he looked down at the other boy.

Graves stiffened. "*You* shut up. They'll chase us whether you're with us or not, Dru, and what part of this do you not *understand?* I'm *not leaving you.*"

"If vampires will attack a whole school full of people trained to fight them to kill me, what makes you think they won't attack a wulfen's house? And . . . Sergej . . . might be on his way too. Come on." I braced myself against the tree. No spike of pain went through my head, but several of the wulfen shivered at the name.

"It's a compound," Andy piped up. "The kin, they believe in the old ways. There's my aunts and the uncles, grandparents, my cousins—"

*Great. More people to die.* "It's a better idea if I just go it alone. I can make it to the next town, get some food and some wheels, and—"

Graves made a spitting sound of annoyance. "Add carjacking or theft to your list of things to do today? No dice, Dru. Look at you, you can't even stand up."

He was right. I held onto the tree. "I could kick *your* ass." But it was bravado. We both knew it, and he shook his hair back and gave me a fey toothy grin. In a couple years that smile would be a heart-stopper.

Who was I kidding? He was a heart-stopper now. Why hadn't I seen it before? Or had it been hiding in him, just waiting to come out?

"Anytime you think you're man enough, sweetheart." He shook himself all over, let go of the tree, and I wondered where the scared kid had gone. The one who had hugged me on the cold stairs while something awful knocked at my front door—something old, and foul, and smelling of rusty blood. "All right, Andy. Lead the way. Tony, Beau, you two carry Shanks. Does he need another shot, Dibs?"

"Can't." The blond boy shook his head. "If I give him more sedative he might get too tired to breathe *or* heal."

The fog pressed close, as if it was listening. It reflected the sunlight oddly, shapes moving in its curtained depths. The wulfen started moving. Graves stepped around the tree and looked down at me. He looked taller, or maybe it was because I was so goddamn tired even though I was awake and mostly upright. The light had grown stronger, and the thopping sound of helicopters faded into the distance. I didn't even know which direction we were going, or where we were.

Two of the wulfen heaved Shanks up. He looked pretty bad. Graves stepped close to me, picked up my left arm, and ducked so it settled across his shoulders. "I'm not leaving anyone behind," he said, fierce and low. "Not anyone. Not anymore."

"I'm sorry." I tried to pitch it low, too. "If I hadn't—"

"Shut up." He took a few experimental steps. Once I let go of the tree, the ground swayed drunkenly underfoot. "Come on."

"Aye-aye, Captain," someone said, and I surprised myself by giggling. The sound was very small and lonely, but Graves looked at me, and the corner of his mouth tilted up a little. Just a little.

The empty places inside me didn't feel quite so big after that.

*I need to borrow something. . . . It will come back, I promise.*

I didn't ask where Christophe was. I was too busy trying to keep upright. And besides, if I had to really admit the truth, I didn't want to know. Not while my wrist pulsed, hot and sore. Not while the world looked like a paper cutout and the space inside my head where the touch should be was glaringly empty. Not while I was still scared, and hungry, and smelling of smoke.

It was better to lean in close to Graves and smell whatever shampoo he'd used before everything went bad. A breath of it clung to him under the smell of outdoors, smoke, and healthy young male who needs his daily shower.

We moved into the weird fog, steadying each other. And vanished like ghosts.

# CHAPTER 23

**T**he woods were a dripping, treacherous wonderland. It got a little warmer, and the trees ran with fat drops of sweat from all the moisture in the air. I wondered about that, but it meant that the helicopters passing over were nothing more than sounds. They got awful close and circled for a while, but faded away as we moved down wooded slopes, over small streams trickling with black water under ice, and slogged through slippery mud.

"At least it's not raining," someone said once.

Someone else snorted. *"Djamphir,"* he said, as if it explained everything.

Maybe it did. How was Christophe doing this?

I hung onto Graves, and slowly I realized the fog—or whoever was behind the fog, keeping us under a curtain of vapor—was watching us.

If I hadn't been so tired and drained I might've seen it sooner. The empty place inside me started feeling a little bit more normal, three-dimensionality returning to the world, and I began to see faces peeking out of the thick white vapor. They were thin, sexless faces with burning deep-socketed eyes and mouths that hung ajar just enough that you could see the fangs.

Just after mid-morning it got pretty bad. No matter how many times I blinked, the faces wouldn't go away. I could walk on my own now, a kind of lurching. There was a whispered conference about what to do with the oxygen tank. I just slung it on my own shoulder and kept carrying it. *Leave no traces*, that was the first rule of being on the run in hostile territory.

One of the boys—Beau, the slim quick redhead—had a package of beef jerky, and we shared that out equally at one stop. Everyone took a small piece and we walked while chewing. The salt in it stung my smoke-rough throat, but a couple of the boys had water bottles and we each got a swallow or two as we walked. It made the jerky into a flavorless cud of salt and ick, but I kept chewing. I was too hungry not to.

Graves had held me up until I could walk on my own. But I veered around so drunkenly he reached down and took my hand, warm fingers slipping through my cold, wet ones. I was worried about my sweating, filthy fingers for about half a second, until my legs made me veer again. I couldn't find my bearings with the world looking as paper-flat as it did. And I was so tired. My head felt like a pumpkin balanced on a stem.

But it was better with him holding my hand.

The faces crowded around. The better I felt, the more the world started looking normal again, the more they clustered around us, their mouths open as they stared at me. Some moved their lips; others vanished into thinning smoke as the sun climbed toward noon.

Yeah. Some normal. Why was it that I only felt like myself when the weirdest shit was happening?

"Fog's thinning," Peter remarked.

This got Shanks's attention. He sucked in a deep, sharp breath, raising his shaggy head a bit. He looked like death warmed over, but at least the blood sticking to him was dried instead of fresh. Terrific bruises swarmed across his face, one eye puffed almost shut. And his eyes were there, not just the whites glaring between his bruised eyelids. "Noon. Sun at its highest."

"Which means Christophe might not be able to cover us from wherever he's hiding during daylight." Graves said it quietly, as if he was just talking to me.

*Oh. That makes sense. Kind of.* My wrist throbbed. I didn't want to peel the bandage back. I didn't want to even look at it, because the thought of that pulling against everything inside me was too horrible. It made me sweat under my four layers and coating of dirt and soot. I itched all over, miserably, but it was a better feeling than the dragging drunken pain *or* the sense of the world having been drained of its entire third dimension.

"I didn't know a *djamphir* could do this." Dibs scrubbed at his cheeks with both hands. He had a little bit of peach-fuzz stubble. A smudge of dirt wandered across his forehead.

"They usually can't, and now he's pretty much crippled until sunset." Peter hopped up on a fallen tree, its moss gleaming with fat pearls of moisture, and glanced back over his shoulder at me. "How much did he take?"

*He means me. How much of* me *did Christophe take?* A wave of dizziness passed through me, hit my heels, and rebounded hard enough to bring bile up into my throat. The remnants of beef jerky clung to my tongue.

Underneath that was the real thought.

*He means how much of my blood.* "I don't know." I had to pack my cheek with chewed beef jerky like a Bible Belt farmer sucking on a wad of tobacco. "It was . . . it was horrible."

"Well, no shit. It's not a pleasant thing to get bit by a sucker of any stripe." Peter hopped down. The rest of them drew closer as the fog thinned. For a group of teenage boys wandering through the woods, they were remarkably quiet. Not a leaf stirred or a stick crackled underneath, unless I stumbled and Graves didn't give me a quick jerk on the hand to bring me back on my keel. "But seriously. How many gulps did he get down?"

*Jesus Christ.* "Th-three. I think." The strange unsteady feeling under my heart was better than the emptiness, too. It was a relief to feel anything other than that soul-destroying numbness.

"That's good, right?" Dibs looked up anxiously. "More than that and you'd be at risk of bonding and the blood-da— "

"Shh!" Peter stopped. Everyone froze. Graves actually stepped close to me before going absolutely still, most of the boys with one ear cocked. Wulfen never look particularly canine unless they've *changed*, but seeing them all holding their heads that way made me think of the RCA dog on some of Gran's old records. A rancid laugh bubbled up inside me. I listened just like they did, blood pounding in my ears, and the sound of another helicopter split the eerie silence.

A nasty little thought came padding into my head on little cat feet.

*A sucker of any stripe, huh? I didn't know* djamphir *drank blood. I suppose that's what the hunger was about. If I drank someone's blood, would I be able to do . . . something? Whatever it is Christophe did? Or what we're guessing he did, since this fog is nowhere near normal?*

Sergej had made the weather change too. He'd made it as dark as night during the day, called up a huge snowstorm. And Christophe was his son.

The whole line of thought made me feel queasy. It was one thing to have something inside yourself ripped out by the roots. It was another thing entirely to think of doing that to someone else. I mean, that made me one of the things from the Real World, all right.

It made me one of those things that my dad would have loaded up his guns and gone hunting after.

*Oh God.* I shivered. Graves squeezed my cold, limp, sweating fingers. The weighted whir of the helicopter sounded different than all the other ones that had passed since morning. Just how I couldn't say, but—

I smelled dirt, a thread of warm perfume, and the colorless fume of violence approaching. A tingling touched my chest, as if the locket was vibrating again. "They're looking for us," I whispered, not knowing I was going to say it until the words slipped free of my lips. "And they're not friendly."

Graves glanced down at me, his mouth opening as if he wanted to ask how I knew. Dibs slid down into a crouch, and before I knew it the rest of them had crouched too, except Graves and me. We stood, and if my knees hadn't been desperately locked trying to keep me upright, I would have fallen down in a heap. Something slid through my head, broken glass and cigarette ash scraping through tender places I hadn't even known were sore, and I flinched, driving my shoulder into his. He didn't move, solid as a rock, and his head tipped up. The fog was thinning in curlicues of steam, and I suddenly smelled a thread of apples and spice mixed with rotting dirt. The scent came in waves, flaring and fading, trying to draw a covering over us.

"Will the bloodfog hold?" Dibs whispered. He looked up at me like I should know, and my throat closed up. I didn't know what to tell him, and the touch quivered inside my head.

The thopping sound got closer. It was hard to tell because of the fog, but it was circling. I could feel it like a sore tooth, nagging inside me.

It was a relief to feel the *touch* throbbing inside me again. I never thought I'd be happy to have that place on my palate open up again. I never thought I'd be so happy to have the thing that made me unable to fit in anywhere coming back.

My teeth turned aching-sensitive inside my salt-dry mouth. My hair tingled, and warmth spilled down my skin.

The fog thinned further. Sunlight intensified, glaring through like a bulb shining through wax paper. *Oh shit.*

"Dru—" Graves's voice cracked. He was staring at me like I'd grown another head.

The aspect flooded me. I took a deep breath, the locket heating up as if held near a candle flame. Had it done this for Dad too? Or just for me? What did it mean?

There was no time to ask, even if there was anyone around who could tell me. The copter's sound grew nearer. A shadow loomed through the membrane of water vapor keeping us safe.

*Come on, Dru. Do something, anything!*

The raw places inside me twitched and twisted. I pulled on them, something that should have been easy as breathing suddenly like lifting a Buick with my bare hands. Blue sky peeped through the shredding fog, and the shape of the copter loomed darker, its downdraft swishing the fog around in vapor trails.

It built up around my hands, my canines sliding free and touching my lower lip. The wad of jerky in my mouth turned into an irritation of salt, but I couldn't worry about that. My belly buzzed, and the smell of spiced apples bloomed around me. Only it was deeper, with an edge of familiar, warm perfume.

The woods around me smelled suddenly like my mother, and

memory crashed inside my head. Memory and new certainty.

*We're going to play a game, Dru.*

"What the fuck—" Peter rose halfway from his crouch.

I jabbed my free hand up, letting out a short cry lost in the sound of the helicopter. The hex—just like the one I'd thrown at a teacher in the Dakotas, a bolt of intent—flew free, sparking and fizzing, and arrowed toward the mechanical shadow. Graves caught me as my legs buckled, and my heart labored in my ears. My ribs flickered, fast shallow breaths, and for a moment the sharp divots of canine teeth touching my lower lip dug in. Warm trickles slid down my chin, and Graves went to his knees trying to hold me up.

There was a weird pinging sound, and the copter veered off, its shark-shadow slicing through the naked tree limbs and thinning vapor. A screech of metal twisting and shearing, and Graves came up in a rush, hauling me with him.

Helicopters are very complex machines. And if you throw one little bit of that complexity off, bad things can happen. It was a tiny hex, barely even worth the name, but Dad would've been proud. *Easy to bring a copter down,* he told me a couple times. *You just remember that, Dru. One little thing goes haywire and alla sudden, whammo!*

Had he known somehow?

My heart hurt at the thought. I would've given just about anything to have him back and dealing with this. He would have sorted this right out.

"Whammo," I whispered, and sagged against Graves. It was only the second hex I'd actually *thrown* in my life. The first one had been a few weeks ago, and I'd almost killed Bletchley, my American history teacher. She'd deserved it, but still.

What was I turning into?

"Jesus." Peter's soft, awestruck whisper. A deep rumble sounded in the distance—thunder, swallowing the screeching sound the copter was making.

*That can't be good for anyone in it.* The smell of rain suddenly rose from the ground, thick and wet, and a huge grinding noise screeched through the clearing. A deep, coughing explosion.

"Ouch," I said, and pressed every muscle down against a retch. The beef jerky was having a hell of a time staying in my mouth. My bones felt floppy. The world receded on a tide of gray shot through with little spangles of blue sky and Graves's voice saying something.

A rending, crashing noise snapped the grayness. Everything got confused, my hands and arms flopping like a rag doll's. My stomach hurt—someone's shoulder was in it, and the world was jouncing up and down.

"Whammo," I whispered again, and the grayness swallowed me whole.

*I think I shouldn't have done that,* I thought hazily, and then I thought no more.

# CHAPTER 24

**came to in** bits and pieces. And I felt like shit. My entire body hurt, my head worst of all. I groaned a little, and sheets shifted. The sound of hard rain on a roof filled up my head, and a crack of thunder made me wince. For a weird vertiginous second I thought I was back in the blue bedroom during the day while rain splashed the windows and the Schola slept.

Then a cool hard hand touched my forehead. "Shhh, *milna*. All's well."

My left wrist gave a little pinging flare of heat and I opened my eyes. For a moment I couldn't see anything and I thought I was blind, but then something clicked. A nightlight near a door-shape went on. It seared through my pupils, and tears welled up. I flinched.

The light clicked off. My wrist turned hot again, two pinpricks of fire. Thunder cracked and boomed overhead again.

"Your head will be sensitive for a little while. Just rest." Gentle words, like I was really sick and he was trying not to upset me.

My mouth was dry. I'd lost the beef jerky somewhere. When I tensed my arms and legs I could feel the bed under me, and pain like a river over my skin. "The others?"

"Safe and sound. Even your *loup-garou*." A glitter of blue eyes showed in the darkness. Christophe's irises were glowing faintly.

"Good . . ." Relief filled me, warred with the pain, and retreated. I exhaled. His hand touched my forehead again, fingertips skating the curve of skull under skin. Then I remembered what he'd done, and tensed even further.

He laughed. It was a small sound, as bitter as Graves's scornful little bark. "More than you bargained for, hm? I'm sorry, I know it hurt. But I only borrowed; I didn't *take*. Remember that."

*Yeah, I don't think I'll ever forget, Christophe.* I sighed and moved my head away from his touch. He leaned back a little, and I heard a creak. A chair by the side of the bed—I *felt* it there without seeing it, hard to describe. My throat was sore, and the locket wasn't doing anything weird. Thank God.

At least the *touch* was still working. I felt like myself again. Beat up and pulled apart, but still me. "Where?"

Like, *Where am I?* Yeah, a totally cliché question, but it was reasonable.

He seemed to understand. "One of the wulfen—Andrew—has kin here. You're in the safest part of the compound. It's night now; by morning you should be all right to travel. Especially with me around."

*Oh, good. But I feel like sleeping in.* "Travel?"

"Your *loup-garou* made a persuasive case for reaching the safety of the city. I'll be able to bear the sun after tonight, when the aura-dark fades." He let out a sharp sigh. The glimmer of his eyes vanished, and the shape of him slumped. "I thought Dylan, at least, would explain a little."

*I think he probably had other things on his mind, Christophe. And I think the history teacher was trying, too.* "Tried. He tried. Look—" There was so much to tell him.

"Sleep." He moved again, and I heard cloth sliding and the creak of the chair again. A breath of apple-scented spice blew across my face. "It's the best thing for you now."

It sounded like a good idea, but I wanted something else. "Graves." I swallowed. My dry throat clicked. At least my mouth wasn't tingling, and my teeth were regular and blunt when I ran my dry rasping tongue across them.

"I told you, he's fine. The prince of the house, here." Christophe's eyes opened again. "You could ask me how I'm feeling. I've had a hard few days too."

*You know, when you put it like that I couldn't care less.* "Go. Away."

"Charming as ever. I'm sorry, Dru."

Then I felt like a bitch. He'd saved my life, hadn't he? Run right into a burning building to get me out. And the fog, that had been him too. And the heat of him against me, a shameful memory that would have made me squirm if I hadn't been so exhausted. "Don't worry about it." I coughed a little. The words scraped hard coming out.

"You think you want water, but it will only make it worse." His tone was very soft. "Nothing will take it away, not even wine. It will fade in a little bit."

The burning in my throat got a little worse. "Do you . . ."

"Me? Always, little bird." Another small laugh. It sounded like it hurt him. "The stronger the *nosferat* strain in your blood, the stronger the bloodhunger. And if a Kouroi ever gives in to it . . ."

I waited. My heart beat hard, in my wrists and my throat. It was really dark in here, and I wondered whose bed I was lying on. We'd made it to safety. A wulfen house.

BETRAYALS

"If you ever give in, it becomes much harder to control. And if you're raised to give it full rein, *kochana*. . . ." He sighed again. The chair creaked a little as he rose and pushed it back. I saw the shadows of posters hanging on the wall, no windows, and the suggestion of a half-open closet sketched in charcoal. It was deathly quiet. "My father raised me to be a scourge instead of a Kouroi." His eyes winked out, and I half-sensed him rubbing at his face. "Dylan brought me to the light, but it was your mother who ensured I stayed. If you don't have a reason to fight it, the hunger will make you an animal worse than the ones we exterminate. Because we are born to be so much more." The vague outline of the door was blacked by his darker shadow. "I'll send in your *loup-garou*."

He sounded so . . . sad.

"Christophe." I couldn't even prop myself up on my elbows. "Wait."

The sense of movement faded. He stood in the door for a long second, then turned. The apple-scented breeze filled my face. He bent down, and the sudden irrational fear that he might bite me again stopped my breathing. His fingertips rested against the locket's warm curve. I felt their weight.

Something soft and warm pressed itself against my mouth. It stayed there for a few seconds, my nose full of pie-smell. Before it even registered, he'd straightened and stepped back. His eyes glowed now, an unholy blue. "If I need a reason now, Dru, it will have to be you."

The door filled up with his shadow, drained away. I moved fretfully. I couldn't even begin to figure this one out. Sleeping sounded really good.

I closed my heavy eyelids again and was gone.

* * *

When I surfaced again it was even quieter and someone lay next to me. He was warm, and took up most of the bed, and I knew who it was even before I accidentally elbowed him and he lunged into wakefulness. He jerked like a fish on a line, half-sitting up and only relaxing once he figured out where he was.

"Jesus—" The word died. "Dru? You okay?"

I coughed. My skin crawled. "Peachy." The starch had come back into my bones, and I felt a million percent better. Best of all, the empty riven places inside my head were no longer throbbing like something had been yanked out. I had a slight headache and I was still god-awful thirsty, but the world was back together again. "Hey."

"There's the floor." He curled up to sit, and blankets moved. Sleeping in clothes always makes you feel bunched-up when morning comes. "If you, you know—"

"Why?" I pushed myself up on my elbows. It was a relief to be able to move. "I mean, we're okay, right? Unless you feel weird about sleeping in the same bed as . . ."

*Oh shit.* I went from feeling pretty okay to feeling totally stupid.

"I thought you'd feel weird about it." But he settled back down. There was only one pillow, and it was scrunched between us. "But, you know."

"Yeah." I didn't, but I was okay with it. "How's Shanks? And everyone?"

"They fixed Shanks up. He just needs some sleep now. It's . . . weird here. Anyway. How are you really?"

I cleared my throat. He was still fully dressed, and I tried to push the pillow over to him but he was having none of it. We settled down, finally, and I breathed him in. Cigarette smoke, healthy young male, the smell that was uniquely his. I needed a shower and my teeth really wanted a good scrubbing, and I was suddenly afraid I had dragonbreath. So I stayed where I was, on my side with my arm under my head, trying not to breathe on him. We were quiet for a little while. The thunder was retreating.

"Some storm," I finally whispered.

"Yeah. Christophe said it was because of messing with the weather system." Graves moved a little bit, lacing his fingers under his head. He was tall enough that I had my face almost in his armpit. It wasn't optimal, but at least he smelled clean and I wouldn't be breathing anywhere he could get a faceful of it. "You should get some more sleep. We're leaving in the morning."

"We?" Meaning, *Who's this we?*

"I'm going with you." Almost sullen. He sighed. "Look, Dru—"

"I hoped you were coming along. Where are we going?" I edged a little bit closer to him. He didn't move away. It was a relief.

"The city. Christophe thinks that if we get you to the central Schola, whoever's trying to double-cross and kill you won't be able to. Dru, I want to ask you something."

The tension came back. "Okay."

I expected something like, *What was it like when he drank your blood?* or *What did you do to that helicopter?* or even . . . I don't know. Something about *djamphir* or wulfen. Something complex.

"Do you like Christophe?" It came out in a whisper. "I mean, really *like* him?"

It took me a second to figure out what he was really asking. *Oh God. Awkward.* "Not, like, *that* way. Jesus. No."

As soon as I said it, I felt like I was lying. Christophe's arms around me, his body hot through his clothes, the spiced-apple smell surrounding me. The broken roughness of his voice as he hugged me, and my lips burning because he'd pressed his mouth against mine.

*If I need a reason, Dru, it will have to be you.*

But there was also his teeth in my wrist, and his scary speed, and the mockery under every word. I was glad it was dark. My cheeks were on fire again, the flush turning my whole body into a lamp in the dark.

I couldn't like Christophe that way, could I? I mean, he'd known my *mother*. And—

"Oh." Did Graves actually sound *relieved*? Thunder rumbled, dissatisfied, in the distance.

"I mean, he knew my mother." I meant to say something different. Like, *He scares me*. But that would be a real blow to my tough-girl image, wouldn't it. And that image was taking a hell of a beating lately.

And if I said it out loud I might say other things. Like, *He doesn't feel like you do when he hugs me*. That would just open up a huge can of worms, wouldn't it?

No. I didn't like Christophe. Not the way he was asking.

At least, I didn't want to. And Graves never had to know about the boathouse, or about anything else. I'd made up my mind.

I was still blushing. Scalding hot.

"Yeah." Quiet agreement. "Can I ask you something else?"

My heart leapt. He sounded serious. "You just did. But go ahead." A slight huff of breath told me he was smiling, and I half-smiled too, in the dark. I waited. Silence stretched out. I finally moved, restlessly. "Are you asleep?"

"No." He moved too, pulling his knees up and turning on his side to present me with his back. "Never mind. It's nothing."

*Oh, dammit.* My heart crashed. Stupid boy. Was he going to ask me if there was someone else I liked?

I lay there in the dark, working up to it. My clothes were irritating, but if I took any of them off nothing would go right. When I edged a little bit closer and slid an arm over him, he stiffened again. I snuggled up close and fit my knees behind his. He was in a T-shirt, so when I breathed out it was a pocket of warmth between his bony shoulder blades.

It felt right. His hair touched mine, and I inhaled. Tucked my arm under my head. It was a little uncomfortable, with my clothes all rucked up and sweat dried on my skin and everything else going on. Still, with the rain on the roof and the way I felt warm inside instead of cold and hurting, I figured I could deal.

It wasn't the scary, fiery warmth of blushing around Christophe. This was a gentler feeling. It was like sitting just the right distance from a campfire, so it warmed you perfectly but not too much. Less hurtful.

Less intense.

I searched for words. "No, I don't *like* Christophe. I'm holding out for someone else."

All the tension went out of us both. He relaxed all at once like a cat, and I felt even warmer inside. Almost gooey.

"Someone else?" His whisper cracked in the middle and I had to smother a laugh.

*Someone who doesn't scare me the way Christophe does. Someone I can count on.* "Yeah. He's a dipshit, but I like him."

"Not that much of a dipshit if you like him that much," he muttered, but I could tell he was smiling.

I yawned hugely. Breathed out, making a spot of heat on his back. The burning in my cheeks and throat, I told myself, would fade. It was dark. He never had to know I was blushing. "No problem, Goth Boy. First one's free."

He snorted a little laugh, and I smiled again. It felt good. My heart went from a shriveled pea to something more, well, heart-size, knocking against my ribs. And I lay there listening to the rain and him breathing for a little while before I fell back into a dark well of sleep.

The flushing heat didn't go away. It followed me down into the dark. But when I woke up in the morning, it was gone.

# CHAPTER 25

The **"compound" was** three long double-storied log cabins built around a wide paved driveway, a huge garage set behind one of them, and a whole bunch of wulfen running around.

I found out I'd been in one of the "cub bedrooms," in the central log cabin. Sleeping arrangements in a wulfen compound are kind of odd—pretty much everyone sleeps where they get tired, and bedrooms are for when you need some privacy. When I woke up in the morning, Graves wasn't there, but he showed up as soon as I found the hall outside the bedroom door leading to a bathroom and four more bedrooms.

"I got you some clean clothes." His hair was wildly mussed, and he smelled like rain, fresh air, and cigarette smoke. His earring twinkled cheerily at me. "You probably want to get cleaned up."

I rubbed sleep-crusties out of my eyes, made a face. "I probably stink."

"Nah. You smell like you." He grinned, green eyes almost twinkling. "Bathroom's in there. Use any toothbrush, they say. There's breakfast when you're ready."

"What time is it?" There weren't any windows, but the sound of rain hadn't gone away. It tapped and slithered against the roof.

He shoved a pile of clothing into my arms. "About seven. You're up early."

"My sleep schedule's all messed up. We leaving soon?" I swallowed a yawn with the last three words, and his grin broadened. Goth Boy looked pretty bouncy, all things considered. "And is there any coffee?"

"Yes, and yes. Christophe sent me to wake you up and get you going. We're leaving in half an hour or so, soon's you're ready and the sun's really up."

I suppressed the urge to ask more questions. "Okay." I pushed hair out of my face. Curls clung to my fingers. I probably looked like the Bride of Frankenstein. "I'll hurry, then."

His hands dropped back down to his sides. He looked at me, I looked at him, and a big stupid grin spread over my face to answer his. "What?" I sounded more aggravated than I really was.

The aggravation only made him grin more broadly. Boys are like that. "Nothing." He turned on his heel, the long dark coat flaring sharply, and all but skipped away.

The bathroom was clean, and I felt squidgy about using someone else's toothbrush, but when your mouth feels like something died in it and you could probably kill a cactus with your breath at twenty paces, it puts a different shine on the sanctity of personal hygiene products. The hot water felt so good on my back I almost cried, and the interesting crop of new bruises and scrapes stung a little. They were healing up more quickly, I thought. But there were so many of them. I looked like a pinto horse.

The new clothes did fit, amazingly. Jeans, panties, two T-shirts—one blue, one gray—and a blue sweater that looked hand-knit. No socks, no bra, and my boots were filthy. But it felt so good to be in clean clothes again I hardly cared, even if the clothes had the odd feeling of being someone else's.

One of the things about dressing in layers is that you almost always have some of your own clothes to put on after a bad night. Unfortunately, mine reeked of smoke and blood and terror, not to mention dirt and sweat. I could almost see the stink lines rising off them. My bag was gone and I wondered where it was.

The question was answered when I opened the bathroom door, an armful of my stinking but neatly folded clothes clutched to my chest, and found Christophe leaning against the wall down the hall. He dangled my bag loosely from one hand and smiled at me, blue eyes glinting. "You can leave those. They're probably ruined."

His gaze dropped down, but I'd tucked the locket away under my shirts. It made me feel better to have it against my skin, even if it was doing some funky stuff lately.

"They'll be fine with some washing." *Besides, I don't have that many clothes left.* I tried not to stare at my bag. My hair was a heavy weight. I'd squeezed all the water I could out of it. "Can I have that, please?"

"Of course." He handed it over and subtracted the pile of clothes from me. "I'll put this in the car, then. You need to eat. Follow me." He set off down the hall toward a door and a set of stairs washed with pearly rainy-morning light.

At least I wasn't blushing. I tried not to think about it. It helped that he was all business. "Why aren't there any windows down here?" I asked his back, bending down to grab my boots.

He didn't even break stride. "The *nosferatu* find it harder to get in. And it means the parents and uncles and aunts can defend the little ones. Come along, Dru."

The kitchen was wide, spacious, filled with light and wulfen. It was a crowd, and I saw my first female wulfen. They moved around the kitchen in perfectly choreographed waves, and some of the boys and girls were carrying plates and platters of food out to a huge dining room with three tables that looked easily fifteen feet long apiece.

"Good morning!" A tall, slim brunette woman wearing an apron over her jeans and sweater stepped out of the bustle. Christophe had disappeared in the chaos. "You must be Dru. It's a pleasure to meet you." She seized my free hand and shook it, took in my bare feet and dirt-clomped boots with one swift look. "I'm Amelia. Welcome to our den."

"Um." The noise and activity were enough to make me blink. "Hello. Hi." Coffee. Eggs sizzling in a pan. Bacon. The good sound of pancakes hitting a hot griddle. And was that orange juice I smelled, and jalapeños? Cheddar cheese?

"Must be overwhelming. This way." She swept back a sheaf of glossy dark-brown hair and pulled me toward the dining room, gracefully avoiding the kids scrambling back and forth. "Oh, good, those fit you! I thought you were just about Danica's size. We'll have some socks around here somewhere, too, don't you worry." She halted and glanced over her shoulder. "We're glad you're here. And we're glad you brought Andy and the young ones."

"I didn't do much bringing," I managed awkwardly. My hair was dripping on the sweater, curls beginning to develop out of the mass. "I was mostly out of it. Graves was—"

"He said it was all you." Her laugh was like bells. "Thanks for bringing Andy to us, and for trusting us. We're loyal."

The way she said it, maybe anxiously, rang a wrong bell in my head. Yesterday was a collage of weird snapshots and disembodied voices, confusing if I thought about it too much. "That's what he—Andy—said. I, um, thanks for letting us sleep here. I—"

How do you tell someone, *Gee thanks for letting us crash, we're probably being chased by mad vampires and a traitor in the Order and you're pretty much risking your lives?* I couldn't figure out the words and something blundered against my knees. When I looked down, a smiling toddler in pajamas over a sagging diaper grinned up at me, her dark eyes merry and her thatch of brown hair rumpled. She grabbed my knee and shrieked.

"Bella!" Amelia scooped her up. "Good God, who's supposed to be watching her?"

"Not me." A passing wulfen girl in a wide broomstick skirt and a yellow sweater deftly took the baby. "But I'll figure something out."

"Bless you, Imogen. Come, *svetocha*, let's get you something to eat. You're not vegan, are you?"

*What?* "No." I watched as the teenager stuck the baby on her hip and plunged into the chaos of the kitchen. The noise level was incredible. "I grew up in Appalachia."

I don't know why I said that.

"Oh, really? That must be where your accent's from." She led me into the dining room proper and smartly rapped an older boy on the head. He let out a yelp. "Get your fingers out of that sugar bowl and finish your eggs! You there, stop torturing your niece. And you, go back and scrub those paws!"

It was like seeing a battlefield general make order out of chaos through sheer force of bellowing. It reminded me of Dad, in a weird way, and my eyes stung. I didn't tell her that whatever accent I had was probably from years spent below the Mason-Dixon line, hunting with Dad.

And I don't think I have an accent, for the record. Everyone up North just talks funny.

She plopped me down at a long table between Graves and Shanks, who was munching on a stack of flapjacks as tall as my hand. Shanks nodded, the blood scrubbed off him and the bruises on his face just faint shadows.

"Jesus, you look better," I blurted.

"Damn straight." He shoveled in a huge bite of syrup-drenched pancakes and Graves slid a plate in front of me.

Eggs. Crispy bacon. Three pancakes. Two wedges of buttered homemade-bread toast. A glass of orange juice, and a big pottery mug of coffee appeared too.

"Eat." Graves's shoulder bumped mine. "It's rude if you don't."

Everyone was showered, in clean clothes, and talking up a storm. It was like lunch at the Schola, only with everyone acting nice instead of the *djamphir* and wulfen growling at each other. The older wulfen ate fast, catcalling and talking back and forth, then picked up their plates and cleaned off a slice of table, taking everything to the kitchen in time for a new person to come in, sit down, and start shoveling in food. Everything ran like clockwork—even the cleanup when a whole jug of syrup got upended somehow. It was incredible to watch, and Graves kept elbowing me and telling me to eat.

I did. I was starving, and the sight of food made me suddenly aware of it. I started eating, and I didn't realize I was gulping down the food until I took a long draft of orange juice and almost choked. My cheeks were wet. Graves handed me a napkin and pointedly didn't look.

I saw Dibs, his head down and his shoulders hunched, and a few of the other boys I knew. Peter was all the way across the room, scowling while he put away a small mountain of grits. He had a fresh black eye. I wondered how he'd gotten it.

There were two more babies, both old enough to sit in high chairs. I saw the one who'd grabbed my knees as she was swiftly buckled in and started chowing down on chopped-up bits of pancake. She grinned and crowed, mashing her baby spoon onto her plate. The other two were babbling, and whoever was closest kept an eye on them and rescued their flung silverware and sippy cups.

Was this what families were like? Or was it just wulfen who ate this way? I liked it better than the Schola, but it was so *noisy*. I wiggled my toes in my boots—Amelia had given me a pair of white tube socks. It was almost pathetic, how much more human a pair of freaking *socks* made me feel. I found myself rubbing at the lump of the locket under my sweater, and made myself put my hand down in my lap like a proper-mannered girl.

I ate until I couldn't hold any more, then sat with my coffee mug and mopped at my cheeks. The tears weren't bad, just hot and embarrassing. I didn't even know why I was leaking. But it was loud and comforting and nobody paid much attention. Shanks was still putting it away at a steady rate—a huge bowl of oatmeal, a mountain of eggs, a generous handful of bacon, and a few more slices of toast.

He saw me watching and swallowed hastily, grinned. "Got to heal up," he said, when he had his mouth clear. "Going with you."

"Oh." I nodded, took a scalding gulp of coffee.

"Stupid asshole thinks he owes me," Graves called in my ear.

"Peter would've left me behind, the bastard," Shanks cheerfully yelled back. "That's why he's all the way over there. I beat him up this morning."

I believed it.

One table freed up and was cleaned with incredible speed, just in time for a group of hard-faced boy wulfen, some of them with wet hair and damp clothes, to come trooping in. All of them looked young, from their early teens to mid-twenties, but you could tell the older ones. It was something subtle—how they moved, or how their eyes were calm instead of dancing with excitement. I couldn't figure it out but I didn't want to stare. Maybe if I had a pad of paper and a pencil I could do a few sketches and find out what it was.

For the first time in two weeks my hands itched to draw, a sudden fierce need. I rubbed my right-hand fingers against the coffee mug, trying to scratch out the sensation.

"They were on watch, running through the woods," Graves yelled in my ear. "They're on vacation from the Schola downstate. Nobody there even *knows* about you."

My stomach closed itself like a fist, and Christophe appeared in the door to the kitchen. An odd almost-silence spread from the table ends nearest him, and Amelia appeared, leaning in and talking intently to him.

It was funny. Even the obviously adult wulfen looked just slightly older than the *djamphir*. Nobody here looked a day over twenty-five, except for around the eyes a bit. I hadn't realized how quickly I'd grown used to being surrounded by teenagers.

I would have wondered where the adults to handle this sort of thing were, but they were here. Just in young-looking bodies.

Christophe nodded, his blond-streaked hair falling carelessly into his eyes. Jewels of water clung to the strands and dewed his face. I dug in my bag and found the transcript, pushing my plate away. The paper crinkled.

I couldn't pull it out here. Jeez.

"Aren't you going to eat more?" Graves almost elbowed me, glanced up to see what I was looking at.

"Full," I said, but my voice wouldn't work quite right. I had to clear my throat and try again. "I'm full."

"Eat while you can." Shanks shoveled in another heaping fork-ful. "Might not get a chance later."

It was good advice, I'd heard Dad say it before. But my stomach had closed down, and I *was* full. Christophe glanced across the room, saw me, and nodded slightly. His expression didn't change. He said something else to Amelia, who pushed her hair out of her face and untied her apron.

Christophe vanished again, and Amelia started across the dining room for us, her forehead furrowed. I pushed my chair back and stood up, scooping up my boots and grabbing my bag. After a few startled seconds, Shanks and Graves did too.

I know that look on an adult's face. It means it's time to go.

# CHAPTER 26

**T**he car was long, lean, and dark blue, older than me but in excellent shape. Dad would've liked it, and I suppressed a desire to pop the hood, because a dark slight wulfen had just slammed it shut and turned on his heel, taking in all of us with a swift glance. His mouth turned down when he saw Christophe, but he covered it well.

"This is Corey. He's our mechanic." Amelia looked proud. "Anything he touches runs like a dream."

The boy wulfen rolled his eyes. "Mom. Jeez."

"It's true," she insisted, and she looked seven different flavors of proud. She hooked an arm over his shoulders and gave him a squeeze. He wriggled away after a few seconds and blushed. You could see he was secretly pleased.

My heart hurt. I took a deep breath and shoved the feeling away.

He wiped his calloused fingers with an oil-stained rag and indicated the car with a short, graceful gesture. "'74 Dodge Dart. She's a good car. Old American heavy metal, run until the doors fall off. Just had a tune-up and an oil change, checked the lights and everything this morning. Fresh tabs, too. So everything's good."

"Very good. I can barely believe it's the same vehicle." Christophe nodded, examining the paint job like he wanted to find rust flakes in it. "We should get going. The longer we stay here, the more dangerous for you."

Amelia shrugged. "The woods are set with traps and we have warning. Other than the Broken"—her mouth firmed up and her eyes turned cold—"nothing's moved all night, and we're well prepared should they find your trail."

*The Broken?* "Ash? He's here?" My heart leapt up into my throat and I pushed down the urge to find a safe place to hide. "Where?"

"He's been following us." Shanks folded his arms. "Cagey little bastard. Slips right through every net."

"He saved my life." I hitched my bag higher up on my shoulder. "Twice, even."

"Nobody's disputing that," Christophe chimed in, darkly. "But it's best not to keep him wandering around here. Let's go, children. Keys?"

Corey tossed them over. "She accelerates well, and the brakes grab. Go easy on them."

Christophe nodded, plucking the keys out of the air and glancing at me. "Good work. Dru, you're in the front seat. You two—"

"Wait a second!" A blond streak crashed out of the rain outside the open garage door and almost plowed into Shanks, who stepped nimbly aside. It was Dibs, his backpack bouncing, shaking the water off in spatters. "Wait for me! I'm coming too!"

"No room." Christophe stalked around the front of the car.

"I'm coming." Dibs glared at him, then darted a quick little glance at me. "Tell him, Dru. I'm going with you. You need us."

"Jesus, Dibs—" Shanks didn't sound like he thought much of the notion.

Graves just looked at me. I raised an eyebrow; he shrugged and dug a pack of cigarettes out of his pocket. His coat was freshly washed, and it looked like someone had ironed it, too. Wonders never ceased.

"We're leaving." Christophe opened the driver's door. "Everyone in."

"Please, Dru." Dibs hopped from foot to foot. He looked as much like a bird as it was possible for a wulf to look. "Please."

Why the hell was he asking me? But since he was, I was going to make the call. I didn't have too many friends, and he'd sat beside me in the lunchroom. "Get in," I told him. "You guys too."

"Three wulfen in the backseat," Christophe muttered. "What are you *thinking*?"

"He's got medical training." I hitched my bag up again. *And he carried me halfway across the state. At least, I think he did.* "He's my friend."

Graves gave me an indecipherable look, and Shanks laughed. I was getting kind of tired of boys treating me like I'd lost my mind. Dibs piled into the car and scooted into the middle of the backseat, where he sat and clutched his backpack protectively.

"Let's *go*." Irritation edged each word. Christophe dropped into the driver's seat and a moment later the engine roused, purring loudly.

"Thank you very much." I sounded really prim. "For everything." *I hope the vampires don't find you.*

Amelia's grin broke out over her face like sunlight, her velvety brown eyes lighting up. Corey stepped back, his gaze running over the car like he wanted a few more hours to tinker with it.

"It is our honor," Amelia said, and it was the weirdest thing—it sounded like she really meant it. People don't often say exactly what they really mean. "Go quickly, and be safe."

I dropped into the front passenger seat. The car was a boat, and Christophe nosed it gently forward into the silver curtain of rain. I waved at Amelia, who hooked her arm over Corey's shoulders and hugged him despite his *"Awwww, Mom!"* wriggling away. Something hot and nameless boiled up in my throat. I swallowed hard twice, tasted pancakes when I burped, and dug in my bag for a piece of gum. I didn't have any, and when I looked up again we had slid smoothly between two of the buildings and were on the paved drive. The place looked deserted, all the windows dark. I wondered if it was intentional.

Christophe muttered something, the car eased through the rain, and the windshield wipers started.

"I hope they'll be okay." I had to fumble with the seat belt. Old seat belts are cranky sometimes. The defroster was on, and the whole car smelled like engine oil and the healthy dry smell of wulfen. And a thin thread of apple pies, blowing in my face when Christophe leaned forward to twist the radio knob.

"I've done what I can to confuse our trail. And to make certain none of *his* trackers survived to report in." His face settled against itself as we threaded down a long single-lane strip of paving starred with unevenly fixed potholes.

"Do you think the vampires will find them?" I twisted to look into the backseat. Dibs sat bolt-upright, blinking owlishly. Shanks had settled back and closed his eyes. Graves stared out his window, his jaw clenched.

"It's not the vampires I'm worried about," Christophe said darkly. The radio crackled. "Find me some music, Dru. We've got a long drive ahead of us."

# CHAPTER 27

**A**fter so long walking it was weird to see the road slipping smoothly away underneath the car. The windshield wipers marked off time, back and forth, and Christophe hummed along with the classic rock station I'd found. He drove the speed limit, too — not a hair over or under. Shanks was breathing softly with his eyes closed, his mouth hanging open a little; Graves stared out the window. Dibs bounced up and down every once in a while, but otherwise kept quiet.

It was, in other words, completely awkward.

Christophe also stuck to the less-traveled roads, not even glancing at a map. If it had been Dad driving, I would've been navigating him. Instead, I sat there uselessly, clutching my bag and staring at the wet world outside the window. Naked trees pressed close to the blacktop, their bare arms reaching out to clutch empty air. Water gleamed on the road, the tires made wet shushing sounds, and Christophe kept turning the radio up in tiny increments when music was on, then turning it down when advertising took over.

Lunch was in a small town on the far end of the county, a pizza place that looked like it had seen better days. All three of the boys in the backseat headed straight for the bathroom as soon as we got a table, which meant I could fish the paper out of my bag as Christophe motioned me into the red vinyl booth.

"Unless you need the facilities too, *kochana*." He ran a hand back through his hair, shaking random drops of rain out.

"I have to talk to you." I dropped down, then handed the sheets of paper over. It all came out in a rush while he looked at me, blue eyes narrowing. "Dylan gave me this, right before everything . . . well, it's important. When Anna showed me the transcript of the call, she wanted me to think you made it. And it was an edited version." I felt like I wasn't making any sense. "She wanted to find out what I knew, too. Dylan said this was the original version of the call. When someone gave my mother's location."

Christophe lowered himself down next to me in the booth and scanned the paper. His mouth turned itself upside-down, the corners pulling toward his jaw. "He gave this to you?" For a moment I thought I saw something close to his true age, eerie on his unlined face.

"When he told me to hide the next time the Restriction bell rang." It was a relief to tell someone, to get at least one secret out of my chest. "It's a good thing he did, too, or they would have caught me in my room."

"They?" His aspect slid over him, his hair sleeking down and turning darker. His fangs peeped out. He took a deep breath and they retreated. I stared at his profile, fascinated.

"Well, the bell for first classes rang. Then, a little while later, the Restriction bell. I hid in a closet and heard them running by. They had to have been *nosferatu*." The word felt strange in my mouth. Even now I was half-lying, keeping a secret.

"Were you going to class like a good girl?"

*No, I was heading for the hills. Why does that even matter?* "I was out of my room. It was like a tomb in there."

The two sheets of paper rustled a bit. His hand was shaking. "Anna." Slowly, thoughtfully. Like the word had a bad taste. He folded the papers back together and handed them to me. "Hm."

"She said you . . ." I swallowed. My throat was dry. "She said you were the one who made that call. I think she wanted me not to trust you."

Christophe stiffened. His fangs peeped out again, retreated. "I would *never*—" he began.

I hurried to cut him off. The flush threatened to rise up my neck again, and I didn't want that. "I already told you I didn't believe her. She wanted me to, and she wanted to know what I knew. If I suspected something, if I'd seen you."

The emotion submerged. It was eerie to watch, his face smoothing out and the blond streaking back into his hair. "So. Milady is meddling."

*Dylan said that too.* "I want to know what's going on."

He opened his mouth, but Dibs appeared at the booth, smoothing his damp hair down. "Can we get pepperoni?"

Christophe dug in his pocket, pulled out three twenty-dollar bills. "Get one meat pizza and one vegetarian, no onions or olives. And five drinks. Off with you."

Dibs took the money and bounded away. Christophe's hand turned into a fist, resting on the table, then relaxed with an effort. The difference between his smoothed-out face and the way he had to force his fingers out and loose was jarring. "Keep this secret. We'll talk later."

It was hard to look tough when my heart was thundering and

I was sweating. I folded my arms and stared at him, uncomfortably wedged in the booth and suddenly aware he was between me and any possible escape. "I want to know *now*."

"I don't know enough myself to tell you anything useful. There is a traitor in the Order. We know that much. Now we know that the traitor is highly placed, and that I wasn't the target. I haven't *been* the target so far, just incidental damage." He ran his tongue along his teeth, and the aspect retreated even further. His eyes were still cold. I wondered why I'd ever thought they could warm up.

"How do you know?" The edge of warmth I felt from him was the uncomfortable sterile heat of the blue-threaded flames. I shivered.

"This is a vendetta. The sins of the parents visited on the children—though your mother was blameless. You have my word on that, at least." In one quick, economical movement, he slid out of the booth. He wasn't looking at my face; he was looking at my chest. At the tiny lump under my sweater. "Put that away. Don't speak of it where others can hear. And for God's sake, Dru . . ."

I waited, but he didn't finish. Instead he stalked away to the counter, where Dibs was all but hopping with impatience and the bored woman working behind the register was punching buttons too slowly.

The aroma of crust and tomato sauce, baking cheese, and the sticky smell that always fills a pizza parlor closed around me. I slid the transcript back in my bag and found out my hands were shaking too.

*Go to the Schola*, he'd said. *You'll be safe there.*

But I wasn't safe anywhere, was I? And I didn't even know *why*. Because someone in the Order had hated my mother enough to want to kill her? And, years later, kill *me*?

Jesus. How could you hate someone that much and still be human? Or even just better than a sucker?

Graves dropped into the booth right next to me. "Hey." He'd

slicked his hair back behind his ears and his face was still dewed with rain from outside. "You okay? You look a little pale."

*Oh, I'm just fine. Not.* I reached down under the table and grabbed his hand, slipping my fingers through his. His skin was warm, and my heart took off pounding in an entirely new way.

"Everything's all wrong." I squeezed his fingers hard. "It's fucking awful."

He squeezed back. A flush crept up into his sallow cheeks. Under the Asian coloring he could really change it up. "Not everything. We're here, right? And we're safe during the day."

"Yeah." A million questions boiled up inside me. Everything from *Do you mind that I ruined your life?* to *Can you imagine hating someone so much you sell them to a sucker?*

"Hey. Whoa." His grip intensified, stopped just short of pain. "Everything's gonna be okay, Dru. It's gonna work out."

"I don't know." I stared at the fake wood of the tabletop, its plastic topping peeling up. "We haven't seen any of the *djamphir* from the school."

"Yeah, I been thinking about that." His tone dropped confidentially. A trickle of customers had started in through the swinging glass door. "Dru, if things happen . . ."

"What kind of things?"

"You know what I'm talking about. If it gets bad, Dru, I'm going with you."

My hand cramped a little. Neither of us let go. He took a deep breath and his eyes met mine squarely, the green circles around his pupils glowing even with the electric lights in here. Rain coated the front window of the pizza parlor, shadows moving like weeds underwater.

"I . . ." Words failed me.

"'Cause I've been thinking. You had your bag and you had three sweaters on. You were heading out."

*Oh Christ.* I opened my mouth. Shut it.

"See, normally I'd get upset about that. But I think you thought you were going to help me out by leaving me someplace you thought was safer for me than you. Right?"

My head fell down into a nod. I picked it back up. My mouth felt like it was hanging open.

"Don't do that." He leaned a little closer, and the rest of the world went away. "Okay? Don't leave me behind."

"They're looking to kill me," I whispered. "You don't get that. It's for real. It's—"

"What do you think I was doing at school, playing footsie?" Irritation made his matching whisper sharp. "You've got a better chance with me, Dru. Don't do something stupid again. If something happens, it's you and me against the world. Got it?"

I was saved by Dibs showing back up at the table. "You're supposed to get your own drinks." He popped a stack of red plastic cups on the table. "I think this is the only place in three states that serves Mr. Pibb. Awesome, huh?"

"Completely." Graves gave my hand another meaningful squeeze under the table, then slid out and grabbed two cups. "Whaddaya want, Dru?"

"Um. Coke. Pepsi. Whatever."

"Not diet?" Dibs wanted to know.

"Are you kidding?" Graves bumped him with a shoulder, but gently. "That shit'll kill you. Back in a flash."

* * *

Dinner was fast food in another weird little town, and the light was failing when Christophe finally found a freeway he liked. "No smoking in the car," he said for the fifteenth time.

I'd kept count.

"Do you really want to see me in nicotine withdrawal?" Graves flicked the lighter, inhaled, and exhaled. His window was down and the sound of wet tires on the road melded with the hum of the engine and the back-and-forth of the windshield wipers, and the Rolling Stones singing about a beast of burden on the radio. "Tell him, Dru."

I rolled my eyes. None of them would see it, but it made me feel better. "Since when was I appointed referee? I hate to ask, Christophe, but how much longer?"

"We're almost to a safe location. Or what passes for one." He rolled his window down a little and wrinkled his nose, and I took a pull off my vanilla milkshake. "Moving after dark isn't a good idea."

"Because that's when the vampires are out," Shanks chimed in, a singsong that managed to be creepy and sarcastic all at once. "And they like to eat little *svetocha*."

"Blow me." I propped one boot on the dashboard. It wasn't like a trip with Dad. He and I could go just about forever without talking, with only my brief comments to navigate him through tangles of overpasses and surface streets.

"Don't make me stop this car." Christophe turned the radio up a little. The Stones faded and the Beach Boys started singing about California girls.

Shanks made a retching noise. "God, when are you going to play some decent music?"

"What's wrong with the Beach Boys? Brian Wilson was a genius." I tapped my foot to the beat.

"Amen," Christophe muttered, and twisted the radio dial another increment. "Now everyone shut up, I have to find this place."

"If you had a map, I could help." I wasn't liking this not-know-ing-where-we-were thing, but Christophe had refused to buy a map when we stopped at a gas station, and I had to save my cash.

I didn't know when I'd need it.

"No need." He slowed down, hit the blinker, cut left across two lanes of traffic, and zoomed us onto a side street. Horns blared behind us, and I almost dropped my milkshake. "We're here."

"God*dam*mit!" I clutched at my waxed-paper cup. "What the *hell* is wrong with you?"

The boys in the back were laughing, troll-like snickers and chuckles. We turned right, then left, and plunged under a canopy of bare branches. It looked like this street had been paved sometime back in the '50s, and the trees marching down either side were wet and black and naked under the iron-gray sky. Dark was approaching.

"Was that *really* necessary?" I popped the top back on my milk-shake—I'd crumpled the cup, dammit. "I mean, really?"

"Streets change." Christophe cut the steering wheel hard again and bumped us up into an overgrown driveway. "I actually wasn't sure until I saw that water tower. All right, kids. Everyone out, and you'll find the garage unlocked. Bobby, open it, if you please."

The boys in back scrambled out in a trice, and I reached for my door handle. The house was narrow and dark, white siding and a peaked roof. It had a glassed-in storm porch, and dead leaves covered the postage-stamp-size front yard. The street was quiet and had the air of genteel shabbiness most really old, expensive neighborhoods do. I'd bet the neighborhood association really went overboard for Christmas and probably held meetings when someone didn't rake their leaves. They must have righteous fits over this place.

"Dru." Christophe reached over and grabbed my wrist. His fingers were warm and very hard, just short of bruising. The milkshake teetered. "You stay."

A slice of darkness opened, Shanks hefting the garage door like it weighed nothing. The car nosed forward as he made little shooing movements with his free hand. He grinned, white teeth flashing.

When the engine shut off, the silence was deafening. It was a familiar silence, though, one I heard every time Dad shut off the car someplace that was supposed to be our new temporary home.

"I think it's best you ward your room tonight. Since you can." Christophe pulled the keys free of the ignition. "And sleep in your clothes."

*I was planning on that anyway.* "Yeah."

"I'll sleep at your door." He gave me a sideways glance, blue eyes firing in the gloom as Shanks pulled the garage door down. There was barely enough room to get the car doors open, and the entire cube of concrete-floored space was empty and bare. "Do you understand?"

*I wouldn't bet a penny on me understanding anything right about now.* I was tired, my entire body ached from all the excitement and sitting in a car for hours and hours, and my stomach was unhappy with the fast food. I never thought I'd be missing school food *or* having to cook my own damn meals, but there it was. "I guess so." I pulled against his hand. "Let go."

"Not until I'm sure you understand. I did not betray your mother, Dru. It . . . it just isn't possible."

Oh. Was *that* what he was talking about? "Yeah, Christophe. At this point, I'm pretty sure it wasn't you."

Graves tapped at the half-open driver's window. "Hey, Christophe. Pop the trunk, will you?"

Christophe let go of me reluctantly, and I yanked the door handle. Dibs already had the door open into something that looked like a utility room, and warm electric light flooded out when he flicked the switch.

"Smells all right." The blond wulf half-turned. "Like nobody's been here in a while, but the lights are on."

"Check every room." Christophe rose out of the car gracefully, and I wrestled my bag out and slammed my door. "Robert?"

"On it." Shanks bounded up the steps and pushed past Dibs. "Stay back, Dibby. Let the professionals work."

Dibs snorted. "Just tell me when I can pee."

I seconded that emotion, and headed for the bright opening. "When will we get to the Schola? I mean, the other Schola?"

"Tomorrow, a little after noon. I want to do it in broad daylight, and I want everyone to be able to see you. That way, you're safer." Christophe took a step forward, and the hot tension invading the air made me stop and look back over my shoulder.

Graves stood near the back of the car, hands in the pockets of his long dark coat. He wasn't looking at Christophe, though. He had his chin tilted up, and he was staring straight at me. His irises were rings of green fire, the pupils reflecting an odd gold-green tint. Like a cat's eyes at night.

Christophe's shoulders stiffened as he stepped forward, right over the barrier between "space" and "someone's personal space." Graves didn't move.

Christophe took another half-step. "You'll have to get out of the way." His tone was deceptively mild, but I've seen so many shoving matches erupt in school hallways. All the signs were there.

Graves lowered his head a little. He stared directly at the *djamphir* for just two seconds longer than he would have if he was being polite, but just a second less than an actual challenge. "Close quarters. Hey, Dru. Wait for me."

I ducked through my bag strap, settling it across my body. "Hurry up, will you?" My voice cracked. For some reason, I didn't want to see the two of them get into the same stupid petty grandstanding I'd seen a million times.

Graves was *loup-garou*, and Christophe was *djamphir*. Werwulfen and *djamphir* pushing each other, the violence and disdain boiling just under the surface. Like jocks and nerds—no, that wasn't quite right. Like two sets of jocks, each with a reason to hate the other. And I didn't so much blame the wulfen. The way the *djamphir* treated them wasn't quite a crime, but it was close.

There was something else between these two boys, though. Something vicious and snarling just under the surface.

It probably had to do with the heat rising up in me, staining my cheeks with fire. I took a deep sharp breath.

Graves turned on his heel. His back was presented like an insult, and he skirted the rest of the car. I stood, watching. When he got to me, he reached down and grabbed my hand. His fingers were warm too, but they didn't hurt.

The sound of the trunk opening was very loud, but when I glanced back, Christophe's head was down. "Samuel. Come help."

*Samuel?* I blinked.

Dibs twitched. "Right. Sure." He hopped past us. The car dripped, its hood ticking as the engine started cooling down, and I decided I really needed to be somewhere else. Rain swept restlessly against the roof.

I pulled Graves up the two steps into the utility room. There was an ugly avocado-green washer and dryer, a big utility sink, and not much more. The kitchen past it was likewise bare, and I felt more than heard Shanks prowling the house.

"What did you do that for?" I whispered, but Graves just grinned.

Not his usual pained half-smile, and not the wide-open sunny grin I liked best on him. No, this was a wide, wolfish grimace, showing every centimeter of tooth he could dredge up.

"Just so he knows, Dru. I'm gonna go help Bobby. Stay here, right?" And he slipped through my fingers and was gone.

*Oh, for the love of—* I couldn't even finish the sentence mentally, it was so ridiculous. Dad used to time me while I swept every new house we moved into; he and I also practiced doing it as a team. Graves was getting all he-man, when a couple months ago he hadn't even known the Real World *existed*.

Yeah, things were changing all right.

I stood in the middle of a kitchen that looked like it had last seen a meal cooked back in the '70s, breathing and listening to the house creak. The windows were full of the bruised, fading light of dusk. I could hear all of them, wulfen and *djamphir* alike.

And I still felt completely alone.

\* \* \*

*The Schola burned around me as I ran, my arms and legs too heavy. It was like running through molasses—not the clear Lucite the world turned into when the muscle inside my head flexed, but a brown-tinged tide of terror dragging at every inch of flesh.*

*They were behind me. I could hear them howling, something between a vampire's glassy, hateful cry and the screams of an enraged werwulf. They ran in lockstep, boots hitting the ground in parade cadence, and the walls cringed and burned away from the sound.*

*There were doors on either side of the hall. I blundered into them, tugging at the knobs, but they were all locked. My fingers scorched, and as I rattled each door I could hear the boys behind them scream-*

*ing. The smoke stung my eyes and filled my nose. And it was my fault they were there, because the things that were after me didn't care who they hurt.*

*It was all my fault, just like Dad. He was dead because I hadn't told him about Gran's owl, and Gran was dead because I was just a kid and couldn't save her, and Mom was dead too because—*

"Dru!" A fierce whisper.

*It was because of me, all because of me, and the growls and shrieks rose as the hallway stretched out into infinity and the jackbooted footsteps got closer. There was no turn in the corridor, and any moment they would be able to see me. The flames hissed and whispered, cackling in dirty little voices that reached inside my head and scraped the curves of my skull dry.*

"Dru! Wake up!" Someone shaking me.

I sat bolt-upright, clawing at empty air, and swallowed a scream. Graves had my shoulder, his fingers biting in as he avoided my thrashing. The mattress in here was thin and cold, set on the empty floor, but it was better than downstairs—at least the bedrooms were carpeted.

"Hey." Graves's eyes gleamed. The blinds on the window weren't tilted up or down, and thin moonlight shone through, fighting with streetlamp light. The rain had stopped. "You were dreaming."

I grabbed for him. He put his arms around me and squeezed. My heart pounded so hard it threatened to come out my throat. He'd unzipped the two sleeping bags and laid his coat over both of us, and it had been surprisingly comfortable until, I guess, I started thrashing and kicked them off. I buried my face in the hollow between his shoulder and neck and breathed him in. Cigarette smoke, whatever deodorant he used, the tang of *loup-garou*.

He held me, and it didn't seem awkward at all until he patted my back clumsily. "Dru."

"What?" My whisper cracked in half, fell down his shirt. I breathed out, back in. *Don't move. Just for a second, don't move. Let me pretend I can count on someone.*

The thought was gone as soon as it showed up; I shoved it hastily away. I was doing a lot of that lately. As a coping mechanism, it sucked.

His arms tightened around me. "There's something outside."

I tilted my head a little, trying to listen. My heart was making too much noise for me to really hear. I gulped in another deep breath and tried to calm down. "What does it sound like?"

There was a sharp creak from the door. As if someone leaning against it had shifted his weight. Christophe hadn't said a single word when Graves followed me up the stairs.

Which was probably a good thing.

"Like it's trying to be quiet. But I can hear it. Breathing, kind of." Graves shifted again, a little uncomfortably. I tried to let go of him, but he still kept holding onto me. My heartbeat started to slow down a little. I was sweating. The thin blue lines of warding in the walls glowed soft and reassuring, not sparking or running together in quick distressed lunges.

*Gran would be proud of me. That's quite a few times I've done wards without her rowan wand.* I swallowed the lump of pain in my throat. The dream lingered inside my head, screams and the burning somehow just as real as Graves's arms around me and the sound of my breathing, quick and hoarse. "Shoes."

"What?" He cocked his head.

"Get your shoes on. And give me mine." I squirmed away from him and found my boots right where I'd put them, right against the mattress. A quick double yank had my feet inside them, and I grabbed for my bag, slid the strap over my head. The gun was still inside. The clicks were very loud as I checked the clip, racked it back in, and slid the safety off.

Graves shrugged into his coat. I let out a soft breath and knee-walked over to the window. My back ached, but not as bad as it could have. Maybe I was healing.

The warm-oil feeling of the aspect smoothed down over me, and the locket pulsed reassuringly. The room got brighter. I almost glanced up to see if the light had turned on. I knew it hadn't, though.

I was just seeing better.

I made it to the wall next to the blinds, cautiously inched myself up, and decided I could peer out there. The room was dark, and nobody would see me looking out—or I hoped they wouldn't.

I peered out and realized what was wrong. There was no taste of wax oranges and danger on my tongue. Whatever was out there wasn't suckers.

So it could be something else. Or it could be, you know, all of us in a strange house and nervous.

*Be quiet, Dru.* The silent imperative nailed me in place, my eyes focused on the narrow slice of roof and tree branches I could see—then, something moved, pouring up over the edge of the roof with scary silent grace.

I let out a soft, wondering breath. The shape was long and lean, fluid with hair. A streak of white moved smoothly on its narrow head.

It was Ash.

He paused on the roof, three paws down and one up in an eerie imitation of the way a cat will stop in mid-stride when something catches its attention. The orange gleams of his eyes shuttered themselves for a moment, and his whole body slumped on three legs.

"What is it?" Graves whispered. I didn't look at him, but I could tell he knew I'd seen something. Maybe it was my face. It certainly felt funny, bones under twitching skin as I froze, peeking out between the slats of the blinds.

The hall outside the bedroom door was deathly quiet. If Christophe was moving, I couldn't hear him.

"Dru?" Graves stepped forward. A floorboard groaned under his feet.

Ash's narrow canine head jerked up and swung around. He stared right at me for what seemed like an endless moment, and the sure voice of instinct spoke inside my head. I took two steps to the side and grabbed the cord, yanking the blinds up with a sound that ripped through the sleeping quiet.

"Dru!" This time it was Christophe sweeping the door open, but I already had the window unlatched. I tugged on it, and wonder of wonders, it wasn't painted shut. It hove up with a screech just as Graves yelled and Christophe swore.

Ash tumbled through the window. He left dark prints on the roof and the sash. Blood looks black at night, and he was covered in it. The liquid length of him hit the floor with a wet thud. The same nameless certainty made me kneel down beside him. Chill night air poured through the window.

Ash made a soft canine sound when I touched his furry head. A half-growling yip that went down at the end, like he was too tired to finish it.

"Dru." Christophe, with the careful tone of an adult telling a kid not to pet the nice foaming-rabid pooch. "Dru, *malutka*, little one, move away." There was a click, and I didn't have to look at him to know he had a gun out. Maybe it was even the shotgun he'd driven Ash off with once before.

*What the hell am I doing?* But Ash had saved my life twice. It didn't feel right to let Christophe shoot him. Just like it hadn't felt right to leave Graves behind once he'd been bitten. "He's hurt."

The wulfen made another tired sound, and turned his head slightly toward me. He sighed. And the uncomfortable thought rose up in me—what if I *had* left Graves behind?

How many times had he saved me, too?

Christophe swallowed, audibly. "Dru, *moja księżniczko*, please. Move away from him."

The hair was amazingly silky where it wasn't matted with water and blood and filth. I touched the white streak and Ash made a sharp, quivering noise. "He's hurt. He saved my life the other—"

"He's dangerous, just like any Broken. And he's probably led them straight to you. Move *away*, and I will end his suffering."

I leaned forward over Ash's head. "Goddammit, Christophe, *listen* to me. We've got to help him. He saved my life, and—"

"He could have done that for any *number* of reasons—"

"So could you." I looked up. His eyes were all but glowing, winter sky. Graves had his hands up and stood to one side, staring fixedly at Christophe's profile and the shotgun. It *was* the shotgun, the same one he'd had before.

And it was pointed right at me. A thin river of prickling fear ran down my spine. The end of a gun looks very big and very black when it's staring you in the face.

"Christophe," Graves said, very quietly. A growl rattled under the words. "Put that fucking shotgun down."

"What are you going to do? Jump me?" Christophe snorted. "Shut up, dogboy, and let the adults talk. Dru, *kochana*, please. I beg you, move away from the animal and let me dispatch him." The spaces between his words got odder, and I wondered again, inconsequentially, how goddamn old he was.

"I'm not going to. We're going to help him." I stared at the shotgun's oiled barrel, its deadly snout. My teeth tingled, turning sharply sensitive. "And I think we'd better do it fast."

The thrumming growl in the room wasn't coming from Ash. A crackle of bones shifting their shape and density brushed the air like the soft sound of a bird's wings.

And the taste of wax oranges bloomed on the back of my tongue. Christophe looked up, a quick birdlike movement, and dropped the shotgun's muzzle toward the floor. "Time to go. He's led them here. God and Hell both *damn* it." He turned sharply on one heel. "*Robert! Samuel! Wake up!*"

It was amazing to hear him bellow. Even more amazing was Graves hunching his shoulders, his eyes glittering green. "Dru?" My name came out half-mangled, because his jaw was changing.

"Come over here." I tried not to sound scared half to death, crouching over a broken, bleeding werwulf. "Help me. He's pretty beat up."

Ash made a convulsive movement. Blood spattered on the floor, and a low hurt sound escaped his muzzle. His teeth looked very sharp, and very white. He sighed, and slumped bonelessly into the floor.

"Graves?" *Oh please don't lose your temper now. Please.*

"Time to *go*," Christophe snarled at the door. "Get downstairs, Dru. Now."

"We're taking him with us." I stared at Graves, willing him to help me out.

The crackling went away. He took two long strides, ending up next to me and the streak-headed werwulf. Knelt down carefully, and I could see how pale he was under his ethnic coloring. His hands shook when he reached down, getting a handful of bloody pelt.

It occurred to me then that Ash was the one who'd bitten Graves.

"Help me get him upright." I wanted to apologize, but there wasn't time.

Because the thin blue lines of warding in the wall had begun to sparkle and run together uneasily, sensing the approach of something inimical.

"Jesus Christ," Graves said, breathlessly, and pulled Ash's arm up. "Okay, Dru. Okay. All right."

*Oh, thank God.* Because I didn't know what I would have done if he hadn't backed me up.

Between the two of us, we got the wulfen heaved up. He hung like wet laundry, and he was heavy and bloody. Christophe's hair was slick and dark as the aspect folded over him, his fangs touching his lower lip and his eyes incandescent.

"If you think I'm going to —" he began.

Graves actually snarled in return, a deep thrumming noise. "Shut the fuck *up* if you're not going to help." He took an experimental step, and Ash's weight got easier to handle. "Come on, Dru."

I let out a sobbing breath of relief. We moved forward, Christophe backed up, and I heard a sharp, hateful cry rise in the distance. It scraped against the inside of my head, and it meant that the vampires had found us. And were moving in.

# Chapter 28

"**W**hat the hell—" Shanks's jaw actually dropped, and Dibs let out a high-pitched squeak that would have been funny if I hadn't been seriously out of breath from hefting an unconscious wulfen down the stairs.

"*Move!*" Christophe barked, and they both lunged into motion. They already had their sleeping bags rolled up and the rest of their stuff together. Dibs shoved everything in Shanks's arms and dug in his bag.

"How are we going to fit that in the car?" Shanks wanted to know, but he was moving. Christophe tossed him the keys. "Shit, I'm driving?"

"Hurry *up*." Christophe turned on his heel. "Get them in the car. Put her in the back, and pick me up in the front yard." Then he was gone, a shimmer hanging in the air where he had just been. The front door opened, and the smell of early-early morning burst down the hall.

Dawn was a long way off, though.

"Come on, chickadees." Shanks headed for the garage, his arms full of gear. "Let's move out."

Ash's head lolled. I almost tipped over, getting him down the steps into the garage, but Dibs stepped forward with a small spitting sound and subtracted the weight from me. I half-fell aside, catching myself against the wall, and heard a crash upstairs that shook the whole house.

Shanks slammed the trunk. More crashes filled the upstairs. "Get *in*! Backseat, Dru. Get in with them!"

Between Dibs and Graves, they got Ash into the backseat. I piled in on the other side, Shanks slammed the driver's-side door, and the engine roused as I squirmed and yanked my own door shut. Thank God the backseat was big—if we'd been driving an import, someone would have been left behind, and that wouldn't have been pretty.

*Wait a second, how are we going to—*

Shanks dropped the car into reverse, popped the parking brake, and smashed the gas.

The garage door was flimsy plywood, and it exploded out in shivers and splinters. The tires bit gravel, Shanks cut the wheel, and we skidded to a stop in the middle of the road, a hair's breadth from plowing into a parked car. He flicked the headlights on and let out a small *whooo!* sound.

"Jesus!" Dibs yelled, digging in his medical kit. "Hold him down!"

Ash was thrashing. His head snapped back and forth in my lap, white teeth champing, and I reached down and grabbed it. Graves folded down over him in the middle, and the passenger-side front door opened.

"*Go!*" Christophe slammed the door and immediately twisted, bracing his knees against the seat. His eyes skated over me as his shoulder moved, and cold air poured into the car. He was rolling the window down.

Shanks dropped it into gear again and hit the accelerator. The car leapt forward. I shot a glance out my window and saw the house was crawling with dark shapes moving far too quickly and eerily graceful to be human. A gleam of blue-tinged flame sparked high up on the roof and blossomed like a flower.

One of the dark shapes leapt onto the lawn and bounded for the car. Everything was going too slow. Ash's teeth snapped, and Christophe had the shotgun braced against his shoulder, kneeling impossibly in the front seat.

The gun spoke once, a roar that sent Ash into more frantic convulsions. My bag, smushed against my side, dug into my ribs. If I could let go of the werwulf in my lap, I could roll down the window and fire at the things chasing us too.

"Calm down." My voice was lost in the roar of the engine. I bent over Ash's head, repeating myself, trying not to yell. "Calm down, calm down, we're trying to help—*ulp!*" The car jolted over a speed bump, the engine roared, and we slewed into a tire-smoking turn.

"Faster!" The shotgun spoke again. Christophe moved, jamming it down next to the seat and producing a very capable-looking .45 semiautomatic. It was a real cannon, and he checked the clip like an expert, too. "*Goddammit, Bobby, break the speed limit!*"

"I *am!*" Shanks yelled back, but the car took a deep breath and leapt forward again, the engine saying, *Yessir, I'm American heavy metal and we can move this thing, yes we can, just give me a second.*

"Calm *down!*" I yelled, and Ash subsided. His head was heavy, and wet with blood, and he smelled awful. The taste of rotting wax oranges inside my mouth crested, and I longed to retch or spit.

Christophe moved. The window was all the way down, and he

pushed his head and shoulders outside.

"What the hell are you *doing*?" Graves's cry was all but lost under the roaring of the wind.

"*Shit!*" Shanks yelled, and I looked up. There were headlights piercing the darkness, and I was confused for a moment before the car started slewing and I realized we were on a one-way street.

In the dark.

Going the wrong way.

And Christophe calmly hooked a leg over the passenger-side headrest, sitting in the window like he'd watched one too many *Dukes of Hazzard* reruns, and started firing behind us.

# CHAPTER 29

"The freeway! Take the freeway!" My elbow whapped Ash's face. I leaned forward and screamed. "Right side, right side, on-ramp! ON-RAMP!"

"SHUT UP!" Shanks yanked the wheel. We hit the on-ramp doing at least seventy, and he swore with astonishing creativity. Streetlamps whizzed by. Something hit the trunk and the car fishtailed, righted itself. I choked, the taste of rotten wax oranges filling my mouth again, and wished I could spit. A spot of fierce cold bloomed on my chest, I flinched.

A tremendous weight crashed down on the back of the car. Graves, Dibs, and I all screamed, a three-part chorus of surprised terror. The glass didn't break completely, and Christophe's gun spoke again as his leg loosened almost free of the headrest. His booted foot narrowly missed my face. I threw my head back and got a confused impression of shadows, red eyes glaring down, a flicker of brazen hair and a spot of orange light with a blue center.

It was the Burner. Her hand was full of flame, and she stared down through the crazy-cracked glass, her eyes full of unholy crimson fire. She screamed, a rising crescendo of hate, and Christophe fired again.

The car zigged and the vampire's weight was thrown away. The entire back window was starred with breakage. The blue-threading flame whispered between the cracks and snuffed itself out as I let out a short puffing breath, my skin tingling with the warmth of the aspect.

Christophe's leg moved again. He slithered back down into the car, and the first thing he did was drop his gun, lean over the seat, and grab my shoulders. "Are you all right? Dru? Are you hurt?"

*What the*— "I'm fine!" I had to pitch my squeaking voice over the roaring wind from the window. Shanks wove in and out of thin traffic. Thankfully, we were going the right way—the only thing in front of us was taillights. "Are you okay?"

He nodded. The aspect receded, blond streaks sliding back through his hair as the wind kissed it. He didn't let go of my shoulders. "Slow down, Robert. That was the Burner, and she will burn no more. Not with half her head gone."

"Yeah. Okay." The wildness filling the car slackened a bit. "Jesus. Are you sure we're clear?"

"Sure enough. But don't stop for a while." Christophe gave me a thorough once-over, and his eyes dropped to the wulfen's head in my lap. Splashes of streetlight and reflected headlamp-shine bounced across his face. "You should have left him behind." His lips shaped the words; they were lost in the slipstream.

My fingers were still tangled in Ash's hair. My chin lifted a little, and my face settled against itself. I stared at Christophe, my gaze moving over his perfectly proportioned features. I could draw him, if I ever had the time and the paper. But how could I capture the way he was looking steadily at me, thoughts moving behind the cold blue of his eyes?

My heart hadn't stopped pounding yet. But, thank God, I didn't blush. I was too terrified. One thin pane of automotive glass between me and a flame-slinging sucker. Jesus.

"He's sedated," Dibs said. "I can't give him more, but that should keep him calm. Why isn't he changing back?"

"He *can't* change back, that's what Broken means." Shanks's dark eyes flicked up to the rearview mirror. It had gotten knocked askew sometime in the last scrambled fifteen minutes, and he adjusted it as the car slowed down a little more, achieving a freeway-respectable sixty instead of a wild looping seventy-plus.

"Shit, really?" Dibs actually flinched, as if he expected Ash to wake up and start making trouble. "Why—I mean, um, this is the one? The one you were talking about? The last Silverhead?"

"Yeah." I nodded, but my eyes never left Christophe's face. "This is Ash. We're going to help him. As much as we can. How far are we from the Schola?"

The *djamphir* let go of me. He studied me for another few moments, then slid down in his seat and rolled his window up. The sudden almost-silence was deafening. "Not long now. Keep heading south. We should hit the expressway in an hour or so."

"I don't suppose we'll be stopping for coffee." Shanks yawned, but he was still glancing in the rearview every now and again. Looking at me? Or at Ash, slumped across everyone's lap in the backseat? At Graves, who had straightened and now stared ahead, a muscle in his jaw ticking? Or at Dibs, who was startlingly pale as he dug in his medical bag?

Or maybe just staring at the back window, where the print of a vampire's fist still reverberated in the cracked glass right over my head, bits of it melting together as if a blowtorch had kissed it. What would have happened if that hand had broken through?

I didn't want to think about it.

"I don't know if we can, with him in the car." Christophe let out a chill little laugh. "Just keep moving until the sun's up. One problem at a time."

It was good advice. I looked down. Ash had stopped bleeding. The rips and gouges in his flesh were starting to close up. It's eerie to see a wulfen heal; you get the feeling that if you look away the skin will twitch and the damage unreel itself like in a bad movie.

Silence and uneasy half-light filled the car. I let out a sharp, long breath. My shoulders ached. I stared at the back of Christophe's head. He ran his fingers back through blond-streaked hair, the high-lights falling into place. How did he look so perfect all the time? It was goddamn unnatural.

But then, so was I, right?

I peeled my left hand away from Ash's blood-clotted fur and reached over. Graves grabbed my fingers, and when he squeezed, a scalding jolt of relief went straight up my arm and exploded in my heart. "We're almost there," I said to the lean hairy face in my lap, to the silence, to Graves, and to my own heart, palpitating inside my rib cage like a squirrel on a wheel. "Everything will be all right."

Nobody else said anything. I suppose I should have been grateful, but instead I just felt shaky and unsteady, like I might start crying. My tough-girl face was gone for good.

* * *

The city painted the sky above it with orange, rapidly turning to gray as the sun came up. Christophe handed two coffees and the herbal tea back; Graves passed Dibs his tea. I took a Styrofoam cup of coffee and tried not to look at Christophe. My hair was a wild mess, and I felt greasy all over. Being jammed up against the door with a werwulf's heavy head in my lap also made my back really unhappy. I was bruised and aching all over.

"Less than a mile," Christophe said, and dug in the bag. "Egg McMuffin, Dru?"

"Ugh." But my stomach protested. I had to eat *something*. "Yeah, I guess. What are we going to do when we get there?"

"You'll have questions to answer. So will other people"—he started doling out packets of wrapped grease—"since they won't know you exist until you show up at their front door. With a Broken, two wulfen, and a *loup-garou*." He even sounded cheerful. "It will be interesting, that's for sure."

Graves handed me an Egg McMuffin and two searing-hot hash browns. His eyebrows had drawn together. "Wait a second. What are you going to be doing while—"

"I don't want to give them another chance to kill me." Christophe gave him another handful of fast food. "And I have other business."

"So you're sending us in somewhere, again, where you know there's a traitor." Graves kept passing food to Dibs. "Nice."

"This is where I thought you were going in the first place." Christophe's tone was deceptively mild. "You two were whisked away to a back-country reform school satellite instead of the one place I could be reasonably sure you were safe. This time I'm going to make sure you get in the front door, and make such a commotion Dru's presence and survival cannot be hidden. Others on the Council and the Schola will begin to ask questions, especially once you're debriefed." He paused. "I don't know quite what they'll make of the Broken, though."

*The Broken. Not even Ash.* And the way he said it was chill and disdainful.

"I'm betting once he cycles through the sedation, he'll start throwing himself at any wall in his way to get back to Sergej." Christophe sighed. "It will be a mercy if he dies."

I took a huge bite of overprocessed English muffin, sausage that had no relationship to meat, and greasy egg. Said nothing.

"You're not going to stick around to sponsor her?" Shanks accepted a McMuffin and tore through the wrapping with his teeth, spat it aside, and kept one hand on the wheel. Traffic was clumping up, since it was morning. "I mean, that's a one-way ticket to—"

"She'll probably insist on you being kept as her guard. There might be a few others eager for the honor." Christophe shrugged, juggled a hash brown from hand to hand. "If Dylan survived, he's probably gotten a report in somehow."

I swallowed hastily. "He said his contacts weren't responding. Like Augustine. He said Augie's disappeared."

"Don't fear for August. He's canny." Christophe set the crackling paper bag aside. The whole car smelled like salt, blood, fast food, and unwashed teenage bodies. Not to mention sick werwulf. Ash twitched as Shanks slammed on the brakes and hit the horn.

"*Moron!*" he yelled. "*Stay in your own goddamn lane!*"

"City driving." Christophe didn't even sound fazed. "In any case, Dru, my concern is getting you in the Schola's doors. Not worrying for Augustine. Six more blocks and a right, Robert."

"I got it." A light turned green ahead. Shanks eased the car forward. I kept eating, barely tasting the food. My hands trembled, and I didn't think it was from hunger.

Traffic parted like waves. The gray, smoky clouds were shredding, and I saw flashes of blue sky. Sunshine meant we were safe. At least from the vampires.

My mother's locket hid under my sweater. It was comfortingly warm, skin-warm. Like normal metal.

"You know who it was." My voice surprised me. "In the tran-script. Christophe, you know."

He shook his head. Took a crunching bite of hash brown. His teeth were as white as Ash's. White as Graves's wide smile now, too. "I *suspect*, Dru. I don't know." A long pause, as another block rolled by. "But I'll find out. And then, God help whoever is playing this game."

*It's not a game. This is my life we're talking about.* I took a scald-ing gulp of coffee. It didn't help. The same nameless instinct that had made me refuse to leave without Ash told me Christophe knew more than he was telling. Though you didn't have to be a genius to figure that out. He *always* knew more than he was telling. "What are you going to do?"

"I've told you. Do you remember? I have a reason now. Turn here, Bobby."

"I know." The car wallowed to the right.

The engine sounded a little unhappy, and I didn't blame it. "Christophe—" My cheeks were on fire again. Why was I blushing like a . . . like a *girl*, for God's sake?

"Hush, Dru. Two blocks up on the left. Do you see it?"

"I see it." Shanks slowed down. "I take it you don't want a chauffeur?"

The *djamphir* laughed. "Why start now? Take care of her, boys." Graves glanced at me.

"Wait a second." I had my hands full of breakfast and Ash was stirring in my lap, little gleams showing under his eyelids. "Don't tell me you're going to—"

Too late. The car almost stopped, Christophe's door opened, and by the time I got half my protest out it had slammed. He darted between two parked cars and vanished down an alley between two brownstones.

"I can't *believe* this." But I could. It was pretty much the way everything was going now.

"Don't worry." Shanks actually stuffed the rest of his muffin in his mouth and chewed two or three times, then gulped. "Shit, he took my coffee. Anyway, Dru, we're home free."

"Yeah." Graves gave me an eloquent sidelong look, just as Shanks sped up a little. The two blocks slid underneath the car's tired tires, and just as he turned left through a half-open wrought-iron gate, sunlight burst down the street, dipping everything in gold. "Home free. Until someone else tries to kill us."

"Great." I almost dropped the McMuffin on Ash's face. Then I began chewing. Whatever happened next, I'd probably need a full stomach to handle it.

A wet black driveway unreeled, trees arching on either side. The tips of their fingering branches held delicate green buds. When we came out of the double line of greenery, sunshine splashed across a huge white stone building. The lawns were immaculate. There were a pair of concrete lions standing guard at the end of the driveway, too, and I thought I saw one of them twitch. But it could have been just the blinding, fresh morning light.

It looked familiar, but I realized the other Schola had been a smaller, grayer copy of this place. It had seemed really grand and imposing, but this was the Real Deal. I swallowed sudden dryness, doused with a last gulp of overcooked coffee. I dropped the cup near my feet and hoped my numb legs would hold me up when we finally got out of the car.

"Thank God," Shanks said, softly. "We're safe."

I looked down at my lap. Ash's eyes had shut again, the gleam under the lids gone now. "I hope so." I finished the last bit of my muffin. Dibs sighed, a sound of pure relief.

Shanks pulled up to the steps leading to the front door. He cut the engine, and I sensed that people inside the big pile of white stone were aware of our arrival. Any moment now the door would open, and we'd have questions to answer and things to do and . . .

The huge, iron-bound double door at the top of the gleaming white stairs was already opening, revealing a slice of darkness inside for just a moment before slim teenage forms boiled out. They were all boys, and all *djamphir*.

Which ones were enemies?

"I sure as hell hope so," I repeated, and reached for the door handle.

*finis*

# DRU ANDERSON'S
# NOT AFRAID OF THE DARK.
## BUT SHE SHOULD BE

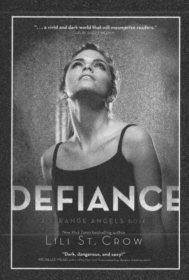